"I absolutely love the writing voice of Kenneth L. Decroo in *Almost Human*. The book is a page turner. Once I started reading it I didn't want to stop. The language is brilliant, and the story most exciting. This is fiction, however, these thoughts might very well be something scientists discuss, and have discussed for a long time. I rarely read thrillers, but really enjoyed this one." Maria Jansson

"I loved the book. It was fast paced, very informative, and never dull. It posed questions about theories of interbreeding within primate species and always kept you looking to the next chapter." Moira A Foster

"Fun, exciting, informative, and thrilling. Almost Human kept me on the edge of my seat from page 1 and just got bigger and better all the way through to the end. In just one book I've become a fan of Ken Decroo's brilliant and intelligent writing. The plot, the characters, the relationships between humans and chimps are just incredible. And then there are those adorable chimps. Excellent piece of work; all in all deserving an A+." Gary Seiler

ALMOST HUMAN

Kenneth L. Decroo

AIA PUBLISHING

DEDICATION

I dedicate this book to my loving wife Tamara Lynn Decroo, who believed in me and this story from the start. This book would not exist if it were not for you asking me to tell just one more story. I love you.

ACKNOWLEDGEMENTS

There are so many people who have helped me along this journey that they are too numerous to list. Indeed, that would be a book in itself. I thank you here and hope this novel is a small memento of our walk together. You know who you are, especially the Playa de Estero people. I would like to acknowledge my mentor, Kathryn Lynn Davis, New York Times bestselling author. Her special, invitational writers' group helped shape this novel and gave me the belief that I was actually a writer. Her patience and guidance always reminded me of the simple fact that writers write. So I kept writing. Many thanks.

I am especially grateful to my editor Tahlia Newland of AIA Publishing for bringing this book to life. Her guidance and professionalism made this book better with each revision. The amazing book cover was done by Velvet Wings Media. And, of course, I would like to give a special acknowledgement to AIA Publishing for selecting my book, my baby, for publication.

Thanks to my dear friends and colleagues Steve and Dorothy Clark for reading the entire manuscript several times. Your insights, encouragement and suggestions kept me returning to this story. This book would not exist were it not for the chimpanzees and other wild animals I have had the great privilege to work with and know, especially Mike and Oliver. Spending time in the company of chimpanzees humbled and inspired me to tell this story. And finally, I want to give special thanks to my parents, Ken and Lois Decroo. You have always been there for me and our family. Your unwavering faith and support gave me the courage to set out on this lonely and arduous path. You have taught me to live life's adventure with courage.

DISCLAIMER

It is unfortunate that we live in a time that a statement like this must be made rather than simply using common sense. This book is fiction. The names of places, institutions, and people are for the story's sake, and so are purely fictional. The events depicted in this story are based on the possibility of things and, of course, did not really happen.

CHAPTER 1

Somewhere off the coast of Equatorial Africa, 1938

Malice brewed far out in the Southern Atlantic where two winds met from different quarters of the world. At first, they stalked each other, blowing blasts between calms as they circled. But in the dying embers of sunset in the empty spaces of the Equator, they combined with a force that turned the calm tropical seas of summer into a cauldron of froth and fury.

A storm gathered. It brooded alone for a while, gathering its force until it sent out the first signals of doom at dawn with steep running swells. They grew in force with each mile, forming giant walls of death which caught the shipping lanes asleep. The captain and crew of the small Soviet cargo ship *Orion* labored up huge, frothing walls. A dark sky poured thundering falls upon her wooden decks, rendering chaos in what seemed like an attempt to clean her of all life. Knotted and tangled wreckage was strewn across her once sanded and swabbed decks.

The ship pitched, struggling to climb the endless advance of waves. When she finally broke clear of the white-capped tops, she took the full force of the howling gale, and then plunged deep into the next swell as though she would dive straight into the bowels of the sea. But each time she slowly righted herself, vibrating the very rivets from her iron skin. She sailed herself.

The helm was dead; for that matter, so was the helmsman and most of the crew. The racket made it hard for the captain to concentrate. Deep-set wrinkles chiseled his weathered face. His jaw clenched. Never had he experienced the force of a sea like this. It felt as though God's wrath was focused on his ship in angry condemnation of the unnatural cargo secreted below her decks. To avoid contact and possible discovery, the *Orion* had wandered about the Mediterranean and the Atlantic like the lost Dutchman, staying clear of ports and shipping lanes, taking on water and supplies in the dead of night on lonely unguarded beaches.

And now his ship was coming apart in the unseasonable storm, screaming and groaning in harmony with the few seamen who still clung to life. Clusters of them held to their stations as the storm worsened. The radio had died, as though it mattered.

The captain had fought many storms and knew the power that came when high winds pushed waves across a thousand miles of open sea. Even now he could feel the great seas fingering the hull for weaknesses as the storm took on renewed fury, sounding as though the devil himself sawed a song of welcome in the rigging above. Nothing seemed to make sense in the confusion. The captain tried to think. He was tired, and the cold numbed him, but he had to concentrate, to fight his terror and get below. He no longer knew their location.

The storm had broken all the glass out of the wheelhouse and washed the instruments away. He peered out at the horizon and saw a great gathering darkness denser than the rest of the sky that seemed to be sucking all that was left afloat into its oblivion. He figured they were far enough off course to open his sealed orders. He had to get below to his cabin and read them. It was his duty. He looked around for help. There was none.

A powerful gust hit the vessel amidships and leaned her to the very rail caps. Men slid down the slippery gunwales, frantically grabbing at flotsam as they dropped, screaming, into the sea. The captain clung to the wheel, trying to hold on for yet another minute, knowing his ship would not recover again. The forward hatch already lay ajar, shipping water. The wind slackened, falling silent with foreboding. They had entered the eye of the storm; their end would meet them when it passed over.

The ship sat dead in the water, her engines probably flooded, her engineers drowned. The captain could imagine what hell had been unleashed below, but that was exactly where he must go. He had to open those sealed orders. Men slowly got to their feet and helped each other to safer parts of the ship, preparing for the coming onslaught. Time was slipping. Life was precious now, measured in heartbeats. The ship boxed her compass as she pitched in the agitated seas. Streams of water flowed over every part of the ship, pouring down the hatches and filling her bowels.

The captain ran down the catwalk of the bridge and slowly moved across the pitching deck towards the main hatch. He slipped down the flooding deck, having difficulty keeping his orientation, and in the end, he swam the last steps. Chaos met him below in the eerie red glow of the emergency lights. What had once been a well-ordered merchant cargo ship, the pride of the Atlantic fleet, had been beaten into a floating wreck. Electrical wires shorted and popped in streams of water. Most of the lights were submerged and dimming as the auxiliary batteries drained, making it hard to see. The dead floated and bobbed in the passageways.

The captain felt lost in his own ship; nothing seemed familiar. Even when he found his way, he had trouble making it through the passageways. Soon his ship would be lost. He wanted out of this closed tomb, to go topside and at least die in the open air above. He'd read his first standing orders when he signed his commission. Now he must read the second set, the sealed orders. But why should he? He was going to die. But he was still captain, a Soviet seaman. Honor required him to carry out his duty. Willing himself against his fear, he raced down the gangways, frantically searching for open passageways. The cabin door had jammed. He tried to stop a seaman making his way topside, but the young man took no heed, stumbling as though in a trance. The captain knew he was alone in this and threw himself against the cabin door, pounding and kicking. He couldn't fail in his last act of command. The ship listed. Torrents of water streamed past him, pulling him off balance. Loose cargo ground deep grooves into the decks while crashing and splintering the bulkheads. The dead piled up like loose cargo.

In a rage against his impotence, he struggled to make a final lunge, slipping against the suction that pulled at his feet. Helped by a wild pitch of the ship, he busted the door open and pushed his way through the splintered wood. The sea poured through widening cracks in the ceiling as the decks parted under the torque of the sea.

There would be little time left now. He searched frantically through the rubble for the keys to his sea chest, and in the end gave up and chopped the top open with the ax he found in the debris on the floor. He searched through logs and charts and found the orders still dry in the waxed envelope. He'd have to read them fast before the dampness made the ink illegible. He tore the heavy wax wrappings off and broke the seal, then wedged himself into a corner where his bunk used to be.

The captain's hands trembled as he re-read the orders. Along with the coordinates of their final destination—useless now—were the words "… protect this cargo at all cost and save all evidence that accompanies it …" meaning do not let those creatures below drown and keep all the records secret. The secrecy, he knew, was only because of those unspoken experiments and the horrible abominations they had created.

He wondered just how the admiralty expected him to accomplish this in a sinking ship.

The captain steeled himself. Orders were orders and had to be followed. He felt the pistol at his side and found it relatively dry. To go farther below was madness, but so were these orders. What had the technicians been doing down there? No one, including himself, had actually seen the creatures, but the whole crew had heard their screams day and night. And they all had heard the rumors and stories. Only the howl of this storm gave them a respite from their cries.

No light remained in the lower decks. He had to make his way by feel and couldn't tell if the cold or the fear numbed him. His last fix on their position had been by sextant almost forty-eight hours before, and they had been dangerously close to the African coast. This storm blew in the direction of its rocky and desolate lee coastline. If he could release whatever was below from their cages and let the ship go aground there just might be a chance. A lot of ifs! He set out for what he realized was his final act of command—free those things.

Finally, he approached the lab door deep in the ship. Screams echoed from behind the door where a sign hung crooked: "Security Area. No Admittance." He opened the door to the full force of the deafening cries that had filled the ship since the beginning of their voyage and stood mesmerized.

"Good mother of God!" he screamed.

A huge, ape-like creature stopped pulling at the latch of the barred door of its cage and pleaded with eyes wild with fear. Others pushed against the bars, whimpering as they beckoned to the captain to help them. But he could not move as he took in the horror of it all. Trapped and panicking as the water flooded around them, at least a dozen others tried to squeeze their way out. The captain reached for his pistol as arms shot out from between the bars and several huge hands grasped the very air around him. He tried to step back but was too late for the ship made a sharp pitch, throwing him into their reach. He felt himself jerked violently to the bars. Hands probed his body before squeezing down on him like steel vices tearing him apart. He felt his arms separating from his body, and the pain overcame his resolution. He watched in horror as a monster pried the keys from his still grasping fingers, unceremoniously tossed his dismembered arm aside, and turned his attention to the lock.

The bars parted as the ship torqued out of shape. A giant shadow squeezed its way through the opened cage door, stepping over the captain as water flooded the cages. Others followed. Cold chestnut eyes stared down at him. His whole body grew cold, numb from shock. He saw but couldn't feel his arm which floated, fingers still twitching, in the crimson flood. He faded with each pump of his heart, barely aware as several others stampeded over his dying body. They paid him no heed as they pushed themselves free.

CHAPTER 2

Forty Years Later

"In closing, I think you will agree that the chimpanzee is our closest relative. In fact, they're more closely related to us than they are to gorillas. Ninety-eight percent of our DNA is the same. We share the same ABO blood type groups. They've successfully received human blood transfusions. They can contract or transmit most of the same diseases found in the human species. Indeed, we differ by only one pair of chromosomes. In the wild the infant nurses from two to four years. Infant dependency is as long as six years. Chimps can live fifty to sixty years. Sexual maturity is nine to twelve years. Gestation is nine months. Sound familiar?"

A few students chuckled and others whispered to each other, sending muffled echoes that broke the momentary silence. Dr. Ken Turner smiled. He always got students thinking with that remark. How many times had he given this same primate lecture? He looked up the aisles of the amphitheater towards the exits—this class was unusually large; at least two hundred students this term. The T.A.'s were going to work their asses off.

Composing his thoughts, he paced the stage as he always did while lecturing. "It's because of these very similarities that chimps have been used in so much research that benefits us: aerospace, bio-medical, and of course, my own work with language acquisition. The more we investigate chimps, the better we see ourselves. We must remember that they are not soft machines, as the experimental psychologists would have us believe. They are thinking, aware, non-human beings. They are, in fact, almost human."

Many of the students nodded in agreement. This always made him feel self-conscious, especially when he noticed he had chalk all over his jeans and jacket. "Damn that chalk."

Sporadic laughter peppered the room, especially from the back.

Ken leaned his long, lanky frame against the lab table and pushed his wire-rimmed glasses up the bridge of his nose, getting yet more chalk on his face. "Are there any questions before we end this evening's lecture?"

Hands went up before he'd finished. He liked this part of class because it was one of the only times he got to speak to and test his students individually. He surveyed the students terraced up around him. *God, they're getting younger all the time; so many different students out there but so few scholars.* How many had he reached in his whole career?

Unlike most of his colleagues, who saw teaching as a necessary evil required by deans to allow them to do research, he loved teaching almost as much as his research. He caught the eye of a fresh young blonde. *God, she looks like the beginning of the Aryan Race.* "Yes you, young lady." He pointed at her. "You have a question?"

She appeared so flustered that she couldn't speak for a moment, seemingly confused as to whether she should brush her hair from her face or shuffle her notes. Finally, she asked her question: "Ah, yes, Professor, I mean Doctor. Is it true that your chimps really talk?"

A few faint giggles broke the silence.

Ken always felt crushed when he realized he'd not gotten through to a student. *How disappointing. So much for beautiful wrapping.* It was not so much *what* she said but *how* that disappointed him. The girl was dumb, and ignorance couldn't be gift-wrapped. "As I've said throughout this course and in my work, chimps are highly intelligent. In fact, in some areas, such as spatial relationships and the like, they probably surpass us. Your question has puzzled scholars since the turn of the century. Many have asked the question, if they can display such intellect, why can't they talk? Indeed, that's how I began my own research."

The lecture hall fell silent except for the occasional cough or stirring of papers. The whole class seemed to lean toward him. Students looked up from their notes, poised for his next words. It always pleased him to see how much this subject matter gripped his students.

"Like most of my colleagues at the time, I was confused as to the nature of language. I'd not distinguished the difference between language and speech. Tell me, can you possess language without speech?"

A murmur swelled among the students. Hands cropped up above the growing chatter. Just as Ken was about to call on a woman towards the back, a tall, lanky young man stood up and answered, "Of course you can."

Silence fell again. Turner recognized the youth as one of those obnoxious students who could recite the content of every lecture but was incapable of putting together an original thought on his own. He remembered him from previous classes but couldn't remember his name at the moment and wondered if that was his way of dismissing him.

The man's skinny frame swayed, and he continued as if he were performing. "Think of the deaf. As you said in your last lecture, there're millions of them around the world who get by without speech." His narrow-set eyes shifted back and forth, and he smiled, obviously enjoying the sound of his own voice. "And they do more than merely get by; they have their own languages whose roots are completely unrelated to spoken languages. They communicate. Those sign languages have histories and origins of their own. They possess their own grammatical structure and are governed by sets of rules much as spoken language is and ..."

When the young man took a breath to continue, Ken cut him off midstream. "Thank you, Mr. ah ..."

"Childs, sir. Gordon Childs."

"Mr. Childs' answer is pertinent to this young lady's question."

Childs smiled smugly at the woman who'd asked the question. She frowned back.

Feeling annoyed, Ken looked past Childs and surveyed the other students. He noticed a young pre-med student in the front row intently copying the class outline Ken had written on the chalkboard. He couldn't have told anyone how he knew the young man's major, but he knew. Years of teaching gave one a certain insight. He caught the med student's attention. "Young man? Yes, you in the sweater. What are your thoughts?"

The boy stirred, clearly taken by surprise, but he managed to keep his composure. "Me?" he asked tentatively.

"Yes, you. Based on today's lecture and the previous answer, what can you tell me about how chimps communicate?"

The young man—a trim kid with fine hair—paused before replying. "They're basically non-verbal. Jane Goodall has observed over fifty signals made with the hands and face by chimpanzees in the wild."

"Precisely! Though chimps do use vocalizations, they rely almost exclusively on gestures, facial expressions and the like to communicate a whole array of emotions, needs, etc. That's why we thought sign language would be articulated through a channel more receptive to your average run-of-the-mill chimp." Ken walked up the center aisle caught up in the subject. "The research I'm doing is giving us insights into how our own language evolved. Chimp behavior is laced with behavioral artifacts that shed light on the antecedents to our own language." He paused, trying to stuff his hands into the pockets of his tight jeans. His tweed sports jacket hung loosely over his tall, thin build. "When you realize that language is a very sophisticated form of communication and that communication is very old and many aspects of it are shared and understood by all mammals, you can see why picking the most intelligent and social of all primates besides humans makes so much sense. They hold the key to how we came to be the way we are today."

He caught himself mid-stride. Laughing and shaking his head, he looked out at his students. "Now I'm really getting ahead of myself. I need to save something for next time." The clamor of students closing their notebooks and packing up filled the hall. He paused, waiting for the students to settle. "Are there any other questions?"

Childs almost jumped up from his seat, startling his classmates, and spoke before Ken had a chance to call on him. "Dr. Turner, sir, given what you say about the close relationship between chimps and us, is it possible that a chimp could breed with a human?"

Nervous laughter broke out.

"Quiet. Please." He raised his hand. The atmosphere had suddenly grown tense and somber. Every student waited for him to answer. *This boy's becoming a real nuisance.* Ken took a closer look at the annoying young man, a bookish sort with sharp, homely features. His gaze darted about furtively. He appeared to be measuring the mood of his fellow students as he waited for a response.

Ken didn't like the boy but couldn't decide if his manner or looks were most displeasing. He didn't like answering questions so close to some of his most guarded secrets. Was this young man's question completely innocent? *Who is he?* "That question has been asked before," he replied, since refusing to answer would make him seem defensive. "Yerkes alluded to it. It was rumored in certain intellectual circles that the Soviets attempted some of this research in the thirties. But the circumstances surrounding this research are very vague and mysterious. I would have to say that—"

"Sir," the young man interrupted, shaking his head, "is it possible? Yes or no."

Ken pressed his lips together and signaled time-out. "Patience, please!" A buzz of quiet conversations and cross-talk

11

filled the lecture theatre. He stared at Childs for a moment, then continued, "I'm getting there. Aside from the ethical questions, there would be considerable technical problems in such an experiment. We will be discussing some of the new *in vitro* techniques in the coming lectures, but they're very new and have not been tried on primates as of yet. As we've seen in our readings, artificial insemination in primates of the same species is very difficult, especially in apes, let alone between species."

Many students squirmed uncomfortably in their seats while others got up to leave. He knew some students would be offended and might complain, which could bring more attention on this topic than he and his colleagues could afford, especially right now. The timing would be disastrous. *The Bible thumpers are going to have to take numbers at the Dean's office tomorrow.* He decided to make a tactical retreat.

"But now we really are getting ahead of ourselves." He glanced at his watch, "Good God! It's ten-thirty already. We'll continue this ... we'll continue our discussion on primate communication on Monday night." He busied himself collecting his notes from the lectern and added. "Don't forget the exam week after next." He shouted over the ruckus of the students gathering themselves to leave, "T.A.s, my office Monday morning at ten."

The clamor of students pouring from the room drowned out the young man's protests. "Sir, Dr. Turner, one moment please." Childs actually pushed his way toward the front against the flow of students exiting.

Well, as my dear wife Mary would say, the best exit is a short one. Ken quickly made for the lab door behind him, acting as though he didn't notice Childs' approach.

***

A tall man in a black-silk shirt and slacks slid up next to Childs as he watched the door shut behind the professor. "It's a shame Dr. Turner didn't have time to *fully* answer your question. I wish we could've heard what he would've said," he said with the hint of an indeterminate accent.

The boy eyed the stranger curiously. "It's very frustrating to be put off like this even though it is a little *late*."

The stranger nodded. "Exactly my thoughts. Sorry; where are my manners? My name is Deter Vandusen, at your service." The stranger made a slight bow. He extended his hand and smiled, revealing a model perfect set of teeth.

Childs took the hand of his new acquaintance and was surprised at the strength of his grip. "My name is Gordon Childs. I don't remember seeing you in this class. Are you a student?"

Vandusen laughed. "God, no. I am ... well ... auditing, you might say. I'm afraid that I'm much too old to be going back to school. Let's just say I'm very interested in Dr. Turner's work and also am disappointed that we ran out of time." Was there just a slight sarcastic tone his voice? This apparent chance meeting made Childs feel uneasy. He felt something menacing about this stranger.

The last of the students were leaving, and Childs didn't like the prospect of being left alone with this Vandusen. This stranger wasn't like the usual people he met around the university. Childs decided to call it a night. He was tired and disappointed. *Perhaps it would be better to consider all of this in the light of a new day.*

"Well, Mr. Vandusen, I really must be off. Classes are early tomorrow, and I still have a long walk home."

Vandusen nodded almost knowingly. "Please, Mr. Childs, I think we have some interests in common. Perhaps I could offer you a coffee and a ride home?"

"What would we have in common?"

Vandusen smirked with one eyebrow cocked. "Determining what Dr. Turner and his people are really up to under the guise of this so-called language project." He paused, and they both watched Ken slip out of the lecture hall. "And helping the right people to recognize your talents, especially in the areas of— hybridization."

Childs and Vandusen left the lecture hall together.

Ken cursed under his breath as he looked for his bike in the darkness outside. *That had been a close one.* This old student lab and its separate door still had a good use after all. It had been a fire exit to the street when the hall had been part of the chemistry department.

Childs' questions worried him. Who was he, really? How much did he know about whom or what they were seeking? Did he know about Oliver? But there was no sense getting paranoid. He was tired and it was late. It was time to get home and check on his chimps.

He threw his leg over his bike and looked up into the dark and moonless sky. The pale points of the stars made everything seem even colder than it was. It felt like snow. But he thought that every time it got a bit nippy. He was, after all, from Southern California. He hoped his assistants had thrown extra blankets to the chimps tonight.

He left the university and raced through the neighborhood streets, the whine of the coasting gears echoing off the brick houses. He thought how different this community and university were from UC, where he'd been educated.

He pedaled hard up the hills behind the town, avoiding Virginia Street and the casinos below, and wound through the darkness, gaining vistas of the neon glow of the Fitzgerald, Mapes, Circus-Circus and sleepless others far below. High above the city, he paused to catch his breath and chuckled. "The biggest little city in the world."

His route took him south toward his research facility—the ranch as he called it. He really did like it here. Why, he wasn't sure. He was in good shape for forty. Riding one-hundred miles a week and fieldwork kept him that way. He pumped a hard pace up the last hill before he reached the summit of the Windy Hill and looked down onto the horse ranches of Holcomb Lane. The earth's fragrance welled up from the valley.

As he raced down into the night toward the ranch, he wondered how his friend Fred was making out in LA. That made him wonder if his grant would be renewed, and then he wondered about other things, many other things.

He still didn't like that boy.

CHAPTER 3

A hot blast of the Santa Ana's filled Dr. Fred Savage's eyes with grit, which scratched when he tried clearing them. Carefully, he made his way down the steep steps of the DC 10, its whining engines winding down. Gusts stirred up the dust and trash off the busy airport runway, surprising him at how hot the evening was and how the force of the wind seemed intent on carrying everything off that was not bolted down. The landing lights barely penetrated a hazy brown sky with no stars. He realized that this haze that burned his lungs must be the smog for which the city was so well known. The sky disappeared as he made his way across the tarmac of LAX.

The trip back from London had been long, and this was the last leg before he could return to Reno. He'd slept little on the bumpy flight and was tired, but he had one more errand to run for Dr. Turner. Was it yet another dead end? There'd been so many. But as they agreed several years before, all leads needed to be followed up. He'd pay a visit to an old animal trainer and the chimp with which he reportedly lived. The image of an old man and chimp living in a trailer like some kind of odd roommates made him smile. He laughed out loud and mouthed their names: Lester and Girlie. They'd been famous once, had performed on Saturday morning children's programs on TV. But more importantly, they might be able to help them in their quest. They might be able to shed light on the dark secret they pursued.

Savage felt uneasy. And it was from more than his fatigue and this awful wind and heavy air. He had the feeling that he was being followed. He'd first noticed it when he boarded his flight in Heathrow. He couldn't be sure he wasn't just being paranoid, but he felt he'd seen the same person or persons several different times in several different settings. Something told him that he'd have to be more careful and alert.

* * *

"Well, old girl, are you gonna bring me that cup of coffee, or what?" The man glanced up from the couch where he sorted through snapshots and news clippings. His movements were slow and deliberate as he picked through the neat piles, sometimes gently lifting a photograph, brittle with age, to the light of a dusty lamp. His hands shook slightly from the tremors of age.

Dishes rattled from the kitchen of the small trailer. Circus and movie posters, acclaiming the past, covered every inch of the dingy paneling.

Ringling Bros. Circus presents Lester and his Charming Chimps.

NOW PERFORMING! Carson and Barnes Circus, Lester's ZOO Revue.

A whole career, rather a whole life, plastered the walls.

Lester frowned. He had pulled all these old boxes out from under the bed because a man named Savage was coming to interview him the next day. Staring at boxes and stacks of his history, he muttered, "I'm not sure why this guy wants to interview an old act like ours. Hell, who even remembers us?"

He pushed a cigar box filled with memories aside. "Ah, good girl. Bring it here."

A chimp ambled toward him, carefully balancing a cup of coffee. Lester took the cup and hugged her.

The chimp went slowly back into the kitchen and brought back her own cup. Her movements were deliberate with no wasted energy. She sat stiffly in a director's chair that had "Girlie" stenciled on the back canvas and sipped her coffee, staring over her cup as Lester rambled on.

He pointed at a yellowed photograph with cracked emulsion. "You remember this show? Let's see, it was you and me, Jody, Oliver—that freak, Danny, and Karen."

He looked closer at the four chimps and a young man and woman in the center ring of a circus. A chimp sat on a tricycle, another of medium size stood on his hands. Two larger ones were jumping rope. The man and woman worked the rope as they waved to a crowd that swelled up around them. They were both in their prime and the woman was beautiful. The chimps wore genie costumes with fezzes, and the man was tall and elegant in a tuxedo. The woman's beauty shone in the fading photo, her eyes sparkling like the sequined gems of her costume. You could tell she was blonde and blue-eyed even though the photo was black and white.

Lester lifted a large magnifying glass from the cluttered table. "Look how beautiful Karen was. We were so young. God, Girlie! Look how big you were. You sure picked up the bike gag quicker than any chimp I ever trained."

Girlie looked back at him, expressionless, as she gulped her coffee with loud slurps. Lester began to leaf through an old scrapbook. "Come here and look at this."

The chimp set her coffee cup down, did a half-hearted somersault out of her chair and jumped up on the couch next to Lester.

"This must have been when we played Berlin just before the war, thirty-five or six. Dr. Goebbels himself was there that night. We were smart, or Karen was, to get out just in time. But we didn't get paid—bastards."

Lester's faded blue eyes moistened, and a single tear ran down his weathered cheek. "They're all gone but you and me, love. We're the last from the old act. God, I miss them, Girlie. I miss the way we were. I miss her." He laid his head on his arms and wept quietly.

The chimp moved stiffly against him and nuzzled.

* * *

It was late when Lester awoke. He found himself nodding off more lately. He was getting old, in his sixties, and his body was beginning to show it. He'd once been tall and distinguished, but now he was bent. His face was wrinkled from so many years outdoors, and his blue eyes had faded to almost gray. He still had a full head of hair, though it was all silver. Time had worked on his body and now was gnawing at his spirit.

He looked around the trailer in the quiet of the night. Girlie slept across from him in her chair, breathing in a shallow rhythm. She was getting old. He wasn't sure but figured her to be near fifty. She was graying around the muzzle, and the black hair covering the rest of her body was thinning. Bones he'd never noticed were beginning to show, especially around her chest and pelvis. In her prime she'd been large for a female, weighing close to one-hundred-and-fifty pounds, but he noticed the most change around her eyes. She had a hollow look that worried him. He feared dying, but he feared dying before her more. They didn't have much money left. His wife's death had been slow and costly. He owned the mobile home and had a small bank account that dwindled with each passing year.

Once they'd been royalty, circus royalty. He and Karen had been married in the center ring in Moscow. Her family had been flyers, trapeze artists, but she took to animal work, and they'd built an act of international stature, starring in some of the biggest circus shows. But that had been a long time ago.

His only remaining friend was Bobby Waiter. Bobby had been born in their Pullman somewhere in Wyoming years ago when they had all been headed for another jump—Canada most likely. Bobby's parents had been on the show with Lester and Karen that year. They were clowns and midgets. The years passed, and they worked together on different shows. Each time they met, Bobby was older, but he never grew. He left the circus after his parents' death. Now he worked as a stunt double for children in the movies.

Lester got quietly up from his chair and stretched the stiffness out as though he were shaking off the gloom. "I'll call

Bobby tomorrow. I need to figure things out. We need a change in our lives." He covered Girlie with a quilt and went down the hall, passing yet more photos, and fell fast asleep in his own bed. He dreamed of performances and applauding crowds. The lights were always especially bright in his dreams these days.

He woke to Girlie sleeping beside him. She'd pulled most of the covers off him to cover herself. As he grabbed some back, he mumbled, "Damn you, Girlie. It's cold."

She glanced at him and rolled back over, pulling on the quilted bedspread.

* * *

It was late morning when he finally stirred, and he was on his second cup of coffee before Girlie came into the living room, dragging a blanket behind her. Her lower lip hung low, exposing her lower teeth, which contrasted the marbled pink and black of her gums. She paid little attention to Lester as she crawled onto a worn and lumpy couch next to a wall heater, which was just taking the chill off the morning. Lester began putting on his suit as Girlie slept. He had agreed to be interviewed, so he was making a deliberate effort to be presentable. *Damn waste of time if you ask me.*

"God, Girlie, all you ever do is sleep." The chimp didn't stir. "I wish I hadn't agreed to this damn interview." He'd developed the habit of talking to the chimp after his wife passed away. He'd always talked to the animals he trained, but with Girlie it had developed into full-blown conversations, though one-way. Still, he believed that she understood much of what he said.

"It might be good to talk to someone new, though. I better call Bobby right now before this guy gets here." He sat at the kitchen counter, picked up his phone book, and leafed through studio numbers and booking agents, many of which were long since scratched out. An old studio directory wall chart hung on a cabinet with Girlie's picture in one of the blocks. When he began to dial, Girlie woke up and climbed up onto the counter. She loved the phone. She liked to hear it ring, hooting in excitement every time, and she liked to put her ear near the receiver as Lester talked, trying to hear the voice on the other end. This morning was no exception.

"Quit it, Girlie, can't you see I'm trying to dial?"

Girlie hooted.

"Hello, Bobby? Damn it, Girlie. This is Lester."

A voice laughed at the other end. "Hell, I know who it is. Who else calls me with a chimp hooting in the goddamn background? How's things, buddy?"

Glancing at the chimp, Lester paused, "Can you come over, Bobby? I need to talk."

Bobby's voice became serious. "Are you guys okay? Lester, what's wrong?"

"Will you shut up?" Lester said. "Sorry, Bobby, not you. Nothing's wrong. Just come over."

Silence at the other end. When Bobby finally spoke, he sounded concerned: "We're shooting today. But I'll be over as soon as we wrap. How's that for a plan?"

Lester smiled in relief. "Whatever turns you on. I'll see you when you get here."

Bobby laughed. "Let me talk to Girlie."

Lester handed over the phone. "He wants to say 'hi'."

Girlie hooted and panted, animated. She danced, slapping the counter with her feet, and took the phone.

Bobby's high-pitched voice shot up another octave. "Hi, Girlie. Take care of that son-of-a-bitch. Give us a big kiss."

She kissed, smacking her lips loudly into the receiver.

Bobby squealed. "Goodbye."

As they hung up, the doorbell buzzed.

Girlie hooted, ran to the door, and started to open it.

"Leave it, Girlie! You'll scare the hell out of him." Lester's voice became commanding, and his whole posture took on the assured presence of a trainer. Pointing his finger toward a chair, he motioned the chimp to sit down. "Sit, girl. Feet down."

Girlie jumped into the chair, crossed her arms, straightened her legs, sitting perfectly still and looking straight ahead.

"Good girl. Now stay."

Lester went to the door and opened it to a stout man in his forties. Of medium height, he had chiseled features which gave him a rugged, outdoor look.

The man smiled and extended his hand; his face wrinkled in well-worn paths. "Lester? Hi, I'm Fred Savage."

Lester took his hand and felt a firm grip with calluses on the man's palms. *Hands that've known hard work.* "Please come in, come in, Dr. Savage." Lester took an immediate liking to the man, though he couldn't explain why, perhaps something in his smile and the calmness of his voice.

"Please call me Fred. I don't go in for all that formality, especially when you have a lifetime of experience with animals. I only went to school for eight years. We have our experience with animals in common, and that's why I'm here. The experience—that's what really counts in trying to understand them."

Lester definitely liked this guy.

Girlie hooted and pranced in her chair, arms outstretched.

"Girlie, damn it all! Where are your manners?" Lester shouted.

Girlie sat back down, whimpering, barely able to contain herself.

Dr. Savage's face lit up. "Hello, Girlie. I sure know who you are. I never missed a show when you still had the series on Saturday mornings." He looked over to Lester. "With your permission, sir?"

Lester knew he wanted to greet her. Chimp etiquette demanded it, but trainer etiquette required he ask permission first. Lester was impressed that he understood the rules.

"Certainly. Al-l-l-l-l—right, Girlie."

Dr. Savage kneeled at the foot of the chair, and they embraced. Girlie placed her opened mouth over his ear and neck and panted, hugging him tightly. Her huge canines left dimples in his skin.

Lester laughed. "There's no doubt about it Doc, she likes you."

Still kneeling, Dr. Savage fumbled in his pockets. "What have I got in my pockets, Girlie?"

She screamed with excitement, looking from Lester to Dr. Savage.

Lester beamed. "It's okay, girl."

In short food grunts that sounded more like dog barks, she searched Dr. Savage's pockets. The barks reached squeals as she found a box of licorice, then she jumped back into her chair, ignoring her newfound friend, all attention devoted to her snack.

Dr. Savage laughed. "How quickly they forget!" Shaking his head, he smiled. "Lester, I've come here to tap your brain. I want to ask you about a rumor I heard some old-timers pass on about you." He'd gotten serious and seemed to choose his words carefully.

Lester put up a hand. "Look, if this is another one of those 'cruelty to animal' deals I—"

"Not at all," Savage interrupted. "It's about a chimp you once trained named Oliver."

Lester nodded. "Okay, what about him?"

"Well, let's see ... I was at Carson and Barnes a few weeks ago. I got talking to a couple of trainers who told me an incredible story about an animal billed as half human and half ape. One of the guys said he'd seen this animal at a carnival years ago, and that he'd never seen anything like it in all his years in the circus. He said you once owned him. Dusty Smith it was. He said he had the elephant show on Ringling that year and that you and your wife had been on the show at the same time with your chimp act."

Lester stared off into space as Girlie rocked on the canvas seat of her chair. "Oh boy, that was a long time ago. I did buy Oliver. Girlie was in the act." Girlie hooted at the sound of her name. "He was different, very strange in the way he looked at you. He walked upright, you know. That asshole Dusty gave an interview in a local paper, in some podunk town in Oklahoma, about him being the bastard of some human and chimp. It caused such an uproar with the locals, I got ran out of town. Asshole!" He looked at Dr. Savage. "Sorry. Dusty that is."

"A lot of chimps walk bipedal sometimes, though, right?" Savage asked.

"Not like this. Oliver did it all the time. Even in his cage when no one was working him. You can train chimps to do it, but this was different. He was a smart son-of-a-bitch, too. Look, I have some pictures of him around here somewhere." Lester sorted through boxes of photographs.

Girlie ambled over and sat between them on the couch.

"Okay. Here we are." Lester picked up an old, curled photo. "It's not the greatest shot, but you can make out how he stood pretty well."

Savage frowned. "How do you explain this? He's perfectly erect. I've never seen such a straight stance in any primate. It's like he has a two by four tied to his back."

Lester stirred. "He *was* very human like, and smart as hell. *Was?* I'm talking like he's dead."

"You mean he's still alive?"

"Unless he died just recently, he is."

"Do you know where he is?"

"I sold him to Fuss Camp's act in sixty-three and he sold him to a real outlaw, who last I heard, was playing a Mexican circus—Sergio something, I think. My guess is he's still down there somewhere with the Circo de las Americas. Someone will know. The animal business is a small world, too small. Why are you so interested in that old chimp? What's he done, now?"

"It's not so much what he's done. It's more like what he may be." Savage rubbed his weathered hands together nervously. Sunlight streamed through the window behind him, highlighting his red hair.

"You don't believe all that silly horseshit about him being half-human, do you?" Lester got up to turn the heaters off.

24

"I don't know what I believe. I'd like to see him." Savage leafed through a dog-eared copy of the *Circus Report* that lay on a weathered steamer-chest that served as a makeshift coffee table. Stickers from all over the world covered its sides and top; some were peeling, revealing the battered leather of a life on the road.

"See him. Why?" Lester busied himself by adjusting a set of sagging blinds before sitting back down next to Girlie.

"To help me satisfy my curiosity. There seems to be something really unique about him. Will you help me find him?"

Lester hesitated before responding, "What do you want us to do?" He put his arm around Girlie.

"Introduce me to people who may know where he is for certain."

Before Lester could answer, Girlie jumped up from the couch and raced to the window, hooting. Then she shot over to the door as it opened.

"Anyone home?" A little man let himself in, a midget perfectly proportioned with fine features. "Hi, Lester, Girlie. Give us a big hug, honey." The man didn't have to kneel to greet her. She completely smothered him. "God, get off me. You're too big".

"Hey, Bobby! Leave your playmate and come here and meet someone. Leave it, Girlie!"

Bobby untangled himself from the ape's embrace, straightening his ruffled clothes. In spite of his diminutive size, he had a presence that filled the room.

"Lester, you look good." Turning away from Lester, he took Savage's outstretched hand and said, "I'm Bobby Waiter."

"It's a pleasure. Fred Savage."

"What's going on, Les? Everything okay?" Bobby seemed to measure his words as he looked around the living room.

"Oh sure, Bobby. We just need to talk later. You remember Oliver, right?"

"God, who could forget that freak of nature? I heard he was in Mexico. Remember when he broke out on you?"

"Which time?"

"What's it take to get a drink around here?" Dropping into a rocker, he sighed. "The shoot was nuts. I thought we'd never wrap."

Lester pointed to the kitchen. "Girlie, bring Bobby a beer!"

Bobby laughed as he pulled the pop-top off a Hamms. Girlie hooted. "This is the best reason I can think of for having these damn, hairy beasts around." He took a long draw and exhaled. "Let's see—Norman, Oklahoma, Barnum and Bailey, Blue Unit. The year Winnie was flying. Remember? What a trapeze act. What an ass. It must have been about sixty or sixty-six. Anyway, it doesn't matter when it was. I'm just finishing my act. Remember, Lester, I had the exploding car routine in those days with my dad and mom."

"It was more like your dad's act, Bobby."

"Whatever. Anyway, Oliver works loose a hinge or something, squeezes out of the damn cage, just before spec. Sorry, Doc, the spec is the parade at the beginning of the circus when all of the acts parade in front of the audience ... this is right as Lester, Karen, and the chimps are performing center ring. That freak was a regular Houdini. Anyway, the next thing we know, that big son-of-a-bitch is running right through the tip." Realizing Dr. Savage was again puzzled, he added, "The tip is the audience."

Dr. Savage nodded with understanding. "Thanks, Bobby. Got it."

"As you can guess, the crowd is panicking," Bobby continued. "I mean this is a situation. Oliver was big and menacing, you know."

Bobby stood and held his hand above his head. "I'm saying *big* even by Big People standards!" Maybe Lester's got a picture of him? This chimp is ugly, you understand, and very dangerous." The smooth boyish lines of Bobby's face wrinkled as he mimicked Oliver. "Anyway, where was I? Oh! Yeah, he runs right through the crowd and out the entrance, his big hairy arms flinging people aside while he steals popcorn and cokes on his way.

"The next thing you know," Bobby paused for effect, "he jumps into the petting zoo and begins fucking a chicken right in front of everyone. I swear on my mother's grave. Cross my heart. Lester, am I exaggerating?"

Bobby looked at Lester but didn't give him a chance to answer. "Mothers are covering their kids' eyes; everyone is screaming. I mean there is absolute panic. This is a damn wreck—Lester running around trying to gather up that big son-of-a-bitch while Karen is trying to control what's left of the act in the ring. But Oliver is having no part of going back to his cage. I mean this chimp has died and gone to Heaven! At which point he begins plucking the poor chicken alive between pumps." Bobby's dark brown eyes filled with tears as he gasped between giggles, his high-pitched voice elevated to barely intelligible squeaks.

Savage watched in amazement while a chimp, a midget, and an old man laughed together about a chimp copulating with a chicken. Only among animal people would this seem normal.

Lester roared with laughter, and between breaths while trying to talk, he waved his hands in cadence. His deep voice oddly contrasted with Bobby's. "This woman runs up to me and asks if I can't save the chicken. I told her I was sorry but it was a goner unless Ollie fell in love with the bastard. It turned out she was the wife of the Baptist minister. We were closed down by both the Humane Society and the Baptist Church. The Animal Rights nuts were out with pickets the very next morning. We went dark in Oklahoma. What a night. God, what a night." Lester paused, taking a bandana out of his back pocket to wipe away the tears. "I haven't had this much fun in ages. God, we had a good run, didn't we Girlie?" Girlie began hooting as soon as she heard her name, her feet and hands pounding the floor in unison.

His mood changed as he frowned and continued, "And that idiot Dusty gave an interview about all that bullshit of Oliver being half human that got us thrown off the show. That stupid bastard."

Savage looked at Bobby. "Did Oliver do anything besides break out of cages?"

Lester answered for him, "Yes. He was nothing but trouble. I only used him in the act for a short time. The other chimps were afraid of him. I couldn't work him within reach of any of them."

"Why?" Savage asked.

Lester rocked on the couch, deep in thought. "It was like he was almost human, only he wasn't. I think he understood our speech."

Savage stood. "That's been said of chimps many times. Did you ever try to communicate with him by using Sign Language or any complex gestures?"

Lester shook his head. "That's just the point. You didn't have to. He knew what you wanted. Like, he could read your mind or something. I don't know. It was eerie."

Savage began to sort through the pile of photographs on the coffee table. "Are there any other photos of him?"

Lester leaned over and handed him a scrapbook. "Try this one. I only used him in the act for a short time, but I've often thought of him since."

Savage looked up from the scrapbook. "Go on."

Lester shook his head. "Well, Doc, you don't mind if I call you Doc, do you?"

Savage waved it off.

Glancing at Bobby, Lester said, "Any time you want to jump in, please don't worry about interrupting me." He rubbed his hands on his thighs and rocked gently. Dark blue veins coiled along the backs of his hands in contrast to his pale skin. "He had a presence that was disturbing. Everyone felt it who ever got close to him. That's why he didn't last long with anyone. I have to say he's the only chimp in my career I really feared. He wasn't aggressive like most big males, mind you. It was like he was holding something terrible back. Like … it was unnatural."

Savage interrupted again. "I still don't understand what you're getting at."

Lester fumbled with a can of snuff, rolling it in his gnarled fingers while tapping it on the makeshift coffee table, deep in thought. The group had grown somber. He finally broke the silence but not the mood. "He was a big, barrel-chest chimp, all male. He was near sighted and squinted at you like Popeye, and almost all his teeth were gone. They'd been pulled. His lower lip hung way down, showing only his gums. He had high cheekbones. His head was very small but proportioned like a person's." Lester pointed at a photograph. "Look for yourself. He didn't have brow ridges like most chimps or much body hair. You could see freckles all over him."

Savage nodded. "He looks almost bald in this picture."

"That's because he was," Bobby said. "But as you know, a lot of chimps are."

"Sure, chimps can have some of these features, but I never heard of one chimp having them all together." Savage picked up the photo again. "He looks like a reflection of a midget in one of those funny house mirrors." He paused. "Sorry Bobby."

Bobby smiled and nodded.

Lester perked up. His head shook with a slight tremor. "That's it. All chimps have features similar to us and some may even have something like baldness that is very human, but Oliver had them all. The other chimps picked up on it. They couldn't figure how to relate to him and so were afraid of him. For that matter, all animals felt it." He nodded to Bobby. "You remember Kemo?"

"I sure as hell do!" Bobby stepped to the center of the living room, his tiny frame erect and arching back as though trying to gain more height, his hands at his side like a showman in the center ring. "I had this horse named Kemo. You know—for Kemo Sabe, in the Lone Ranger. I used him for stunts when I doubled for kids." His eyes twinkled as he winked at Dr. Savage. "Does that surprise you? Anyway, I had him broke and trained to do some tricks—the usual, like falling, limping, rearing, all that stuff. When I wasn't using him in a shoot, which was pretty much most of the time, I loaned him out for hazing in camel and ostrich races."

Savage looked from one to the other. He couldn't make out if they were putting him on. "You're kidding; races with camels and ostriches?"

Bobby rolled his eyes. "Well, yes. You see, there's a lot of call for them around the country, playing country fairs, rodeos, that kind of stuff—events for cities, charities and what have you."

Savage frowned, puzzled. "What's this got to do with the horse?"

"Oh! Well, the point. I used Kemo to haze camels and ostriches in these races. During the race I'd be riding in the middle of this craziness, trying to keep everything happening. I've seen Kemo take a mouth full of feathers right out of a big ostriches' butt, his ears all lain down. Doc, he was open for business. Kemo was one tough stud horse." Bobby used his hands to mime Kemo taking a bite as he stepped over Girlie's toys that lay on the rug.

"Sorry, Doc, I guess I'm wa-a-a-a-y off the point. The point is ... shit what is the point, Lester? Oh, never mind! Oh, yeah ... I boarded him on a ranch that was fuller than the goddamned Ark with every wild animal you could imagine. This horse worked in Circuses, on movie sets, carnivals, and that horse wasn't afraid of anything in this world or at least our side of it. Was he, Lester?"

Lester shook his head. "Not 'til he ran into Oliver. Bobby forgot to mention that we used to ride chimps on his back for parades. Anyway, we got this stupid idea one day, Bobby and me. Why don't we put Oliver on Kemo's back? I think we were trying to get some job, a commercial, maybe. The word was out that this production company, Needham, Harper, maybe, would pay big if someone could make it happen."

"So, what happened?" Savage asked.

"It didn't," Bobby said. "We bring Oliver out of his cage. He's bristling. He gets real agitated when he sees Kemo. Now Kemo takes one look at Oliver and rears up. He's really scared. He gets all white-eyed and bolts for the stable. We go running after him. Well, I go and Lester stays with Ollie. When I got to Kemo's stall, he was dead. I swear, dead."

Lester broke in, "He died of fright. It was awful. That ended that bright idea."

All four sat silently for a moment.

Savage reached into his jacket and pulled out a small notebook. "Do you guys mind if I make some notes before I forget some of this?"

"Hell no, Doc. Next time bring a recorder."

Savage began making notes.

While Savage was engrossed in writing in his notebook, Girlie leaned against him, hanging over his shoulder and watching him intently. Every once in a while, she brushed his ear with her finger. Savage would absently brush back as though a fly was irritating him.

"Do you think she knows what's going on?" Bobby asked. "I mean really knows."

Girlie's eyes followed Savage's hand as he scribbled, her face wrinkled in concentration making her look even older.

"Why do you think I keep working them? After sixty years I still don't know for sure. Just when you think they don't, they do some incredible thing that makes you believe in them, makes you want to try to close the gap some more. It's got to be hard for them, Bobby. They have a foot in both worlds: ours and theirs. They're driven more by instinct then we are. I think that's their real downfall. It keeps them too honest. They're wonderful animals though—so close to us, yet so different."

Finally, Lester said, "Let's step out on the porch."

It was strange how easily the transition happened. One moment Dr. Savage was a visitor, a guest, and the next, it seemed natural to leave him and Girlie together on the couch. It's that way with animal people. Through the interaction with each other's animals, they appraised each other's worth and built trust. It was a quick process that happened automatically, subconsciously, without fanfare. The life of animal people is very complex and subtle. But Savage knew the rules because he knew how to work animals as well as he knew his books. That combination was rare and highly valued.

Bobby and Lester moved out onto the porch under the stars and talked long into the evening. They fell into the rhythm of old friends who'd campaigned long together. They still watched Savage and Girlie as they fell into a similar rhythm, though they didn't have any more than a common understanding of each other's worlds. The night closed, comforting Lester. He didn't have the fears and feel the vulnerability of the night before. They talked mainly of the past, but Bobby's gentle humor brought him back to the present.

"Take the man to the Luncheon Club, Lester. Don't worry about old memories. It's time to make some new ones. Hell, you and Girlie finally have someone new to play with. Think of it. He hasn't heard any of your stories. It'll be months before you have to start lying!"

Lester stomped the weathered wood deck and scraped the rusting slider open. "Spoken from experience, huh, Bobby?"

"What do you always say, Lester? Whatever makes you happy? You know what they say about you circus people." Bobby followed him to the door. He lowered his voice inside. "I'll go with you guys if you want."

Lester laughed. "Bobby, don't do me any favors. And don't forget you grew up in the circus, Mr. Movie mogul."

Bobby smiled. "It's not a favor. I'm interested in this guy. Maybe there's more than we thought to this Oliver deal".

"I'm not sure that it's so much we didn't take notice of Oliver. It's we didn't want to believe it or worried someone would take him away if it was true. Anyway, that was a long time ago."

"No, it hasn't been that long ago. Unless he died in the last year, Oliver is still alive, and you and Girlie are for sure, but

Karen is gone. You can't hole up in this trailer park and expect to get any of it back. I'm sorry if I'm hurting you, buddy, but I love you both." Bobby put his hand on Lester. "You have more to do, I think." They both stood quiet, gazing into the darkness, as only close friends can do who didn't fear a silence falling between them.

Savage's voice startled them out of their thoughts. They looked into the blinding light streaming out, just making out his silhouette.

"Excuse me, Lester? Where do you keep your monkey chow?"

Girlie was food grunting in the background.

Bobby laughed. "Hey, what about us, too?"

Dinner was as lively an affair as Lester could remember.

* * *

Savage stayed late into the evening talking and joking, and Girlie was fast asleep when he finally said his good-byes and started down the gravel driveway toward his rental car. The little trailer park was quiet. Light seeping out of the crooked blinds of some of the trailers helped him make his way. He heard muffled voices and laughs drift from behind the thin walls as he walked through the darkness. Sounds took on an ominous meaning at that time of night; a bark was more than a dog.

He smiled and said to no one. "Bumps and thumps in the night".

All the secrecy of their investigations kept him on edge. Once again, he had the feeling that he wasn't alone. But why, he wasn't sure. He believed they were being very careful in their movements and inquiries since they'd decided to go down this slippery road that would put them on the wrong side of the university administration. But the broader ethical boundaries they might cross eclipsed these concerns.

He thought back to Lester. They had an amazing culture, circus people. They were so used to being outcasts on the fringes of society that they were incredibly tolerant—so tolerant they could have something like Oliver in their midst and not question it.

After the Circus Luncheon Club, he planned to fly home to Reno and report back to Dr. Turner. He hoped he'd have good news.

He shook his head to clear the shadows, smiling to himself as he got into his rental. "A chimp copulating with a chicken, camel and ostrich races, indeed." *What next?*

CHAPTER 4

When Dr. Savage picked up Bobby and Lester late the next morning, they rode together deep in thought, mulling over the conversations from the night before. Savage had been accepted into their association with little ceremony. Both Lester and Bobby could see that he knew his way around chimps. And Girlie really liked him, which was enough for them.

Bobby broke the silence first. "Doc, you're going to have to kind of listen and let us find out more about Oliver. These people warm to strangers a little slower than us. Turn left at the light." Bobby looked over at Lester, whose mood had become sullen the closer they got to their destination. "And no dragging up old grudges with Dusty, if he's there, or anyone else. I think Oliver screwing the chicken got you thrown off the show, not Dusty's interview with those locals."

Lester stirred. "God, will you listen to him, Doc? Who put you in charge? How 'bout you worry about yourself."

Bobby exhaled in frustration. "I'm just saying that we'll get nowhere if you drag up old news. He or Hunt are likely to know something. Straight down the alley here." Bobby pointed at a little parking lot that set off the alley across from Phillipie's in downtown Los Angeles. An old man standing at the entrance, acting as self-appointed security guard, motioned them in.

Bobby waved at him. "Hey, you old coot, why don't you get a real job!" The old man smiled and bowed.

Lester looked the other way.

Ignoring Lester's mood, Bobby continued, "That's Smooth, Lester. You remember him? What a bear act he had back in the day." He turned to Savage. "You see what I mean. That's exactly what I'm talking about. Lester's the only one I know who can't get along at that place. Christ! That was rude not to wave back at old Smooth."

"My God! I'm not going to worry about hurting the feelings of a bunch of 'has-beens', especially that old asshole. He was always around Karen when I was on the road."

"Doc, he's going to screw this up, I swear. The only reason anyone put up with him was they didn't want to hurt Karen's feelings. He's a—" Bobby stopped mid-stream. "Hell. I'm sorry Lester. I didn't mean that."

Lester shook his head and broke the strained silence. "Karen always fit me in. She put everyone at ease. Right here, by the trash cans, Doc."

Up the hill sat the few remaining pagoda roofs that had resisted the modernization of China Town. In the other direction, Union Station, the grand old station of the thirties and forties, remained unchanged.

They formed an odd group as they crossed the street, dodging traffic and ignoring the panhandlers and pedestrians who stopped to stare when they entered the door that lead downstairs into another time.

By Los Angeles standards, the French dip joint known as Phillipie's was an old establishment, since it had been around since before World War II. On the third Wednesday of every month, the Circus Luncheon Club met in the basement. Over the clamor of the lunch crowd, circus performers, young and old, employed or unemployed, famous or infamous lunched together to share their unique culture and fellowship. It was *the* place if you found yourself in LA to get news, hear the latest gossip, find work, or just simply be among your own kind.

Circus people were much like gypsies—in fact, many were. They had traditions that went back centuries and lived by different laws of conduct. They kept to themselves, seeming always to be "just passing through."

This place with its sawdust floors, its rows of long, wooden tables and benches, its clientele, who ranged from the homeless to yuppies on their lunch hour, was the perfect setting for a people who liked to blend into the crowd—a people you only noticed in the center ring when the circus was in town.

Lester and his wife had once been regulars. But after Karen's death Lester had found it hard to go—too familiar, too many memories. Bobby Waiter went occasionally. But, he too, had drifted away. Now he had more in common with the movie crowd.

But when you returned after a long absence, you were always welcome. All jealousies, rivalries, and disagreements were set aside, at least for a few minutes. This was neutral ground. You were among your peers, your family. You were also surprised to find out that most everyone knew exactly what you'd been up to. It was a small world.

People crowded around a long deli counter, muscling for a turn at French dips, coleslaw, and cheesecake. It took a moment to adjust to the contrast between the dim light of the restaurant and the bright streams of mid-morning sunlight that spilled through the greasy glass doors.

The sawdust covered floors and rows of long tables made it appear like a soup kitchen of the Great Depression. The place was full and business was booming. Old ladies in their starched uniforms, hair pinned neatly in buns, looking as though they had always worked there, shouted orders above the din and sliced up various meats as they built juicy dips on homemade French rolls. The aroma made Savage hungry.

Around the corner out of sight from the order counter sat several long, wooden tables with red-Formica tops, and some paneled, dark-walnut booths hugged the walls. While simple in design, obviously much care and craftsmanship had gone into their construction. They'd been made before mass production by the hands of someone who cared. The enclosed booths formed small, private dining areas. Pictures of various circus personalities adorned the walls.

The tables had folded cards with handwritten notes in various styles proclaiming, "Reserved for the Paul Engles Circus Luncheon Club." It felt to Savage as though he'd stumbled into a circus museum maintained by a haphazard curator who had little regard for grouping like things together. Memorabilia that went back to the last century covered the walls—paintings, old training gear, and circus props as well as the photos. Some had little typed captions explaining their significance. Others just hung there waiting for you to guess their stories.

"Looks like we're the early birds," Bobby said. "Come on, Lester, let's get a booth. Doc, why don't you come with me, so we can beat the rush and order our lunch. I know what Mr. Personality wants."

"Idiot," Lester hissed under his breath as he settled into a booth and moved the place card over to an adjacent table.

Bobby ignored him and led the way. They weaved through the throngs of customers toward the counter, past the cashier on the left, and joined one of the many queues.

"You never know who's going to be here. I hope Dusty shows. But if he doesn't, someone will know about old Oliver. Everyone keeps in touch, except Lester, of course. Big surprise! He's really having trouble with this, but he'll get over it." Bobby seemed to know everyone, and the few he didn't, he talked to as though they were old friends. All the servers knew him by name, and they bantered back and forth.

Their booth filled along with the other reserved tables. Bobby's face lit up as they reached the long table. "My God, everyone's here." He set down the tray and worked among the chairs, greeting everyone. "Hello. Hello."

Savage stood hypnotized. He'd never seen such an accumulation of characters. From the flamboyant to the reserved, in small groups or alone, they milled around the tables and booths. Lester fell into deep conversation with the whole group at his booth. Bobby kissed some, hugged others, but in one way or another made his way around to everyone.

He finally settled down next to a couple near the head of the table and motioned Savage over. "Doc, bring that tray and sit with us over here." Clearly everyone was pleased to see Bobby. Jabs flew back and forth across the table. Some ate, while others were still getting their orders. People flowed in a constant stream around the tables as late arrivals were greeted with renewed energy.

When Savage approached the table, various people smiled or nodded acknowledgment as he passed. They seemed used to strangers amongst them, showing him a mild curiosity.

Bobby patted the space next to him. "Have a seat, Doc. I've got some people for you to meet."

The couple sitting next to Bobby smiled. At first glance they seemed mismatched. The woman, small and lean, like a gymnast, appeared to be in her early forties. Savage discovered that she was a trapeze artist, a flyer as they referred to themselves. Her black, silky hair flowed down to her shoulders, and her soft, dark eyes betrayed her gypsy heritage. Savage thought her very beautiful and her smile disarming. She emanated the perpetual youth of someone who'd always done what she pleased. She rose to meet him. "Dr. Savage, I'm Winnie McCay."

"*The* Winnie McCay, if you please," Bobby said. "Winnie is probably the greatest living flyer, Doc. She's just come off a season with Barnum and Bailey, Blue Unit." He grabbed an older gentleman standing behind Winnie and said, "And this old hide here is Winnie's lesser half, Chester Cable. Chester's a juggler of some repute. He's in the Guinness Book of world records for juggling a table with his feet or something like that."

Chester's face wrinkled into a smile and his huge hand grasped Savage's outstretched hand like a vice. "Well, you're right—something like that, Bobby. So, you're the man interested in Oliver. Come, put that tray down."

Just as Savage was settling in, a young man pushed in between him and Winnie. "Excuse me, guys. Winnie, someone's got to start this meeting before they all wander off like last time.

We need to sign up acts for the Benefit."

Winnie sighed, looked over at Savage, and gently patted the young man's shoulder. "This handsome young man is Hunt Bushnell. Hunt, meet Doc."

Hunt smiled and lowered his voice. "A pleasure. So, you're the professor looking for Oliver." The tall young man had groomed himself to look like the magician Harry Blackstone Jr., closely cropped goatee and all. A bird trainer by trade, he was also the vice-president of the Luncheon Club, but because the president was on the road with his chimp act, he found himself in the dubious position of trying to the run the club without stepping on toes. A lot of the old timers saw him as an upstart. So, Hunt went through this ritual of conferring with one of the more established members before he called the meeting to order. The strategy worked because if the rest of the members saw him first speak to someone like Winnie, they were more likely to pay attention to him. He rapped his knuckles on the table. "Excuse me please. Your attention, please."

The group at Lester's booth laughed at some jest while a few more late arrivals greeted everyone all over again. Savage thought the chaos appeared much like a graduate student party.

Hunt tried again. A born showman with a center ring voice, once on a roll, the most seasoned audience liked to hear his voice, almost as much as he did.

Winnie smiled at Hunt, gently squeezed his arm, then stood. Everyone stopped talking and quickly returned to their seats. In an instant, all was quiet. It was that simple.

She sat down without saying a word, and Hunt began. "Thanks, Winnie. As some of you probably already know, the Children's Hospital Benefit will be the twenty-fifth of next month. We're going to sign up acts today. I hope we can count on you animal people. Dusty?" Hunt looked over at Lester's group.

A large man, who could have doubled for the actor Wallace Beery, waved back with a smile and a nod.

"Thank you, Dusty. We can always count on you and your

elephants. Now, people, could we have a show of hands?"

And so began a lengthy discussion that ebbed back and forth as to which acts would appear and in what order. The most heated discussion took place in this latter area, but after a few hours and gallons of coffee, all seemed satisfied.

At this point, at the close of the meeting, Winnie leaned over and whispered, "Doc, I've asked a few friends who knew about Oliver to join us in our trailer. Can you come over? Some of us are wintering out at the Wild Animal Training Center in Norco. It's about an hour drive from here. Dusty's coming over and is willing to help if we can keep him and Lester from getting into it. We think we know where he is." Winnie stood to greet a latecomer and Lester's group fell silent.

CHAPTER 5

"I really wouldn't worry too much, Dr. Melon. Dr. Turner is often late after his evening lecture. He probably got tied up with questions after class. He's very devoted to his students."

Mary wondered how many times she'd used that excuse. What an idiot he was sometimes. *The whole NSF site committee is here waiting to meet him, and he's probably spinning theories to a bunch of first year undergraduates, who haven't a clue what he's talking about. He's got no concept of time or priorities.* How could he not realize that these four men represented the funding behind his work, the National, *Goddamn*, Science Foundation?

"It's admirable that Dr. Turner takes such an interest in his students," Dr. Melon said. "But it's getting late, and I'm sure we have a full day, tomorrow. We had hoped to see Dr. Turner tonight to map out some sort of itinerary for our visit. Actually, many of the facilities we visit print one up. It's really quite helpful, you know."

Did Mary pick up a slight sarcasm? It was hard to tell with Melon. He spoke, most of the time, devoid of emotion. His voice sounded over rehearsed, bored ... *He* was boring. "I really wouldn't expect that kind of sequential approach from Dr. Turner. He's more simultaneous and intuitive then that ..."

Shit! Why'd I say that? That's really going to set him off.

She could tell he was growing impatient. A tall, grave-looking man in his early sixties, his manner and reputation indicated someone used to getting his own way.

"Perhaps so ..." He stood, rocking on his heels, hands in

his pocket, looking down his nose over his wire-rimmed, glasses.

He looked like an emaciated penguin.

"But still we have no idea what we're doing tomorrow morning." His voice rose, catching the attention of several people in the living room. "I'm tired and would like to go to bed. I'm as open-minded as the next person, but you people seem to have a complete disregard for other people's time." Harvard educated, he had all the usual prejudices against West Coast universities.

She found his habit of squinting his eyes as he spoke more annoying than disturbing, but it grew worse as the evening progressed. There was nothing physically attractive about the man. He resembled a scarecrow with big, protruding ears, and his coarse-black body hair contrasted against his pasty skin. But his long, thin hands bothered her the most. Pale and soft-looking like a china doll, they'd clearly never known physical work. In fact, his whole body lacked tone, shape or interest. He looked very much at home indoors, one of those people who'd probably looked ill all of his life.

The chimps would have a field day with this guy. Mary smiled to herself. She really wanted to tell this couch lizard that in all probability Ken had completely forgotten about him and his little site committee visit. He was likely at this very moment pontificating to some undergrads over a beer.

She looked around the large living room buzzing with small groups of research assistants, TAs, grad students, a select few undergrads, the site committee and their support team. There was still real enthusiasm among them. Ken's work brought that out in even the most skeptical scholars. His enthusiasm showed in every aspect of what he did and could be positively contagious.

The other three members of Dr. Melon's group still seemed interested in the log books, videos, and especially three young female grad students they had cornered in the video room. She laughed and whispered, "Poor things."

How could this guy not see all of this? At the same moment, she realized it had nothing to do with her husband's work. This man was jealous of anything or any idea he didn't directly control. Or was it more than that? He had been skeptical of the chimp project from its inception, so much so that he'd put the whole project in jeopardy when he wrote a dissenting recommendation for continuing their funding three years previously. Mary's suspicious nature had prompted her to do some research on him and his background, but, so far, she'd found nothing concrete. Instincts, however, lead her to believe that he had a hidden agenda and would use any excuse to try to shut down their work. Her Irish-Italian practicality surfaced; he was going to take a lot of work.

These visits had to be endured every three years, like a penance. The committee had become increasingly hostile over the past few years as Ken's work received more attention in the academic community and paradoxically became more controversial. She still had trouble getting used to the petty bickering and jealousies of intellectuals. They doted over their research like mother hens over their eggs.

This particular committee was tough. All the members seemed to have some connection to Melon. They'd either been a student of his or worked for him at some time in their careers. She always did a little investigating into their backgrounds and interests—a little insurance against Ken's naiveté.

Ken truly thought that his work would stand on its own merits and that politics had little to do with grants. It was just this innocence that had attracted her to him. She'd left her profession as a Hollywood director, her home in Malibu, and her friends to be with him. It'd been a hard adjustment. One she'd often doubted was going to work. Reno was, after all, a long way from Hollywood.

Ken was an absolute contradiction to anyone who really knew him. He had no practicality in the day-to-day business of life. He simply had no organization. His presence could bring total chaos to the most ordered operation or schedule.

University administrative assistants had nightmares about him. Department secretaries screeched in terror at his approach. But when it came to his research, he was a completely different person. His field notes and observations were ordered and filed with meticulous detail. He was never late to a lecture, yet he was often hours late to a dinner party. In the real world he just didn't make much sense to her. It was as though he lived on a completely different plane, one parallel to hers. He was unique, an original. Different from any other man she knew.

She smiled to herself. He didn't take himself seriously like these people. He could be really goofy at times. He just didn't fit. His colleagues constantly underestimated him because of his easy-going manner—until they saw him chain up a 180-pound chimp and work it through a temper tantrum. He had a desirable blending of physical attractiveness and mental wit, a renaissance man in a world of specialists.

The first greeting hoots jarred her out of her thoughts. The chimps' timeless, primeval cries of welcome echoed in the stillness of the night. Dr. Turner was home. This chaos was a nightly ritual of genuine respect these animals had for him. The big males hooted deeply as they pounded the steel cages with a resounding force that made one feel frail and vulnerable. The females shrieked above them in rising octaves that ended in pitches that only the bats could hear. Mary could recognize the individual chimps' repertoire of greetings.

The whole room buzzed with excitement. Conversations ceased mid-stream and were replaced with laughter and surprised cries. Mary thought Ken would've commented on what a good example of non-linguistic content everyone was displaying. Most of the visitors appeared uneasy. The staff reassured them that the chimps had not all escaped and were heading their way to take revenge.

Mary laughed to herself at how contagious these greetings were. Ken was always pointing out the similarities between chimps and people. His comparisons offended a lot of people, even a lot of the people in this room, who unknowingly were showing these very similarities tonight. You just couldn't live this kind of life if you took yourself too seriously.

She walked across the room as everyone settled with the quieting of the chimps. She could hear Ken hooting back at the chimps, panting and food grunting. The usual comments were flying around the room: "Which one's the ape;" "Talk about an entrance;" "What a drum roll."

God, I wish these people would get some new material.

"Excuse me a moment," she said, "I'll see if Dr. Turner needs any help." She didn't direct her comment to anyone in particular; she just wanted to get outside, away from all these eggheads. Her eyes had trouble adjusting to the darkness outside the house. She never tired of the stillness of the ranch after dark. A fresh breeze tonight brought the chill of the Sierras with it. They'd have to take special precautions to insure the chimps would be warm. She looked back at the house and thought how soundproof it was. Only muffled sounds drifted out, unintelligible. Light streamed from the big bay window of the family room, making it appear like an aquarium. The people inside didn't seem real in this stillness.

The Milky Way banded the Nevada sky, settling her feelings. The chimps were settling down as well. She loved the stars here. Ken had shown her all the different constellations and planets, but it was their colors that amazed her. LA didn't have many stars, let alone ones with colors.

Where is he? I'm going to kill him. She walked toward the chimp quarters. "Ken, where are you?" She could hear Mike food grunting and changed direction toward his cage. "Ken! Damn it. Where are you"! She knew that if he was communicating with Mike, a bomb could go off, and he'd be totally unaware. Signing with chimps took a great deal of concentration, which she understood but was not too forgiving of tonight.

He'd left her with a room full of "Poindexters" waiting for him. "Tea, cookies, and me can only last so long, and he's still screwing around," she said to no one in particular. "Ken, damn it, answer me."

Mike answered her with a hoot. "Oou, Oou, Awh, Awh, Ha, Ha." He held out his hand to her as he panted. Ken stood in front of the animal. He turned in her direction, but completely engrossed with Mike, he turned back. That always pissed her off, but tonight it was beyond belief.

She signed to Mike. "Hi, Mike."

Mike jumped up and down, hooting and pounding the cage. He danced for joy as he signed. "Play. Play. You. Me. Sweet. Drink. Play."

Mary shook her head and signed, "Not now, Mike. Bedtime—"

"You. Bed. Now." Mike whimpered, making his lips into a trumpet. "Ooh. Ooh. Hurry play. Candy. Me. Mike." He tapped his chest with his index finger, making hollow thumping sounds.

Mary frowned at Ken. "You're incredible. How can you screw up things so easily? Don't you know what's going on in your own house? How can you do this?"

Ken looked up, apparently completely confused. "Why what's the problem?"

"Are you serious? I'm so sick of you leaving me holding the bag with those over-educated idiots. What's wrong with you? Ken, these people pay the bills. This is the committee that reports back to NSF to fund your whole project."

Ken looked further confused, paused, very thoughtful, and shook his head. "No, that's next Friday. I'm sure of it."

Mary exhaled loudly. He still didn't understand what was happening. "Then who are all those people in our family room?"

Finally, as though he'd just arrived after a long absence from some place far away, he got it. "Shit. I've got to get up there. Will you tuck Mike in?"

Mary nodded and entered his cage. "With pleasure … Sometimes I think Mike's the only one who knows what he's doing around here." She stretched out her arms. "Mike, come here. Give me big hug."

Mike ambled up into her arms and panted in her ear. Both turned and watched Ken striding up toward the house. The light from the windows silhouetted him as he brushed his hair back and stopped to dust his clothes off in fits, like some mime entertainer. The light blinded them both as he opened the door and disappeared.

She shook her head. "God, Mike ... He's hopeless." She turned with Mike in her arms and walked up toward his den box.

* * *

All eyes turned to Ken when he entered. He thought to himself that it really didn't feel like his place filled with all these people and the furniture rearranged. God, how could he have missed all these preparations? *Mary must have worked her ass off.* But he couldn't think about that right now, he was in big trouble. He had to concentrate on the business at hand.

He promised himself that from now on he'd pay more attention to what was going on around him. *Shit, I don't even know who's supposed to be here or the names of the half these damn people.*

It didn't take him long before he caught Melon's frowning gaze from across the room. He smiled, and when it became apparent that it'd take him some time to make his way through the crowded room, he feigned an apologetic gesture. He moved through the crowd, greeting various guests and exchanging shakes and embraces.

Thank God for primate greeting behavior.

Out of the corner of his eye he saw what he guessed to be the whole site committee plus entourage making progress toward him. He just had time to make himself a drink at the bar.

Whisky in hand, he looked up again. Dr. Melon and company were pushing through with purpose. *Closing in on their prey.*

"If a thing's got to be done, it may as well be done, right?" he said to no one in particular. He took a gulp of his drink, set it down and turned toward his destiny, alone. *Where the hell is Mary?*

Melon approached with expressionless eyes, like steel ball bearings. He reminded Ken of a shark during a feeding frenzy. The students and guests parted for him like Moses and the Red Sea.

Turner smiled. "Ah, Dr. Melon, at last. It seemed as though I'd never get away this evening." He flashed his most endearing and ingratiating smile as he reached out to shake Melon's hand.

Melon hesitated between anger and confusion, then seemed to settle on confusion. "So it would seem." He grasped Ken's hand. Ken's mind raced over all the things they'd discussed and demonstrated last visit and desperately tried to remember what he'd promised to do as a result of that visit.

I need more time. Hell, I need Mary. He glanced about the cluster of students that gravitated around them and caught the eye of one of his grad students, a pretty young woman from Mexico City. "Consuelo, will you please bring us Dr. Melon's last reprint? It's on my desk in the study."

"Yes, professor." She strode off toward his study.

Ken's gaze followed her out of the room and then returned to Melon. "I really must congratulate you on your recent article. It was most insightful to postulate such a close correlation between semiotic behavior and classic symbiotic relationships.

Melon's face softened just slightly around the eyes. "Well. Dr. Turner, I'm pleased you feel that way. Few scholars have grasped the important distinction between the two."

Including you, Ken thought. "How true, how true … Ah, here's Consuelo now."

She handed him the reprint while brushing her hair back with her other hand. She caught his gaze with a twinkle in her eye.

I wonder if she's on to me. "Thank you." He smiled, then turned his attention back to Melon. "Dr. Melon …" he paused to hand him the reprint, "I wonder if you could elaborate on your definition of semiotic behavior? I've required your article in my Animal Communication seminar this term." Sweeping his arm around the room in a lazy motion, he continued, "Many of these bright, shiny eyes and faces are in that very seminar."

Laughter joined his chuckle. The room buzzed as grad students gathered around them.

Melon took the bait. "Well, of course, it is a very complicated topic." He looked around at the eager, attentive faces and then glanced at his watch. "But I think we could take a few minutes and I could summarize the main points of my theory and show how that relates to my definition ..." Melon drew a deep breath, then began.

Ken had the man on the run. *It'll be awhile before he looks at his watch again.*

Students pressed in around them, their attention focused on Melon, and Ken made it appear as if they were pushing him out of the inner circle of discussion. He maneuvered himself behind Melon and quietly slipped out of the room toward the kitchen. At the kitchen door he caught Consuelo's eye and subtly motioned to her to follow. She picked up his meaning quickly, joined him in the kitchen, and began pouring herself a cup of coffee.

Beneath the noise of the party, he whispered, barely moving his lips," Find Mary as quickly as possible, and Mark if he's still about, and bring them to my study." Consuelo made the slightest nod and left. There's a quick young lady, he thought, as he left the kitchen by way of an opposite door that lead into the living room.

The room was dark. They rarely used it for functions such as this, it being too small and intimate. He heard a rustling on the couch as he passed through it toward the hall that lead back to his study. Two figures practically jumped up at him in the dark.

"Dr. Turner!" Mark's English accent strained with a combination of embarrassment and surprise.

"Jesus! What the hell are you doing popping up like a Jack-in-the-Box? You scared the hell out of me. Follow me, both of you."

Mark Chaney and a young, attractive student untangled

themselves and got up. "Look, Dr. Turner. We didn't mean to offend you or—"

"Quiet! Just follow me." Turner motioned them along.

They glanced at each other and followed sheepishly in single file down the dark hallway. Muffled voices drifted up the hall from the party. Ken led them down another hall and disappeared into his study. Mary and Consuelo stood to welcome them as they entered.

Mary was about to speak when Ken interrupted her. "Close the door and sit down, please, everyone."

Mary shook her head. "This isn't one of your seminars, Ken. Please lose the drama."

"You don't seem to understand," he replied. "The whole site committee is here, and we're not ready." He paced in front of them.

"Yes, *we* are." Mary and Consuelo looked at each other, smiling.

"Oh really! Then how do we propose to tour them tomorrow and schedule demonstrations. It was disastrous last time. It'll take us weeks to prepare." Ken frowned. "I can't understand how this happened. We really need to plan better."

Mary looked in the direction of Mark and his girlfriend. "Mark, do you hear this. Look at him. I wish I had this all on film. If you must know *we* do have a plan. *We* just didn't include you this time. We learned from the last visit the chaos you added to our planning."

"What do you propose to do tomorrow?" Ken asked, ignoring her reference to chaos.

"We propose to follow our itinerary."

They all smiled at him, except for Mark's friend who seemed confused.

"What itinerary?" Ken was really at a loss now.

"Mark, if you please."

Mark stood and walked over to the file cabinets. His girlfriend stuck close to him; she seemed nervous and unaccustomed to such close contact between faculty and staff.

Ken recognized her now. She was in the medical school. That explained much of her reserve. They made an attractive pair: she, a tall blond with beautiful hazel eyes, and Mark, a good-looking Englishman—a bit shorter than her, but his red hair and blue eyes made up for it. Then of course he had an Oxford accent. Intellectual women loved an accent; especially in the Queen's English. He, also, noticed Consuelo's eyes darken as she stared at Mark.

So, Mark's at it again. I'm going to have to have a talk with that boy.

Ken caught the young lady's eye and smiled. "What's your name?"

She smiled and seemed to relax a bit. "Kristen, sir." She had a clear accent, perhaps from Denmark.

Consuelo's eyes hardened.

Mary interrupted. "Kristen, will you please hand Dr. Turner the folder Mark's holding?"

Kristen grabbed the folder from Mark and bought it to Ken, avoiding Consuelo.

"Thank you." He opened a thick folder and leafed through it. They'd thought of everything. Chimp feeding schedules, log entries, demonstrations, itineraries, lectures and presentations, video screenings, and dinner schedules. The folder reminded him of the handouts given at academic conventions.

Ken shook his head, chuckling. "My God, you've thought of everything. So, what do we start with tomorrow? A magic show?"

"I think the double-blind experiment with Mike." Mary smiled and caught his eye.

All but Kristen and Ken nodded in agreement. "Well, they won't be able to say our presentation is rehearsed. We'll call a project meeting tomorrow morning at eight. Shall we?" Ken motioned them toward the door. "As Mary always says; 'it's show time.'"

As the group left his study, he grasped Mark's arm and paused until they were alone. "Make sure there's no mention of Oliver or the whereabouts of Dr. Savage. Understand?"

Mark nodded.

When he reentered the meeting room, Melon rushed him at the door. "See here, Turner. Where've you been off to? We really need to know what's on tap for tomorrow. We've come a long way and are tired."

"Yes. Yes. It's all in here. I popped off just now to get you and your people the itineraries for your visit." Ken handed copies to the committee members.

"What? You have programs for us." Melon snatched one out of one of his colleague's hands and leafed through it. "Why, this is excellent. I really can't tell you how surprised I am at this organization considering ... most impressive, Turner."

"Why do you say that? As everyone knows, I'm a stickler for order and efficient use of time." His students, those within hearing, shot looks at each other in disbelief. Unheeding, he continued, raising his voice above their mummer, "I'm very disappointed in you people. Why didn't someone give Dr. Melon and his committee the itinerary in my absence?" He looked around the room, making sure not to catch anyone's eyes. Many of the students looked completely confused, unsure of their own ears.

Mary leaned up next to him and whispered, "Ken, don't push it."

* * *

Melon and his party stood in the gravel parking area in front of the ranch. He shivered in the cold mountain air and looked back at the main house and the grounds of the facility as his people gathered around him. In a sarcastic tone, he addressed the committee, "I think Dr. Turner has done pretty well for himself with our money—think of what this facility and those animals are worth." The rest of the group nodded in unison. "He's not fooling anyone with his pretext to be solely interested in pure research while ignoring the significant applied aspects of his work. I have taken the liberty of engaging a representative from the Department of Defense to consult with us, a Mr. Vandusen and his team. He has been very helpful in keeping us informed on Dr. Turner's real motivations." Melon paced in front of them, and his voice grew conspiratorial. "To think of the resources he's wasting here." He swept his hand in the direction of the chimp cages and quarters. "I'm told by Vandusen that there're enormous benefits that could be gained by putting those animals to work for the military. Lives could be saved—lives. What a waste; I'm not going to allow it." He paused for effect. "Pure research, indeed!"

A chimp, as though on cue, broke the silence of the evening with a hoot.

One of the members with enough courage to interrupt Melon's venting asked, "So what do you propose?"

Melon startled as though out of a trance. "We're all professionals here and know good research from bad and are charged with the fiduciary responsibly for the foundation. We have the power to recommend not funding his work. I think without funding the animals, at least, would become the property of the university in cooperation with the foundation—us."

"But would the foundation go along with this?" the same member said.

Melon smiled malevolently. "We *are* the foundation, especially if there's a unanimous recommendation not to continue funding." He made eye contact with each and every member. "I went to great lengths to hand pick this committee."

Several members were visibly uneasy with this line of discussion. Dr. Melon was a very powerful man in their world and could make or break careers.

Seeming to sense their line of thought, he dismissed them: "Let's get out of this fantasyland and get some rest. Tomorrow is an important day for us and an opportunity to do some good."

They had much to think about as they climbed into their van for the long trip back to town. Each had to balance the ethics of what Melon proposed with the future of their careers. It was now obvious why they'd been selected to this powerful committee. They each owed Melon something large.

CHAPTER 6

Ken's chimp facility stood in the shadow of the Sierras in the middle of what had once been the finest grazing land in Nevada. The panorama of the mountains and rolling grasses gave a western feel, in a Bonanza-Wagon Train sort of way. Horse ranches of wealthy casino families and a few remaining old-timers quilted the valley. This was a haven where old money could embrace the lifestyle that had made them, where they could ignore the new development and "progress" of downtown Reno but still remain close to their money.

Ken lived at the facility and fondly referred to it as "the ranch." And it was just that, though little remained of the original buildings built in the late 1880's. It was now a hodgepodge of architectural styles reflecting the different needs and tastes of a variety of previous owners.

It started as a cattle ranch, but as the economics of the fifties needed recreation more than beef, it evolved into a dude ranch. Then, in the sixties, as gambling grew in the "The Biggest Little City in the World", the ranch became more of brothel then a dude ranch. Between owners and pinches with the law, it swung back into legitimacy as cottages for people getting divorces Nevada style. But as divorce laws loosened around the country, few couples needed to come to Nevada anymore and the place came up for sale just as Ken received a large NSF grant to expand his linguistic research with the chimps. Needing more room, he bought it in the early sixties and converted it to his research facility—a good move on his part as in just a few years, South Reno, west of the 395, had become high rent.

The property's history made it amply adapted to his plans. The main ranch house, a stately Victorian of white clapboard and green trim, nestled in an orchard of apples and pears on the remaining thirty acres of the once-grand spread. Ken moved into the house, and Mary made it a home. The various barns and outbuildings were put to use by his staff as the project grew. The hay barn left over from the cattle days was renovated into an indoor play area for the chimps. The cottages used in the dude ranch days housed the chimps in human-like, domestic settings, and the apartments that had once housed those ending their broken dreams, now housed research assistants.

These apartments were the oddest part of the facility. Built in the sixties, they didn't fit with the rest of the setting. The six, motel-style rooms with bathrooms and a community kitchen looked over a now-empty swimming pool. Ken didn't like swimming pools and often threatened to fill it in, much to the consternation of his staff who held out hope of someday restoring it to its past glory.

Young graduate students, who'd been lucky enough to get on the project, lived in these apartments. They came from all over the world, sporting pedigrees from the finest universities, wishing to be in the frontline of what many felt was the *moon shot* of the social sciences. They fed, clothed, and cared for the project chimps, and were in Ken's words, Human Companions, or in the student's own words, HC's. Ken didn't like the more commonly used terms of trainer or handler, thinking it to imply a manipulation of the chimp's behavior by the accompanying person.

The chimps had an HC with them every waking hour. These young students fed them, clothed them, played with them, fought with them, and, all the while, recorded data. They kept a running account of all the signs the chimp generated and the context in which they were observed.

Only American Sign Language (ASL), as used by the deaf, was used around the chimps. That the chimps had responded in kind shook the foundations of science, questioning the very definition of language.

Ken's research challenged the traditional premise that the possession of language was what separated humans from the rest of the animal kingdom. These animals were acquiring language and using it to make sense of the world.

The members of this project sensed the power of this endeavor. They approached their work with excitement, but also the long hours, physical danger, and intellectual demands of being a student and researcher simultaneously caused an intolerable amount of stress. The turnover was considerable during the first year. But for those who stayed, a very close and secret community of practice had developed of which Ken was a stranger.

These young people had developed their own slang and acronyms surrounding the project. They held parties, gave awards, and passed on the oral history of the project as seen through their eyes.

Ken's friend and colleague, Dr Fred. Savage, was closer to the students' ages. He knew and understood their world, shared in it, and kept their confidences. While these students respected and admired him, seeing him as a more competent peer, they came close to worshiping Ken. He was, in their eyes, a genius, and they forgave his many eccentricities.

Various other buildings were used as shops, labs, and living-quarters for more senior members of the staff, the Ph.D. candidates and the post docs who headed different facets of Ken's overall research.

A two-story cottage, set fifty yards across the main drive from Ken's quarters, was the only other real house on the ranch. It'd been the foreman's quarters in the old days and had been remodeled in the sixties to look like a scaled-up doll house, for God knows what reason, and that was what everybody called it, the "Doll House."

The vacant downstairs served as storage for obsolete and broken instruments, and upstairs housed Savage when he was in town. Though technically on Ken's staff as the staff ethnologist, he was rarely seen in the flesh and had spent most of the last six months in the rain forests of Southern Mexico and Brazil studying Jaguars. An expert in animal communication, in particular cross-species communication, his work was considered brilliant, but he was thought to be eccentric by those who knew him. Rather than following the normal conventions of dress and decorum expected of professors, he wore different hats and clothes he'd collected during his travels to distant parts of the world while conducting his fieldwork. He treated everyone the same, whether they be a university president or a custodian, and spent his free time in a working-class bar called Franks Café.

Savage was Ken's best friend. They'd gone to graduate school together. Stories of his exploits in the field and in the local bars had begun circulating around the university community again, so Ken expected him back any day now.

Each morning for the last week, he had walked over to the Doll House half expecting to find his friend having his morning coffee with some young grad student on the upstairs balcony while enjoying the view of the Sierras and watching the horses play in the neighboring pastures.

Ken always started his morning rounds while the chimps were still sleeping. It gave him time to collect his thoughts and plan his day. This late-autumn morning, made crisp by new snow high up in the mountains, was special. He was ready to demonstrate his double-blind test for sign language vocabulary with his brightest chimp, Mike, to the site committee. He smiled as he thought of how well the evening before had gone with this committee.

What a lot of crap, but thank God for Mary.

He took in the sweeping panorama of the Sierras and breathed the crisp, clean air into his lungs. It felt great to be young, alive and free to do work he loved.

He thought that what he did was a special kind of travel, like wandering into the vast empty spaces of an early \nineteenth century world map with all those blank, white spaces that read "unexplored." His chimps were like windows into non-human perception, guides into those unexplored spaces. Nothing could be this good.

His feet crushed the frozen gravel, and his breath fogged as he caught the whiff of coffee brewing. Probably one of his students over at the apartments. Everything was still.

The calm before the storm.

He headed down the walkway toward the Playroom, walking very quietly by Moja's cabin so as not to wake her. One of the older chimps in his project, she'd grown more difficult to handle with each passing year, a frustrating part of working with chimps. Like humans, their intelligence grew as they developed physically, but they also became stronger, and their chimp instincts often got in the way of their language development. No one seemed to have a solution to this dilemma, and it had serious consequences for his work.

Mark ambled around the corner of the building just as Turner reached the door. "Good morning, Dr. Turner," Mark said nervously. "Listen, about last night in the living room, I really would like to explain."

Ken shook his head. "Not now, Mark. You'll wake the chimps." He pointed to the Playroom door. "Come inside. Let's get ready for the double-blind test."

The Playroom had been converted from an old shop and finished off with drywall. Masses of toys cluttered the floor. Some were proper toys like those you'd buy in a store, but most were objects that had not sold at garage sales and army surplus stores and the like: headless dolls, broken cameras, remnants of parachutes, plastic pipes, ammunition boxes, an array of wrenches and bolts, junk in general which the chimps loved.

A two-way mirror hung on one wall so that researchers could view the chimps from an adjacent room, the Observation Room. A projection screen situated below this observation mirror allowed a chimp to look at what was projected on it and communicate with a researcher, an HC, without the person being able to see what was on the screen.

Ken had designed this venue and these procedures to ensure that someone could not cue the chimp intentionally or unintentionally by seeing what the chimp saw. In research circles, this cueing was referred to as the "Cleaver Hans" error. Named for a turn-of-the century circus act in which a horse was thought to be able to solve addition and subtraction problems by counting or striking his hoof the number of the answer.

Cleaver Hans had created quite a stir until a scientist of the time had noticed that his trainer had given subtle non-verbal cues as the horse neared the correct answer by slightly, leaning toward the horse in anticipation of giving him a reward. The horse used the subtle moves, nods and like of the trainer to solve the problem rather than possessing any actual mathematical ability. Ken thought it disappointing but very observant on the horse's part.

No one ever determined if these non-verbal cues were intentional or not. Savage had once confided to Ken that he'd always believed that the scientists and the press of the day had missed the real point. It was amazing, to him, that this horse was astute enough to read human non-verbal communication to such a level as to be able to display the correct answer. Though an amazing display of cross-species communication, it would be a disastrous outcome for his project, to say the least.

At the last site visit Melon had expressed concern over the subjective practice of having researchers recording on paper what they thought the chimps were signing. He feared a "Cleaver Hans" error might exist in his work. The committee had accepted that "something like language was going on" but questioned just how much of it the researchers themselves prompted or cued in the way circus trainers gave subtle cues to elicit tricks from their performing animals. These remarks had enraged Ken, but, just the same, he knew how important it was to dispel these claims or concerns with a solid, empirical test that could not be disputed.

Hence, Ken's double-blind test, the scourge of his graduate students, who had spent long hours building it over the last several years, testing it and refining it. Ken had seemed almost obsessed with this test, pushing the entire project to contribute to its design and execution. And now it was time to display it to Melon and the site committee.

Mark started cleaning up the room and put order to the toys as Ken loaded the slide carousel next door in the Observation Room. He returned shortly carrying the slide carousel and observed Mark at the other end at work with the toys. "Mark, don't do … Look, leave everything as it is."

Ken stood looking about the room. Nothing escaped his gaze. He surveyed from ceiling to floor slowly and deliberately and moved his head around the room, visualizing Mike at play. He imagined him lumbering over to the screen with the handler and searched for what he thought might be distractions to the purpose at hand. Finally, he looked back to Mark and said, "If Mike comes into this room and finds it well ordered, he may get suspicious. He's used to this place looking like a bomb went off." He took another look at the area where Mike would sit, and if all went well, the test would determine the future of his entire project. Frowning, he looked at Mark again. "Don't do anything different from a normal testing day. I worry that Mike will pick up on our nervousness."

Mark glanced at Ken's mismatched socks and smiled when he realized that he had two different boots on as well.

"I don't see what's so funny about this damn 'dog and pony show' that we have to do every Goddamn three years for a bunch of pencil pushers. God, I hate this." Ken breathed faster, his voice reaching a pitch that conveyed his raising sense of urgency, his fear that everything was not ready.

Mark ignored him and moved to the areas of the room he always picked-up before a test, mainly around the doors and windows. "Not to worry, Professor. Mike, at least, will shine during all this. He likes doing the test—bloody showoff".

Ken nodded but hesitated. "I hope you're right. He can be very difficult sometimes if he senses we really want him to do something. Remember last fall when I tried to video him for that press group?"

Mark smiled. "Yes, but remember there's an adage among animal people that goes something like, the secret to working an animal is you have to be smarter than the animal you're working. I reckon the old boy who thought that up had to deal with the likes of Mike, and I'd say we have a sizable brain trust here to deal with that little bugger."

Ken smiled. "Right. Remember when you dropped your keys in his cabin and he stole them?"

"Actually, I was hoping that was all forgotten. Yes, the little devil let himself out and then commenced to liberate all his friends. The whole bloody thing was recorded on the security video. It took me a fortnight to bribe Consuelo out of it." They both tried to control their laughter as Mark continued, "It could've been worse … he had the bloody master key on that ring!"

Laughter echoed off the walls, amplified by the concrete floor of the Playroom. Mark caught Ken's eye, his English reserve restored. "It'll be fine, really. He's sharp as a pin this morning."

"Yes, understood, but sometimes he gets that evil look in his eyes, and you can almost see the horns growing out of his head." They both stared off into space for a moment, thinking of all the carnage Mike had caused in the past and what he was capable of inflicting on Melon and his team aside from botching the double-blind test.

Motivated by these thoughts, both stirred into action. "We're going to have to really watch that little devil today, Mark," Ken said as the continued to clean up. "At least one thing can be said about this work."

Mark looked up at him and said in a serious tone, "What's that, Professor?"

"It is never, ever boring!" They laughed again, louder.

Mary came through the Observation Room door, smiling. "My God, did I just hear laughter in here or was that hyperventilating? Ah, hi Mark—keeping our fearless leader away from red alerts, I hope?" Mary referred to Ken's propensity to add drama and chaos to the simplest tasks as "red alerts" of which her husband was famous to almost the level of legend at the Ranch. It was common knowledge that there'd been fewer since their marriage. His grad students didn't know if they should be pleased or disappointed with the absence of these outbursts. They sometimes actually missed the Commedia dell'Arte flavor of the old days before Mary.

"Oh, by the way," she added, "Consuelo just phoned. The committee has just left their motel."

Ken gasped. "Christ, Mary! Are you having them watched?"

Mary busied herself about the room picking and stacking what the chimps had dumped in their play. Speaking over her shoulder, she said, "Why is there some sort of code among you academics against it? It's obvious you haven't been to many film festivals." She continued at her work, sorting some National Geographic magazines strewn on the floor, fallout from some chimp chase game. "Anyway, I won't go quite that far. Just say that Consuelo likes to stay informed and decided to have breakfast at the Bagel Factory across from where they're staying." She looked over her shoulder at them and smiled while brushing a strand of red hair back from her deep-green eyes. "You guys better get back to the house or you'll be late to your own meeting—as though that would be a surprise."

As they filed out of the Playroom, she paused and looked back over the room, hands on her hips as though it were one of her movie sets with cameras ready to roll. She nodded. "This works."

Ken's long strides paced him up the drive ahead of them. Anxious to reach the house and the impending meeting, he was already mumbling to himself, head down in thought.

Mary leaned close to Mark, a practiced move. "Stick close to him today, Mark. You have a calming effect on him."

Mark nodded. "He's wearing two different boots today. And then, there's his bloody, mismatched socks."

"Great," she whispered, then raced off through the garden toward the back door.

* * *

Nothing this side of purgatory takes as long as a university meeting, and this meeting was no exception. The usual gathering and assortment of faculty members, junior and senior, grad students, and post-docs would filibuster to prove they were clever, and often arguments broke out that had little to do with the purpose or direction of the meeting.

To get anything done required a strong personality that could keep everyone on track. The worst of these meetings was when Ken decided to lead it himself. He could lead when it was important to his research, but this morning's meeting had lasted past its scheduled forty-five minutes and had become bogged down. An aside comment had sparked him to give an impromptu lecture on New World monkey locomotion. The room echoed with competing voices wishing to be heard. All views were singular and loud.

Melon and the site committee walked right into all this turmoil. No one took heed of him as he stood, rocking on his heels, looking around expectantly, nor did anyone see Mary and Mark catch Melon and his committee as they stood confused by the door and lead them outside for a walk around the facility to *get them orientated*. This was done over the committee's protest as they competed to point out that most of them had been at the facility before. But Melon soon pulled everyone in line when he informed them that the tour was part of the newly *revised* itinerary that Consuelo had just delivered to him with her best low-cut blouse and a smile that took you to the south of things.

Meanwhile, the meeting finally died under its own weight with no one really knowing what was expected of them other than to "act in your usual professional manner" and to direct any specific questions to Mary. Several grad students immediately asked where they could find her. Everyone left charged with enthusiasm though many were not sure to what purpose to put it.

Consuelo caught Ken at the door and directed him to the Playroom. The stage seemed set, and he thought that it wasn't often in one's career that everything you've worked for rides on the outcome of one single event. Everyone can remember such a time: a turning point, a critical moment of clarity. This was just such a time for the future of his project. "The hell with it!"

He didn't speak again as they walked down the gravel driveway past the cottages toward the Playroom. Moja, one of the chimps, hooted a greeting at him as they passed her cottage. Ken paused for a moment at her window and signed, "Moja. Good girl?"

She panted with a play face. "Me. Me. Good. Play. Play. You. Me." A play face is the happiest you'll ever see a chimp. Their mouth is open and panting with real unadulterated revelry. They're showing all their teeth, almost smiling in a human sense. You can't help but laugh, as well, especially when they look back with that relaxed countenance of pure joy.

Ken grinned, never tired of this display. "Play. Late. Goodbye."

Moja whimpered. "Play. Play. Chase. Now."

Her HC came up to the window smiling. "Time. Eat." Moja began food grunting and looked away.

Ken signed goodbye again and continued down to the Playroom, thinking about the difference between instinct and intelligence. This time he entered the Playroom from the back, into the Observation Room.

The Ranch began to bustle with activity. Students came and went from the crowded little Observation Room with expectant faces. Mary and Consuelo gave Melon and his closest associates the grand tour of the equipment and procedures. Ken leaned against a wall, watching Mike and his HC playing through a two-way mirror. He didn't see the horns growing this morning. In fact, Mike was in a very cooperative mood, helping his HC stack and put things away when he was finished playing with them.

The HC working with Mike, a tall, lanky boy from the Midwest, was one of the best in the project. Ken's cynicism rose for the moment as he reflected that the boy wasn't good because of his training and education but rather because he'd grown up on a farm. He was simply good with animals. Ken felt uncomfortable when he thought along these lines. So much for the School of Animal Behavior. He laughed and shook his head. *Why not just grow up on a farm and save all that expense of money and time?*

Mike got into the swing of things; naming things for the HC as he moved around the room. *The transition from play to work is what chimps display better than we'll ever know.*

The boy subtly worked his way toward the projection screen and two-way mirror for the double-blind test. Ken realized that the HC was not only good with animals but also intelligent and subtle. He must make a note of that and talk to the boy later or perhaps Mark already recognized his talent.

"What? What? That?" the boy signed to Mike, pointing at a picture of a cat in a magazine he held. Mike took the magazine and leaned on one arm as he lowered his forehead onto the open page. His lower lip hung loosely down, and then he puckered and made kissing noises at the picture. Tapping the page with his knuckles, he signed, "That. Cat."

The HC nodded. "Good boy! Yes. That. Cat."

Mike bounced around the table, hooting and stomping his feet on the magazine. He drummed the table, and his hoots grew louder and higher pitched. At the peak of the display, he swept his long arms under his body while jumping up and awkwardly flinging the magazine across the room. Pages settled around the room. Seeming satisfied, he hunched down on the table and looked over his shoulder toward the mirror.

The boy beckoned him over to the chairs in front of the projection screen. Mike ambled over and lay lazily into an over-stuffed chair. The test began without fanfare. Melon and the site committee who'd quietly filed into the Observation Room pressed against the two-way mirror. They'd been warned that if Mike heard noises from behind the wall, he'd very likely get distracted. Some of Melon's group began taking notes while others activated a video recorder they'd hastily set up on a tripod.

The HC was really good. He was so wrapped up in his duties that it became apparent that he'd completely forgotten about the presence of the observers. Mike worked through twenty or so pictures before he became distracted and left his chair to play. It took a while and much skill on the HC's part before he could be persuaded to continue the test, but eventually it was over and Mike went to one of the windows of the Playroom and signed, "Out."

The HC followed Mike and signed, "Who. Out?"

Mike panted. "Me. Mike. Out. Hurry." With a play face, he tapped gently on the HC's arm while shaking his head up and down, then signed again, "Out. Out." He took hold of the HC's hand and led him to the door.

Melon and the rest stood mesmerized for several heartbeats before he finally broke the silence. "Dr. Turner, this is quite remarkable." He looked at one of his assistants. "Do we have this on video?" They exchanged sly, knowing looks.

A short, dark-haired man with glasses that kept sliding down his nose stirred nervously and replied in what seemed an over-rehearsed tone. "Well no, sir. I didn't realize that you wanted the test recorded—you never told me to record."

Melon smirked. "I'm sorry Doctor but could we have the chimp do the test again? I need this data for our files back in Washington."

Ken looked at Melon in disbelief. "What? Let me get this straight. Your people wanted this on video and let us put Mike through the whole Goddamn test without recording?" His voice raised a pitch as his whole body tensed, hands clenching into fists. "I'll tell you what you can do with your fucking video," he shouted.

His grad students saw a *red alert* coming and made a mass exodus from the Observation Room.

Mary broke into the room against the flow out the door. "That really won't be necessary, Dr. Melon. We recorded everything from three angles with our own cameras. Mary handed him three cassettes. "I think this will make provocative viewing back at the motel. And we have backup copies should you have any other technical difficulties." She used her most disarming smile and locked onto Melon's stare, eyes shining as she jerked back her dark-red hair and combed it with her fingers. Like so many lesser gods and producers before him, she drew him into her spell—a spell Ken knew well and had willingly embraced long ago.

"Thank you, Doctor … ah, Mrs. Turner. I'm sorry for the inconvenience. I can't think what my people were doing during this amaz—this display of inter-species communication. I'm sure this will be adequate."

Melon and company gathered up their belongings and beat a hasty retreat out of the room as Ken continued to glare.

Mary watched Melon gingerly close the door on his way out, then turned to Ken. They stared at each other for a moment. Ken seemed transfixed but then worked through his conflicting emotions and realized what had just happened. "Good old, Mike. God, he was better than usual."

"He may have just financed your project—and judging from that little Poindexter's reaction, for a long, long time. It's going to be difficult for them to discredit us with this evidence." She held more cassettes up in the air. "You might want to thank our little stealth crew of grad students for having a few extra cameras rolling." Mary hopped up on a counter and swung her shapely legs back and forth. Her voice became more serious as she continued, "It was rather unfortunate *and* convenient for them that Dr. Melon's flunkies didn't get Mike's performance on tape. Don't you think?"

Mark broke into their thoughts. "Interesting; the red recording light was blinking on his camera the whole time."

Mary nodded. "With what we gave them on tape and the fact that they may miraculously discover that their camera did actually work, there should be little doubt that Mike is able to use language to communicate with us. Oh, and I plan to send copies to the Foundation just in case they misplaced the ones we gave them." She slid off the counter and moved closer to Ken. "Did I do right?"

They both burst into laughter and embraced. Mark shook his head and beat a quick retreat out the room. They could hear Mike on the other side of the room bouncing off the walls and they laughed again, louder.

* * *

The committee had a hard time following Melon's brisk pace out the gates of the ranch. He ignored the greetings of the staff and students they passed along the way.

Melon's jaw clinched tight. "We're going to have to do something about that woman."

An assistant totting the camera equipment asked what the whole committee was nervously thinking, "Like what?"

Melon's face hardened. The steel in his eyes disturbed his colleagues. "Plan B. It's time to call in our consultants. I'll set up a meeting in Reno."

CHAPTER 7

The Wild Animal Training Center was a legend in the movie business. Movie producers called the company when they needed animals for a show. Savage felt excited to be headed for it now.

Girlie slept in the far back of the Wagoner in a bed of blankets that she'd meticulously arranged at the beginning of the trip. The shape and her method of construction had reminded Savage of Jane Goodall's descriptions of wild chimps in the treetops of the Gombe Stream. She neatly made a nest by pulling blankets from beneath her seat and wrapping them in a ring around her, then she bedded down and pulled one over her body.

She'd been excited at the beginning of the trip, jumping between windows, startling passers-by with her hoots, but now she slept deeply with part of a blanket over her eyes to block the late afternoon sun that streamed through the side window.

The training center, located on several acres along the Santa Ana River, housed some five hundred odd and wild animals and was also used as locations for many movies and commercials.

What he knew of the Training Center's Director, Dr. Chris Raven intrigued Savage. A professor like Savage, Raven had caused a stir when he left his tenure track position at the university to begin a career as a technical adviser in the movies. Many in the academic community had condemned his actions as irresponsible, even as selling out. He was still thought of as a traitor by many, but Savage had never felt that way. He'd envied Raven the chance to get away from the stifling structure of academia. Rumors said he'd almost been brought up on ethics charges for some very questionable remarks he'd made at the Paris Convention, referencing some preliminary research he'd been conducting that had focused on the inter-specific breeding between humans and great apes.

Bobby and Lester had filled Savage in about the training center. Some of the best trainers in the business worked there, and many more, especially circus people, wintered over, using the grounds and facilities to hone their acts. Over the years, it'd become a stopover for animal people on the road. At any given time, several trainers would be pre-training for different projects and others might be just stopping over. Winnie and Chester wintered at the training center every year as did Hunt. Raven also conducted a school for would-be trainers.

They turned off the highway and started down a winding dirt road. It had been a long day. Savage squinted up from his papers as the car negotiated the first bumps. A sign in dark-red letters read, WILD ANIMAL TRAINING CENTER. DO NOT ENTER. VIOLATORS WILL BE EATEN! The road stayed on the bluffs overlooking the Santa Ana River. At first, it looked like a typical ranch. Alfalfa and oat-hay fields stretched out across the lower fields in uniform patchwork. Tractors and other farm implements worked the fields. Irrigation pipes fed great spouting rain birds. The smell of fresh cut hay filled the air, mixed with the musky odor of the riverbed. The road continued for a few miles before they caught first sight of the compound.

Bobby broke the silence. "That's the main building of the compound up there on the hill. This all used to be a duck hunting club in the old days. Hollywood stars and politicians used to fly in during different hunting seasons. You can still see the old runway up there by where all that hay is stacked."

The main building had the look of a huge California ranch-style home of the late forties. It had a covered porch that wrapped around, giving it a Western look.

This was true country living, Savage thought.

Dusk was just setting in as they turned down the main road. Savage was startled by the familiar greeting hoots of the chimps. He could just make out their cages through rows of trees and bamboo that lined the drive. He thought how similar compounds were to one another. Not just the layout but the sounds and smells. This could have easily been Ken's ranch in Reno except for the sounds of lions roaring. A sound Savage had always likened to someone hand-sawing wood. The rich aroma of manure from the hoof stock corrals filled him with nostalgia for his country upbringing; that smell, so rich with the earth, always gave him peace.

The place bustled with activity. Several keepers carried buckets of food to their respective charges while others hosed down concrete cage floors. All seemed intent on their work and took only a passing notice as the car pulled up under a tree in front of a sign marked VISITORS PARK HERE. PLEASE CHECK IN AT THE OFFICE.

A young man in his twenties greeted them as they climbed out of the car. "Bobby, what brings you all the way from Hollywood?"

Savage laughed as Bobby introduced him. "I think Bobby must know everyone in the world."

The young man beamed when he saw Lester at the back of the Wagoner, attending to Girlie. "Now, this really makes my day, in fact my whole week." He walked over to Lester and they shook hands and embraced. Girlie hooted and jumped into the young man's arms.

Bobby laughed. "We best leave old friends to catch up."

Bobby and Savage continued through the main gate as the young man shouted after them that they were expected and that Dr. Raven was with the others. Savage wondered who the others were.

They continued down a sidewalk and entered a large building.

"The trainers call this the Clubhouse," Bobby said as they entered a room cluttered with reptile cages and various teaching aids.

A fireplace and hearth made of local river stone and large enough that Bobby could've walked into it without ducking sat on one wall—presumably a carryover from the duck hunting days. Books filled the room, stacked haphazardly on tables or neatly stowed in shelves along the walls. It took a while for Savage's eyes to adjust to the dim light. Only the heating lamps of the reptile cages and the fire from the hearth lit the room. A flock of Canada Geese flying in perfect formation hung from the high cathedral ceiling, a tribute to the art of taxidermy.

Another leftover from the Hunting Club days.

He could almost picture the likes of John Wayne and William Holden in this grand setting, warming up next to the fire after a long day of hunting in the wetlands below. He noticed that their autographed pictures hung with countless others around the room.

Bobby took them up to a tall man. "Dr. Raven I've brought you some dinner guests."

"Well, indeed you have." Raven smiled and extended his hand to Savage, who immediately felt the strength and energy in his firm grip. Raven seemed genuinely pleased they'd come.

Bobby looked at Lester and Girlie who'd just caught up and whispered, "And so it begins."

Lester nodded. "Yes, but what I wonder."

"I've wanted to meet you for some time, Dr. Savage," Raven said. "And now, where should I find you but at my very own door step." He looked at the rest of them and shook his head. "And accompanied by this odd assortment. Better be careful or you'll end up like me and run away to the circus—they're a bad influence; I'm warning you."

Savage smiled. "I could do worse."

Raven beamed. "See, that's just what I mean." He waited for everyone to leave the Clubhouse and lowered his voice just above a whisper, "Rumor has it that you people are searching for Oliver."

"Well, the good Professor is for sure," Bobby said. "As for me, I'm just along for the ride."

Raven nodded knowingly, "Really. You seemed to be an awfully busy passenger." He looked back at Savage. "Would you care to take a tour of the compound?"

"With pleasure."

Bobby smiled. "I'll catch up with you guys. I think I'll see where they'll be bunking Girlie and then go raid the food prep refrigerators."

"Very good, but save some room for tonight. We've planned quite a little shin-dig for you and your fellow passengers."

They left through the double French doors of the Clubhouse. Savage paused a moment, letting his eyes grow accustomed to the dusk. Low garden lights that dimly outlined a network of pathways lit the walkways.

Signs designated different areas, but they were hardly necessary. The sounds echoing from various parts of the compound would guide him. He heard the chimps near-by, food grunting and panting. The high-pitched trumpeting of elephants and the roars of the lions as they prepared to bed down came from farther away. He wondered how many compounds he'd toured in different parts of the world during his career. It told him so much about the people who were there, and he always learned something new to add to his own practice.

The last light faded as a full moon rose. The birdlike chirps of capuchin and spider monkeys came from the rows of monkey cages they walked past. The howlers made Savage feel as if he were in the jungle again. Baboons barked from farther up the walk, and familiar greeting hoots rose from the chimp area.

Raven walked over to a telephone pole and engaged the lights for the chimp cages. Chimps were everywhere. The lights reflected off the damp, freshly hosed cage floors. Floodlights atop other poles surrounded the entire area. The greeting hoots rose to total pandemonium as the bigger chimps began their displays. The sound was deafening, frightening, even for Savage, who'd never seen so many chimps in one place, and some of these were the largest chimps he'd ever encountered. They pounded the heavy bars of their cages with unnerving, primeval power that seemed to shake the very slabs on which they were mounted.

Savage tried to count the cages and the chimps in them, but fund it hard to get an exact count. A large cage stood in the center surrounded by banks of smaller cages. The large cage housed at least thirty fully mature chimps that looked to be in breeding pairs. The smaller cages housed smaller chimps or isolated pairs of mothers nursing infants.

Before realizing it, he was drawn to one of the smaller cages that sat back in the shadow out of the main area. He approached the dim cage, seeing movement back in the corner. Something lurked in the darkness.

Raven moved in behind him and whispered, "So you're drawn to this cage? Watch closely and remember what you see in there. That creature is Danny, said to be Oliver's brother."

Savage's eyebrows rose in surprise. "He must be a better kept secret than Oliver."

"He's not really much of a secret among animal trainers nor his brother." Raven laughed. "You really need to get out more, Fred."

A large form moved out of the shadows toward them. He stood bipedal and didn't display like the others. He just peered at them in a stoic, almost unnatural quiet as he placed his giant hand out into a classic begging gesture.

Raven stepped quickly forward and whispered, "I needn't warn you not to take his hand." He looked at Danny. "Hey boy, are you hungry or just man-fishing tonight?" Danny stared at them and whimpered, then extended his whole arm out toward them.

Raven and Savage exchanged looks and laughed. "Boy, he deserves an Academy Award for this performance. He sure is interested in you, Fred." The two scientists stepped closer to the cage, just out of reach to get a better look.

Raven cautioned him again. "Careful. Danny is a master at straining people through the bars. Have you ever seen a chimp with less pronounced brow ridges?"

"No, but it's his bipedalism I don't understand. Why would he walk upright like that if he wasn't required to? I mean, if not reinforced. Lester and Bobby said Oliver did the same thing."

Raven nodded in agreement. "It still doesn't necessarily mean he's carrying human genes. He simply could've been taught to do that. You know nurture over nature as the old argument goes."

"Of course, that's possible, but still, do you think that the behavior would be so ingrained that it'd continue even when not reinforced?"

"Obviously in the absence of biological data little can be substantiated." Raven smiled at Savage almost laughing.

Savage suddenly understood. "You've got data, don't you? You've run some tests? Before he could answer, the clamor of a dinner bell rang out across the compound. The clang kicked up a deafening chorus in unison to the ringing.

"Let's go to dinner before we all go deaf." Raven motioned to the group and led the way.

Raven and Savage once again found themselves alone together as they walked.

Raven paused to watch a group of male capuchins lunging at them as the females and adolescents huddled back in a corner. "Danny came to us from a small regional circus several years ago. You know the usual thing. He'd gotten too big to work and someone got hurt. First his trainer wanted to sell him to us, but, as it usually goes, when we tell these guys we're not interested in another big psychotic chimp who wants to pull peoples arms off their bodies, they're then willing to pay us to take the chimp off their hands. We always try to get as much information as possible. You know, paperwork, permits, vet records, etc. but there's usually very little. Most of these old-school trainers have little more than their stories to give. He finally gave us Danny without any money changing hands. He was just relieved to be rid of him. He had no paperwork of any kind. No bill of sale, transfer records, nothing, nada." Raven paused as some handlers passed close by.

"So, we don't know if the trainer even owned the chimp?" Savage asked.

Raven nodded. "In the legal sense, yes, but there was no question about it when you watched them together. And there are very few ownership disputes over these big chimps. Well, sometimes there can be heated debates over who doesn't and therefore has no liability when something goes wrong. It's a common problem with these show business chimps. They live too long and get too big. Inevitably, at some point, they get too dangerous to work. There are not a lot of places to dispose of these guys, and in many instances, trainers have actually put them down. But in most cases, the bond is too strong between them, and the trainers really want the best for them. But it was Dusty who filled us in on Danny and Oliver's history. You met him at the Luncheon Club. We'll talk with him this evening so he can fill you in."

Lester and Bobby walked up the path towards them, interrupting Savage's thoughts. "Girlie is an adult chimp who has grown quite large, but it doesn't seem to be a problem between her and Lester."

"Indeed not. They're unique. But don't let his age fool you. Lester is still probably the best chimp trainer alive; perhaps, the best who ever lived."

"And Girlie is one in a thousand."

Raven smiled. "More like one in a million. I've seen only few like her in my whole career. Ah, but speak of the devil, or more accurately, 'devils' plural. Alas, the search party has arrived."

Bobby ran up to them. "Hey, what the hell you doing up here? I wanted to eat without you, but mister personality here thought we should form a search party. Let's go. We're hungry, and Raven here seems to be so integral to this place that everyone's reluctant to eat without his eminence. I told your ranch manager—a humorless sort—that we could probably manage the project without you guys. She just stared, or rather glared, wouldn't you say, Lester?"

"What do you mean by Mister Personality?" Lester snapped.

Bobby waved his hand at Lester as though dismissing him. "You're no help. Christ, you guys feed your animals on a better schedule than your people. You ought to start a fat farm out here."

Both scientists laughed.

"Okay, Bobby. Peace," Raven said. "I haven't caught this much hell since I was married. With your permission, Fred, we'll postpone the rest of this until after dinner.

Savage nodded, but felt frustrated. He would've gladly missed dinner to hear the rest of Oliver and Danny's story. But if he'd learned anything about life from his years of fieldwork, it was patience. *Everything comes to us in its own time.*

They filed down the path and worked their way toward the Clubhouse. The staff and company had set up a dining area on the front veranda. Several picnic tables had been scooted together to form a long table. A large kitchen window had been opened and the screen removed, making it convenient to pass dishes through. They caught the aroma of baked bread and spaghetti sauce.

On the lawn in front of the veranda, the young man who had first received them set up a large barbeque made of two oil-drum halves welded together. Piles of various fowl and game sat on the cart next to him. Dressing out the meat of animals that had died from injuries was common practice at the compound. On a facility that had over five-hundred animals, one never

79

lacked exotic meat for dinner. The barbeques at the WATC were legendary, and tonight was no exception: steaks of emu, wallaby, ostrich, camel, crocodile, and water buffalo lay stacked beside more traditional cuts of beef, pork and chicken.

Over the years, some of the trainers, including Raven, had developed marinades and side sauces that distinguished these exotic meats. It all fit into the tradition of wasting nothing.

Many zoos had stopped this practice in an attempt to placate some small but vocal animal rights groups, some of which had reached a near militant posture. But the WATC was a private facility and accepted no public funds or non-profit donations. Even in the not-for-profit concerns, such as the wildlife rehabilitation program or public-school presentations they accepted no donations. Raven felt very strongly about this. He'd not forgotten the money games and politics he'd left behind in academia and took great pride in his independence.

Savage thought about the politics and strings attached to the money they received from government grants to keep their chimpanzee language project limping along up at the University of Nevada and envied Raven's freedom. The more shadowy elements of the government had often approached his friend and colleague, Ken Turner. Representatives from the Department of Defense and even the CIA had come to visit them over the years with enormous offers that seemed too good to be true: they decided, in fact, that they were. The people who approached them with these offers scared them. Savage and Turner sensed a deeper intent than they represented with all their smiles and best wishes to help.

The milling of small groups of trainers, handlers, students and guests as they filed in the direction of dinner, stirred him out of his thoughts. The apparent good spirits of everyone impressed Savage, and he said so. He thought Raven's reply interesting:

"We have far fewer misfits in this business than most, especially the pompous sorts who are full of themselves." Raven took a place as they entered a line by the barbeque, then continued, "Training is nothing more than a form of communication—a complicated one for sure, but communication just the same—and the basis of communication is mutual trust, respect and love."

The aroma of the cooking steaks blended with rich marinades that blew over them in gusts. The cooking juices cracked and hissed as the meat was flipped, causing a riot of fragrant smoke and flame, smelling of mesquite.

"Well, I hope we live long enough to sample some of those steaks," Bobby called out. "What's it going to take to get someone to get this line moving?" Apparently, everyone had been waiting for them to clear the cooking area, reluctant to cut ahead while Raven was so engrossed. They appeared relieved when Bobby broke the spell.

Dinner took on a festive air and lasted well into the evening. Most of the cooking and clean-up duties seemed to be self-appointed.

Savage thought that, here at least, too many cooks did not seem to spoil the broth.

Girlie seemed to be widely known and in great demand around the table and with clusters of diners who'd come late and settled on the lawn. And just as everyone was digging into seconds, someone let a younger chimp out to play with her. This added a level of chaos that these seasoned animal people took in stride in spite of spilled drinks and dumped plates. But after a particularly destructive chase down the middle of the dinner table, Raven ordered the chimps to the lawn with the handlers and students.

Laughing he said, "I have come to believe after years of study that chimp play is most appreciated by young trainers, students and, of course, mothers."

With Raven in continual demand throughout dinner, there'd been little opportunity for any serious discussion about Oliver or Danny, the chimp who might be his brother. As the evening wore on and people thinned out, Savage found himself seated with Lester, Bobby, Raven, Winnie, and Dusty. Winnie and

Dusty seemed tenser than when he'd first met them at the Luncheon Club. The tone of the evening shifted to a more serious mood as the dinner party wound down and people said their goodbyes.

Raven brought the discussion back to Oliver by drawing Dusty into their conversation. A large robust man in his sixties, Dusty was famous among animal trainers, thought of by many of his peers to be the greatest living elephant trainer. He had a wide face with a wider belly that jiggled when he laughed, which he did often. And his laugh was legendary. His face creased into wrinkles that hid his closed eyes as he let out booming belly laughs that could be heard across the compound. Savage noticed that both Lester and Dusty were conspicuous in their mutual acknowledgement by ignoring one another.

"So, Dr. Savage it seems to me that you think there may be some merit to the rumors that Oliver is—how should I say?—a hybrid, a product of interbreeding between a human and a chimp." This caused a buzz among their small group.

Savage collected his thoughts. "I'm not sure. It's just that we've heard rumors of these sorts of creatures for years and yet have never been able to substantiate anything. There have been, of course, many hoaxes, living Piltdown men, if you will but—"

"Excuse me, Doc," Bobby asked, "but what do you mean by Piltdown?"

"It was a very elaborate fraud perpetrated several years ago. A claim was made that the missing link had been found—our common ancestor. It was later determined that it was a hoax; a skeleton had been constructed out of various hominid bones.

"The animals we find in various sideshows, billing them as half human and half chimp have always proved to be products of this same sort of thing. You know, sometimes clever but usually pretty obvious mixtures of makeup, staging and training. The motivation in these cases is pretty basic, a quick buck and then move on. The typical audience is usually naive and never gets a chance to verify any of the claims."

Winnie broke from side conversations with Dusty and asked, "So why do you keep investigating these shows if you know they're fake."

"I ask myself that question after each disappointment, but it's so tempting when you know it's scientifically possible, though ethically questionable, to produce them, and under the right circumstances it wouldn't require very advanced technology."

Dusty placed a hand on Winnie and used her as a brace. It was unclear to Savage whether he was always this unsteady or if he'd just had drunk too much wine. "I remember rumors about this when I was a boy working as elephant groomer on Ringling," he said. "There was a trainer with a chimp act named ... Simon or something like that. I can't remember for sure. But—"

Lester interrupted: "Simon and his flying chimps—great act in its day. He and his wife had them doing all kinds of trapeze gags; really good stuff and funny."

Dusty nodded. "I remember Simon talking, while we were watering the elephants, about two really scary chimp-like animals being imported by a Belgium trader. He was asking a large sum, claiming they'd been captured in the Congo and that they were half human; *humanzees*, I think he called them. We all thought it was a bunch of horseshit by another asshole trader."

"Traders of those days would say and do anything to make a sale," Lester said, "especially the ones from Belgium."

Savage nodded slowly. "Well, let's see. Where was I?"

Winnie smiled at him. "We seemed to have gotten off track, here. You were answering my question and talking about how possible it was to breed a chimp with a human."

Savage was struck again by how beautiful Winnie was, especially in the moonlight. Her skin had a bronze, smooth sheen and her eyes were disarming. Simply put, she was a very attractive woman. Exotic was closer to the mark. "Yes. In fact, many of us feel experiments may have been conducted in the thirties by the Soviets."

A murmur rose from the group.

"Excuse me, Dr. Savage," Raven said, "who do you mean by 'many of us'?"

Savage hesitated a moment. He looked around the group that remained, unsure how much he should be divulging. He realized how little he knew about any of these people.

Lester and Dusty were deep in thought, paying little attention to the conversation, but he knew they were a bigger part of this story then they realized and still had a part to play. He stared across the table at Winnie, Lester and Bobby and knew he could trust them as much as they'd trusted him. They were circus people who were used to living with very dark secrets.

Raven clearly knew more than he was saying, and Savage felt comfortable talking to him. He felt it was more than a coincidence that brought him together with this particular group, this particular night. More than that, he somehow knew that these people were used to keeping secrets and anything he said would not leave them.

He started tentatively, "I have a colleague, a friend actually, Dr. Turner, Ken Turner." He glanced at Raven. "I'm sure you've heard of him. He's doing the definitive work on inter-specific communication. He has been teaching ASL … eh, American Sign Language to chimpanzees. His work has received a lot of notice in the scientific community and in the popular press. Of course, as you would expect, not all this attention has been favorable." Savage fidgeted with his napkin, tying it into small knots. "I'm sure I don't have to emphasize that any association with what we're discussing here tonight would be harmful to him professionally."

Dusty stirred out of his thoughts. "That's what I was trying to get at Doc. This kind of thing wouldn't be good for any of us, either. I can tell you that animal training, especially the entertainment side of it, attracts every kook that ever thought he saw a UFO or thinks he can read an animal's mind. I don't know why, but it's a fact." He looked over at Raven. "I'm sure you remember that student of yours who told me she could walk through walls. What was her name?"

Raven shook his head. "If we start dwelling on every outer-limits type we've known, I don't think we'll get anywhere here tonight. Please, Dr. Savage continue."

"Well, during the course of Dr. Turner's research he stumbled onto an obscure but interesting set of facts. In the early twenties or so, a group of Soviet scientists may have conducted some preliminary breeding experiments between chimps and humans. There were few details other than that the experiments were to have been conducted on board a ship at sea that was thought to have mysteriously disappeared off the coast of Africa. No more has been written about this, but there have been sketchy rumors and vague references that there could have been survivors."

Everyone began talking at once. It was apparent to Savage that this kind of information was, at least in principle, not new to them. There'd always been rumors of the existence of these kinds of creatures. The circus had a great oral history. Much information passed from show to show around the world. Everyone seemed so engrossed in their own discussions that they had forgotten him for the moment.

"I can tell you right now we need Hunt here," Winnie said, getting control of the group, which seemed to be her role. She addressed Savage. "Hunt is a kind of historian when it comes to our world. He's the only one I know who has taken the time to record anything about the circus, the real history as passed on from generation to generation by circus families, not the typical books you'd pick up in a bookstore. You can see that all of us have heard things but never really thought much about it, but if you want to know particulars about who said what at what time to whom, he's your man."

"Where is he tonight, anyway?" Raven asked.

"Hunt's up north in San Francisco for the weekend," Winnie replied. Dusty smirked, and Winnie continued, "Whatever anyone thinks about Hunt's ... shall we say, lifestyle choices, he's the best bird trainer in the business and a very good friend of mine." She paused to let her last words sink in. "There'll be plenty of time to talk to him later. Dr. Savage, you were saying?"

"We've been mainly focusing on chimps that would now be about fifty-years old since that would be about how old any survivors would be today. However, we'll checkout all leads as time permits. I do most of the footwork since Dr. Turner wanted to keep his distance and has a compound to run." Looking at Lester, he continued, "I'd heard indirectly from someone who'd talked with Dusty here that you'd once owned Oliver. I found a newspaper article recently that made some pretty far-fetched claims about him and decided to follow it up, see if I couldn't find him and run some tests." Savage looked at Raven, who was whispering to Lester. "You never know what you're going to find out on these missions, and now I'm led to believe that Oliver had a brother and that he's here in the form of Danny."

Raven broke from his conversation with Lester. "We ran his DNA from blood and hair samples, but the results were inconclusive. We can't tell if Danny's aberrations are a result of mutations, training or cross-breeding."

"I've seen both Danny and Oliver," Bobby said, "as has most everyone here, and I can't say that any of us would call them Frankensteins or anything like that. They're different for sure but—"

Dusty interrupted, glaring at Lester: "They're both goddamn menaces and should be put down."

Raven waved Dusty off. "It'd be difficult to predict what one would get with a cross between people and chimps, but the outcome would vary extensively because of the random nature of gene combinations. It wouldn't be much different from any other kind of hybridization. You'd get traits from both parents that might produce an offspring resembling one or the other or both, depending on the blend of recessive and dominant genes."

"Have any of you seen wolf hybrids?" Savage asked. "I'm sure you must've seen them on some compound."

Raven nodded. "We have them here."

Savage noticed the young man who'd cooked the meat on the barbeque building a fire in a clearing near them. Several students placed chairs around the ring and put the final touches on the evening clean-up. He continued only when sure they were out of earshot: "I'm sure most of you have noticed that a litter of these hybrids varies in both physical and behavioral characteristics. Some will look and act very much like wild wolves while others in the same litter will seem in most respects just your standard, garden-variety domestic dog."

He paused before continuing, "Then, of course, we get the mix of traits. We call this cross-wiring. That's when the animal gets mixed genetic signals. Being neither dog nor wolf, but rather something in between, his instinctual traits are confused and unreliable. He simply does not know who he is. If you throw all this together with adolescence and the accompanying hormones, you've got a *wreck* on your hands, as Bobby would say." He smiled at Bobby who was so intent on whispering with Lester, that he didn't notice his name being mentioned.

The young man who Savage had noticed building the fire stepped forward and whispered something into Raven's ear.

"Ah. Thank you, Brian," Raven said. "It seems we are invited to relax around the fire, if you all would care to join me."

The group got up and moved towards the fire. Many stopped to stretch or stomp the evening chill from them before making themselves comfortable around the fire.

The flames popped and crackled, sending sparks far up into the clear fall sky. Its flames sparkled through the holes of the old, washing-machine drum that contained it. A peacock sent out its eerie cry across the compound—a call Savage had always likened to a human crying for help.

The mood grew more subdued and somber as the fire danced shadows around them. Everyone seemed to be involved with their own thoughts. Each attempted to avoid the shifting smoke, but the smell of the wood fire washed over them.

Lester seemed impressed by Savage's observations. "I'm worried about what you think is remarkable, Doc. You're talking about making some sort of monster like Frankenstein here. I don't like thinking about something as smart as a man but as strong as an ape. It's crazy Doc, it's dangerous."

Everyone talked at once and paid little attention to each other. They all seemed to share Lester's concern, including Dusty. Raven stood and raised his voice over the group: "Please, people. We're getting ahead of ourselves. We've inconclusive data concerning Danny, and no one in this group has seen Oliver for ten years. I think that before we begin gathering the village people to go light torches and grab pitchforks, we ought to hear him out."

The group settled down and awaited Savage's reply.

"Thanks. I should be clear about one thing. We're not purposing to do these kinds of experiments. We're simply trying to confirm if they were conducted before. If these kinds of offspring exist they'd give great insights into a number of disciplines of science. Think what it could mean to the sciences of genetics, medicine, or the behavioral sciences to mention just a few. The possibilities are unlimited."

A silence, a kind of introspection revisited the group.

Savage continued, "What's really important tonight?" He looked toward the horizon and back at Dusty. "Or what's left of it, is to locate Oliver. It's a long shot, but based on what I've read and what Lester and Bobby have said, I think it'd be worth finding him."

Dusty nodded to Lester. "Lester knew him the longest, I'd say, at least eight or nine seasons."

"That's true. But I told you all that back at the trailer. The last I heard he was playing in a Mexican circus."

"El Circo de las Americanas, to be exact," Dusty said but seeming reluctant to share the information. "He was in the Lancer act with Sergio Ramirez last I heard."

Frowns, head shakes, and sad expressions indicated that everyone felt upset by the news.

Bobby frowned. "That's not good news. No one, ape or human, deserves to be near that guy. He's the worst of a really bad lot."

Savage shifted in his chair. "I'm not sure I want to know what you mean by a bad lot."

"There are some trainers that should not be around animals," Lester explained, "and he's one of them. He uses a lead pipe to make up for his lack of talent."

Savage was beginning to get the point. "Are you saying he's heavy handed?"

Everyone looked at Lester. "It's beyond that, Doc. He's a goddamn sadist. He enjoys beating them. I'd have never sold him if I thought he'd end up with that crazy asshole."

Bobby patted Lester on the back. "Take it easy, guy. You had no idea where he was going?"

Dusty got up from his chair. "Well, it's getting late, girls. I've got to get up early tomorrow." He looked over at Lester. "Some of us still work for a living." Lester started to say something but Winnie nudged him again. "I can tell you this, Doc. That circus plays spots way South this time of the year. It's a rinky-dink little circus and will be hard to find until it gets close to the border again. Talk to Hunt. I think he knows the itinerary of every circus in the world."

Dusty's departure spurred most of the group into activity. Savage shook hands with several people as they said their goodbyes until only he and Raven remained by the fire's fading warmth.

Raven smiled at Savage. "Well, here we are again. I think most everyone bought what I said about Danny."

Savage watched as the last of the stragglers faded into the night. "What do you mean?" I thought you said the tests were inconclusive."

Raven stared into the darkness in the direction of the chimp cages. "I lied. He has forty-seven chromosomes—one less than a human, one more than a chimp."

Savage followed his gaze. A growing mist crept up onto the bluffs from the river below, obscuring the chimp cages. A barn owl broke the muffled silence with cloaked hoots. "Holy Christ ..." was all he could manage at first. He stared directly into Raven's eyes. "I lied, too. Under the right circumstances, we would do the experiments, if we found suitable subjects."

Raven touched Savage almost sympathetically. "Why would you risk everything to conduct such an unethical experiment?"

Savage stood and paused before answering, "Curiosity I think ... Wouldn't you want to create a new species that possessed the very best traits of both humans and chimps. God, think of what we could learn ... I really don't know why this has grown on me so—it's like an itch I can't scratch—I know it's crazy." He turned and walked away, fading, like a sleepwalking ghost, into the patches of fog that rolled through the grounds.

CHAPTER 8

Raven spent the morning over coffee bringing Savage up to date on what they'd found out about Danny. They sat in a newer model Airstream trailer. The early morning sun accentuated the grain of the natural wood cabinets and table where they sat. "The tests results suggest he isn't fertile," Raven said, "and our attempts to breed him here have been unsuccessful. But you know as well as I do, that this could be as much behavioral as biological."

Apparently, Raven had friends at a local medical school and had managed to convince them that he needed assistance in his breeding program. They'd run several basic tests on samples of blood, hair, and sperm he'd given them. Danny's samples had been slipped into this group. But these had been broad-spectrum tests that only gave gross indications. The results had given them little to go on except for two things: Danny's chromosome count appeared to fall between a chimpanzee and human; and he might be sterile. The lab itself had attributed the chromosome count to some kind of sample error and had dismissed it. Raven had been reluctant to bring further attention to the abnormality and had not pursued it. Without samples from Oliver, they were not able to make comparisons.

"This is very exciting," Savage said. "But I know you're aware that while variation in the number of chromosome pairs and the production of sterile offspring are indicative of hybridization, this phenomenon can be caused from many other less-exciting things."

"Of course, but remember, Fred, you saw him last night, and you've seen enough chimps in your career to know something doesn't add up." Raven looked at him quizzically. "Am I right?"

"Yes. We need to run more tests and more accurate ones. Dr. Turner has an assistant up in Reno, an English guy—a post doctorate from Kent named Mark Chaney. The man's brilliant by all accounts in the area of chimpanzee histology and reproduction."

"So, what's he doing in a language project? Can he be trusted?" Raven asked.

"Yes. He's very loyal to Ken. I understand he got into some real problems in England, something to do with a female student. She was Arabic—royalty no less. Ken sponsored him over here and got him out of that situation just in time. But aside from that, he has an excellent professional reputation. You know, well published, guest lecturer and all that. He's got access to just about any lab we'd want as long as we can keep him out of trouble of the other sort."

Raven laughed. "Sounds like he'd fit right in. You know, I've been thinking. If either Danny or Oliver is fertile we jump a full generation ahead in the experiment."

Savage took a few heartbeats to let this set in. "That only matters if we were planning to conduct those kinds of experiments. I think we're getting a little ahead of ourselves here. Perhaps we should try to find Oliver and talk to the good people up in Reno about running some proper tests on Danny."

A knock at the trailer door startled them out of their thoughts.

Raven sighed and shook his head. "Just when things were getting interesting." He got up from the small dinette table at which they'd been sitting and opened the door to Bobby.

"So here you are. Christ, I've been looking all over this damn place for you two." He looked quizzically at both of them. "I just wanted to let you guys know that Lester is getting antsy to leave. You can't believe it but with a whole compound, eleven-hundred acres, Dusty and Lester haven't been more than ten feet apart all morning. Hell, those old guys like to bicker."

"Well, how could we miss something as entertaining as those two old coots at each other?" Raven patted Bobby on the back and lowered his voice. "Keep them busy a little longer, please. We're going to take another look at Danny."

Bobby picked up the seriousness in his tone. "Sure thing." He walked off in the direction of the elephant barn.

The two scientists made their way to the chimp cages. Savage thought how different the compound looked in the morning light—so much more normal when it wasn't cloaked in darkness. But the sounds and smell were the same. They just seemed less intense.

The training center was a busy place by day, and when they reached the chimps, the whole facility echoed with their greeting and thundering displays. It was deafening.

Savage thought there must be every size, sex, and color possible in these cages. He looked from cage to cage, seeing chimps with white faces, some bald, others with big, floppy ears. He saw short, squatty chimps; tall, lanky ones, and even some of the rarest of all, the pigmy chimp, Pan Paniscus. The variation seemed limitless.

Several handlers hosed down the larger cages, while pairs of trainers walked large studio chimps down paths leading to training areas. The large chimps were always walked with two trainers. The lead trainer controlled the animal by holding both the chimps' hand and a lead chain that was hooked to either a neck or waist collar. The back-up trainer carried a cane and watched for people and stray animals that might surprise them. Occasionally the back-up would announce their movements to other trainers who didn't notice them approaching. "Clear for Clyde" or "Chimp coming through" or "Behind you."

Savage left Raven talking with his head chimp trainer and wandered on towards Danny's enclosure. In the daylight, he could see the layout of the area more easily. Danny's quarters sat behind the rest of the caging area, nestled in a cluster of mulberry trees.

As he approached the cage, he noticed that Danny hadn't come out of his sleeping box. The exercise cage he'd seen him in the night before seemed strangely deserted. He leaned against the bars for a closer look. Various toys and pieces of food littered the floor, much like those any chimp would leave around, but the wall closet to the door caught his attention. At first it looked like rows of tiny dots, but when he drew nearer, he found, to his surprise, two rows of mashed flies, all neatly pressed one after another to make two on the top and six imprints on the bottom. Each fly was evenly spaced and had been methodically oriented in the same direction.

The macabre display reminded him of accounts he'd read about the behavior of prisoners left in solitary confinement too long. It certainly didn't resemble anything he'd ever observed chimps doing. He felt compelled to have a closer look, to touch it as though it were a piece of art. He started to reach into the cage to touch it when a strange foreboding stopped him. He felt a menace directed toward him from the other side of the cage, a brooding within the shadows of the den box. In an instant he realized that Danny wasn't sleeping but watching him from the darkness within, and, further, Savage was in great danger; he was within reach.

Several things happened at once and much too quickly: he leaped back from the bars with all the force in his legs he could muster; almost in unison a blur streaked across the floor of the cage toward him and arrived just an instant late. Danny clanged into the iron door with such force that it could be heard clear on the other side of the compound. Two giant arms shot through the bars and two huge hands closed like traps in the space he'd occupied seconds before.

Chaos broke out in the nearby cages as he gathered himself up from the grass. At first, he thought the debris landing around him was a result of the other chimps joining Danny in the attack, but as he looked around, he realized that they were aiming at Danny's cage, not him. Danny ran back and forth upright, lips tightly pressed together, pounding his giant fists against the bars of his cage. His hair stood on end in classic piloerection making him appear even larger.

Savage didn't want to think how close he'd come to being dismembered. Raven came running up with a pistol drawn and had to shout above the cries of the chimps: "Christ, Fred, I saw that! Are you all right? What were you thinking? Damn, that was wa-a-a-y too close."

Trainers arrived from all directions. Some were armed with canes while others carried fire extinguishers and shovels. All looked frightened, and none came empty handed. Dusty and Lester brought up the rear. They'd come all the way from the other side of the ranch armed with axes.

Dusty looked at both of them and then leveled on Raven. "You're going to get someone killed with that goddamn freak. I've told you that you need put that freak of nature down!"

Lester looked at the hinges of the door. "You better check this cage over, completely." He looked over at Savage. "You know better than to get that close to a cage." Seeming to forget their feud, he nudged Dusty and pointed at Danny. "He's worse than Oliver." He walked over to the cage axe in hand. "Get in your house." Lester pointed at the entrance to the den box. Danny grimaced showing all his teeth and backed toward the opening in the box while making high-pitched cries.

Savage thought those were the first chimp behaviors he'd seen Danny make—displaying classic fear and submission behavior to Lester. He was showing respect, making it clear that he knew Lester and accepted Lester as dominant. Danny went into his box. Savage knew that a chimp in a cage wouldn't obey anyone he didn't believe could come in and discipline him.

Bobby walked up the path towards them.

"Where have you been, Bobby?" Lester yelled.

"Where the hell do you think? I locked myself in Dusty's trailer." That seemed to relieve the tension and everyone broke into laughter.

"Okay, everyone. Thanks for responding so quickly." Raven looked at Bobby, "Especially you, Bobby. He holstered his .45 under his vest and looked at Savage. "You can't deal with Danny like any chimp you're used to. Well, from the looks of you, I don't think I've got to say anymore."

Savage was trembling. "That was the closest call in my career."

Raven nodded.

* * *

The excitement of the morning had delayed their departure, and it was afternoon before Savage stepped out of the little guest trailer ready to leave. What he saw across the compound at Danny's cage mesmerized him. Lester stood in the cage with his hand out-stretched, and Danny, grimacing in fear and respect, placed an object in the trainer's hand.

Footsteps behind him startled Savage. He turned.

Dusty joined him and pointed toward the cage. "That man is the greatest chimp trainer who ever lived." His face wrinkled as he smiled. "But don't tell him I said so."

"Your secret's safe with me."

They stood in awe as they watched Lester give Danny a long hug, as though he were just another chimp. He did this alone and without fanfare.

Savage was struck by Lester's stature as he walked toward where they stood watching. It was that of a young man.

Dusty lightly punched Lester's arm.

Lester nodded to both of them and said, "I think you lost something, Doc. It's going to need a new band." Lester handed Savage his tattered watch.

* * *

When he boarded the plane to Reno late that afternoon, Savage could barely keep his eyes open. Lester, Girlie, and Bobby had headed back to L.A., and, to his great surprise, Dusty had hitched a ride with them.

Raven had driven him to the airport in Ontario and sent him off with a file on Danny, and he'd also agreed to get in touch with Hunt Bushnell while he was still in San Francisco and see if they could meet in Reno.

It seemed that after years of disappointments and dead-end hoaxes, he was finally onto something. He had much to tell his colleagues back at the University of Nevada, Reno.

It'd be good to get back home. He wondered how Ken's site visit had turned out.

CHAPTER 9

Night had fallen by the time Vandusen finally made his way back to town. It wasn't advisable to keep the General waiting, but the tourist traffic on Virginia Street had slowed to a crawl, and to further complicate things, he had trouble threading his company-issued, dark-blue sedan through all the tourists and up to the front of valet parking at the casino entrance.

Vandusen squinted into the bright lights that lit up the front of Fitzgerald's and could just make out the marquee that hung directly above him. He smiled as he read the reason for all the crowds—opening night for Tony Bennett. He loved Tony, and it seemed he wasn't alone. Downtown was packed. He was struck by how much like Vegas this once-sleepy, little cow town was becoming.

A uniformed valet startled him when the boy ran up to get his keys. Opening the door, he whispered, "The General's waiting upstairs in the penthouse."

"Why the hell you jumping out at people!" Vandusen growled. His Eastern-European accent was more distinct than usual due to the surprise.

The valet slunk back, crestfallen.

Vandusen didn't like people running up on him, especially when he was reporting on Company business. And even more, it made him nervous when strangers knew his doings.

Two men in dark suits smiled at each other knowingly as they waited out front by the entrance. From the tiny earphones neatly inserted into their left ears, he figured them to be either deaf or some kind of undercover agents. He could just make out the thin black wires that disappeared into their collars.

Not very subtle.

A lot more of these types had shown up in Reno lately. They nodded acknowledgement, and without a word, entered the casino, one on each side of him.

"Gentlemen," Vandusen said in a controlled but sarcastic tone.

They worked their way through the crowds of gamblers seemingly intent on finding the next big payoff. One of the agents nodded in the direction of the crap tables. "Jesus, the natives are restless tonight."

Vandusen made a closer inspection of his escorts. They looked the part of government agents, stamped out of the same mold: both with sandy hair and blue eyes, tall but not too tall. To a trained eye, they stood out in their attempt to blend in.

Dedicated to doing their job, their alert eyes scanned the room like hawks. The pasty hue of their skin contrasted with the dark blue of their matching suits and thin black ties. They could've been Ivy League graduates if not for the earpieces.

He chuckled, acknowledging the agent's comment, and then taunted them, "Nice suits."

On the other hand, dressed in his grey, pin-striped suit and four-hundred-dollar Florsheims, Vandusen looked more like a stockbroker than a government agent. Tall and lean, he towered over his guides by several inches. His brown eyes, olive skin, and slick, black hair hinted of his European heritage.

He marveled at the layout of the smoked-filled casino. You had to walk right through the gambling areas to get to the elevators that led to the upper floors. The place was designed to prey upon human weakness with the intent of parting awestruck tourists from their money.

What a joint. What a perfect place for a con.

Bright lights glared down on the green-velvet gaming tables from enormous crystal chandeliers that hung a story above from gilded ceilings. All the crystal and gold spoke of opulence. He still remembered reading with awe how much it'd cost to build this place. But judging from the amount these marks were dropping on the tables tonight, the casino probably had made it back in the first year.

"Brilliant," he whispered to himself.

"What's brilliant?" one of the agents asked.

He realized he'd been thinking aloud again and had been over heard. He needed to be more careful about that. He was getting careless. Maybe he'd spent too much time in these boondocks. He looked at the agent on his right. "Nothing, forget about it. I was just thinking about how smart the people were who designed this place."

The agent gave him a blank look and didn't reply. *No use explaining it to either of these two.* He'd worked with hundreds of these government types. They were not deep thinkers at this level. If something wasn't related to following orders, getting laid, eating, sleeping, or shitting—and mainly in that order—they wouldn't waste much energy on it. But while they weren't philosophers, these guys could be quite innovative when it came to taking care of "government business." He understood that their real asset was following the General's orders without question.

The excitement of the pit areas was contagious, even to him, especially as they passed the crap tables. "And it's a four; four the hard way! Hey, we have a winner. Place your bets, place your bets." Screams and howls punctuated the rattle of dice bouncing with a muffled clatter across the padded tables, making or breaking hopes and dreams.

Shapely Kino girls in short, skin-tight dresses that looked to be painted on scurried around the players revealing more than their personalities as they leaned over to pick up chips and dispense free drinks while flirting for more commerce. Young and beautiful, they were mostly college girls from the local university working their way through school. He smiled, fondly remembering all the girls he'd personally helped with tuition over the years.

Bells and sirens echoed above the whoops of winners as coins rained out of the metal throats of slot machines and rattled into plastic buckets held by players impatient to put their winnings back in.

He remembered reading in a newspaper article that it was the slots that paid the house the most these days. The article said a casino had only to install them and collect the money. So automatic, so efficient; no need to set the marks up and take them down, just put a machine in their path.

Where's the fun in that?

He nodded in the direction of the agents, and, amazed at all the action for a weeknight, said, "You're right. This place is jumping tonight." His old street instincts kicked in as he sized up all the fat marks in the building sporting nametags and Shriner hats.

Lambs ready for slaughter.

But he knew the rule. No running cons on company time, especially when the General was in charge. He took a last wistful look before stepping into the elevator. "Beautiful."

One of the agents pulled out a key that put them on an express climb to the penthouse. They shot up sixteen floors above the city lights of Reno in seconds. The agents just had enough time to pat him down. They nodded at him and, without a word being said, he assumed the position. His hands smeared the mirrored walls of the elevator as he leaned spread eagle.

Just like the movies.

It was routine, nothing personal. Everybody who came to report to the General on company business knew the drill.

The doors slid open to a tiled alcove. One of the agents handed a waiting marine a Smith & Weston 357. The marine looked Vandusen up and down and compared him to his identification card. After making a phone call, he motioned him into a large, sunken living room surrounded by giant picture windows that framed a panorama of the evening skyline. It was beautiful, a breath-taking view in every direction.

Vandusen wondered how the General had convinced Langley that a penthouse in a luxury hotel was an appropriate location for the control room of this operation. As he took off his coat, a door opened from across the room, and the General stepped in.

"Mr. Vandusen! Come on over here and join us for a debriefing."

Us referred to three of the General's adjuncts who sat in the middle of the living room by a fireplace. They appeared to be hard men who'd not smiled in a very long time.

The General pointed to one of the couches next to the fireplace. "Please, make yourself comfortable."

One of the agents moved to sit next to where the General had indicated. The others straightened, covering some files they'd been studying.

The General looked different out of uniform. Of average height, his graying temples gave him a distinguished look despite his off-the-rack suit, which hung loosely on his thin frame. He had the appearance of someone working very hard to look ordinary.

Vandusen noticed, for the first time, two other men in the far corner by a bank of phones. They looked out of place. His field instincts told him they were military trying to pass as civilians.

"Do you mind if I smoke, sir?" Vandusen asked.

The General smiled and pushed an ashtray across the table. "Smoke 'em if you got 'em."

He fingered a pack of Lucky's, tapping them in his palm before pulling one out with his lips.

The General waited until he'd settled with his smoke, then asked, "So how's our college boy doing?"

"I think we can help him get inside. We're going to brief him on his part in this operation and help him make contact with Dr. Turner's colleague Dr—"

"Dr. Savage," the General interrupted, "who's returning from a mysterious trip down in LA. Our people say he was visiting several undesirable types, circus people. We've had contact with these types before and found them very unreliable."

"Yes, sir," Vandusen continued. "As usual you're on top of the operation. We've got people on the players surrounding Turner. We just need someone inside on a day to day basis."

The General nodded knowingly. "Good. So, he's going to play ball with us? What about the rest over there?"

"We have people inside the administration of the school. We're sponsoring Dr. Melon and his committee. They review Turner's facility for funding and are working with us. They're on the payroll. But Dr. Turner's people aren't going to cooperate with us, I'm sorry to say, which poses a big problem. We can't afford any publicity, so we have to move carefully." He shot a glance at the two men standing in the back of the room. "But this graduate student, Childs, may be useful. He fits our profile: a loner, unpopular, and not employed. He feels unappreciated and unaccepted by his colleagues. He'll cooperate. My guess is he has no other options."

"What's his motivation? Money, power, a past …"

"Praise and approval—if you can believe it. He'll work cheap."

The General stood abruptly and made his way across the room to the gentlemen Vandusen had noticed. "But we're getting ahead of ourselves. These are friends of mine." He pointed to the men in the corner. "They worked with the company back in sixty-three on that sticky little business down in Cuba."

Vandusen realized immediately that they were specialists, probably from the muscle side of the organization. He remembered "that sticky little business" very well after spending several months as a guest of Castro's government when he and his associates were abandoned in a cane field by "friends" like these. Their military haircuts and bad shoes gave them away as field operatives. He wondered how they were connected to this business here in Reno.

He stood to greet them as they approached. If the General recommended them, that was enough for him. "I was in Cuba. Welcome to Nevada." He noticed them stiffen when he mentioned Cuba. So, they, too, had their little secrets.

"Let's just say we're a couple of consultants for the Government interested in the battlefield uses of bio-medical research. The General has asked us for a little help," one of the men said.

He knew that'd be the most he'd get out of them. These guys were trained to be vague. They got that way from living in the shadows. "I'm sorry but you have me at a disadvantage," Vandusen said. "I seem to have come into this in the middle. What's your role in this operation?"

They hesitated, deciding how much to say, apparently not used to direct questions.

The General spoke for them: "They may come in handy if we find we need to jump start this operation by getting a little more hands-on."

Vandusen was struck again by how much alike these types appeared. They probably were recruited right out of Officers Candidate School at Fort Benning. The big difference between these two agents was that one had a jagged scar that deformed the bridge of his nose.

Everyone shook hands cordially while exchanging pleasantries, but they were wary of each other, like the first round of a boxing match—testing and searching for weaknesses.

What was the General thinking? These guys would turn us over in a heartbeat.

"So, when can I meet this young man?" the General asked.

"How 'bout tonight? I told him to meet me for dinner downstairs. We want to get him ready for his little *chance* meeting with Savage at the airport."

The General nodded, seeming pleased. "We might want to have a little talk with the wife of the good doctor as well. We need to get this project under our control like yesterday. Langley's getting impatient."

Vandusen stood. "With your permission I will arrange everything. I think we can get most of this wrapped up in the next two days, sir."

The General gave one sharp nod and pointed toward a bank of phones.

* * *

The General and Vandusen had just started in on their deli sandwiches when the two agents that had originally escorted him into the casino entered the deli. They scanned the little restaurant looking for their table. A third, smaller man rushed in behind them, out of breath. He seemed more intent on pocketing his car keys than joining them in their search. Just as the little man was finished fooling with his keys, the other two caught sight of Vandusen and the General and made their way toward the table.

Childs followed tentatively, casting nervous glances around the dining room. Vandusen motioned for Childs to sit down. "Mr. Childs, I'd like you meet someone who is sympathetic to your problem and can help you."

The General extended his hand. "We meet at last."

Childs clumsily reached across the table and shook hands, almost knocking their drinks over. "I'm so pleased to meet you. Mr. Vandusen suggested you might be able to help me with the "powers that be" to get a position where my training would be of use."

The General smiled sympathetically. "I understand you've been trying to get on Dr. Turner's project with little success—and you a person of such talents, I'm told."

Childs relaxed as the General lightly patted his arm.

Vandusen never ceased to marvel at how good the General was. With just a smile, a nod and a pat, he had Childs actually believing that they really cared about his future. He was a subtle chameleon.

The General continued his mastery: "So when can we get together with these people and help them see the errors of their ways and convince them about how important it is to get you on board with them."

"You can find Dr. Turner and his colleague Dr. Savage at Franks Bar most any evening," Childs replied eagerly. "If you ask me, they spend more time in that dive than conducting research."

"So, who's minding the store when they're away?" The General looked from Childs to Vandusen.

Childs answered before Vandusen could speak. "Good question. I think his wife and a few keepers. The house is probably empty except for Mrs. Turner, Mary that is."

Vandusen and the General exchanged knowing looks. It would be a perfect time to pay a little visit to Turner's wife as well as stop by Franks bar.

Kill two birds with one stone ... Divide and conquer.

The General took on a sympathetic tone as he looked over at Vandusen. "Why, that's very irresponsible, don't you think?"

"I'll arrange for some visits after Childs has had the opportunity to meet Dr. Savage at the airport, sir." Getting up, he motioned the two agents to follow him.

The General leaned forward. "Now, Mr. Childs, let's get to know each other a little better, and then you can set off." The General paused. His last question sounded more like an order. "You're free tonight, aren't you?"

CHAPTER 10

Savage fell asleep almost immediately after takeoff from Ontario. He shifted and turned in the uncomfortable airline seat in a fitful sleep full of dreams. The person at the window finally moved, leaving him to his dreams and both seats.

Between the late nights and the excitement of his two encounters with Danny, he'd hardly been able to keep his eyes open on the way to the airport. Raven had made conversation the entire way, but it'd been mostly small talk about mutual friends in the academic community. They both seemed reluctant to further their previous discussions in front of the young man driving. Or was it more comfortable to talk of such deeds cloaked in the shadow of night?

His dreams had been disturbing, vivid. He'd dreamt himself on a large cargo ship in a raging storm. Deafening, panicked cries of apes rose from the hold. The ship seemed inexplicably headed towards a rocky coast where giant waves broke. He could just make out the dense jungle that loomed up from the shoreline, and the rank, humid air carried the strong aroma of decay. He ran through the passageways of the ship, trying to warn someone of the impending danger, but the ship was abandoned except for the shrill cries echoing up from below.

He awakened to the bustle of preparations for their final approach into Reno. Clouds streaked by the window as they made their steep descent, shrouding everything except part of the wing from view. They broke out of the clouds as the plane made a sharp bank, and Mt. Rose and the whole panorama of the Sierras came into view with a glimpse of Lake Tahoe beyond.

As the plane finished its final bank, he saw the layout of the town. On the outskirts looking eastward, stood the newly completed MGM Grand and five other new casinos that had been completed in the last year.

By all accounts Reno was a boomtown once again, as evidenced by the new housing developments that were spreading out from the edge of town. He could just make out the older downtown with its out dated casinos and hotels. Old standbys like Circus Circus, Mepps, Fitzgerald's, and the Cal-Neva Club still lured tourists off old Virginia St. but in dwindling numbers. The new, gleaming Reno that had appeared where once had been grazing land just outside of town had brought a new kind of person with new money and ideas.

Savage had returned to the closest thing he knew to be home and family. He smiled to himself as the wheels touched down with a jar. He'd covered a lot of territory in the last few days. After so many years of running down false leads around the world, he was finally on to something. He'd found some really promising clues, but more importantly, he'd discovered a world peopled with his own kind. He laughed to himself as he thought back to the antics of Bobby Waiter and Hunt Bushnell.

What color and flavor these animal people had compared to the stark rigidity of academia. He'd discovered the term *animal people* and had realized that he was one of them; that was where he fit. For varying motives, these people who risked their lives working and training wild animals had much in common with each other. They shared a culture. They shared a bond. He had more in common with these people he'd just met than he had with colleagues he'd worked with for years. Was it the animals that bonded them together? Or was it the secret they all shared? Circus people were a people of secrets, and they kept them well.

His friend Ken would be pleased. He'd found out about Danny and had a lead on Oliver. That is if he was still in business. He wondered again how the NSF site visit had gone and pondered all the possible things that could've gone wrong. Especially, if Ken was left with the committee too long on his own. He was a positive genius at doing or saying the wrong thing politically.

A smile crossed his face as he thought of Mary orchestrating the activities to avoid just that possibility. What would Ken do without her? For that matter, what would he do without her steady organization and humor in the face of government and university politics?

It'll be good to get home.

Neither he nor Ken had had very promising careers until Mary had come into the picture. If you didn't know the politics of raising money, you wouldn't go very far in academic circles. Universities not only received prestige from research grants but more importantly sizable cuts for "overhead," right off the top.

Money, even in the ivory towers of academia, made the world go around, especially in their world of labs and field research, and Mary knew just how to play the game. Seemingly, she had made the transition from Hollywood to academia effortlessly.

He waited for most of the passengers to disembark before stepping into the cold fall air, so different from L.A. and parts south. He'd not called anyone before leaving and hence no one waited for him. He preferred it that way. It gave him a little more time to transition slowly back to the world of deans, students, and university bureaucracy, a little ritual he'd been doing since his graduate days when there'd been no one to call anyway.

The airport still kept its small-town charm despite the fact that the whole town was booming. So far it had not expanded to handle the growing onslaught of tourists anxious to lose their money at the new casinos; hence the place was packed.

Departing tourists piled with bags of souvenirs from Tahoe, Truckee, and Virginia City sat in small, gray-carpeted waiting areas, nursing their hangovers and praying for their planes to take them back to work. Seated in avocado-green, vinyl upholstery and chrome chairs, their travel clothes clashing, they looked dazed, taking little notice of the excitement of the new arrivals swarming around them.

Free from the cares of their parents who worried how they were going to pay for the gambling that came with the cheap rooms and ninety-nine cent prime rib, children pressed against large, plate-glass windows, squealing at the roar of jets taking off and landing.

Slim young women in trim airline uniforms, small hats tilted to one side of their perfectly styled hairdos, watched over the tired and the lost from behind smooth Formica counters. With smiles seemingly glued to their flawlessly made-up faces, they gave comfort and directions to the confused and hungry. He thought them beautiful to behold, like gorgeous works of art. One model-like beauty caught him admiring her; she smiled and winked at him. He smiled back.

God, I love this town.

He laughed as he almost took pity on these poor lambs lining up to be slaughtered by the dealers, Keno waitresses, hostesses, pit bosses, and you name it. Certainly a new energy flooded into this little airport, but it would all be short lived, as the "Biggest Little City in the World" would soon go the way of Las Vegas and Atlantic City. Life as they had known it up here at the foot of the Eastern Sierras was changing fast.

He wondered how all this growth would affect their little animal compound and the research they'd worked so hard to keep out of the attention of mainstream politics. New streams of money flowed into the university, big streams of money, and new faces smiling with big endowments, but he knew all too well that big endowments rarely came without strings attached, and the underworld was never very far away from this kind of money.

As he made his way through crowds of tourists waiting to claim their baggage, he heard someone calling his name. "Dr. Savage, excuse me; Dr. Savage, sir." He turned and could just make out a tall, lanky man weaving his way tentatively through the airport crowd. He waited while the young man pressed his way, bumping and apologizing, to where he stood by the baggage carousel. An ungainly sort of person, seemingly all arms and legs, the young man looked somewhat familiar, but Savage couldn't place him.

The fellow ambled up to him with an awkward gait that appeared to be a combination of poor coordination and affected subservience. It struck Savage how utterly unattractive he found this person with sharp, hawk-like features and a face pitted with acne. Boils erupted in purple contrast to his pasty white skin, and his close-set eyes shifted about, never making contact. His sickly yellow hue gave him the look of someone who didn't get outside much.

"I'm Gordon Childs. Your colleague Dr. Turner is my professor in primatology."

Savage frowned. Something about the man's demeanor didn't feel right. He was almost too accommodating, too polite, as though he was trying too hard to appear something he was not. His tone of voice had a sardonic quality, and something about his manner made Savage distrust him immediately. But since he'd been under a lot of strain from his adventures, his judgment could be overly suspicious, so he decided to be polite. "Have we met before, eh, Mr. Childs?"

Childs shifted from one foot to the other, avoiding making eye contact. "Not exactly. I attended your lecture on biological and behavioral differences between Pan paniscus and Pan troglodytes. We, ah, the students, found your field observations fascinating, especially regarding the differences in copulation styles between the two species."

"That was last year in Dr. Turner's course. I'd just returned from the Congo if my memory serves me correctly." Savage paused, making ready for a polite exit, but Childs broke in:

"Can I give you a lift somewhere?" Before he could answer, Childs reached for his bags and directed him to the parking area. "My car is not far from here, just through these doors."

Reluctantly Savage followed the young man out of the terminal. "I really wouldn't want to put you out, Mr. Childs. I can make a phone call, really." He knew Childs was pressing himself on him but attributed it to the eagerness graduate students often show trying to get senior faculty members to take notice of them. But there was something else about him, something that wasn't quite right. Did this young man have this effect on everyone, or was it just fatigue from his travels making him over sensitive to strangers?

The bustle of passengers thinned out as they left the terminal and headed for the outside parking lot. He paused at the curb to cross traffic, looked up at the panorama of the Sierras, and filled his lungs with crisp, fall air. Reno had grown and was losing much of its small-town atmosphere, but it still had the flavor of the West and the beauty of the mountains.

Childs took little notice of his surroundings, seeming anxious to press on. His unsightly gait reminded Savage of a spider, but he resigned himself to endure this nervous, self-conscious young man long enough to secure a ride to the Ranch.

Childs drove a little better than he walked. After some trouble starting his VW bus, he drove, with the machine coughing and lurching, toward South Reno with deliberation. Traffic clogged Virginia Street as a result of the seemingly continuous road construction that was attempting to convert old Route 395 into enough lanes to accommodate the growing traffic. Dodging potholes and ditches, they made slow progress through the squeezed lanes.

"This is really quite exciting for me, sir ... to have you all to myself, almost captive so to speak." Childs spoke nonstop in a steady and relentless stream of nervous one-way drabble.

Savage looked at him quizzically but didn't have time to respond before Childs continued:

"I'm sorry; you see I'm doing it now. I'm talking too much. I always do this when I'm nervous. I can't shut up."

His nervousness made Savage want to compensate by trying to put the young man at ease. "Really Childs, I won't bite, you know. Why don't you tell me a little about your research?" This usually put the most nervous of students at ease or at least focused them, but it also subjected him to being a captive listener to someone lecturing about something they were very much enthused about while he wasn't.

He was surprised, however, when Childs dove into a field he found not only interesting but also related, though somewhat distantly, to his own investigations: the copulation styles of various primates. Childs made him nervous, though, when he mentioned his interest in the possibility of distinct species interbreeding in the wild. "I attempted to question Dr. Turner several times about his thoughts on this subject, but I almost got the idea he was avoiding me."

Savage felt uneasy with the direction their conversation was taking. "Dr. Turner is very busy these days and, of course, preoccupied with the NSF people."

"Of course." Childs gave him a side glance.

Had he detected an air of sarcasm from Childs? He was getting very irritated with this awkward young man. "It is my belief that this kind of cross-breeding is more likely to occur in captivity than in the wild, but in either case it would be quite rare."

"Certainly rare, but possible, is that what you're saying?" Childs seemed unable to shift gears without grinding them. Fortunately, however, it distracted him and broke his train of thought.

Childs slowed to turn against traffic and for a moment devoted his attention to finding a break in the steady flow heading into Reno from the South on 395.

Savage decided to take advantage of the loll in conversation to put an end to the discussion. "There are few cases of species naturally interbreeding with another in the wild. We're not talking about probable behavior here but rather theory. There is a big difference, young man."

Childs finally found a break in traffic and sped onto a narrow country road that led to Ken's ranch. "What about coyotes breeding with domestic dogs?" Childs looked more at him than the road, seeming to grow agitated with him attempting to control the conversation. The van veered dangerously close to the irrigation ditches that dropped off each side.

Savage found himself pushing an imaginary brake pedal with his right foot and thought it best to calm Childs in the hopes he'd pay more attention to his driving, "I would say coyotes are more likely to eat a dog than breed with one, but there may be cases. Most of the data is anecdotal in any case and while *Canis latrans* is a very adaptable species, remember he's well down the phylogeny from primates. So, I think we are pretty far off the mark here, Mr. Childs".

"But you would concede that if it happens with some species in the wild, it could happen with humans and chimps, in theory at least?"

Savage could see in which direction this conversation was heading, and he was also concerned with the direction the van was taking as it hit an unusually large pothole. "I know there are African legends to this effect, but frankly I find it very unlikely. It's far more likely to happen in the controlled setting of the laboratory than in the wild." *Shit!* He caught himself too late as he realized that this conversation had strayed way too close to his recent investigations. Had he caught a hint of satisfaction in Childs' manner? He wished their ride together would come to an end, but not in a ditch.

"So, you would concede that under the right laboratory conditions it would be possible create a hybrid species between humans and chimpanzees?" Childs became animated. The VW swerved, seemingly under its own guidance, as the young man paid more attention to Savage than the road.

"But for what reason? What would be the point of such a set of experiments?" Savage reached for the wheel as they headed for the ditch.

That brought Childs' attention back to driving. He slowed and, much to Savage's relief, put both hands back on the wheel. "Reason? My God! Think of it? Having the power to create a creature larger and stronger than a chimp and as intelligent as a human. It would be a super race!" Childs seemed to be talking to himself, as though he were thinking aloud. He caught Savage's gaze, once again taking his attention off the road. "The military or ... CIA would support that kind of research with all the resources of the government. I ... we could name our own ticket ... for life."

Savage shook his head, appalled. "That, young man, is exactly why that sort of research should never be done. It is unethical to say the least!" Savage raised his voice and grabbed the wheel, steering them out of harm's way.

Childs seemed to suddenly catch himself mid-stream in the flow of their discussion. "But of course! Of course, it shouldn't be done, Dr. Savage. I thought we were just speculating." Childs once again attended to the road and lowered his voice. "Really, sir, what do you take me for? No need to get upset."

Childs seemed genuinely hurt. But Savage thought he was over playing it, like a bad actor in a melodrama. Was it his fatigue, Childs' driving, or the fact that he wasn't sure of his own motives regarding such research? Was Childs touching too close to home when he spoke of the gain from such research? "Really, Mr. Childs, your driving has upset me. I would be grateful if you paid more attention to the road. I'm very tired and would like to make it home in one piece." Did he detect a glimmer of suppressed anger cross the young man's face? He couldn't be sure.

"Ah and here we are! Safe and sound." Childs slowed the van and turned his blinker on in an exaggerated deliberation.

Savage felt relieved to catch the first glimpse of the green roofs of the Ken's compound. He thought it interesting that Childs seemed to know his way there. "Have you been to the compound before?"

"I've been by it a few times, but I've never had the chance to go inside. Is it possible to get a tour after I drop you off?" Childs voice sounded modulated and guarded, almost contrived.

So that was the reason for him being so helpful.

"I'm not sure it's possible unannounced, but I'll ask." Now Savage was irritated. Clearly Childs had used him to get inside and close to Ken.

He probably wants a job ... little sneak.

On the way up the main drive to the facility, they saw several Human Companions (HCs) at work and playing with their chimps. Childs pulled up in front of Ken's small apartment, better known on the compound as the Doll House.

He knows exactly where I live—interesting.

Ken crossed the drive that separated the main house from where they stood in front of the Doll House. His gait hesitated when he realized he wasn't alone. "So the wayward traveler returns!" he called and strode towards them.

Savage exited the van, and he and Ken embraced, ignoring Childs for a moment.

Childs climbed out of the vehicle, watching them closely. "I happened to be at the airport and was lucky enough to find Dr. Savage in need of a ride."

"Thank you for bringing my friend back. That was a lucky coincidence. How was it you were at the airport?"

"I like to people watch and the airport is a great place to do that. You never know who might show up."

Ken narrowed his eyes slightly. The young man's answer seemed over-rehearsed. Suddenly, he remembered him as the irritating pest from his evening lecture. Trying to hide his dislike for the young man, he smiled and extended his hand. "Well, thanks again for getting my colleague here safe and sound. I'm sure you'll excuse us as Dr. Savage must be very tired after his adventures, and I have work to do."

"Dr. Savage promised me a tour."

"I didn't say that," Savage retorted. "I said I'd ask if it was convenient."

Ken sighed, wondering how he found himself in the situation of trying to rid himself of Childs a second time in less than a week. He didn't believe in coincidences and felt suspicious of the boy's motives. "Very well, go up to the office and tell Dr. Chaney that I asked him to give you a tour".

Childs looked crestfallen. "I had hoped *you* could show me around."

"While I'd love to, I'm short of time and must still prepare for this evening's lecture— perhaps another time."

Childs mumbled something under his breath as he walked toward the main house.

Savage watched Childs depart. "Interesting, don't you think?"

"What's that?"

"Our new-found friend seems to know exactly where to find Mark and drove directly to my place without the need of directions."

They looked at each other knowingly. "Excuse me while I escort our new friend over to where he belongs." Ken followed after Childs.

When Childs and Ken neared the house, Ken called out for Mark. He came to the door and frowned upon seeing Childs. "And who do we have here?"

"A good Samaritan if you will, Mr. Chaney. This is Mr. Childs who was kind enough to give Dr. Savage a lift from the airport and would like to honor us with a visit. He has requested a tour."

"Has he now? Well, let's have a look around, Mr. Childs."

Ken whispered to Mark, "Short and Sweet, Mark, and keep him out of the labs and hospital. Let us know as soon as he's gone—as soon. I want him out of here before Fred and I head for Franks."

"No worries." Mark put on his best poker face, barely moving his lips, gave a wink and caught up to Childs who had wandered ahead toward the main house. "Now, Mr. Childs, this way, shall we?" They walked toward the large hay barn where a particularly pretty young HC was exercising her chimp.

Ken walked back to where he'd left Savage frowning. He didn't notice the car out on the main road slowing as it passed the driveway.

* * *

The two men in the car smiled at each other as they watched Mark and Childs reach the hay barn.

The driver absently rubbed the scar across the ridge of his nose. "Well, it looks like Mr. Vandusen was right, our young friend might be useful. He's inside." His cold eyes followed the men as they entered the barn.

Ken turned and walked back up the drive toward them.

"Let's get back to the casino," the driver said and drove on. "Our friend will be along soon enough, or at least he'd better; we have a date at Franks. Isn't that what it's called?" He made his thumb and finger into a gun, pointed it back in the direction of the hay barn, then lowered his thumb. "Bang." He blew on his index finger, as though it were a gun barrel, and laughed through his nose.

The other agent smiled, "Now, that's no way to treat a potential partner."

CHAPTER 11

The lights of the little circus glowed in the tropical night sky, casting giant shadows that danced against the walls of the decaying old church. Two ancient generators roared from behind the mission walls, struggling to power up the little circus and drowning out the echoes of the surrounding jungle. Bobby could just make out the entrance to a small village cemetery that shared a clearing.

He followed a crowd of peasants who apparently knew that the way to the circus was along a stone-lined path that snaked through the cemetery. He picked his way through the head stones, bumping into villagers who paused to briefly pay their respects to departed relatives and friends. Giant bats darted low, dodging, like fleeting spirits, around the villagers' heads, as they chased insects drawn by the lights. It seemed everyone in the village, living and dead, was out to see El Circo de las Americas.

It was October 31st and depending on where you lived in Mexico, it was either the beginning of *el dia de los muertos* or the Eve. In this little village, they reserved the 31st for all the relatives who'd died in accidents, *los accidentes*. By the number of peasants pausing in the cemetery, it seemed everyone in this little village must've lost a loved one to an accident. Bobby negotiated past families picnicking in the dim light of hundreds of flickering candles set on and around the chiseled-stone monuments of the rich or the weathered-wooden crosses of the poor.

He wondered at the groups laughing, picnicking, and drinking at their family plots, all clustered around their loved-ones. The adults busied themselves cleaning and tidying up while the children laughed and played with one another. He smiled and shook his head, speaking to no one in particular, "God, where do all these people come from?"

A voice came out of the darkness: "Some come from heaven. But they come mostly from Purgatory, *senor*."

Bobby stopped and turned in the direction of the voice. A small man stepped out of the darkness smiling. "I am Alejandro, *senor*. Are you in need of a guide?" The light from the circus just caught his profile and cast a huge shadow against the mission wall, contrasting with his diminutive, Mayan frame. He stood almost even with Bobby. His eyes gleamed as he flashed a full-tooth grin of ivory and gold and extended his hand.

Bobby took his hand and smiled tentatively, detecting tenseness in the tiny man. Years in show business had made him suspicious of friendly strangers. "Thanks for your kind offer but I think I've found what I'm looking for. This is the place to see the *famous* Circus of the Americas, isn't it?" Bobby put a sardonic emphasis on the word famous.

Alejandro laughed. "It is for sure, but you may be disappointed. I regret to say that El Circo de las Americas is not what it used to be, or all it seems."

Bobby detected a hint of sarcasm veiled behind his accent.

The tiny man nodded his head knowingly as though he could read Bobby's uneasiness. "As you wish, *senor*. I will follow you just the same as it seems our paths are heading in the same direction, at least as far as the circus, and who knows you may still find me useful."

Bobby nodded politely and continued down the path, making his way toward the circus. He'd learned long ago in his travels not to insult the locals. He quickened his pace, though, hoping to put some distance between him and this strange little man in the hopes it would discourage further conversation.

He could just make out the glow of the big top through the jungle. It seemed to hover above them, on a hill by the mission. The lights inside made it appear as a huge, colorful lantern sitting ajar atop the trees.

Quiet, little groups of villagers finished with paying their respects to the dead made their way through the starlit cemetery, each picking separate routes. They whispered as they strolled, uncommonly subdued by the spirits of the cemetery and awed by the circus.

The little village of Palenque was silhouetted against the tropical night awash with a surreal aura. Bobby thought the spirits were alive tonight. He smiled to himself as he wondered about all the little circuses that were going through the same ageless ritual of bringing magic and marvels to isolated little hamlets around the globe. He felt at home even in this far-away place. He was going to the circus, and the circus was the closest thing to roots and a home he'd ever had or would ever have.

The circus had arrived early in the afternoon. Advance men with big gold-toothed smiles had swept into the little village, spreading pesos and promises. The villagers had stared with startled doe-like eyes when the great elephant ambled down the cobble-stone streets towards the church at the center of town, preparing to pull the ropes that would raise the faded big top.

Much had happened since the afternoon. The circus was open now, and everyone within ten miles of the village pushed their way down the crowded pathways to get a good seat. The little, dusty clearing next to the mission had been transformed into a place of wonder. Villagers stood in front of the main entrance, gawking at the menagerie of animals grazing and pacing within their enclosures. The ruins of the Temple of the Inscriptions could just be made out rising out of the jungle, looking as though it were an intentional backdrop to this little affair.

Clowns and jugglers worked the growing crowd, startling them with magic tricks and blasts of fire from their smiling mouths. The real magic was parting these poor villagers from their few horded pesos.

Tickets were selling fast around the front of the tent. Most of the villagers gathered next to colorful, antique circus wagons that contained pacing lions and tigers behind rusting bars. An elephant swayed from leg to leg, pulling at the chain around her rear leg just behind and out of reach of the cat cages.

Huge, colorful banners served as a backdrop, screening the broken-down, horse-drawn trailers that this little circus used to limp from town to town. They depicted visions of a grander circus, a circus that this one had never been and never would be.

The Circus of the Americas was a small, worn company of second-rate players and has-beens—discards from better companies and better times. This collection of cast-off people and animals traveled from town to town at the speed an elephant could walk and graze. It was a circus of the infirmed and addicted, of the lost and failed, disguised in costumes of sequins and glitter.

Misty the elephant was their prize possession. Her owner, Sergio Rameriz, had been a cat trainer in Europe for a Berlin Circus but had had to disappear after one of his tigers pushed past him while he was rehearsing and killed a little girl. He'd had the foresight to not leave empty handed. Sergio was no fool. The circus had probably stopped waiting for him to return from the vet with Misty and the gate receipts.

The Spanish gypsy had many skills. Chance had brought him to Mexico after leaving another circus that had got him to the other side of the world before it'd gone broke. He joined up with the Circus of Americas just in time to disappear from probing questions and now found himself slipping into anonymity, traveling around, from country to country, through Latin America under a borrowed name and papers.

Conveniently for him, circuses just passed through, and no one ever really checked them much, especially in Mexico. Sergio was methodically remaking himself, which was not unusual in the byways of Southern Mexico where people traveling through rarely had much to say about their past. Sergio and Misty were the top billing and had slowly gotten the biggest take of the gate, but it was never enough. He was becoming restless, and this little company of petty thieves was taking him nowhere.

As luck would have it, an unfortunate accident had taken the life of this circus' original owner, and Sergio became their new one. It seems the former owner and Sergio had become close friends, confidants. But they both drank too much and sometimes shared secrets, unhealthy secrets. One night, after many shots of tequila, the two of them took a walk, arm in arm, into the jungle singing and laughing. Sergio came back alone. He had many skills.

After the circus owner's mysterious disappearance, Sergio presented signed papers that made him the new owner, and it appeared he'd also inherited all the man's belongings. No one dared contest this new arrangement. Among the photographs, costumes, and papers that the owner had stored in his trailer, he'd found what looked to be a deed to a farm that appeared to be located in the jungles of the Congo. This new turn of events had planted hope that, if he played his cards right, he might be able to really disappear and disappear in comfort with a few extra pesos or pounds in his pocket.

When he went through all the owner's belongings, he found many strange things. The most interesting were old photographs of what appeared to be strange ape-like creatures. He wondered if they had been or were housed down there and if they were worth any money. He wondered about many things.

The photographs of these creatures unnerved him. They reminded him of Oliver. He'd sold Oliver to this very owner when he first joined the company. He remembered how glad he'd been to rid himself of that menace, but, at the same time, how anxious the owner had seemed to close their deal and ship him off.

It'd seemed strange that the man was willing to pay so much for an old chimp that couldn't be worked anymore because of his habit of pulling people's arms off their bodies. But he'd needed money at the time and thought that if the owner was stupid enough to believe all that crap of him being half-human, he deserved to be screwed. It now made sense where he must've ended up. He'd have to pay a little visit down there and see if his old friend Oliver was there. What a reunion that would be. He'd beat that freak of nature again, just for fun.

Other papers among the photographs had looked to be written in Russian. He needed to find someone who could tell him what they said. The only person he knew who spoke Russian was that idiot bear trainer. He'd have to make friends with him and get him to translate the documents. If there was anything of value that needed to be kept secret, they could always take a little walk into the jungle. His black gypsy eyes darkened, and he smiled, thinking how fun it would be. He'd not delay taking care of this. Who knew, there could be enough money to get him out of this shit hole, this limbo, this purgatory, and give him a new life.

Sergio had felt uneasy all day. He'd been having dreams lately, dreams of discovery and incarceration. He had a habit of looking at the audience from behind the curtains before each show. You never knew who might be in the crowd, and it was good to know who was around. His nervous eyes swept across the crowd in the bleachers. It was going to be a full house tonight. *A good tip.*

The ringmaster joined him and, as though reading his mind, said, "Some of them might actually appreciate our show. Better yet, some of these peasants may even have some money. Goddamn, *campasenos.*" The ringmaster nudged Sergio and ever so slightly nodded toward the front box seats closest to the center ring. "It looks like we have some guests tonight. You may have to welcome them after the show or, better yet, take them on one of your little one-way walks."

Sergio ignored the ringmaster's comment. His cold eyes stared in the direction he'd indicated and hardened. He fumbled in his pocket and was reassured by what he felt there.

The ringmaster walked away and smiled back. "A Boy Scout is always prepared."

Sergio thought he might have to be taking a lot of people for walks if they didn't start minding their own damn business. He was beginning to think that this little part of the world was becoming way too crowded.

* * *

The trip to San Francisco was worth it; Hunt must know where every circus is in the world at any given time. Bobby smiled as he realized that for fifty pesos—less than two dollars US—he had the best seat in the circus, a program, plus a bag of churros. He reached into his jacket pocket and pulled out a small silver flask.

Now I'm set.

To Bobby's irritation Alejandro slid into the box next to him. "We are lucky to get such good seats, amigo."

Bobby nodded back at him and pretended to read his program.

Alejandro laughed. "Oh, so you read Spanish. That's very good, for sure. No wonder you don't need a guide." He continued to chuckle.

Bobby ignored him and kept at his program—printed on cheap paper with ink that smudged at the touch in the humid air. He could tell by the frayed edges that it'd been picked up off the ground and recycled, as was common the world over with shows that worked from performance to performance to stay afloat. Every centavo counted. The date, time and location of the show were stamped on a sticker that'd been placed over other stickers at the top of the program. He thought it very economical. He, also, thought of all the expense and waste practiced on his own shows in Hollywood.

His fingers blackened with each turn of the page. While he couldn't understand the text word for word, he understood it by context as programs the world over promoted the same things. Dark, grainy pictures with bragging bios of the stars included words like *magnifico, supremo, excelente,* words Bobby had seen after his own name.

The small world of the circus closed in around him. Even without the text he would've recognized Misty the elephant. In a really poor photograph, Misty stared back at him, one foot and trunk up.

He'd been with Lester years ago in Circus Berlin when he'd met her and her trainer. He remembered that she'd disappeared under mysterious circumstances, but mysterious circumstances were common in the circus world. Those who lived the life learned early to keep to themselves and not ask too many questions.

He continued to flip the pages of the little program and immediately recognized the photo of the short gypsy but not the name printed next to it. He'd come to the right place. Hunt was right about Sergio being in the show. He wondered if he was right about the rest of the story. He would have to be very careful, he cautioned himself.

Interesting that the brief bio mentioned nothing about his performances in Europe. The story came back to him now. Lester had told the story of how Sergio and Misty had disappeared after a show in Berlin. Everyone had marveled at how anyone could disappear with an elephant. He thought it ironic that Sergio would've ended up with Oliver.

On the next page was a listing for what Bobby made out to be a bear act. It had a picture of a big, bearded man in a caveman costume posing with a large, brown bear standing on its haunches. Bobby found it hard to make out details from the picture because it was so smudged. He had to hold it up to the light.

Alejandro leaned across the flimsy partition that separated the box seats. "Ah, looks like we are in for a treat tonight; the Three-Legged Bear Act is coming for our enjoyment all the way from the Soviet Union or so it says in the program you're holding."

Bobby smiled back. "Well, it's probably the only three-legged bear act in the world, and here we are." Bobby thought he might need this guy after all. He looked up from his program and realized that the big top was filling up. A brassy band began to play and the glare of the house lights dimmed.

The ringmaster stepped into the center ring and announced the performers of the little circus as they paraded into the ring. Bobby wondered how many Specs he'd seen or been in during his career. He had an overwhelming feeling of nostalgia as he watched the various performers smile, wave, and bow to the audience. Each act had its own style of presenting itself to the *tip*, the audience.

Spec was a tradition in circuses around the world. Its purpose was to introduce the acts at the beginning of the show and build the excitement. While this little circus was following this timeless tradition, it was not building much excitement, not until Misty the elephant came into the ring. The crowd went wild when the trainer had her lift her trunk and leg and then bow. As Sergio turned with Misty to exit the ring, both faced Bobby in the center light, and Bobby couldn't help but nod at him. He noticed just the slightest flicker of recognition cross the trainer's face before he led Misty out of the light.

Alejandro smiled and nodded toward center ring. "It is touching to run into old friends so far from home ..." The music drowned him out as the first act was announced. "Well, here we go. He is saying the world-famous Three-Legged Bear Act is about to perform for our pleasure."

Bobby thought it a sad little act. More than that; it was terrible. The trainer tried several times to get the bear to go up the rickety old steps of a playground slide and slide down the other side. The old bear ambled apathetically on three legs. Bobby wondered how the poor thing had lost his front leg. The act was so bad it was comical.

Finally, in desperation, the trainer climbed up the ladder, placing bits of food on several steps, his big bulk shaking the whole slide. The audience roared with laughter when the bear slowly worked its way up the steps eating the snacks but then turned around and came back down the way he'd come rather than go down the slide.

The trainer tried again. This time he placed even more bits of food strategically all the way up to the top. When the bear reached the top, lured by the food, the trainer slid down the front to the bottom. His leopard leotards rode up the crack of his huge, hairy buttocks, showing more than the crowd wanted to see. Cat calls and moans rose up interspersed with laughter. The trainer ignored the crowd as he tried to race around to the bottom of the steps before the bear turned around again. He picked up a long stick he apparently had laying by the slide and used it to push the bear down the slide. Bobby now realized that this was the act—sadly, all of it. He thought it a pathetic piece of training. In fact, it was not really training at all, but ironically the crowd loved it.

Alejandro looked over at Bobby. "Well, was it worth coming all the way down from El Norte to visit this little village and see such a grand spectacle? Perhaps you're looking for someone to discover and put in one of your movies?"

"How do you know where I come from?"

"It's my business to know, Mr. Bobby Waiter of Studio City, California."

The acts continued to play center ring. Each seemed to be worse than the previous. The crowd, however, was enthusiastic. The fact that tequila began traveling from hand to hand, up and down the rows, may have had something to do with it. Much of this was lost on Bobby as he tried to figure out this little man sitting next to him. "I'm sorry, have we met before? How is it you know who I am?"

"Let's just say our interests are one for the present. I'm investigating the strange disappearance of the previous owner of this little disaster of a circus. I work for ..." A little brass band led by several loud trumpets interrupted their conversation. The crowd cheered and rose to their feet as the ringmaster announced Misty the Elephant and her trainer Sergio Rameriz. Alejandro watched Sergio intently as he performed his act. "It is interesting how good he has become as an elephant trainer when you consider he was not much of a cat trainer."

Bobby looked again at this mysterious little man sitting in the next box seat, so intense and not much taller than him. Meeting someone close to his height was unusual, as he'd lived his whole life as a Little Person always looking up at people who towered over him. But mostly he felt very uncomfortable about his probing questions and his knowing looks. He tried to think of everything Lester and Hunt had told him about what had happened in Berlin so long ago and wondered how all this connected to his search for Oliver. How did this little man fit into the puzzle?

When he came back from his thoughts, he realized that Sergio had been staring in their direction. Their eyes met briefly, and he felt Sergio's stare change to a menacing glare, bold and threatening. The gypsy looked from Bobby to Alejandro, paying little attention to his work in the ring. Bobby felt as though something very evil was visiting this little corner of the world, a chill welled up in his very core, and, not for the last time, he felt very alone and confused—and a long way from home.

"It might be to our mutual advantage if we paid a little visit to our friend's trailer before this show is over. From the look he gave us, I'd say time is running out, and you might feel more comfortable with a guide." Alejandro spoke fast and almost in a whisper, barely moving his lips as he starred back at Sergio.

"Who are you? What is it you think you know about me and my visit here?'

Alejandro smiled. "Still playing coy, are we? Let's just say I'm the only friend you have right now in this stinking little village. I think maybe you'll agree we are a long way from the bright lights of Hollywood. Time is slipping, my friend. He's going to bolt, for sure. So, are you in or out?"

"Why should I care?"

The little man pulled him near and whispered, "Oliver."

Bobby stared at the name. "Let's take this outside."

* * *

Sergio watched as they left the crowed big top. He gripped his fingers around the elephant hook and with his other hand, fumbled in his pocket for the large switchblade. He thought again that this little circus was getting way too crowded and it was time to thin it out a bit. He didn't like chance meetings, especially when they included outsiders.

Bobby knew something wasn't right when they slipped out of the tent through a large flap manned by an usher. He caught a last glimpse of Sergio hunched over, watching them as they ducked under the drape. "This is not a good start." Bobby nudged Alejandro to look back toward the center ring and Sergio.

"Let's take a look around the grounds while everyone is busy." Alejandro led the way around the back of the big top where the performers had their trailers.

"We just might get lucky and get a chance to talk with our favorite elephant trainer before he disappears again."

Their eyes had trouble adjusting to the darkness. Bobby could just make out a cluster of haphazard trailers ahead. As they neared, a large man stepped out of the darkness, blocking their way. "Who are you? This is a closed area."

"I am Inspector Alejandro Rivera of the Federal Police. My associate and I are looking for Sergio Ramirez's trailer. We have business with him." He held out a badge with his ID.

Bobby finally realized that his suspicions were correct about their meeting not being chance. This situation was unraveling very quickly.

The guard looked skeptically at them, especially Bobby, and seemed to hesitate on what to do next. "He's performing right now. You'll have to wait until the show is over and I can get him."

"We're waiting for no one. If you don't want to end up in jail, I suggest you show us to his trailer right now."

Now, the man appeared really confused. He shifted his weight between his huge feet while clenching his fists. He had the meaty look of a weight lifter and the rough manner of a barroom bouncer.

Alejandro lifted his shirttail above the butt of his pistol. "Now if you will be so kind as to show us the way, we would be most grateful," he said in a less-terse voice.

They stood for what seemed like several heartbeats until finally the man nodded and led the way to the wagons behind the circus. He stopped at the largest one. The area was dark except for a glow cast by a colorful string of lights that outlined the trailer. They could just make out the steps leading up to an oval wood door.

As they approached the trailer, Alejandro pulled his pistol and motioned the guard into the trailer ahead of them. They remained silent, somehow understanding that they'd crossed a line and there'd be no going back.

Bobby sighed and wondered how he'd gotten into this mess but more importantly how he was going to get the hell out. "Is the gun really necessary?"

"Yes—you, too, Bobby." He waved him into the trailer behind the guard.

"Christ. Am I under arrest?"

The little detective didn't reply.

Bobby could just make out the dim glow of a small kerosene lamp that lit the inside of the trailer. He turned it up. Its oily smell competed with the rank air.

Alejandro nodded to the guard. "Sit down." Looking over to Bobby, he added, "Let's take a look around."

Furniture and boxes crammed the trailer. It had a surprising amount of room, but every inch of it was full. Costumes hung from hooks in the ceiling, and piles of papers were stacked about. It had the look of a place that was temporarily storing valuables for more than one person. Stacked boxes had crudely scribbled names on them, and Bobby realized that some of the names were from previous associates of Sergio's—associates who would probably not be coming back to claim their valuables.

Alejandro moved about the room as though looking for something in particular. Every once in a while, he looked back toward Bobby and the guard, who was tense and glowering. "Bobby, check the door."

It was too dark outside to see anything, but he could still hear the brassy little band playing from the tent. Muffled stirrings of animals in their cages and corrals came out of the darkness. He shut the door again.

Alejandro kneeled over a large, battered old travel trunk with broken leather handles. Hotel and steamer stickers from around the world peeled off from all sides. Alejandro looked very closely at a particularly large label written in a sloppy illiterate hand that was barely legible. Perhaps Sergio's hand.

"I think we may have found a clue to both our little riddles."

"Why? What does it say?" Bobby gave the man in the chair a wide berth and leaned over Alejandro's shoulder.

"Oliver."

Alejandro pointed the gun at the man and sternly asked, "Do you have the keys to this?"

The guard glared back without a word and lowered his head, staring at the gun.

"Probably not, considering how I think most of this stuff got here." He lowered the pistol and looked back to Bobby. "Take a look around and see if you can find any keys or something to break this damn thing open with. I think we're running out of time."

The big man in the chair leered knowingly and leaned forward while looking at an old clock on a cluttered desk across from him.

"Judging from the smirk on this mute's ugly face, I think we are out of time. Check outside … I don't hear any more music … do you?"

The door jerked from Bobby's hand, making him fall forward and block the doorway. Sergio tried to kick him out of the way, knocking the breath from him. Bobby clawed at his kicks, tripping him up. A knife skidded across the trailer floor. Sergio grabbed him by the neck while pinning his little body down with his knee. The Gypsy's fingers closed on his throat like a vise, relentless and unremitting, while he reached for the loose knife with his free hand. Choking, Bobby flayed his legs as he tried to break free, but he was no match for such savage violence. His kicks weakened as he feebly attempted to free himself from the grip. Sergio was actually smiling down at him, lost in the joy of his work. Bobby was past panic. Everything was fading.

Out of the corner of his eye, he saw the guard leap from the chair and smother Alejandro's little frame as he tried to reach Bobby. In his last moments of consciousness, the room filled with a bright flash and deafening blast. The cracks of God's thunder, he thought, then the world went dark.

CHAPTER 12

"Can you hear me?"

Bobby awoke to someone shaking him. Alejandro's small, dark face came in and out of focus. He could smell, almost taste, the pungent odor of gunpowder. His whole body tingled as the room slowly grew brighter and sharper. But when he tried to prop himself up on one arm, the room spun so fast that he felt twinges of nausea. His head throbbed painfully to the rhythm of his racing heartbeats.

"Jesus! What the hell happened?" Bobby wobbled as, with Alejandro's help, he tried to stand up. A second, stronger wave of nausea sent him stumbling to the door of the trailer. Alejandro steadied him while he retched and vomited into the darkness.

"How do you feel?" Alejandro looked nervously around. "You don't look so hot, my friend."

"Thanks for the reassuring words! Just let me walk around a little and catch my breath." He walked in slow circles outside the trailer in the darkness, taking deep breaths while Alejandro sat on the steps watching.

"You know, you can't stay around here any longer." Alejandro cocked his head slightly listening to the brassy music drifting out from the big top. "Believe me, you don't want to be around when my men join in with the locals to investigate this mess. All hell's going to break loose."

Bobby stopped rubbing his head. "But aren't you the police?"

Alejandro pointed into the trailer. "I *am* the police, but that's not going to help. Consider this, you're a foreigner ... a gringo—and about to be wrapped up in this and several other messy deaths, which we now know are murders." The light streaming out of the partially ajar door revealed a body, limp on the floor. "You need to get the hell out of Mexico, and I mean like right now."

Bobby frowned. "I'm not going anywhere until I have a look inside. I didn't come all this way to run off just when we may've found some real clues about Oliver." Bobby caught himself too late. He wished he hadn't admitted knowing who Oliver was in front of this mysterious little detective. Before Alejandro could reply, he started up the steps to the trailer.

Alejandro followed just behind, shaking his head. "You'll be less enthusiastic if you land in jail in Mexico City, believe me!"

"Well, then help me. I want a chance to go through his belongings for any clues of where Ol ... what I came here for—please!" He stepped awkwardly over Sergio's body and froze at the sight of the bodyguard slumped in the chair in front of them. "You shot them both?" He stood between the two motionless bodies, trying not to stare. Sergio's eyes were still partly open, glinting menacingly, even in death. Bobby felt another wave of nausea welling up and swallowed several times.

"It's a pretty common reaction, at least in this country, to shoot a criminal when he attacks a policeman. It was *self-defense*. But what's important is that this finally wraps up a case I've been working on for two years." Pointing at Sergio he continued, "And I have my man right here, case closed. No complicated trial or loose ends—if *you* don't complicate things by hanging around.

Alejandro motioned to the large chest in the center of the room. "See if you can find what you're looking for before you become a loose-end, yourself. When the show ends out there, this place is going to be crawling with people, which I guarantee will include the local police."

He came over to help Bobby pry open the trunk. "It'll be very hard to keep you out of this. I may be the police, but I'm no miracle worker! So, get to work so we can get you on your way."

The two turned their attention to the trunk and its contents. It was packed with mementos from all the little walks Sergio took with newfound friends—friends who mysteriously did not return with him. They soon discovered he'd taken one of those walks with the previous owner of the circus. Upon digging through a large pile of letters and photographs, they found evidence suggesting that Sergio had brought Oliver to the circus, but he was no longer there. He'd been transported to Africa.

The music grew louder from the big top. Bobby knew from his years of living and working the circus that the grand finale was on and soon the show would be over. He figured no one had heard the shots over the noise of the band and announcer. They'd been very lucky so far.

Bobby quickly gathered any material that seemed to be about Oliver. Photographs of what looked to be a whole compound clustered in the jungle stunned him. Many of them had short captions scribbled on the backs indicating locations and dates. They were neatly organized in stacks and bound together with hemp string. He didn't have time to examine them properly so he grabbed what he could, stuffing his backpack.

An old, brittle photograph that lay in the bottom of a shoebox caught his eye. It looked as though it'd been casually tossed in after the rest had been bound. He blew a layer of dust off its back and gently waved it in the air, which set him into a fit of sneezing. He could barely make out a faint inscription scribbled in pencil. Some of the letters were so smudged with age that he couldn't read them, but when he turned it over, he, once again, looked into the piecing glare of someone he'd feared from long ago—Oliver.

He flipped it back over and tried again: *Oli...r, 1956...G...ne, Africa.* A flood of emotions and images overwhelmed him. His voice quivered as he slowly filled in the blanks, "Oliver, 1956, Guinea, Africa."

"Can you help me get somewhere where I can get to an airport? I think I've located the whereabouts of an old acquaintance that some friends of mine are very interested in visiting."

Alejandro nodded as he continued to stand watch at the door. "As long as you're out of my jurisdiction by morning, and you're out of here right now. The shows over in more ways than one." The music had stopped, and they heard footsteps in the darkness. Alejandro sprung into to action. "Now *vamonos*!"

* * *

Bobby had to find a post office and chance sending Dr. Turner the documents he'd salvaged from Sergio's trailer; and he had to do it right away. Alejandro had made it clear that it'd not be good to be found with any evidence that could connect him to the incident of the night before.

He had just a little time while Alejandro made arrangements to get him out of the village and on his way to Mexico City where it'd be easy for him to disappear and fly to anywhere in the world without much notice.

And where would that be?

The little detective had gravely told him he wasn't sure how long he could keep him out of all this.

A vendor in the park proudly pointed out that the town did indeed have a post office and that it was housed inside a stationary store down a street on the opposite side of where they stood. He gave Bobby confusing directions in broken English.

After referring to his dog-eared Spanish phrase book and weaving through the market crowd, Bobby figured he was standing in front of the right place. The haphazard display of school supplies and fading stationary gave him a further clue. A little, rusting sign hung above the door that read *Oficina, de Cerroes*. Bobby mouthed the words in his best broken high-school Spanish, said "post office," to no one in particular and quickly ducked in.

He found the little counter in the back of the shop that housed the makeshift post office—nothing more than a few cartons of incoming and outgoing mail. The shopkeeper helped him package the documents and photos by selling him what he needed, then waited patiently as Bobby hastily scribbled a note to Dr. Turner. When he was sealing the envelope and putting it in the box with the other things, he realized he didn't have Turner's home address. He hastily scribbled, "University of Nevada, Reno, Nevada USA C/O Dr. Ken Turner."

He stared anxiously at the box; it would have to do. Time was running out. The shopkeeper took the box and Bobby's pesos with little interest. A soccer game blared on a radio and the man was clearly anxious to get back to the stool beside it.

Soon after, Bobby and Alejandro stood beside the bus to Mexico City by way of Tuxla Gutierrez, Pueblo, and Vera Cruz, watching the passengers board.

"Remember my friend," Alejandro said as they parted, shaking hands, "stay with this bus until you arrive in Mexico City." He smiled, looking around the bus. "You'll have plenty of time to figure your next move."

Alejandro seemed nervous as he scanned the little terminal and climbed into the bus with Bobby. The detective read a sign above the bus driver and laughed. "Well, my friend, you're in good hands." He pointed at the visor above the driver's seat where a small picture of Jesus Christ ascending into the heavens hung and translated: "Jesus Cristo is my copilot. Give my regards to Senor Hunt."

Bobby stared at him with a quizzical look.

"It seems like you circus people are always in need of help." He nodded once to Bobby and left the bus.

The ancient, second-class vehicle coughed into life, and Bobby watched the mysterious little man who'd aided him in this faraway place disappear as the bus lurched forward into the unknown. *What next?*

CHAPTER 13

Fred Savage always felt comfortable when he stepped into Frank's Bar and Cafe. The good old-fashioned hangout attracted a wide range of clientele, from blue-collar factory workers to university professors. Around since the forties, its glory days had long since passed. Yet it had a simple charm that kept Savage coming back. It's peeling walls with cartoon-like murals depicting bar life stirred memories of his misspent youth as a grad student. Legend had it that a past patron whose identity was long since lost had done the drawings to make good on an unpaid bar tab. And from the quantity of them, he must have had a large tab.

Savage had frequented Frank's since first coming to Reno in '78. He saw it as a place to unwind from the politics of the university. The upper echelon of the U didn't make it to this side of town—on the other side of the tracks, way down in the working-class district nestled in among decaying warehouses and small repair shops.

Young working artists and writers along with untenured faculty found they could relax and mix with working people whose conversation ran more social than professional. But more importantly, Frank's was a place where you could meet someone unnoticed for a quiet rendezvous. People here minded their own business.

He stood for a moment, his eyes adjusting as the door swung closed behind him, shutting off the glare of the midday sun. The glare briefly silhouetted his stout, compact frame. A few patrons looked up from their mugs and plates but quickly returned to their steaming bowls of chili and generous burgers, showing little interest in him.

Scotty, the bartender, nodded in the direction of a back booth by the bathrooms while he dried a tray of mugs. The bartender knew most everyone who came in and who they belonged to. The place was deep with people on their lunch breaks: no nonsense working people who'd made it halfway through the workday and were set on getting through the rest with as little hassle as possible. The place echoed with the hum of conversation and laughter, the noise of rattling plates from back in the kitchen and the sharp crack of pool-cue shots. Burgers sizzled, sending out an aroma that mixed with large steaming bowls of chili, making Savage hungry. A jukebox struggled to be heard above the bustle. He wondered at how coincidental yet fitting the present selection was as Bruce Springsteen belted out, *Born in the USA-A-A-A-A-A.*

He thought how different the patronage was during the day compared to the evening when he usually hung out. Most sensible working people went home to their families in the evening. Intellectuals like him took over the place in the evening. They had no real home to go to so they stayed late. He made his way down one side of a long U-shaped bar as Scotty took orders and tapped beer. They slapped hands as he passed.

Savage finally spotted his friend Ken Turner sitting in the back and made his way toward him, weaving through a maze of tightly spaced tables and chairs. Many of the customers greeted him with mild recognition and friendly nudges.

The glow of a 'Hamms of Sky Blue Water' beer sign that hung behind the burgundy Naugahyde booth where Ken slouched faintly illuminated his friend's thin, angular features. The sign seemed oddly out of place with its scene of a canoe beached next to a camp on the edge of a crystal-clear lake.

Savage grinned as he looked at the sign. "A Hamms would go pretty good right now."

Ken stood to greet him. "Sure thing," he said as they embraced, then he motioned to Scotty and shouted, "Give us a pitcher that's been brewed in the *Land of Sky Blue Water*." He paused as they sat. "So, how'd it go down South?" he asked, searching Savage's face.

Savage waited until the busty young waitress slopped a frosted pitcher of beer with two rattling glasses on the table and left with their lunch orders. "We're in the game, I think." He leaned over and whispered, "Dr. Raven may have Oliver's brother at his compound. His name is Danny. I met a number of trainers who'd be willing to work with us. It turns out that Raven's a big fan of yours."

"You saw him, this Danny?"

"I almost went hands on with him. He's a goddamn menace." Savage took a sip of his beer. "We'd have to do more investigation, but it's very likely he's what they say he is."

"What'd you mean by a menace?"

"He almost strained me through the bars. He's a real bad boy."

The same young server returned and slid their lunch in front of them. She smiled at Ken, touching his hand lightly. "Will there be anything else, Professor?"

He smiled back. "We're fine, thanks."

"How's Mary?" Savage smiled briefly as he watched what he figured to be one of their students sway away.

"She's working at the compound. We left her entertaining your guest, Mr. Childs. She's going to join us later this evening when she dumps him."

Fred frowned at the mention of the boy's name. "I don't think that was a chance meeting at the airport."

"Really? So, what do you think he's up to?" Ken asked.

"I think he's trying to get in with us to spy around. His interests likely go beyond our communication work, and I don't think he's working alone. He's absolutely obsessed with the idea of cross-breeding chimps and humans—really the whole area of hybridization of species."

"He popped up at my evening lecture last week. I don't like that boy." Ken frowned. "He could be working with the administration of the university or maybe agents in the government or both to find out how far we've actually gone beyond our published work. They may want to put us and our chimps to work in an applied area rather than pure research." Ken put special emphasis on the word *applied*, which unsettled Savage.

"What're you talking about?" Savage paused to refill their beers. He waited for the rich cream-colored foam to settle back down into the amber liquid. "Remember, I helped write our grant. We're being supported to investigate the cognitive and linguistic abilities of chimpanzees—right? That's pure research. There's nothing applied about it."

"Exactly, but receiving government funds makes our work public record, and there're those who'd speculate on how to apply our work to their own purposes for good or ill." Ken looked around and lowered his voice to a conspiratorial tone: "Several of the primate projects have been approached recently by people supposedly representing the government—and it seems to always be right after an NSF site visit." Ken tore nervously at a napkin.

"It's that little worm Melon, isn't it?" Savage spit out Melon's name.

Ken ignored the reference. "The common thread in these inquiries has been exploring ways to apply this work for the benefit of the Department of Defense or the Intelligence community. The worst thing is that these people have been getting more and more, how should I say, aggressive in their inquiries."

"They can do that?" Savage asked.

"Of course, they're the Goddamn government. They can do whatever they want." Ken's voice sounded strained.

Savage became agitated. "No, I mean, do you think they can find uses for chimps that meet their purposes?"

"They already have. The Air Force is using chimps for part of the space program; the National Institute of Health and Medicine is using them for all kinds of medical research, and the Navy is conducting studies with dolphins. So, we'd be a perfect candidate for the Army, I should think." Ken emphasized each point by thumping his knuckles on the table.

"Does it ever stop? We've had enough trouble with the university wanting to use our chimps for medical research, and now this. Christ!" Savage's raised voice caught the attention of a couple of diners.

Ken lowered his voice. "Believe me, Fred, the university will not be our allies in this debate. As they say, 'money talks and nobody ...'" Ken's voice trailed off.

Savage, continued, ignoring Ken's cue to lower his voice, "I can't see how they would be very useful in war."

"Arming or disarming mines might be one use ..." Ken collected his thoughts. "But you're probably right. The present stage of our research primarily focuses on communication." He leaned towards Savage and whispered, "But if you added what we're both been talking about here, hybridization, that would be a different story. Think if they got their military minds wrapped around what we're investigating with Oliver."

Savage nodded, looked around, and finally lowered his voice: "If you look at the hybridization of other species from wolves and dogs to tigers and lions it's often the case that you get a kind of hybrid vitality. That's what Dr. Raven and I were talking about this morning before I left to come here."

"Bingo, very often the offspring are greater in size, strength and intelligence."

Savage frowned. "And sometimes, though rarely, they're even fertile."

Ken nodded. "If you crossed a human with a chimp you might get some real 'hybrid vitality' as you say—an animal with the intelligence and size of a human and the strength of a chimp—a kind of superhuman. I can see where that kind of creature could be quite useful on the battlefield, and, worse, the army would probably be reluctant to classify them as humans thus making them very expendable."

Savage became agitated. "Shit, I never thought of that. Since they wouldn't technically be human, whole colonies of them could be raised for a variety of uses outside the normal ethical bounds of research."

Ken shook his head in disgust. "Think of the uses these creatures could be put to in battlefield medicine—they could be farmed for their organs."

"Exactly, since one donor would be human there might be less possibility of rejection when using one of their organs in a transplant. Remember recently the operation Dr. Christian Bernard performed in South Africa? He did a successful heart transplant in a human patient using a baboon heart. Unfortunately, the heart was rejected after a few weeks and the patient died."

"Organ rejection might not be the case with a creature more closely related to humans like a hybrid." Ken gazed into space. "But I think I most fear a cross that possesses the traits of an adult chimp's temperament with the size of a human or bigger."

"That would be a real cross-wired monster; a damn Frankenstein," Savage exclaimed, "a Danny but bigger and, God forbid, smarter." They paused, collecting their thoughts as they visualized various combinations.

What seemed like the whole university soccer team came bursting through the door, hooting and howling their excitement over their win against their cross-town rival, CHIVAS.

Ken smirked, glancing up as the captain did a jig, hands waving in the air. The rest of the team surrounded him, jumping and hooting out of control. Several of the patrons got up to leave, shaking their heads and mumbling under their breath, so Scotty tried to calm the team down. "It would depend on exactly what parts of human intelligence ended up in such a hybrid ... certainly not the kind we have displayed here." His tone mocked the serious style of one of his lectures.

Savage laughed and replied sarcastically, "I think any one of our chimps has a larger working vocabulary than any one of these guys." They both laughed and then attended to the rest of their lunch and more Hamms.

Ken and Savage became so engrossed in their conversation that they lost track of time. They had much to catch up on. When they finally did take notice, they surmised that evening was fast approaching, even though Frank's had no clocks or windows. More students and other university types had supplanted the noon crowd, filling most of the tables or lining the walls on both sides of the room as they cued up to play pool. The room became noisier with the growing crowd.

Several coeds clustered around a middle-aged man wearing a beret. He seemed out of place in a bar full of students and young professors. Ken noticed Savage watching the interaction as the ladies laughed at something the man had said. "Old Harry is holding court again it would seem—instead of writing."

Savage shook his head. "What a waste of talent. He was a promising young writer, but now he's a one book writer."

"But Harry spends most of his waking hours here, and he knows everyone. He may be useful, especially concerning what Childs is up to. We'll have to have a word with him soon. But let's finish our business. It's getting too busy in here."

The two scientists were more careful as they continued their discussion. Visits from students who recognized them often interrupted them. The notoriety of their research had made them celebrities of sorts in academia, especially at a small campus like theirs, and especially among the young students. The University of Nevada, Reno had been elevated to headline news as a result of their sociolinguistic research, moving their once-obscure School of Psychology into the big show. They were getting attention from both the academic and popular press. The importance of their work had been described as "the moon shot of the social sciences" by one of the science commentators in the press.

They soon realized that they'd have to finish their discussion soon as there were just too many interruptions, not to mention ears too close to their table. Ken paused as a group of his students left to play pool. "What do you make of Dr. Raven and his claim concerning Oliver's apparently lost brother?"

"I can't say for sure," Savage replied. "We don't have all the pieces to the puzzle, but we have enough to make some decisions as to our next steps. Danny and Oliver apparently were in the same circus act twenty or so years ago, and many of the people I met both at the Circus Luncheon Club and the Wild Animal Training Center remembered them. Lester actually worked with both of them." He paused as a server cleared their table and took orders for dinner. "Dr. Raven told me that he ran some DNA tests on Danny and his chromosome count is 47.'

Turner blinked, startled by this news; excitement lit up his eyes. "That's significant, Fred! It places him firmly between a human and a chimp. Why haven't you told me this before?"

"I'm unsure of the validly of the results. First, we've only Raven's word and we don't really know him."

"Raven has had a colorful background for sure, but I think a good scientific reputation. What's really bothering you, Fred?" Turner asked.

"There could've been an error in the testing. It was all done on the down low—clandestine—and it's only one test." Fred fidgeted.

"But there's something else bothering you?"

"Yes. Danny's very different to be sure—but not as different as I would've expected."

Ken nodded knowingly. He seemed to sense the direction of logic that Savage was taking. "Well—there would be a wide range of variation among the offspring depending on the genes of the parental donors, and, as with all hybridization, it would take generations of selecting for particular traits to shape a specific outcome—much as it is in the breeding of dogs or cats.

If you consider the apparent age of both Danny and Oliver, they could've been the first generation of the experiments that happened in the twenties."

"I know all of that ... really ... I think I'm disturbed by the whole ethical issue surrounding these kinds of experiments, and I guess I'm torn between the wonder of this and the horror of it—I want to be really sure of our direction and motives." Savage held Ken's eyes. "Ken, we've known each other for over twenty years and you're my best friend. We're on the same page with this—right?

Ken responded without hesitation, "Yes, we are. We're not the ones doing these experiments or proposing to." Ken paused, collecting his thoughts as though he wanted to pick his words carefully. "We want to know if it's been done or is being done. And if so, we want to know by whom and to what end— and if these creatures exist we need to make sure scientists with ethics determine their outcome, not individuals or institutions motivated by self-interest." He was silent for a moment, deep in thought. "They would need protecting."

Savage relaxed, relieved. "So, what's the next step?"

"I think we need to take a closer look at Danny and find Oliver. Do you think Dr. Raven will help?"

"Yes. He shared a lot of information considering we just met. I think he's looking for support, and as I said before, he has a huge respect for you and the work we're doing."

Before Ken could respond, they were startled by the thump of a fat manila envelope landing on the table between them. They looked up; Mark and Consuelo stood there, looking serious.

Mark couldn't contain himself. "Bobby sent us some interesting documents from his travels. I just picked them up at the Post Office. Apparently, they were miss-addressed. It seems he's run away to the circus again." He slid into the booth while Consuelo intercepted the young server who'd just arrived with dinner. "I hope you don't mind. I took a preliminary look— there're some astounding photographs and other documents that are unfortunately in Russian. Who do we know who reads Russian?"

Ken started to open the envelope but hesitated. "I don't think this is the place to open this. When Mary gets here we should go back to the compound where we can have some privacy." Ken looked toward the door. "Where's Mary?" he asked Mark. "I thought you said she was coming with you guys."

"I left her to walk our new friend, Mr. Childs, out to his car so I could get here on time," Mark replied.

Consuelo broke in, "When I drove by the compound to see if you needed a ride, I saw her with Childs, talking to two other men in a car in front of the compound." She paused. "I didn't think much about it. I just thought he was up to his usual pestering."

Ken frowned. "How long ago was that?"

"A good hour before we got here," she continued nervously. "I found Mark in the Psych department over at school." Consuelo's voice faltered as she read the concern on everyone's face. "Is everything okay? Did I do something wrong?"

"I don't know." Ken frowned as he fumbled in his pockets, pulling out wadded bills and piles of change. "I'd better call her."

"Indeed. Let's do," Mark said, frowning. "Childs seems harmless enough, but I didn't like how our little visit with him went this afternoon. He asked entirely too many questions about inter-specific breeding, and he kept prying into our staffing and asking to see more of the facility. He seemed edgy, more nervous than usual."

"She's probably just running late, as usual." Ken's voice had a forced levity to it.

The booths now were full of students drinking and flirting with each other. The remaining tradesmen sat along the counter together as if in a last stand to claim at least one part of the place as theirs. Scotty was still working and holding court; his tall thin body bent over, pouring beers and wiping up the counter as he carried on several conversations at once. Many of the old guys were still in their work clothes, caps pushed back on their heads as they drank and smoked. They mixed with the students mainly at the pool tables. The soccer team apparently had decided to make it a night and was in full swing, hooting and hollering as they downed shots of Wild Turkey.

Ken walked to the pay phone that hung on the wall next to a mural of a male pool player aiming a shot toward a woman's buttocks as she sat unaware on the edge of the table.

"What'd you make of those two characters?" Mark pointed at two strangers who'd just slipped in among the bustle of a group of students leaving. They stood a moment at the door adjusting to the dim light that filtered through the cigarette smoke.

Ken returned in time to hear Mark's question. "I recognize the tall guy on the left. He was at my lecture last week." He spoke through his teeth as he sat back down. "I didn't get a hold of Mary."

"Yes, I saw him, too," Mark said. "He was talking to Childs after your lecture."

They watched while the two strangers surveyed the crowded bar as though searching for someone. The taller stranger elbowed the one Mark recognized and nodded his head in the direction of their booth. The strangers whispered intently together as they approached.

"Mierda!" Consuelo leaned toward Savage and whispered, "They're the ones who were in the car in front of the compound, the ones I saw Mary and Childs talking to. I might be able to get out through the kitchen and get some help."

"Call Mary," Ken whispered urgently.

She made for the bar before he or any of them could say more. The crowd immediately swallowed her petite form. The two were so intent on closing the distance to their booth that they missed her in the crowd.

Scotty, who seldom missed anything, lifted a small, hinged part of the counter for Consuelo as he looked past her; his narrow-set eyes followed the strangers' every move. He picked up a tray of glasses and nonchalantly followed Consuelo into the kitchen.

The two arrived, pinning Ken, Mark and Savage in the booth. "Well, what have we here; a little pow-wow?" Vandusen's voice held a note of sarcasm, mixed with a slight accent, possibly Eastern European. "Dr. Turner, you're a hard man to catch up to." Smiling at Ken, he continued, "Mr. Childs actually believes you've been avoiding him." He glanced at his associate. "So, we decided to take a chance of finding you here—though according to Mr. Childs, it wasn't much of a gamble—finding you here, that is. He's been most helpful and informative." Vandusen put his hand on the shoulder of the man standing next to him. "I'd like to introduce a colleague. He represents interests in the Government—important interests, that it seems you've been ignoring, Dr. Turner."

The stranger stepped forward. Apparently sizing up the situation, he wore a deadpan expression except for a growing malice in his eyes. "We're tired of trying to run you assholes down." He almost hissed his words, his whole manner that of someone working very hard to control himself.

Vandusen leveled his gaze on Ken. "As you can tell, Mr. Bauer is not much on formalities and manners. He likes to get right to the point. He's a man of action, so to speak."

Bauer's eyes hardened as he looked at the three of them.

"Fuck this. I've got work to do. I don't have to put up with this," Mark muttered under his breath as he started to stand, but Bauer quickly stepped forward agilely blocking his way.

"I wouldn't leave just yet, Mr. Chaney. Mind if we sit down?" Before anyone answered, Vandusen and Bauer slid into the booth on opposite sides.

Mark frowned, taken aback by the mention of his name by a stranger. *Childs must have been very informative—the little shit.*

Vandusen looked at the envelope Ken held and leaned toward him. "I see you're doing a little homework? Now, we're going to have a word with you, and you're going to listen, but it would be best if we retired to your facility."

Ken slipped the envelope under his arm.

Bauer's shirt had lifted when he slid into the booth, revealing the black handle of a pistol tucked into his jeans. Bauer smirked when Ken glanced at the weapon and deftly covered it up. "Now, do we have your attention?"

Ken settled back, moved the envelope out of sight under the table and mumbled, "fuck" under his breath.

Vandusen looked around the table, satisfied that they'd made their point. "Mr. Childs thinks you've been investigating a little more than communication in your research lately and that you may be getting close to solving a mystery that has confounded many of the people we represent for the last forty or so years." He looked from where the envelope had been to Ken's eyes. "The people we represent think your expertise and your animals could be of considerable use to them."

Ken and Savage exchanged an uneasy glance for an instant before Ken confronted Vandusen. "I don't know what you're talking about. Are you threatening us? You wouldn't do anything in a public place like this. We're having a private conversation, and you're harassing us." Ken started to stand.

"But your wife isn't, how did you put it, in a public place." Bauer paused to let this information sink in. He smiled menacingly. "So, if that's how you want to play this, fine. We'll just have to have a talk with your wife instead and my guess is that could be quite entertaining."

Turner's jaw locked. "So, you are threatening me."

Vandusen waved his hand, interrupting him. "Our associates have stopped by for a short visit and a word with her since we've had such a difficult time meeting with you. We've nothing to gain in harming her—at this point.

Ken didn't miss his emphasis on, *at this point.*

"I suggest we go check on her," Vandusen continued, "and share a little information at the same time. Maybe after that, you can give us a short tour of your facility. We'd love to meet those famous monkeys of yours." He stared in the vicinity of where Ken had put the envelope.

Ken tightened his hold. He sensed that his accoster was speculating on its contents. He paused for several heartbeats, trying to remember who was on duty at this time in the evening and if Mary was alone.

Vandusen continued, his voice measured and controlled, as if sensing Ken's indecision, "Really, we can save a whole lot of time by just taking a short drive to your place and clearing everything up. The organization we represent has deep pockets that could fund your research for many years to come or cut it overnight." He paused to let this information sink in. "I understand you're waiting on the findings of your most recent NSF site visit. Dr. Melon is a good friend of the Company. We have helped him on several occasions, and I'm sure we could put a good word in for you—or perhaps it'd be better to meet with your wife?"

Ken sensed that the man's veiled threats were very real and didn't like to think of what "clearing everything up" might mean from men with guns.

Vandusen signaled Bauer to get up. "What do you say we get Dr. Turner reunited with his wife and the rest of you back to your important work?"

Ken stood and motioned for his colleagues to do the same. He didn't like the prospect of leaving with these men but felt they were quickly running out of options.

As everyone got up to leave, Mark caught sight of Scotty coming in from the kitchen. He glanced at him for an instant. *Was that a slight head shake? Shit! Was he trying to signal them?* He looked around furtively as they walked across the room toward the front door. *We can't leave with these men, but what about Mary? Is she safe?* Aside from innuendos, they hadn't actually done anything to them. He frantically tried to think of a way to not leave but not make matters worse for everyone. Their progress slowed as they had trouble making their way as a group, through the evening crowd. His mind raced. Where had Consuelo gone? Had she grasped their whole predicament? Had she found Mary?

When they neared the door, Scotty's booming voice startled them. "Dr. Turner!" he yelled above the crowd. "Phone. It's your wife!"

Laughter and "ahs" broke out around the room, especially from various soccer players.

The team captain laughed the loudest. "Your wife's calling, Doc! How sweet!"

Ken turned back toward the bar, but Vandusen grasped his arm. Scotty hurriedly pushed through the crowd toward them carrying a black phone above his head; a long cord trailed behind which hampered his progress as it tangled or was stepped on. Ken glared at Vandusen and tried to jerk his arm free as Scotty reached them.

"As I said, it's your wife." He surveyed the group suspiciously. "Everything alright here?"

Vandusen and Bauer hesitated. Bauer reached under his shirt, but Vandusen shook his head. He looked at Ken. "Remember the only way out of here is with us."

Ken jerked his arm free and took the phone. After a moment of listening, he turned to the rest of the group, barely controlling his anger. "Mary is at home in the company of some of Washoe County Sheriff's finest. Apparently, we had some trespassers on the facility this afternoon. Consuelo is on her way here with the cavalry". He leveled his gaze on Vandusen. "I think we'll pass on your invitation. We're going to wait here for Consuelo and the authorities."

Vandusen and Bauer looked at each other in confusion. Both reached under their shirts.

Mark knew he had to act and act quickly. He caught the eye of the captain who was still laughing at them and shouted,

"So—are you girls ready to play a real team like Manchester United?"

The captain froze for a moment as if he didn't believe his ears, then the whole team pushed forward. One of the taller members shouted back in an Australian accent, "Hey, why don't you bloody Pommies come play in our country and see what happens?"

The entire bar fell silent, sensing the tension as they waited for Mark's response. "Unfortunately, I don't have a criminal record. Isn't that compulsory to immigrating to Australia? You bloody puff!"

In his drunken state, it took several seconds for the entire insult to sink in, but when it did the Aussie charged forward, followed by the rest of the team. They pushed and shoved through the crowd, closing in on Mark and company. When the Aussie stopped inches away from Mark, he pushed the Australian back into the captain who stumbled into several by-standers. This enraged the entire soccer team and assorted drunken fans, who charged in, shouting insults against Manchester and the whole of England.

Mark threw the first punch just as the door flew open with the entire CHIVAS Latin American Travel team looking for revenge for the beating they'd received on the field that afternoon. Between swings, Mark caught sight of Consuelo trailing in with several of the players as they made their way toward them.

A beer glass grazed Vandusen, hitting one of the CHIVAS team members squarely in the forehead. Holding his bleeding forehead, he kicked Vandusen in the groin, thinking he had thrown it. Vandusen dropped to the floor like a dead spider.

Bauer seemed confused as to whether to help his associate or chase down Ken and company who were scattering in the melee. As he reached for his gun, the goalie for the U tackled him, sending the pistol skidding across the floor. The fight, rather the brawl, began in earnest.

Scotty ducked below the counter to avoid flying glasses and pool balls and dialed 911. This was not his first fight at Franks.

The fight between the teams quickly evolved into a free-for-all as people lost track of who was on which side. The whole place erupted in chaos.

Ken and Savage dodged past two players wrestling on the floor as their girlfriends tried to pull them apart. One of the girls got punched in the face for her effort. The other girl grabbed a broken pool cue off the floor and began beating the man off her boyfriend. When he rolled off, moaning and holding his head, she turned on the girl she'd punched, who lay spread-eagle on the floor unconscious.

Consuelo along with two players from CHIVAS grabbed Fred, Mark and Ken, and protected them as they moved across the room through the thick of the fight towards the kitchen. Mark barely ducked below a flying bar stool which splintered next to them. He shoved two players who were choking each other out of the way as they slowly made progress. They reached the swinging doors to the kitchen, and Mark caught sight of Vandusen and Bauer trying to fight their way towards them.

Scotty stood and defended the bar and their retreat with a baseball bat. He grinned briefly at them as they passed and said, "Don't worry, I've got your backs. Mary is waiting for you guys somewhere outside. Now get the hell out of here!"

"We owe you, Scotty," Mark called back as they slipped through the backdoor into the alley.

Scotty shoved the bat into Bauer's chest of as he tried to climb over the counter. "Yes, you do," he shouted. "It'll be on your tab. Now get out of here. The police are coming!"

As though on cue, the police rushed in the front, swinging nightsticks and shouting instructions to cease and desist, but the brawl showed no signs of subsiding. A large officer pushed his way through to Scotty, shouting so he could be heard over the noise, "Scotty, how in the hell did this get started?"

"Those two started it all." Scotty pointed at Vandusen and Bauer.

* * *

It felt like stepping out of a storm when the service door slammed behind them. They found themselves in the quiet of the evening on a loading dock among trashcans and empty beer kegs. They followed Consuelo and her friends down an alley that twisted and turned in the darkness and stopped several times to consult with each other as to the way, while listening to see if they were being followed. Each time they stopped, they heard only dogs barking in the distance.

At one point, they crossed a concrete flood channel by balancing across a single plank, one at a time. After reaching the other side, they waited as one of the soccer players with Consuelo pulled the plank over to their side.

Ken bent over, trying to catch his breath, and could barely ask, "Where the hell are we?"

Consuelo and the two soccer players huddled together, whispering longer than usual as they looked around, trying to get their bearings. The group stood at a junction that went either along the canal or back onto an empty street that dead-ended directly in front of them. Ken's Spanish was good enough to know they were confused and couldn't decide which direction in which they should continue.

Savage had also caught the flow of the conversation. "Apparently they're wondering the same thing. But I'd rather spend the night lost right here than where we just came from."

The sound of Mary's familiar voice relieved their concern. "We have a better place for you to spend the night, Fred." She stepped into the dim light of a lamp hanging over them from a telephone pole and motioned everyone to gather around her. "Right, Consuelo?"

Consuelo smiled as Ken and Mary embraced. They looked into each other's eyes for a long time until Mary stepped back. "Well, you don't look the worse for wear, sweetheart." She looked around at all of them. "I'm not sure how this would've played out if Mark hadn't created a diversion. Well done."

Mark nodded. "I wasn't really thinking. I saw Scotty's signal, so I figured you were okay. I took a chance—but how did you know that?"

"Believe me, Mark, we were hoping … actually counting on that." Mary motioned to Consuelo. "This girl has a lot of faith in you. She's been busy while you were entertaining your guests at Frank's. You have her to thank for the reinforcements—oh, and Scotty kept us in the loop."

Consuelo looked down as if embarrassed.

Not for the first time, Mark thought what a striking beauty Consuelo was with her raven, silky hair and glowing, bronzed skin. She was a refined Mexicana, slim and flowing. But just as importantly, she was warm and soft, which contrasted to her sharp, piercing mind. He stepped over and gave her a long embrace while everyone smiled. He felt her body stiffen, then yield, which moved him.

"What about the compound and the chimps? I don't think these guys are going to just go home tonight." Ken sounded worried, and he looked back into the darkness, as if half expecting Vandusen to loom out of the darkness.

Mary nodded. "First things, first. Let's get out of this light. No sense being center stage in this alley. We have a car waiting down the street." She nodded toward Consuelo and her friends, "Please tell your friends we're in their debt."

They followed Consuelo and the two soccer players down the empty street until they reached Mary's Mercedes. Everyone congratulated each other and thanked Consuelo's friends.

"I hate to put a damper on the festivities," Ken said, "but we've been very lucky tonight, and Vandusen and company could still be out there somewhere—as I said before, what about the compound and the chimps?"

"Let's go home," Mary said, her voice somber.

No one spoke as Mary drove through the darkness of early morning. She chose the backcountry roads instead of Virginia Street, which took longer but felt safer.

Only when they were winding through the familiar horse ranches near home did Ken realize how tired he really was. Mark and Consuelo sat in the back, sleeping in each other's arms, and Fred stared off into the darkness, deep in thought. It was quiet except for the hum of the engine.

Mary, intent on driving, looked straight ahead, her fine features profiled in the faint light of dawn. She looked beautiful against the soft light. He still wondered at how different they were and yet how close. She seemed to sense him staring and smiled without looking his way. The breeze from the window fluttered her flowing, rich-red hair. She tilted her head toward him and said softly, "I love you."

They held each other's eyes for an instant, just long enough for him to marvel again at how striking they were, hazel with hints of gold. He thought just then that he'd never seen anything more beautiful. He reached over and touched her.

He nodded off several times between fingering the envelope he held tightly. He wondered how Bobby was fairing so far from home and what clues sat in his lap, then sleep finally took him.

CHAPTER 14

Ken awoke to the rattling of cups and running water. The aroma of coffee always got him moving. He'd slept deep considering what had happened to them the night before.

Exhaustion. And he ached all over.

He stretched and swung his legs off the bed, then tried to piece together the events of the evening and sort what he thought had actually happened from what he may have dreamt since it all seemed so surreal. They'd arrived exhausted at dawn. Mary had shepherded them to their beds and thoughts.

Mary's familiar voice called him back to the present. "Well, you've proven one thing this morning, Ken. The dead can rise again."

Mary and Consuelo laughed hard as they busied themselves making breakfast in the kitchen.

"Hallelujah!" Mark walked out of the bathroom, his thick red hair disheveled. Looking worse for wear after the strain of last evening's events, he picked his way carefully, barefoot, through the jetsam of Mary's latest renovation project. She was remodeling the kitchen.

Electrical wires hung from an open ceiling, requiring Consuelo and Mary to bob and weave as they busied themselves with eggs and bacon. Partially constructed walls defined the kitchen. Pots hung from a weathered, red-brick wall behind a huge stainless Wolf restaurant stove. The mixture of the finished and the unfinished made their voices echo off the brick and cement underlying the old ranch house.

Adjacent to the makeshift kitchen sat a large dining area with a giant picture window that took in all the Sierras and an apple orchard that was a favorite with the chimps. It was late in the morning so the handlers were letting the chimps play in the trees as they snacked and threw apples.

Ken felt glad to be back home and relieved that the routine of the ranch was carrying on. "Well, it looks like we're all awake, finally." He surveyed the latest damage from Mary's remodel as he negotiated through wheelbarrows and ladders toward the kitchen. He gave Mary a hug from behind, pinning her arms so she couldn't reach her work at the stove.

She leaned her head back against him. "Pull the OJ out of the fridge, please." Ken had to look twice because the refrigerator had been moved to make room for the demolition of a wall.

Everyone sat around a large redwood picnic table that somehow looked out of place against the stainless kitchen. "So, what are we going to do now about these goons?" Ken talked between bites. He realized he was very hungry.

Mary passed some toast to Mark. "Move the chimps and us out of here. You know, get out of Dodge ASAP."

"I think that's easier said than done. These assholes have guns and could show up at any minute." Ken looked around, half expecting Vandusen and Bauer break through the door at any minute.

Shaking her head, Mary went over to a phone that lay on the floor between them. She talked for a minute, then hung up, smiling. "Just like we planned. Scotty is a really good friend. He told the police that your new friends, these 'goons' as you call them, started the whole ruckus at Frank's. Scotty is filing charges." Mary looked over at Mark. "Not against you love. The police took them away in handcuffs. It seems they couldn't explain why they were carrying concealed weapons without a permit." Relieved, everyone broke into laughter. "Let's make another call." After a few minutes, she hung up and made a thumbs-up gesture. "They're in the Washoe County jail as we speak, and I don't think they're anxious to get any more press just yet. Anyway, no one has come to bail them out. My guess is someone's going to have to come all the way out from Langley."

Savage rattled around the kitchen, digging up seconds. "Who are these guys?"

Mary raced back into the kitchen. "Let me help you with that before you ruin my Nambe." She picked up a wooden serving spoon and pushed him aside. "I have friends in the Sheriff's Department that seem to think they're some kind of government contractors."

"What do you mean? Like Watergate types?" Consuelo cleared the table with Mark's help.

"Something like that." Mary sat back down.

"They mentioned the 'Company' last night." Ken frowned as he picked up the envelope from the table. "Let's have a look at what Bobby sent us."

"The CIA, that's what you mean by the Company, right?" Mary watched as Ken began spreading the contents out on the table. "What've you got there?"

Ken delicately picked up what appeared to be an old leather-bound notebook, several stacks of faded and curled photographs, and a pile of letters bound together with a faded red ribbon. "Well, the first thing I can tell you, even though I don't read much Russian beyond scientific nomenclature, is that all these documents were written by the same hand, and it's probably an educated hand—excellent penmanship. Mrs. Rich, my third-grade teacher would've been very impressed."

Mark squeezed in between them. "So, who do we know who reads Russian?"

Ken didn't look up from his examination. "It's not so much who reads it as who we can trust who reads it." As he set the envelope aside, he paused a moment and broke into a smile, looking at Mary. "Remember that director you brought around the ranch last year who was so taken by the chimps?"

Mark laughed. "He was all goo-goo over them. He wanted to come live with them."

Ken still smiled. "Correct me if I'm wrong, but wasn't he from Mother Russia?"

"You mean Yuri?" Mary asked nonchalantly. "Yes, he speaks Russian. He's a Russian Jew but doesn't have much love for the old country." She watched them gather around the contents of the envelope.

Ken nodded thoughtfully and reached over to the stack of photographs he'd organized. "Look at these!"

They all leaned forward. He gingerly picked up a photograph by its curled edge. A very large, ape-like creature standing erect, stared into the camera.

Savage thought the eyes the most striking aspect of the photo. They were piercing, intense and very intelligent. "I've seen eyes like these before!" he said, startling the others with the intensity of his voice.

"What do you mean?" Ken asked.

"I saw the same intensity and malice from the darkness of Danny's cage."

Everyone leaned forward and took a closer look at all the photographs. They surmised from details in the pictures that they'd all been taken at the same compound. Further, the backgrounds of some of the photos led them to believe that this compound was in a tropical area.

Mark discovered the faint penciled inscription on the back of one of the photos. "Thysville ... Thysville, Africa ... Central Africa, I think!"

Ken's hands trembled with excitement as he hastily sorted through more, looking for clues. "There seems to be at least six different creatures here. Look at the variation. Some are almost chimp-like while others are more like this big fellow."

Savage picked up several more photos and spread them out. "Yes. That would make sense. Like we were saying last night, you get considerable variation in the early generations of hybridization. Some will have the cluster of traits that resemble one or the other of the donors or they can be entirely different." He reached out for the photo that Ken had first picked up. "Now, here's a very big boy. If you compare him with the wheelbarrow in the background, I'd make him out to be close to six-feet tall, and his traits are very human-like. Look at that set of genitals." The entire group sat in silence for a moment.

Mark picked up the notebook and letters, frowning as he called to Mary, "Exactly where's that guy you know who reads Russian?"

Ken nodded and lay the rest of the contents on the table. "Mary. Can we trust this producer friend of yours?"

"Yes. After what he made on the last picture I directed for him, he owes me his career. I'll make a call." Mary pulled her phone book out of her purse.

Gucci, of course. Ken grinned as he watched her dig through it.

Mary looked back at him as she dialed. "So, we're feeling a little better. What's so funny?"

"Nothing." He busied himself sorting through the rest of the photos. "Mark, don't you have a friend in the library who works in archives? We need someone experienced in gleaning information out of historical documents like these letters and photos."

* * *

After a good hour of making calls Mary hung up the phone. "Yuri will be here this afternoon and Mark's friend, Tamara, is on her way. She took a little convincing, however." She pointed at Mark. "Apparently, they're not dating anymore."

Mark, who was sorting through the pile of correspondence, looked sheepishly over his shoulder and said nothing.

Savage grinned. Consuelo didn't.

Mary shook her head. "I suggest we clean up and get ready for guests." She picked a couple of coffee cups off the table and turned towards the kitchen, then stopped and looked back. "Oh, I just got a call from one of the handlers. Mike is raising holy hell and is on the roof of the hay barn and won't come down. Apparently, he's throwing roof tiles at the parked cars and with pretty good aim."

Mark and Ken looked at each other and simultaneously yelled, "Shit!"

They flew out the kitchen door.

Mary smiled. "Leave it to Mike to get things back to normal."

Savage followed, but not until he'd cleaned his second plate.

CHAPTER 15

"He's definitely off the reservation." Savage handed the scribbled note back to Ken as Mark looked on. They were all concerned. The last anyone had heard from Bobby was several days earlier when he'd called from a little village in Chiapas, the most southern state in Mexico. The connection had been poor, but Savage had managed to make out that Bobby had found the Circus of the Americas and was planning to take a look as soon as he'd arranged transportation.

A few weeks later, the envelope containing the photos had arrived, sent by mail, which was very risky and unlike Bobby, who preferred to do things safely. It'd taken awhile to reach them as the address wasn't complete, and except for the hastily scribbled note, there'd been no other communication.

Ken read the note aloud: "It's not safe here. I'll be in touch." It was hastily signed, "Bobby W." The group fell silent for a moment. Mary left the room.

"I wish I'd gone down with him," Savage said. "I never liked him poking around there, all alone."

"We really didn't have much say, Fred. He took off after talking with Hunt. I'm sure he's all right or we wouldn't have received this." Ken held up the envelope. "And you, yourself, said he's a very resourceful guy."

Ken noticed Yuri and Mary standing a short distance away. He wondered how long they'd been there and how much of their conversation Yuri had heard. "Yuri! It's wonderful that you could come."

"Anything to help the chimps," he replied. The afternoon sunlight streaming through the living room window reflected off his bald head as he bowed slightly and shook Ken's hand.

Ken stifled a smile as he remembered how Mary had once described Yuri's head as a bobbing cue ball. "You remember Dr. Chaney—Mark—I think."

Mark and Savage stood, dwarfing the rotund little man dressed immaculately in seersucker slacks and a lime-green turtle neck sweater.

His face wrinkled into a smile upon recognizing Mark. "Yes. Dr. Chaney. He was the nice young man who was kind enough to let me play with the chimps last time."

There was an awkward silence as Ken collected his thoughts, deciding how to bridge the subject of why they'd invited him. He'd asked Mary to keep it vague until they spoke with Yuri face-to-face.

Mary broke the silence before Ken could speak. "Yuri. We need your help on something that is very … how should I put it? Delicate."

Yuri lowered his voice in a conspiratorial manner: "Of course, Mary." He looked back at Ken expectantly.

Ken picked up the logbook that lay among the other documents they'd spread on the table. "We have some documents we'd like you to translate. Maybe we could begin with this? Everything we talk about today is confidential."

Yuri nodded, and without saying a word took the tattered log. The rest busied themselves with the other documents and photos as he settled in for a long read.

* * *

Yuri exhaled loudly and stretched, then looked from face to face. Ken and company had worked quietly as he'd read the log in its entirety. They'd whispered occasionally but for the most part had watched him with apprehension.

He removed his wire-rimmed glasses before he spoke, looking at Mary: "I don't think I ever told you the circumstances surrounding my immigrating to this country." He continued before Mary could reply, "My father had to leave to escape Stalin and the OGPU, the predecessor of the KBG. Our family lived in Kazakhstan where father had been exiled after serving time in the Gulag." Yuri paused as he tried to control his emotions. "Father was a doctor and a scientist. This is not the first time I've heard about such doings. I once overheard my father talking about these unspeakable experiments. But I never believed that even the Soviets would be capable of this kind of abomination—not until now." He shook his head, staring into space.

"So, what's in the log that makes you bring this up?" Ken asked in a strained voice.

"They're talking about the results and what to do with the off-spring from breeding chimpanzees with humans." Yuri looked at him with wide-eyes.

"So exactly what's it say?" Ken, along with the rest, pulled up chairs, surrounding him.

Yuri looked closely at them. "I can see this is not entirely a surprise to all of you." Before they could respond he continued, "It's a laboratory log from the merchant vessel, *Orion*, dating from about August to November 1929. It's hard to say exactly, some of the pages are missing or too damaged to read. It looks like it was submerged in water. Some of the pages are stuck together, and the ink in places is smeared. There are reports on its cargo, an animal cargo. Much of it talks about routine operations, but not all of it." He thumbed toward the back of the log, then stopped. "Here's a separate section. The senior scientist, I think, writes about the care of creatures he refers to as 'almost human'". Yuri paused to let what he'd just said sink in.

"There's a daily report on this animal cargo," he continued. "It appears the ship was under secret orders from the Kremlin to transport a whole colony of these creatures from the Soviet

Union to Guinea, Africa. Apparently, they were smuggling the animals away from the Sukhumi Monkey Colony where the experiments had been shut down for some reason. It's very detailed, written, as I said, by someone in authority. He recorded and summarized the daily reports of the scientists who were on board caring for these things."

Ken interrupted: "The Sukhumi Monkey Colony was a Soviet primate center created just after the Bolshevik Revolution during the rise of Stalin."

Yuri continued to leaf through the logbook. "There's a name that keeps coming up, Ilya Ivanov."

"Ah, now we have a real aristocrat!" Ken exclaimed excitedly. "Ivanov was an early expert in artificial insemination and worked, if I remember correctly, for the Bolshevik elite, inseminating thousands of domestic animals at several centers he opened up in the Soviet Union. Later he began research into creating domestic hybrids."

Savage broke in: "The Soviet Union was in desperate need of millions of strong cattle to help transform their economy. He was in the right place at the right time to get his research supported."

Mark looked up from his work at the table and added, "For a time, he was the darling of Stalin and the Social Marxists who could be very generous in their support of any research that might further the Revolution."

"But not all of his research was dedicated exclusively to farm animals," Ken said. "It's been rumored that he tried to artificially inseminate human and ape females with the other species' sperm. This would've been in the late twenties, I think."

"From the looks of these entries, 1927." Yuri pointed to a page in the log.

"Interesting," Ken said. "I thought he'd fallen out of favor by then and been arrested by Stalin's people. Most people believe he was discredited and subsequently exiled. I thought he died sometime in the early thirties."

"Hmm, something doesn't add up, then." Yuri held up the logbook. "He's referred to in here several times as being alive and well on board the *Orion* during the same time period."

Ken motioned to the stack of letters. "Let's take a look at these letters. Maybe there's something in them that'll give us a clue as to why that ship was headed for Africa with a whole colony of hybrids. But most importantly, we need to know for sure if Ivanov was actually on board." He handed Yuri the letters and the rest of them continued to sort through the photographs.

Suddenly the outside door burst open and a chimpanzee raced in with Consuelo and another handler chasing him. The chimp's hoarse exhales accentuated a classic chimp laugh. His pursuers didn't seem to be enjoying the chase as much as him. He leaped onto the table, spewing their neatly sorted piles of photographs on the floor.

"Goddamn it, Mike!" Ken stood and pointed at a chair next to him. "Leave it! Sit."

Mike whimpered, but did as commanded. He barely contained himself, wiggling in the chair, almost tipping it over.

"I'm sorry," Consuelo said. "He's been a hellion all afternoon. No one can get him to listen. He heard your voices while we were trying to take him for a walk." Her stern manner set Mike to hooting.

"Bad boy!" Ken frowned and accentuated "bad" by raising his voice but lowering its tone.

Mike began to cry and reached out his hand in a bagging gesture. In fast facetted gestures he signed, "SORRY, SORRY ... MIKE, GOOD BOY ... SORRY .... GOOD ..."

Ken purposely ignored him by turning his back, and with the help of the rest of the group, gathered up the mess of letters and photographs.

Mike finally settled into his chair, his cries subsiding into barely audible hoots. His large expressive lips formed a trumpet shape as he mimed a final hoot and intently watched Ken's every move.

The group worked quickly, stacking and sorting. Mike occasionally reached his hand out in a begging gesture and signed, "PLAY." For the most part the group ignored him so as not to reinforce his previous behavior.

Ken stopped his work and held a large portrait of an especially large creature whose dark, menacing eyes stared back into the camera. Ken wondered how the photographer had had the nerve to focus. Though chimp-like, it was enormous, dwarfing the man who stood just out of reach, shotgun in hand. It stood erect, and with its balding head and sparse body hair, it reminded him of a very large Oliver. The others stopped their work, staring at the photo mesmerized.

Consuelo broke the spell. "Look at Mike," she whispered.

Mike's hair stood on end and he grimaced, showing all his teeth as he stared at the photo.

"That's a classic *fear grimace*," Ken whispered to Yuri.

Mike let out a series of high-pitched screeches, jumped into Mark's arms, and followed that with a loud bark which brought everyone to their feet and Mary running back into the room. The primeval *waa bark* he used was instinctual and had been used by chimps for the twenty-million years they'd walked the planet as a species.

It stirred raw fear in all of them, reinforcing the close kinship humans shared with chimpanzees. They'd never heard Mike make that sound before. Ken had even thought that being born in captivity and raised domestically had not given his chimps the opportunity to acquire it as they would in the wild. But that image of the creature had stirred something deep and frightening in Mike that sparked some ancient wiring deep in his subconscious. The archetypal sound unnerved them all.

"Easy, Mike," Mark said, choking from Mike's grip. Mike was no longer a captive, signing chimp with feet in both the wild and human worlds. He was a wild chimp of the Gombe stream, and he was frightened and therefore dangerous.

Consuelo quickly turned the photograph over and covered the rest of the pile, but Mike continued to panic. He hugged

Mark desperately as the others gathered around and reached the back of his hand out to each person for reassurance, panting between screeches.

Yuri stood back near the door in terror. Until that moment, he'd thought of the chimps as human-like, as depicted in the movies, something amusing. He now realized that even the small ones like Mike could be extremely dangerous when stirred.

Mike's reaction unsettled them all. Up until now their investigation had been an abstraction, like a history project. Now they knew that there was an evil in all of this that cut to the core of what made them human.

Mike settled as fast as he'd riled up. He began grooming himself and played with a shoe Mark handed him. He made slight kissing noises and shook his head as he played with the laces and signed, "SHOE."

Consuelo, still visibly shaken, sighed. "He's a little devil—I can see the horns growing just under his hairy little head."

Ken, jittery from the adrenaline, tried not to smile.

* * *

Ken thought Tamara a striking beauty. He remembered first seeing the tall, lean woman with blue eyes and blond hair from her Swedish heritage at the University library in the Archives department. Mary showed her in and she entered the room emitting a calm grace that put Ken at ease in spite of what they'd all been through; she seemed to have a similar effect on everyone except Mark who was visibly nervous around her.

She strolled across the room, greeting everyone except Mark, and after conferring with Ken, immediately went to work on the photos, armed with a large magnifying glass and several reference books.

Consuelo's eyes followed her every move, seldom straying except to look at Mark who conspicuously avoided them both. Ken decided he wouldn't want to be in Mark's predicament of being in the same room with two rivaling romantic interests.

Tamara placed photographs into separate piles while she referred to different reference books she had piled around her. She kept comparing a few of the photos with each other. Savage sat next to her, conferring in whispers. Ken thought that she was either so absorbed in her work as not to notice Consuelo's attention or a very good actor.

Yuri sat alone at the opposite end of the table, reading. Ken couldn't tell if his frown was from the content of the letters or concentration. Wrinkles migrated up from his forehead, invading the bald region of his head.

At this point Ken was the only one without a job. Mark had left with Mike and a trainer for a second try at exercising him. He definitely felt the odd man out so he busied himself helping Mary prepare a late lunch. They worked quietly in the makeshift kitchen trying not to disturb anyone.

Tamara was first to break the silence that had become unbearable. "I'll need more time to glean all the information out of these photos, but there's a lot of obvious information that may be helpful to you."

The rest gathered around, including Mark who'd just returned. Tamara cast a cold glance at him and continued, "I can tell by the resolution and emulsion that these photos were probably taken in the late twenties to early thirties." She waited for comments. Ken nodded for her to continue. "By the look of the vegetation in the background I'd place them in equatorial Africa probably on the coast."

"How can you tell these are on the coast?" Ken asked.

Tamara smiled, shaking her head. "The fishing nets in the background of this photo might indicate it, but also the sand on the pathways in the background. If you look closely with a magnifying glass you can see fragments of shells." She picked up several photos. "These were taken with a large-view camera with excellent depth of field. The resolution is very fine—even the distant backgrounds are in focus." She handed Ken the magnifying glass and a photo. "The photographer was obviously trying to record everything."

Can these be enlarged and still have detail?" Mark asked.

"As I said the resolution is excellent, very fine. We'll certainly be able to make out the detail in the distant background of these."

Ken realized she'd been stacking photos by many different categories. He'd assumed she'd used the content as the criteria but now realized she'd set several aside that she planned to blowup to make out the background.

"Do you mind?" He reached to pick up the stack to which she referred. She nodded affirmatively. He could just make out buildings on the hills in the background. "If we can get a better look at the architecture of those buildings, we might be able to place the region where these were taken."

"Exactly—my guess is that it's the old Belgium Congo."

"What makes you say that?" Savage leaned over her shoulder, looking at the photo she held.

"Take a look at the hat the man with the shotgun is wearing—oh, and also his belt buckle and the shotgun he's holding." She leafed through one of her reference books that showed pages of military memorabilia and handed Fred the magnifying glass. "Look at the markings on the plate below the barrel just above his hand."

Savage studied the photograph while the others looked on with growing interests.

Tamara continued, "Those are proof markings of the gun maker Charles Galand." She continued to thumb through the pages of a worn and dog-eared reference volume. "Here we are. According to this entry he was a gunsmith located at Rue Lamarck in Liege from 1919 to 1930."

"That doesn't in itself put them in the Belgian Congo," Ken said. "The man could've bought the shotgun anywhere."

"True but have a closer look at the man's clothing. It's an old military tunic. You can just make out an emblem on his shoulder."

Ken took the magnifying glass for a closer look. "Yes, it looks to be a dark rectangle with a single star."

"Like this?" Tamara pointed at a picture on a page of flags.

Ken checked. "Yes, just like that."

"That's the flag of Congo Free State, a colony of Belgium— better known as the Belgiam Congo. He might've been a veteran of the First World War serving in equatorial Africa. You know, the Africa later made famous by Stanley and Livingston and Joseph Conrad." She seemed pleased with herself and was certainly enjoying the search after getting over the initial shock of seeing the photos of the hybrids.

They spent the afternoon examining the contents of the envelope Bobby had sent them and were amazed at how much information Tamara could glean out of a pile of faded old photographs. Several pictures included local natives, and from their dress she was able, by cross-referencing them with her books, to identify them as members of local tribes of the Congo River Basin. In one photo, she identified a set of baskets as belonging to a coastal tribe living near where the Congo flowed into the Atlantic in a town called Banana.

Ken thought it fitting that all clues were drawing them to the continent of Africa—a place that held the secrets to the dawn of humans, as illuminated by Dr. Leaky—and more specifically the Congo region where two species of Chimpanzees, Pan Paniscus and Pan Troglodytes, still lived in the wild, as described by Jane Goodall. Even today it was a wild and lawlessness frontier, one that had not changed much since the Belgians had left it in ruins after scouring it of most of its treasures.

But it was Yuri who really made them realize that their search would have to continue in the Congo. He handed Ken a stack of letters and, barely containing his horror, said, "Keep these letters safe. They hold horrible secrets. The Soviets sent Ivanov to Guinea, it was his plan to inseminate African women with chimpanzee sperm. But according to these letters his plans didn't seem to pan out. He had the support of the governor and the local governments but only under the condition that the women would cooperate willingly. I guess money can't buy everything. It seems the women wouldn't participate in these lurid experiments."

"Why would the Soviets want to do such experiments? It's monstrous and unethical," Consuelo pointed out.

"It seems that Ivanov and the socialists were interested in something called—there's an English word here, Heterosis," Yuri said.

"Heterosis, hybrid vigor." Savage frowned. "Heterosis levels can be higher as a result of cross-breeding, creating what is often referred to as hybrid vigor: the vigor of the off-spring can be greater than that of the parental lines."

"In what ways?" Consuelo asked.

Ken answered her: "In many ways. It is hard to predict. The off-spring can be larger, stronger, more intelligent, many things."

Yuri spoke next: "That would fit the designs of Stalin and his henchmen. The Bolsheviks had a disdain for the belief in God. They thought that nature should serve man, Soviet Man. They wouldn't have been bothered by ethical issues or Judeo-Christian beliefs concerning this sort of endeavor." Yuri's voice trembled. "Stalin would have found many uses for these *hybrids* as you call them. He could have added them to the rest of his cadre of slaves."

"My God," Savage exclaimed. "No wonder Vandusen and his pals are so interested in these experiments. It's a kind of biological warfare isn't it?" He watched a grad student play with Mike in the front of the window. "I hate to think what would happen to our chimps if those assholes ever got control of our work."

Looking at Yuri, Ken asked, "So are you saying that the *Orion* somehow ended up in Guinea?"

"That's what's confusing in these letters. They seem to be headed for there with support of the Soviets, but when it doesn't work out, they leave and leave with the whole of the province after them. It's unclear where they go from there at least in the letters and log." He paused for effect. "I think that's what puts Ivanov on the *Orion*."

"But thanks to Tamara, I think we have some idea where they went next," Ken said. "Based on these photographs, I think they somehow ended up at the mouth of the Congo River."

The telephone rang, startling them. They could hear Mary's voice but couldn't make out what she was saying. She walked in just as Turner was about to check on her. "Well, I just got a call from a friend at the courthouse. Our friends made bail. And you won't believe who posted it."

CHAPTER 16

"Who posted bail?" Ken asked.

The group waited for Mary to answer. The afternoon sunlight streamed through the big picture window, framing the apple orchard outside. A thick green lawn, strewed with apples the chimps had knocked loose in their play, aproned the rows of trees. Ken thought it a strange contrast to the stuffiness inside and wanted to get out into the fresh air.

"Dr. Melon and his associates!" She slammed the receiver down so hard that it rang like a struck bell and stormed out of the room. Her parting words were, "I need a drink."

Irish-Italian, redhead with flaming green eyes; what do you expect? She was beautiful when angry but violent.

"That little weasel." Mark mimed twisting Melon's neck off.

"Well, that explains why we've had so much trouble with him." Savage walked around the room swearing under his breath. "The Melon and Vandusen crews make strange bedfellows, don't you think?"

Ken frowned. "Not really. They both want to cash in on our work, just for different gains. People like them are parasites who take advantage of other people's hard work."

The sound of ice rattling and glasses jingling interrupted their conversation. Mary rolled in a heavily laden liquor cart that looked to be left over from the old, dude ranch days. Brassy and ornate, it fit with the rest of the décor of the room—gaudy.

Mary's remodeling hadn't quite reached this room, yet.

Mark got up from the worn-leather couch where he'd been sitting with Consuelo and made two scotch and waters.

Ken noticed that Mark seemed to be paying more attention to this beautiful young lady since Tamara had left the grounds. *There's a story there.*

"At our expense," Mark said.

"At the chimp's expense, you mean. They're the real losers in this," Ken cautioned.

Everyone nodded silently in unison.

"Dr. Turner, we need to get out of here right away before those goons decide to pay us another visit." Consuelo squeezed Mark's arm tightly and leaned against him for protection.

They all looked around nervously half expecting Vandusen and his crew to come busting in at any second.

Mary took a long sip of her martini. "I wouldn't worry too much about that. I think our escapades last night bought us a little time. They've blown their cover now. I don't think we have much to fear in the short run. The local authorities are onto them. So, they'll have to be careful and try a different tact." Mary picked up the phone. "I'll make a few calls while Ken plans our next move." She looked directly at him.

As if on cue Ken stirred into action. "Well, it's the end of the spring term, which works in our favor. No one would miss us until we reconvene for the fall semester." He spoke as though thinking aloud.

"What do you mean *miss us*?" Mark asked.

"I think we should take Mike and the rest of the signing chimps on a road trip. We need to leave and leave soon." Ken spoke slowly with determination. "What do think, Fred?"

"Sounds good. As you know, Dr. Raven has invited us down for a visit, and he certainly has the room and the ability to help us transport some of the chimps. Perhaps, we should take him up on his kind invitation." Savage fumbled through his wallet, searching for Raven's card, which he handed to Ken.

Mary turned on two old, western-style lamps with rawhide shades to add a little extra illumination to the fading late-afternoon light.

"Thanks, Mary." Savage continued, "He has a number of special horse trailers that are fitted with chimp cages. He uses them to transport his larger apes to movie sets. Mike, of course, could ride with us." Savage paused to let them absorb the information. "From the outside they look like any other trailer you'd expect to see around here. Hell, this is ranch country. No one will even notice."

Ken picked up the phone. "I'll call him, right now." He motioned the rest out and into action. "You need to pack for yourselves and the chimps. We're taking only the four signing chimps besides Mike. They're the only ones of value to these people. But pack lightly and fast. I think we have about a day's grace before all hells going to break loose."

"People are going to get suspicious if we just haul ass out to here. We need a cover story," Mark said as he and Consuelo left the room holding hands.

Ken put his arm around Mary. "Will you stay here a few days and cover for us? Mark's right; it needs to appear as though everything is normal."

Mary laughed. "Like that's ever the case around here."

Ken ignored her joke. "The rest of the staff needs to think we've gone off to a conference or something, that we're using the chimps for a demonstration. I don't know. You'll think of something. You know, make up one of your stories like when you're brushing off an actor who wants work. We need some time to figure all this out without Vandusen or Melon and university administration breathing down our necks."

"Or the police," Savage interjected.

Ken and Mary looked at each other a without speaking as the others filed out.

Mary nodded in agreement, unusually silent, as though the gravity of the situation was finally sinking in.

Ken began to dial.

The next twenty-four hours were hectic as they waited for Dr. Raven's people. Moving the chimps and half the crew right under the noses of other workers and staff at the ranch took a lot of work. They had to be subtle in their packing and planning, careful not to be observed as doing anything out of the norm.

Ken dropped several asides in his conversations with the rest of the staff during his rounds that suggested that they'd be leaving for an important confidential meeting where they'd use some of the chimps for demonstrations. This wasn't out of the ordinary. They'd done it at different conferences or fundraisers in the past. He kept the details vague as to where they were going and exactly when by indicating that this opportunity was still very much "up in the air."

He and Raven spoke several times and decided that it was best to lay low down at the WATC. It would give them a chance to share information.

"Besides, your chimps and people will hardly be noticed. We're gearing up for a big movie in Africa. People will just think you're somehow involved," Raven said. "I'll send two trucks up your way today."

And it was decided; simple as that.

When the trucks and trailers finally arrived, Ken instructed everyone to wait until dark before loading. He sent everyone on the ranch home early with the excuse that Mary and he would be staying in for the evening and leaving early the next morning.

They'd been very lucky so far as no one from the sheriff's office, university or anyone representing Vandusen had made contact, but Ken had a sense of foreboding and felt they had to work fast and slip out of town. He also knew it was better to take a little longer if they could leave undetected.

The whole team was exhausted when he finally said his goodbyes to Mary. They tried to speak over the loud clatter of an idling diesel and thought better of it. Instead, they walked a short distance away to get clear of the noise and pungent fumes.

Mary tried to keep their parting light, but both knew that when Ken drove off with the chimps, they'd be stepping into a whirlwind of events beyond their control. Worse, they were not sure when they'd see each other again.

"So, do you have enough clothes?" Mary actually sounded worried, which surprised Ken. She was usually so calm under pressure, making light of everything.

"Sweetheart, it's not like I'm going away to war." Ken pulled her close. He felt her warm and toned body yield. The sweet fragrance of Opium was intoxicating.

"Are you sure?" Mary trembled.

He couldn't be sure if it was from the night air or fear, and he found himself in the strangely reverse position of trying to calm her. "I'll call you along the way."

"Use a pay phone. And don't say anything that will give your location away. I still think they haven't figured out our connection to Dr. Raven, at least not yet. I wouldn't be surprised if they had our phones tapped soon," she said nervously.

"I think you've been watching too many James Bond movies."

Mary ignored his comment. "I think this plan will work. I doubt they'll figure out that some of the chimps are missing. I don't think any of them actually know how many chimps we have or could pick Mike out of a lineup."

"Okay, mom."

"Ken, stop kidding around; this is serious."

For reasons he couldn't explain, he felt strangely excited at the prospect of heading out on the road, in spite of all the danger. It surprised him. After a several long embraces and false starts between equally long kisses, he jumped into the waiting truck and slammed the door. It roared into action, belching a cloud of smoke.

Mary watched the caravan of trucks and trailers slowly bounce down the dusty drive toward the lights on 395 and south. She wept quietly and caressed herself against the chill blowing off the mountains.

It was going to be a long, cold evening, followed by how many more, she wondered.

She collected herself and bravely turned toward a dark and empty house wondering what tomorrow would bring. She felt dampness in the air and the smell of rain. The leaves rustled in the darkness with each gust, making her edgy. Clouds covered the moon intermittently making it difficult to pick her way.

She was already planning for her new role as the brave wife holding down the fort until her husband returned. She was going to have to make it appear that everything was in order and it was business as usual at the ranch.

She had to buy them enough time to straighten out this mess. The plan was for her to get out of Dodge in a day or two and join Ken before Vandusen and his cronies had time to regroup. They figured he and Bauer had dropped out of sight for a while, which would give them time.

None of them, including Mary, realized just how dangerous that role would turn out to be.

CHAPTER 17

Ken found the trip down 395 uneventful compared to the excitement of the last few days. He, along with Mark, Consuelo and Savage, successfully made it out of Reno, "without any more drama," as Mary would put it.

They rambled South in the big rigs sent up by Dr. Raven, stopping every few hours in convenient but secluded spots along the Eastern Sierras. This gave them a chance to stretch their legs, water and feed the chimps, and do the same for themselves. They picked this route because it was rural and they could blend in. Their cargo of chimps was concealed in two large gooseneck horse trailers that had cages installed inside. Ken had commented that it was really quite enjoyable to be out on the open road again in spite of their circumstances. He would refer to it later as "a picnic on wheels." To make sure they weren't noticed, they stopped in the smallest towns they could find, and there were many: Independence, Big Pine, Lone Pine, Lee Vining, and Randsburg, to name a few. Rigs much like the ones they were driving lined every little restaurant, rest stop or truck stop they found, making it easy to blend in and keep moving south.

They traded seats often so conversation was not boring during their slow progress along the winding and undulating two-lane highway. But in time, they talked themselves out and became caught up in their own thoughts as the moonlit countryside streamed by.

At dawn they found themselves crossing the vast Mojave Desert. Ken was struck by the contrast between the rich-green foothills along the Sierras they'd just left and the stark, dusty emptiness of the desert with its Joshua trees and ruler-straight highway.

As agreed, he called Mary several times in route to check in. So far, all seemed to be going as planned. No one had visited the ranch. In fact, Mary's inside sources at the Sheriff's department reported that Vandusen and Bauer had skipped town after making bail.

Ken was surprised that she'd not heard from Melon or the university administration. Everything seemed to be moving along so normally that he wondered if any of this mad dash south had really been necessary.

The two drivers that Raven sent knew their business. They'd pointed their rigs down the 395 and drove like clockwork, only stopping when asked. Both wore the typical uniform of rodeo cowboys with their faded and creased Wrangler jeans, wide-brimmed, straw Resistol hats, and Tony Lama lizard-skinned boots. They wore large silver belt buckles with "Wild Animal Training Center" inlaid in turquoise.

Ken liked that they kept their attention on the road and didn't ask questions. They seemed more preoccupied with packing their lower lips with Copenhagen snuff than making small talk. They blended in very well in this part of rural California—a California that didn't fit the Hollywood stereotype. In contrast, Mark, Ken, Savage and Consuelo stood out in these sparsely populated towns of farmers, cowboys and miners.

As they neared the end of this leg of their journey, they stopped for coffee and the biscuits and gravy special in the Cajon Pass just outside of San Bernardino. The early morning light painted the mountains that surrounded them as they stepped into the Summit Inn. The wind blew in strong gusts, causing them to lean in its direction.

"Well, we've made good progress." Ken downed his third cup of coffee, feeling in high spirits.

"Raven wants to talk to the drivers," Mark said when he returned from a payphone booth. Frowning, he stepped over to the drivers, who were sitting at the counter joking with a plump waitress as they attacked the breakfast special. To them, picking up the chimps was just another job in staging for an upcoming movie in Africa. Ken had noticed that they were regulars in the few cafes and filling stations in which they'd stopped and seemed to cause no suspicion among the locals.

"Is something wrong?" Ken asked Mark.

"It seems there's a couple of unmarked cars parked at the main gate of the compound. He wants to guide us in a back way. Apparently, there's a back door."

"Dr. Raven is full of surprises." A familiar dread revisited the group as they sat silently sipping their coffee.

* * *

"Goddamn it!" The driver exclaimed. The front rig seemed to be leading their caravan too fast. The two rigs only just had time to make a bumpy transition to a muddy, single-track farm road that led off across dairy pastures and thoroughbred ranches toward the dense foliage of what looked to be a river bottom. The driver skillfully negotiated the muddy puddles and slippery ruts with one hand on the steering wheel, while the other was occupied with holding a Styrofoam cup he used at intervals to spit the juice off his wad of snuff. The big rig shifted and slid heavily, making the chimps cry out in excitement. The driver seemed accustomed to dirt roads, however, and concentrated on the narrowing track ahead.

The rich riverside vegetation closed in around them, making it seem like late afternoon rather than mid-morning. The cover disturbed Ken, and he wondered how long they'd be jostled before reaching the Training Center. He'd lost all bearings of where they were but somehow felt that was a good thing if they wanted to arrive undetected and safe. But still he felt uneasy about being so isolated with people he didn't know. The group

186

had become somber since they'd heard of the unknown sentries waiting out front of Raven's facility.

Suddenly the driver slammed on the brakes, locking up the wheels of the rig. They came to a skidding halt just before a wide, rushing river. The road disappeared into it.

"This can't be good!" Ken cried.

The driver smiled nonchalantly. "This happens sometimes. It must've dumped while we were gone."

"Hell, what are we going to do now?" Ken hung out the window, craning his head back up the trail.

It would be a long way to back up.

"You can exercise the chimps if you like until the others get here." The driver's answer seemed matter-of-fact as he swung out of the truck and busied himself opening one of the toolboxes from below the cab.

Where the hell are the others, Ken wondered.

Mark stepped out of the other truck as it slid to a stop just behind them, blocking them in. Mark and Ken huddled together and peered across the rushing water where they could just make out in the shadows where the road continued. A sign sat on the opposite bank of the river. Mark read it aloud: "Private Property. Keep out by order of the Wild Animal Training Center and the Hidden Valley Wildlife Area. Violators will be eaten."

"Great! This isn't the reception I expected." Ken frowned and approached Mike's cage in the back of the trailer.

Mark handed him a bag of Monkey Chow, and Mike started all the chimps hooting when he saw the prospect of food. But Mark and Ken continued to watch the drivers who seemed to ignore them, intent on gathering various lengths of rope and chain.

"This would be a great place for an ambush," Mark whispered.

Consuelo and Savage joined them, nodding in agreement.

The distinct, pungent odor of rotting vegetation lingered in the stillness. A flock of ravens broke the silence with their cackle as they swooped just above the cottonwoods that surrounded them. Indecisive as to what to do next, Ken and his colleagues shot furtive glances toward the drivers as they went through the motions of feeding chimps. The animals' food grunts and hoots took away all possibility of staying secret.

Ken opened his mouth to quiet them but was startled by the noise of something very large and determined breaking through the thick bamboo that lined the river, followed by a loud, piercing trumpet. The team froze at the sight of three massive African elephants breaking out of the thickets onto the open bank of the river. They trumpeted again before plunging into the river on the opposite side and frothing their way toward them.

Ken broke into a smile at the sight of Dusty, Hunt, and Bobby riding, mahout-style, on the backs of the massive creatures. It took just one glance to see that Dusty was in charge. While Hunt and Bobby sat on their own elephants, Dusty, on the back elephant, called out commands to the herd. "Move on; Move on. Good boys!"

The two drivers waited as all three splashed out of the water before them and stood with rivulets pouring off their massive bulks.

"Down!" Dusty commanded in a resounding voice.

In unison all three kneeled so their cargo could scramble off, then stood again with his last command: "All right."

Ken noticed that Dusty drew out the "All". Even now in their present circumstances, he couldn't help but be fascinated with the techniques of a fellow trainer. That must be why they had so much trust between each other even though they'd known each other for only a short while. He felt guilty for his recent suspicion.

"That's a long friggin' way to ride on one of these smelly, hay burners!" Bobby beamed as he they hugged each other. "All's well so far. Now let's get you all to the ranch!" He paused and lowered his voice secretively, "We need to be careful. We're pretty sure we're being watched up on the mesa." Bobby's little finger pointed up and in the direction of the Training Center.

So began some of the most amazing feats of animal handling and engineering that Ken had ever witnessed. Or in Bobby's words, "Towing two fully-loaded trucks and trailers circus style."

It'd rained over the last several days, and all the roads into the ranch were slippery with mud, but this back way was particularly difficult; since it served only as a last-ditch emergency exit—or in this case an entrance—it wasn't maintained regularly.

The drivers and trainers, working under Dusty's direction, chained up each truck and trailer and hooked all three elephants in a single-file train using a harness made for just such an occasion and slowly pulled each rig across the river and along the long and windy, narrow road, greasy with sloppy clay. It was a slow process, taking the full attention and skill of all involved, but they finally came up the last hill and caught site of the Clubhouse.

Raven met them at the elephant barn as they unhooked. They decided to leave the chimps in the horse trailers until evening when they could move them into the center of the compound under the cover of darkness. Ken, Savage, Consuelo, and Mark moved quickly into the Clubhouse.

They made it to the training center without any pursuit, but it was clear that the WATC was under suspicion. It seemed to all of them that Vandusen and company had a long reach.

* * *

The WATC trainers had a fire crackling in the Clubhouse as it was spring and evening was setting in. The handlers worked under limited light as a precaution against prying eyes.

To avoid suspicion, Raven had told them he was concerned that some of the competition could be spying on their doings. The business could be brutal so this was believable. Incidents of thefts and actual poisoning of animals had occurred in the past, thought to be perpetrated by trainers who hadn't been hired or competing companies that didn't get a contract. But, in actuality, Raven was well liked in the business, being generous with his knowledge, contacts and even financially on occasion. But this was a great cover story just the same and allowed them to keep their doings out of sight.

"I don't think our chimps are going to be safe anywhere in the U.S." Ken stomped the mud from his boots, splattering splotches on the giant stone hearth. "I mean—how can we keep safe from these thugs? They *are* the Goddamn government."

"We could take ourselves and the chimps out of the country for a while—at least until we can clear things up." Mark looked at Raven as he spoke as though this wasn't the first time they'd discussed this idea.

Ken looked at them with surprise.

Raven smiled. "I'm afraid you've caught Mark and I talking out of school about this. What I'm thinking is …" He paused and looked around the room to be sure they were alone. "We have this movie going where we'll be transporting a shit load of animals, including chimps, to Africa."

It took a moment for the idea to set in, but Ken got the significance. "We not only get the chimps far away from here, but we'd be exactly where we need to be to follow Oliver and the rest of this mystery." Ken began pacing the room, leaving a trail of mud tracks. "We couldn't have planned this better. But how will we get the paperwork done in time?"

Raven smiled. "One thing I've learned from traveling animals around the world is that they all look alike to the average customs official. We'll move them under the paper of some of my chimps. It's really very simple." Looking a little guilty, he continued, "I must admit this wouldn't be the first time I've done it."

"Is that legal?" Ken asked naively.

Raven laughed along with the others. "About as legal as what happened to you up in Reno." He paused and took a serious tone. "So, if we're all on the same page, I suggest we get busy readying our new 'movie' chimps and their trainers to be on their way to the Dark Continent." Staring at Consuelo, Ken, and Savage he asked, "You all have your passports, right?"

CHAPTER 18

The Wild Animal Training Center was in a flurry of activity the morning after Ken and his company arrived. The evening before had been uneventful with everyone retiring early to get ready for the final push before they'd move the chimps along with trainers and assorted other animals and gear to Africa.

The logistics surrounding a movie with animal stars was staggering. Travel cages had to be built. Training equipment, food, and vet supplies had to be packed. And the paperwork had to be ready and in order for all personnel and animals to travel. This required jumping through the countless hoops of federal and state agencies and foreign consulates. It was a staggering task to meet all the requirements and had to be planned months or sometimes even years in advance of the first scene being filmed.

And all the equipment and animals had to be staged in such a way as to keep it secure and accessible. Every detail had to be thought of, considering they'd be on location for the next six months in the middle of the jungle. If they didn't bring it, they wouldn't have it. And if they didn't pack it right, they wouldn't find it.

But Raven and his crew knew their business and wasted little time in staging every item, animal, and person for the trip. The lawn in front of the Clubhouse looked like a huge garage sale with items laid out in rows with labels attached with packing instructions. Handlers scurried around arranging and rearranging equipment.

The greatest challenge had been to substitute Ken's chimps for those with valid paperwork and get Ken and his crew their passports. Mary had to collect them along with immunization cards without raising suspicion. She overnighted everything down to them, not daring to risk coming herself. On top of all these preparations, the trainers worked their animals daily to put on the behaviors required by the script.

The director, along with his entourage, planned to pay a final visit before their scheduled departure to check on the progress of their "pre-training," as it was called in the business. Tensions were high as they made ready for the visit and their impending departure. Making a movie was an expensive proposition, especially with animals. It cost close to $80,000 a day to make one, so the trainers had to be sure their animals could perform what they promised.

"There's a caravan of Land Rovers coming down the road," Mark called out as he gazed up the long drive. "You'd think they're on a bloody safari by the looks of how they're kitted out." Shaking his head, he handed a worn set of field glasses to Raven.

"Okay, everyone, it's show time. Let's get cracking!" Raven took off in the direction of the chimp cages followed by the rest of the trainers, leaving Mark alone in the middle of the drive.

The lead Rover pulled up. A small, rotund man stepped out as the dust settled around them. He extended his hand. "Good morning. Could you direct me to Dr. Raven?" Several crewmembers joined in around him, obviously excited to be out of town and the usual studio routine.

Mark was taken aback by how many people had emptied out of the vehicles. He smiled, reminded of one of those clown cars in the circus. They all seemed to be in costume, dressed in matching khakis and safari hats. He grasped with both hands the outstretched hand of James Hill, the director.

Beaming, Mark said, "It's a real pleasure, Mr. Hill. I'm a great fan." Mark knew his work and loved it. James Hill was a well-known director from London. He was genuinely pleased to meet him. Almost star struck.

Hill looked Mark up and down. "And from the UK— by your speech."

"Kent."

"Sheppard's Bush." They shook hands with enthusiasm, as fellow countrymen would often do who'd met by chance, far from home.

"I should like to get on with this demonstration straight away. We're meeting with the producers back in town this evening."

"No worries. I can take you over to the training area after you and your company have had a chance to freshen up." The group followed Mark into the clubhouse.

* * *

"Ah, here you are!" Raven beckoned Mark, the director, and his company over to a row of empty chimp cages. "We're ready for you."

When the crew surrounded Raven expectantly, Mark could tell that this cluster of movie people had settled into their surroundings. They were all business.

Raven paused, looking from face to face, as though sizing them up or, as Mark thought, for dramatic effect. "I've been thinking that rather than run through all the behaviors with all the animals, we might take the toughest scene in the movie and run our star chimp, Doc, through the behaviors." The crew hesitated, looking toward James Hill, but relaxed when he nodded in agreement. Everyone immediately fell into action. A young boyish-looking woman handed the director a thick, dog-eared script. A young man ran up with a folding canvas chair with "Mr. Hill, Director" inscribed on a back panel. Two trainers went off in the direction of the chimp area to fetch, Doc, the star chimp, and some of his co-stars.

Everyone seemed to know their job despite their new surroundings. *Impressive!* Mark thought it must be a big part of the work to be adaptable and innovative. The hoarse greeting hoots of several chimps stirred him from his thoughts. They ambled along with their trainers, glancing curiously from side to side as they approached the movie crew. The rest of the chimps they'd left made the usual racket.

The crew set up cameras, shiny boards, and lights. A generator fired up, startling the chimps and their trainers, who quickly got back to the task at hand without a beat. Raven moved in closely behind the camera operator, who leaned intently over his gear. Grips lifted several empty, steel-bared cages and moved them into the scene under the direction of the set designer and assistant director, or AD as they are not so affectionately called in the business.

Hill raised his voice above the noise of the controlled chaos, "Come on people we have got to go!"

People darted in and out of the developing scene, shifting the direction of lights and moving props without ever seeming to bump into each other. The transformation of several piles of props and equipment into a scene from the script took less than an hour. Mark found it amazing, almost magical. The chimps sat patiently with their trainers just off the set, watching the activity unfold.

Ken had been exercising Mike when he was drawn to the activity of the group. He and Mike stood off to one side, watching with interest. Mike jumped as a crew member popped in behind them, bringing two chairs, assuming they were part of the show.

The lighting director moved around under lights, holding out a meter.

The AD called out on a bullhorn, "Places everyone—five minutes. It's an animal shot, people. No rehearsal!"

The set designer stepped in to make a final check of how things were arranged and raced over to confer with the director.

The rest of the crew clustered around their equipment, speaking in whispers before settling in anticipation.

Several trainers, including Raven, brought three chimps along with Doc onto the set. Clearly these chimps and trainers knew their craft as they required little communication. The chimps seemed to know their marks, needing little prompting. Two of the chimps had been placed in the empty cages with secured padlocks on the doors. A ring of keys was left on the floor of the cage in which Doc was placed. Each trainer held up his hand, giving the command for the chimps to hold their positions. The chimps stood, not moving, staring at their trainers for their next cue.

The director nodded to the AD whose bellowing voice carried over the set, "Quiet on the Set!" He made a final scan and looked to the cameraman and his assistant. "Roll Camera!"

The very pretty assistant shouted, "We're rolling!"

The AD looked in the direction of the soundmen hovering over their recorder, earphones in place, "Roll sound!"

His assistant nodded, clutching his earphones against one ear, "Speed!"

A young man darted past the AD, held a clap stick in front of the camera lens, and waited on the director.

Hill nodded and shouted in a commanding voice, "Mark it!"

The boy responded in rapid succession, "Pre-training sequence, WATC, scene 1. Mark!" Then he clapped the sticks together in a loud report.

The chimps knew their business. The trainers stepped out of camera range to allow them to perform the sequence they'd been practicing for months. Doc ambled on all fours across the cage and picked up the keys. Standing up, bipedal, he awkwardly made his way to the lock where he tried each key until he got it open. The other chimps watched as he worked his way to each of them and laboriously opened each of their cages, upon which they made their way to Raven who was just off camera. The trainers quickly gathered up their charges, praising them and rewarding them in whispers.

"Good boy, Doc," Raven whispered.

All the chimps got a can of apple juice and a handful of M&Ms for their efforts.

"Cut!" Hill moved excitedly toward Raven and Doc. "Wow! You really did it!" He called over to the cameraman who was replaying video and checking his Panavision. "Do we have it?"

The cameraman and his assistant nodded in unison. "It's in the can."

"Both film and video?"

"Yep."

"Print it! I need that video footage to schmooze our producers this afternoon back in town." His hazel eyes gleamed with excitement. He watched the crew sweeping over the set, getting everything ready for another take. Doc and the other chimps sat in their chairs, eating fruit leathers and sipping their apple juice.

"Okay, people. That's a wrap for today. Let's get back to town!"

"All right, everyone. You heard the man. It's a wrap. Let's break down and get moving!"

The soundmen moved off with the trainers and chimps as they needed to record the chimps making their usual hooting noises and sounds of opening and closing the steel doors of the cages. The editors would need to cut these sounds into various scenes. The rest of the crew got busy wrapping the set and loading up.

The trainers had put the chimps back in the steel cages and were about to unlock the door, when Mike pulled away from Ken and reached for the keys in a trainer's hand. The startled trainer looked over to Ken. He nodded. Mike took the keys and ambled to the cages, then sat in front of the door, deep in concentration, sorting through the keys. He looked up at the lock, rocking on his haunches. Just when Ken moved to take the keys back, Mike climbed up the door and tried the keys until he unlocked it.

The trainers stared, amazed. Raven leaned in behind Ken and whispered, "It looks like we now have a backup for Doc."

"Just when you think you've seen everything a chimp can do," Lester said, "they surprise you with something like this." He studied both professors' reactions. "From your looks I'm guessing no one trained Mike to do that."

Ken was startled out of his thoughts. "Hell, since you opened the one cage, you might as well let the others out." He made the sign for "open" and pointed at the other cage.

CHAPTER 19

Raven elbowed Ken as they approached the customs desk. "I'll do all the talking." He gave a knowing look to the rest of the trainers as they awkwardly followed, each pushing heavy transfer cages. The chimps hooted with every bump, echoing in the cavernous Customs House. And there were many, as the hard rollers seemed to find every imperfection in the concrete deck. They slowly made their way past rows of crates all stenciled with different destinations.

Raven mentioned that they were lucky today, as they seemed to be the only animals attempting to clear customs. A bored forklift operator waited on his idling machine for the go ahead to load their animals and equipment onto the Flying Tigers cargo plane that sat waiting on the tarmac.

Ken noticed that there was none of the usual banter between the trainers that he'd grown accustomed to. Everybody was on edge. They were playing a high stakes game by substituting Mike and the other research chimps for some of the movie chimps. He knew the law as well as anyone. What they were doing was smuggling and could definitely land them all in jail, or worse, get the chimps confiscated by the very people from whom they were running. The wave of anxiety that threatened to overtake Ken stalled mid-stream as they approached the inspection desk.

Barely glancing up from his paperwork, a small, rotund lieutenant addressed them, "Have your certificates of health, passports, and animal permits ready when the agent comes to inspect your animals." An American flag hung limply behind the little man, partially obstructing a faded and torn poster of the US Customs mission statement. Ken could just make out something about "service with courtesy" and was struck by its irony in this particular situation.

But the trainers knew their work and quickly got the documents ready for each cage. Each chimp had to be cleared separately, so the process would be lengthy and one careless comment could unravel their whole plan, and worse, they would be under the scrutiny for hours. One slip-up would cost Raven the movie and Ken his getaway.

With a nod from the lieutenant, an agent began working his way around each cage, which set the chimps off. But their deafening hoots seemed to be helping their plan by keeping the inspecting officer a good distance back from the cages, making it difficult to actually see clearly inside.

Sweat gleamed off the agent's forehead and stained his white, short-sleeved shirt. His dark, thinning hair contrasted against the pasty white of his skin. It was obvious from the blotchiness on his skin and his pear-shaped body that he spent most of his time inside, out of the light of the sun, counting and inspecting. He had a nervous habit of tapping his pencil against his clipboard, apparently bored with the process, but, fortunately, he seemed more interested in comparing the number of animals to the number on the manifest rather than actually identifying them. He seemed to just want to get through the process. Standing well back, he peered into each travel cage and, between taps, marked the manifest on his clipboard.

As the officer slowly worked his way to each trainer, Ken began to relax a little, taking in his surroundings with more interest. The volume of material parked in this warehouse amazed him. He wondered how the government kept track of it all.

During a rare loll in the chimp cries, a muffled cough shifted his attention above where several armed officers patrolled a catwalk. He stiffened when he noticed a man leaning over the rail intently observing them through field glasses. The man was dressed differently than the rest of the officials, wearing a suit rather than a uniform.

When the man noticed Ken observing him, he quickly put the binoculars down and spoke into a handheld radio. A radio sitting on the lieutenant's desk squawked, startling Ken, and when the lieutenant finished his conversation, his whole manner changed. He mustered several more officers to join the inspection. Now they seemed more interested and certainly more aggressive. They checked and rechecked the bills of lading and the manifest sheets thoroughly and meticulously. While they were more thorough, they didn't seem to be in any hurry, working their way methodically to each trainer and travel cage.

Ken did as he'd been told and stayed out of the way as this whole process was completely foreign to him. Clearly Raven was in his element and stayed on hand with additional paperwork or explanations when needed, which was often, as the lieutenant now orchestrated the entire inspection.

Concerned at the shift in everyone's interest after the apparent radio communication, Ken wondered if they were responding to some tip or just being thorough. He didn't believe in coincidences and wondered what had been said on those radios. A sense of dread revisited him when he observed the plain-clothes agent leaning with one hand against a wall speaking on a phone. But he felt that, at the moment, the best approach was to still stay out of the way and watch.

Watch and wait. If they were busted now, there'd not be much they could do right in the cargo terminal of Los Angeles International Airport with armed custom agents crawling all over. They were going to have to play this out to the bitter end.

The hours crept by and evening set in, but even though the whole process was nerve wracking, Ken grew accustomed to it and continued to take in his surroundings. The plain-clothes man was on the phone constantly watching every move they made. Finally, when Ken thought he could stand it no more and would crack, the lieutenant gave the forklift operator a nod and the slow and delicate process of loading finally began.

This caused a heated discussion between the plain-clothes agent and the lieutenant. Ken couldn't make out what was being said though he could hear shouts. It ended with the lieutenant throwing his hands up and walking away and the plain-clothes man returning to the phone.

The loading process was a touchy operation as the chimps were now in an uproar, shaking their cages, which made it difficult for the operator to balance each cage on the forks and lift them into the waiting cargo door of the plane. Trainers tried riding on top the cages in an attempt to reassure them.

Raven seemed to be everywhere, barking orders. "Careful with that damn machine! You're not loading sakes of potatoes here. These are valuable movie animals. God damn it!"

"Mark, get your hands out of your pockets and help tie that cage onto the forks or do I have to do it myself!"

Obviously Raven and his trainers had done this before, as they needed little communication between them, but Ken and Mark felt clumsy and out of place, always seeming to be in the way. Finally, after getting yelled at by almost everyone in the building, they stepped back out of the way. Mark lit a pipe that got him into further trouble.

This made the lieutenant suspicious. He eased over and asked, "Are you boys new to this?"

Mark looked mutely at Ken, but Ken was quick to respond, "Why, yes. Actually, we're technical advisors—not trainers."

This seemed to appease him for the moment. He walked away shaking his head. "Hell, technical advisors—whatever that is. It seems like in your business anyone who stands around and does nothing is rewarded with a big title."

Just as the trainers were about to gather up the last of their personal belongings to load onto the plane, they had yet another delay. The plain-clothes agent raced down to stop them. He decided he needed to personally inspect everything they were carrying on board. It appeared that he was stalling.

This completely exasperated Raven, who strode over to him shouting, "Can't you people do more than one thing at a time? We were holding our luggage in our goddamned hands when your people came through and inspected the cages the first time! Christ Almighty! It costs eighty grand a day to make a movie and you've already cost us a day."

Ken hadn't been able to tell Raven what he'd observed or share his suspicions, which seemed fortuitous. Raven might have been more guarded with his temper had he known. Clearly, this man didn't want to be out in the open and this scene was making him uneasy. The man looked around now, noticing that everyone in their vicinity, including the forklift operator, had stopped working to watch this exchange.

Raven finally noticed the agent's uneasiness and for the first time looked him up and down. "Just who in the hell are you, exactly? Why, you're not even in uniform!" The man hesitated. "Let me see your badge, Goddamn it!" Trainers and agents quickly closed in from all directions. Just as the officers started to intervene, the trainers escorted Raven away.

The man beat a hasty retreat, wanting to get back into the shadows as quickly as possible. Exasperated, the lieutenant finally ordered everyone onto the plane.

So much for incognito, Ken thought as he followed the others across the warm tarmac of the runway. The high-pitched whine of the jet engines warming up squelched any further discussion.

Ken climbed aboard, turned down one of the jump seats that lined each side of the cargo plane and sat down, exhausted.

Raven staked out a spot on the metal decking by laying out a foam mattress and his sleeping bag. He still muttered to himself, apparently not finished with the argument.

After making a final check of all the tie downs on each cage, the rest of them followed suit. It'd been a long and stressful day. Ken could barely keep his eyes open as the jet finally was cleared for takeoff and roared out of LA International Cargo Terminal headed for Africa by way of Ramsgate. They'd made their escape, safe and sound. But how secretly and for how long?"

* * *

The ranch manager slowly reread the search warrant as the young sheriff stood by and Vandusen glared. Confused, he looked around for help, but there was none as he'd been left solely in charge of the WATC while everyone else was on the movie. "I don't understand what you're after. There are no chimps left here. They left this morning with their trainers for a movie we're doing in Africa. I'm sure you've heard about it. It's gonna be the biggest chimp movie since Tarzan. James Hill is the director."

"Well, just the same I have a warrant to search these premises for stolen animal property and these persons." The sheriff produced a set of photos of four university chimps including Mike and Ken Turner, Mark Chaney and Consuelo.

The ranch manager's hands shook as he shuffled through the photos. Vandusen watched him intently. The manager handed the photos back to the sheriff and repeated more empathically, "I told you, there are no chimps at the ranch right now, and, anyway, these aren't ours."

Vandusen broke in, stepping past the sheriff, "So you're saying you've never seen these chimps or these people before?" He sensed the man was nervous about something. But he wasn't sure if he was just nervous talking to the law, like many citizens, or because he was lying.

The two men stood in silence, staring at each other until the sheriff felt uncomfortable. "Shall we take a look around?"

Vandusen shook his head. "No. They're not here. But I think I know where to find them."

CHAPTER 20

"Welcome to Africa!" GuGu stared right through them with his dark, dead eyes. A faded, camouflage t-shirt that read *Take no prisoners* above a skull and crossed rifles canopied with a parachute hung loosely on his small but muscular frame. Sweat stains outlined wide salty bands that'd nearly eroded the cloth from under each arm.

It was sweltering out of the air conditioning of the plane. The rich, verdant green of the jungle closed in around them, shrinking the runways and terminal. Waves of heat rose from the tarmac where they stood. Ken looked at the dark-azure sky which contrasted with huge, billowing clouds that brought little relief from the humidity. An Air France commercial plane took off, stirring a flock of thousands of grey parrots.

Now this is Africa.

The smell of rotting vegetation followed them into the terminal, mixed with the perspiration and urine inside. Rot and decay seemed to permeate the whole building. They could just make out through the smeared and dirty windows the bustling activity of gangs of black men off-loading the parked planes. They pushed huge handcarts across the melting tarmac. Inside was a clamoring of humanity, a Babel of the languages of trade. French, Pidgin French, Swahili, and countless other European and native dialects bombarded Ken's senses. He thought it right out of one of the old adventure movies of the forties he was so fond of.

Raven grasped GuGu's hand enthusiastically. Ken caught a glimpse of a faded French Foreign Legion tattoo on GuGu's outstretched forearm before it was pinned from sight between their embrace. They both stepped back, pausing to look each other over. It was apparent they were good friends.

GuGu smirked, and in a thick Belgium accent sardonically observed, "You're a long ways from California, Doctor."

"Yes, and with your help we're going to make a movie and some serious money."

"Now that's what I like to hear!" The little Belgian paused for a moment, and looking around to make sure they would not be overheard, lowered his voice. "And I believe you have need for some of my other services."

"We do and will," Raven whispered and pointed at the men off-loading the chimps. "We'll need you to do one of your juggling acts you're so good at. We need to make this movie but lose some chimps while doing so; and right under the noses of some very—well, how should I put it, nosey people."

"Nosey people with or without guns?"

"With."

"*With* is going to cost you, my friend."

"Money we have. Hell, we're making a movie." Both men laughed.

GuGu abruptly yelled something in Swahili to the men helping the trainers lower the chimp cages, then he whispered to Ken, "Leave everything to me, my friend."

Sometime later, GuGu and a tall lanky African uniformed in knee high shorts and a khaki military blouse emerged from an office behind the crowded customs desk. A sign hung ajar on the office door that read "Capitaine de Police."

GuGu slapped the officer vigorously on the back in a jovial manner, but the captain seemed hesitant and suspicious. Obviously, he was a reluctant player who'd succumbed to GuGu's powers of persuasion. Ken could only guess what scheme they'd developed. GuGu continued to whisper in the tall African's ear as the solemn policeman nodded slightly, looking around the room furtively. He wore a tall fez with a tassel that distractingly swished with each jerk of his head.

Ken didn't want to be part of GuGu's doings; preferring to leave everything African to this energetic Belgian. The other workers in the terminal kept to their business, ignoring this interaction and, for that matter, the very presence of the chimps and their entourage.

"So, what do you think of our new-found partner?" Ken asked Mark as they looked on.

"He seems almost too helpful, but Raven seems to trust him."

"Apparently they're old chums, but I'm not sure how that will carry over to us."

"I don't like him." Savage walked up, frowning, as he watched GuGu glad-handing everyone in uniform.

They slowly made their way out of the building with GuGu orchestrating their departure, chimps and all their belongings in tow.

"Time will tell—time will tell," Ken mumbled almost to himself as he followed what had become an entourage.

* * *

"Everything's arranged!" GuGu announced, his face animated. Indicating a chart, he presented his plans to head down the coast, then paused, presumably to let the good news sink in. His forehead wrinkled, seeming disappointed that he'd had little effect on the group. "There is one problem, however."

"What's that?" Ken asked. He'd been waiting for the other shoe to drop since they left with GuGu for the coast to find a boat.

GuGu hesitated, taking time to pick his words. "There's no place to leave your chimps that is safe. This whole region is a black market for the animal trade and money can buy anything here, and I do mean anything. There are no secrets. and the word is out that you're here." He waited for their reaction but continued when he still received none, "No one can be trusted."

Including you, Ken thought. *Tell me something I don't know.*

The group looked at GuGu suspiciously and continued to brood.

Appearing uncomfortable with the silence, GuGu pushed on, "Actually, there's one more thing. The owner will only let the boat I found go if I accompany you."

This last news was too much for the group and he finally got a reaction. They all began talking at once. The gist of which was that none of them had a good feeling about this new information.

The discussion became so heated they didn't notice Raven walk up. "I'd feel better if he did go with you." GuGu looked relieved as Raven continued, "Obviously, I'm going to stay with the movie along with my people. I don't like the thought of you roaming along the African coast alone without a guide. It's not safe."

GuGu nodded in agreement. "This part of the world is no place for a group of outsiders like you to be wandering around without a guide. You need someone with local knowledge."

"Besides," Raven continued, "it'll be good to have someone like me remain behind in case you're followed. We can stay in contact by radio."

It suddenly dawned on Ken how much they'd grown to depend on Raven. They'd been so focused on getting to Africa that he'd not given much thought to their next steps and had just assumed that Raven would be with them to the end, whatever that was. While it made sense to take GuGu, he still felt uneasy about bringing him into their confidence. There was something about the Belgian that made him suspicious despite Raven's support. But in the end, he realized they had little choice.

As Consuelo put it, "If Raven can't or won't come, then who else?"

* * *

GuGu had been right when he'd observed that you could get just about anything in Free Town. They stood on a decaying wharf, looking up at the rusting hulk of a motor yacht. A

Spanish flag hung limply off the stern above the faded and chipped name, *Si Como No.*

We're really in for it now, Ken thought.

He turned to the others, breaking them out of the spell. "Let's get Mike and Girlie out of the sun somewhere up on this rust bucket. They'll need to be fed and watered."

Lester stirred into action. "I'll take care of that."

Mark and Consuelo followed him up the sagging gangplank.

Bobby and Hunt watched as GuGu directed several workers in the loading of their supplies. The Spanish Captain leaned on the rail above them, shouting orders in both Spanish and Arabic.

"So, can we trust these guys?" Bobby asked.

Hunt shook his head. "I don't like the look of them—especially that Spaniard."

Ken frowned. "You better get used to them. Unfortunately, GuGu and the Captain come with the yacht."

* * *

"The coast in that area is very rocky and there are other dangers," Omar, the captain, said with a Spanish accent. A black Moor with sharp Arabic features, he was trim and compact and wore a black turtleneck with epaulettes in spite of the evening heat. He pushed his white merchant hat back, accentuating his potted forehead.

The group leaned over a worn chart that draped the table in the wheelhouse. A damp mildew smell competed against the oily pungency of a dimly glowing kerosene lamp. Their eyes strained as they tried to follow the captain's gnarled index finger as it traced the proposed route down the coast in search of the *Orion.*

Omar was clearly suspicious, and he asked not-so-subtle questions about why they were searching for this particular wreck, the *Orion.* He'd not been convinced when Ken had told him they were doing historical research and not treasure hunting. As though he'd not heard a word they'd said Omar suddenly asked, "Will you need any of my men to help carry off the salvaged cargo?"

Exasperated, Ken replied, "No! I told you. There is no *cargo*. We're simply trying to solve an historical mystery"

Omar smiled knowingly and seemed unconvinced.

That set Bobby off. "Maybe we should get another boat."

They put out to sea at dawn. Wispy clouds streaked with pink and orange painted the horizon. The sea was dark and oily. The ship humped up on the swells as they left the crumbling breakwater. They turned south and looked out to sea, skirting the coast on their left.

Bobby recited as they stood in silence at the rail, "Red sky in the morning, sailors take warning. Red—"

"Great, Bobby." Hunt stumbled to the roll of the ship as he made his way towards the ladder to the wheelhouse.

"Let's check on our new partners and see if they know what they're doing," Ken said looking up at the bridge.

The rest followed in silence.

CHAPTER 21

The last couple of weeks traveling from the movie location to where they stood had put them on edge, and Ken feared they all might unravel from the strain of their search. After procuring a vessel that would accommodate their needs to house them and store their equipment, they'd clawed along the coast, searching for any bays or coves that might fit the log entries Bobby had found. They had some rough Lat/Longs, Latitudes and Longitudes, that placed the ship's last location near the mouth of the Congo River in the Atlantic. So that's where they'd started their search a week before.

The battered wreck leaned half buried on the beach; a stranded derelict, alone in this far corner of the world. Ken could just make out her shape in the fading light. Large combers broke with resounding thuds over her tangled decks, swallowing her up with a shroud of foam. With each receding wave, water rushed out of jagged, gaping holes in the hull, like seeping wounds.

It had been a near death experience, for Ken's group, to enter the mouth of this hidden cove. They had to shoot through a raging surf line in their little dinghy to land on the steep beach where they stood. There'd be no returning tonight. It was good they'd brought gear to camp as a precaution.

Ken could just make out their mother ship, the *Si Como No,* through the hissing spray of the breakers. She lay anchored on the leeward side of the one of the small coastal islands that stood a mile or so out. He wondered how Lester, Girlie and Mike were faring with GuGu and the captain out there without the rest of them aboard.

They felt more secure leaving Lester on board with the chimps for their first scouting of this lonely beach with its large and ominous wreck. There'd been many dead ends over the last several weeks and each had been a disappointment besides being dangerous. They couldn't believe how many wrecks strewed this lonely coast. But this one had looked very promising through the binoculars, being of the right size and in the right location based on the logbook that Bobby had procured with such risk in Mexico. That seemed so very long ago, but, in reality, it'd been less than two months since they pored over the cache of material Bobby had sent them back in Reno.

So much had happened to them, thought Ken, wondering if this adventure was really worth it with all the risk. He was at least glad to leave the confines of their ship, but after running the mouth of the cove and viewing the wilds of where he stood, he was having second thoughts. The *Si Como No* had become their home for the last week as they searched along this deserted coast for the wreck of the *Orion*. He wondered when and if they'd ever return to it.

They'd been lucky to find this little cove tucked away in this lonely part of Africa. The jungle formed a dense, dark-green barrier that made it unapproachable from land. Several islands that formed little more than a string of rocks blocked the cove from view from the sea. It'd been a challenge to follow the meandering channel that weaved through an archipelago of ship-devouring rocks to reach the relative safety of the cove. And, even then, the huge rolling waves at the mouth of the cove made it dangerous and difficult to land on the beach.

Ken wondered how such a large cargo ship could've made her way into this little cove to end up wrecked on this forgotten beach. It'd not been by chance. Someone with great skill had intended to bring her in here despite all obstacles.

For what reason and for how long had she lain here? If this was indeed the *Orion* ... he knew the reason—this wreck could be the very vessel that, so long ago, had transported Soviet scientists intent on breeding humans with chimpanzees.

Ken watched his little landing party of Hunt, Bobby, Savage, Mark and Consuelo as, in the fading light, they struggled to pull their inflatable dinghy up the steep slope of the beach where they'd been unceremoniously pitched into the soft sand by the powerful shore break.

The group valiantly fought against the violent undertow that pulled them back toward the sea. Each wave floated everyone and everything briefly before sucking them all back toward the sea, leaving them to fight against the suction of the dissolving, sinking sand as they slowly worked toward the harder ground at the edge of the jungle.

Hunt stood waving and motioning. He seemed to be shouting directions to them, but Ken couldn't hear him over the roar of the surf. He could just make out the slim, supple form of Consuelo who stood hunched over, hands on her knees, apparently catching her breath as the struggle with the dinghy continued.

Luckily, they were working their way in on a rising tide or they'd never make it. The larger waves in the set helped them make progress.

It's good they're working together so well.

Ken's attention strayed from the little drama on the beach to examine where they'd landed. He scanned the landscape from atop a large, slippery rock just above the incoming waves. Large rollers broke below him, carrying a strong smell of brine with their spray. His skin tingled as salt deposits dried on his cheeks in the tropical heat, like perspiration in reverse.

The jungle grew in close around the rusting ship, covering it with vines that ran along her twisted decks like huge tentacles that weaved through what was once the wheel house, as though intent on covering it from view. Ken realized how hard it would be for anyone to locate this cove, let alone this wreck, from land, air or sea had it not been for the maps and documents Bobby had found.

The last light of day left the dying embers of the setting sun on the darkening waters. A school of baitfish slapped the oily water in unison just off shore. A dark shadow followed just behind. Ken thought, not for the last time, that he didn't like this place despite the prospects. After years of searching, they might have actually found the lost Soviet ship, *Orion*, but they'd have to wait until the morning to verify their hopes. It was late. It'd been a long journey; they were tired and finished searching for the day.

Ken struggled up the sandy beach to rejoin the rest of the group, hearing faint jungle sounds over the breaking combers.

The whole place had an unwholesome feel to it, like a brooding malice, but everything added up from the records Bobby had found. This ship here, in front of them now, if it was the *Orion*, had until now seemingly been swallowed up by time, crew and all, while carrying her unspeakable cargo.

But this stretch of abandoned African coast with its uncharted rocks and shoals had most likely snagged many unsuspecting vessels over the centuries. The light and the tides would be better in the morning; then they could investigate. He made a note to unpack his tide charts.

He didn't like the idea of camping on this beach so near the dark silhouette of the wreck, and he didn't like the idea of spending the night so vulnerable away from the safety of their ship. They'd tried all day to reach Raven with the ship's radio but to no avail. It didn't feel good to be so far from home and out of contact, but they were losing light and it wouldn't be safe to try to run the waves back to their ship.

Patience.

"Let's make camp up there by the tree line, above the high-tide mark were the sand is firmer," he said as he rejoined the others,

The group seemed subdued for being so close to what might be the goal they'd been seeking for so long. They quietly pitched tents and built a small fire just under the trees. Even Bobby had nothing to say.

The wind died with the setting sun. The tide reached its peak and slackened, bringing a quiet to the place. The waves lay down now that the tide filled the little cove. He made a note to himself that high tide, slack would be the best time to try to run the waves back to the ship.

Without the wind, the air, filled with the over-powering sweet smell of rotting vegetation, grew stifling and humid. The stars began to appear, competing against the afterglow of the sun, now gone from this part of the world. A colorful spectacle of purple hues streaked the sky as dusk swallowed the canvas of high-flying clouds.

No one spoke as they focused on helping Hunt and Consuelo prepare the evening meal of freeze-dried beef stroganoff. Stirrings and muffled cries came from deep in the trees. An especially loud and prolonged rustling startled them.

Bobby broke the silence. "Let's build a bigger fire."

Ken could just make out his small silhouette as he moved into the darkness of the trees, stooping along the way to gather sticks.

Hunt followed after him. "Bobby, damn it. Stay in the light. I don't like the looks of it in there."

"You'll like it less without light when this fire dies out. I'm just trying to find more dry sticks. Why don't you come and give me a hand?" Bobby slipped into the darkness, seemingly swallowed by the jungle.

Hunt hesitated just under the trees and looked back at the group. "Will somebody talk some sense into this stubborn midget?"

Ken motioned towards Savage. "Fred. Please. Grab a flashlight and make sure he doesn't fall into a hole or get lost."

Rifle in hand, Savage was already up and jogging towards where Bobby had disappeared. He paused at the edge of the trees and frowned. "Save some dinner for us." From his tone, it was apparent he wasn't enjoying these new developments. The light from his flashlight disappeared the second he stepped under the canopy of the trees. After a few moments his muffled voice could just be heard: "Hey, there's a trail in here and it looks used!"

The group moved out of the light of the fire toward his voice and peered into the darkness. When their eyes adjusted, they just made out a clean, sandy trail cutting straight into the jungle. The light from the fire cast a glow for a few yards up the trail before the blackness swallowed it. They stood in silence for what seemed like an eternity before Savage's flashlight reappeared up the trail, bouncing to his gait.

"Someone made this path and, moreover, is still using it. Take a look at this." He stepped back into the firelight, gingerly cradling a large, flat piece of bark in both hands. It'd been recently peeled off the trunk of a tree of considerable circumference. The edges were cut smooth as though with a tool, but what struck them all was the neatly ordered rows of dead ants pressed on the smooth bark. "I've seen this before." Savage's voice quivered with excitement.

They didn't notice Bobby standing behind them holding a bundle of sticks. "I found a pile of kindling in the clearing a few yards up the path by a fire ring, a fire ring mind you." The group jumped at his voice.

"Damn it, Bobby!" Ken squared on the whole group. "I want all of you to stay close to the fire and together. No one is to stray from the group until we get the lay of the land around here. We could have company." Everyone looked around nervously as they walked back toward the fire. Bobby kneeled and began stoking it bright.

Savage kneeled beside Bobby, helping him. "I wouldn't use all of that just now. I think it'll be a long night, and we'll want the glow of a fire while it's dark."

Bobby nodded in agreement. "I had the feeling I was being watched. That's why I came back so fast. What the hell's gotten into you all?"

"Remember the rows of flies Danny made back at the WATC?"

Bobby nudged him. "Let's have a look at the artwork."

Savage laid the bark out beside the fire for everyone to see. The group huddled around it, close to the fire in spite of the heat. He traced the pattern on the bark, being careful not to actually touch it, much like he would've treated a delicate artifact. "I count six in the top row and two in the bottom— that's exactly the pattern we found in Danny's cage the day he almost strained me through the bars." The group stared in silence as the fire crackled and added heat to the humid equatorial air.

Bobby jarred them out of their thoughts. "We definitely need a bigger fire!"

Ken gazed out into the blackness of the night. He realized that while the glare of the fire made them feel secure, it blinded their view and made them very exposed.

"We're setting watches tonight. Bobby you're first." Ignoring Bobby's grumbling, Ken continued, "Has anyone radioed Lester?" No one answered. Ken picked up the radio and walked over to his tent.

The rest of the group finished setting up camp and making dinner. No one seemed anxious to retire to their tents though they'd had a long and strenuous day. They sat around the fire deep in thought, feeling safer sitting close together. The eerie sounds of the jungle grew louder with the darkness, filling the air. The stars sparkled in the black sky as the fire died down to a glow.

One by one without fanfare everyone retired to their tents, leaving Bobby and Savage sitting together.

Bobby threw another limb into the fire, sending sparks into the air to compete with the canopy of stars above them. "What do you make of the clearing where I found the kindling? It definitely was made by someone, and the wood was in a neat pile by a fire ring." Bobby paused and lowered his voice, "A friggin' fire ring, Fred."

"We'll know more in the light of day. Get some sleep." Savage stood abruptly and headed for his tent.

Bobby stared after him, shaking his head, and whispered, "Great." He stoked the coals into flames.

They slept in their tents even though the lank air made them all want to sleep outside, but they'd learned that the tents gave them the only refuge from the relentless feeding of insects.

Bobby had made them all laugh when he'd said, "The insects in these parts are so big they have facial expressions." The tents also gave them a feeling of security that defied logic, but just the same they all felt secluded and secret from the prying eyes of the jungle.

The fire died, as did the wind and the sound of the waves. Bobby could hear every crack and thump in the night. The sounds of the jungle echoed across the beach from deep within its heart. Rustlings and cries woke him to his duty several times throughout the night, keeping him on edge. After Hunt relieved him, he'd had fitful dreams that stole his rest, and he woke in the morning tired and nervous.

Nevertheless, he was the first up and made a point to wake everyone else as he rifled through their bags. He could hear the others stirring in their tents.

"Rise and shine, ladies! No rest for the wicked." Bobby's high-pitched voice set what sounded to be a whole troop of macaques howling, thus waking the last holdouts.

Ken unzipped his tent first. He walked to the edge of the tree line, stretching and yawning, and just as he was about to respond to a call of nature, he shouted, "Well, it seems we had visitors last night or early this morning."

Bobby joined him at the back of the tents, and they looked down at a large hominid-like footprint, at least sixteen inches in size, imprinted in the sand.

Savage arrived with his camera and took a shot. "I think some of us were sleeping more than guarding last night." He measured the print with a small tape he was in the habit of carrying in his pocket. "Judging from the size of this, we're looking at something very large, and it's not a chimp. This is a human-like walking foot, not like any great ape. Notice the flatness of the print, the indentation of a ball that defines a big toe. As I said, this is a foot for walking upright, not for grasping or quadrupedal locomotion."

"Plain English, Doc," Hunt yelled as he busied himself unpacking a food box.

"He's saying that who or whatever made this print most likely walked on two feet and was more humanlike than chimp like." Ken kneeled for a closer look and eyed the distance from the print and his tent. "It got very close last night."

"*They*, I'd say," Bobby pointed at several other prints of different sizes and shapes near the fire ring. The sand around the camp and their equipment had been disturbed. "Has anyone made contact with Lester?" Bobby stared at where their inflatable dinghy had been staked out. They could see drag marks before it had, apparently, been lifted and carried away up the path they'd found the evening before. More of the same prints marked the sand.

"It's clear that not everyone was awake during their watch," Ken said. Bobby and Hunt looked guiltily at each other. "Let's get some pictures of these prints before we start walking all over them. I'm going to speak with Lester."

The rest stood silently watching Savage photograph the footprints. They figured there were six different sets belonging to six different animals or as Bobby reminded them, "Six different things."

Several hours passed before they'd finished their work and packed camp; then they argued as to whether they should explore the wreck or try to find their dinghy up the trail. Ken settled the dispute by reminding them of their purpose. "We've traveled too far searching for the wreck of the *Orion*. We shouldn't forget what we came for. The trail will be here when we get back, and we have another dinghy that Lester will bring."

"But will we still be here, I wonder?" Bobby looked at an especially big footprint by the fire ring.

"I've asked Lester to bring Girlie and Mike on shore. They can stand guard on the camp while we investigate the wreck. He can keep an eye on our vessel and man the radio."

Bobby gazed up the trail. "I hope you told him to bring his pistol."

"Now let's get going." Ken took off toward the wreck.

CHAPTER 22

The president's office was plusher than those of the endless stream of deans they'd been referred to all day. It had large bay windows looking out on the grassy commons of the university. The afternoon light streamed in, highlighting the rich academic appointments of the spacious office that marked his position. The large mahogany desk and bookshelves that surrounded the little administrator seemed to swallow him. He listened nervously on the phone while Melon paced furiously in front of him.

The bureaucratic run-around had been exasperating after all the money the grant he represented had brought into this little shit hole of a university way out in the west. Being stonewalled in such a way was infuriating. He and his committee represented the National fucking Science Foundation, and, by God, he was going to get some action.

They'd descended on Ken's own department, the Psychology Department, that very morning, sending its secretaries and administrators into a flurry. Everyone seemed to run for cover. Finally, after talking to the head of this and the head of that, they got to the department chair who claimed he hadn't a clue as to where Ken was or, more importantly, the chimps where, other than that he was on a six-month sabbatical leave which would last through the summer and fall. They had the nerve to refer him back to the compound and Ken's wife. This had been beyond belief.

The president put the phone down and smiled apologetically. "I'm afraid we simply don't know where Dr. Turner is presently."

Melon leveled his glare and leaned on his desk. "So, you're telling me that Dr. Turner has left for parts unknown with valuable animal property owned by your university and bought with NSF money without even a word and without permission?"

The president squirmed in his high-backed leather chair. "We don't have a university policy that requires him to keep us informed of his whereabouts while on sabbatical."

"Really!" Melon held his hand out to an assistant who fumbled through his briefcase and handed him a thick document. Melon put his flimsy wire-rimmed glasses on the tip of his nose and began to read, "Section 3.2. It is further agreed that the said grantee, Dr. Turner, will keep the grantor, NSF and its agents, including the sponsoring institution, UNR, informed of transfers of all property procured by the grant funds, including a detailed inventory of where said property is housed."

This set the whole office in a buzz of bureaucratic activity. The little man seemed to shrink into his chair, as though attempting to hide, before he stirred into action by shouting into his intercom, summoning assistants and assistants' assistants who popped in and out while Melon and his committee stood by fuming.

The final outcome of all the day's effort was that Melon could fill out a formal complaint and file it with the provost who would forward it to the university police. The University Administrative Council would then decide on a course of action.

This set Melon into a rage. Pointing at the president, he shouted, "May I remind you that your university receives a sizable overhead account for overseeing the administration of this grant which, I must say, you have been not just remiss with but totally negligent. You should be fired!"

Melon and the NSF committee stood in front of their van in the university parking lot after being escorted off the premises by the university police. Melon hastily filled out the complaint form on the hood of their vehicle and, hands trembling, gave it to an assistant to hand to an officer who silently stood by.

Melon surprised the driver when he instructed him to turn the opposite way to their motel, make his way through the traffic downtown and drop him off on casino row on Virginia Street just down from the bridge at Truckee River. "I need to get some air and dinner on my own. Go back to the motel and check on the others. I'll find my own way home."

He walked along the river under the trees and found a bench in a clearing that served as a wild park. He was surprised to see someone walking up with Childs.

"Ah, Dr. Melon there you are. I wasn't sure if you'd be able to get free with all that mess at school."

Melon frowned, looking past Childs to Vandusen. "I thought you wanted to meet me alone."

"I'm afraid I pulled rank on your colleague." Vandusen noticed that Melon flinched at the use of the word colleague in referring to Childs but pressed on by flashing a department of defense badge. He laughed to himself while Melon took a long look at his ID and badge, and marveled at how good the organization was getting at making these counterfeit badges. "I'm sorry," he continued. "I've taken you by surprise. Our agency is conducting an investigation that includes Dr. Turner and his operation. We're having a difficult time interviewing him, and now he seems to have evaporated into thin air, which brings me to the both of you, I'm afraid."

"Your guess is as good as mine as to where he is." Melon was clearly uncomfortable with these new developments.

"I know where they went," Childs offered tentatively.

Both waited for him to continue.

"Ah. I paid a visit to their facility, and after being stonewalled by Dr. Turner's wife, Mary, decided to talk with some of the handlers on my way out, Human Companions, they call them. Anyway, it seems two large trucks from the Wild Animal Training Center came in several days ago in the dead of night, and Dr. Turner and most of his assistants headed south on 395 with Mike and several of the other signing chimps."

"What would a group of scientists and their research animals be doing down on a movie compound in Southern California?" Melon asked.

"They're making a movie?" Childs answered incredulously.

Vandusen smiled to himself. Clearly Melon didn't know the extent of the question he was asking. "I know this. The WATC is doing a movie in Africa, and I think that's where we're going to find Turner."

Melon looked flabbergasted. "But why would they go to Africa?"

Childs smirked but said nothing when Vandusen glared at him.

"Dr. Melon," Vandusen replied, "let us worry about that. We'll get the chimps back if you help us move them to a more important research project that is critical to national security, and I assure you it'll not only be profitable to you personally but also professionally. The agency will be very grateful."

"But what research would that be?"

Vandusen smiled. "It is top secret so unfortunately I can't share that with you, yet, but I assure you we take good care of our country's patriots—we're less generous with the country's enemies." Vandusen's manner changed as he emphasized the last sentence, giving Melon a menacing look.

Melon frowned, taken aback. "I assure you I'm here to help. What can I do?"

"Back off your search and let the professionals do their job, but you keep the pressure on the university. Let us know what you need in resources to accomplish that."

Vandusen handed him a card. "Call this number day or night, and don't be shy to ask for anything."

Melon stood staring at the card in the fading light as Childs and Vandusen faded into the shadows of the trees from where they came.

Vandusen put his arm on Childs' shoulder. "Start packing. We're headed to Africa."

CHAPTER 23

They hesitated, looking up from the base of the ship, each wondering how they'd scale the side. The rusted wreck was overgrown with low-hanging trees and vines. After years in the elements, all markings had disappeared.

The low tide made it easy for them to walk around the hull. After several tries to climb up, they took the anchor and rope from the dinghy in which Lester, Girlie, and Mike had come ashore and gave it to Girlie to climb up the side. Mike looked on with his head cocked in interest.

With shouts and gestures, Lester encouraged her to climb up to the deck, and with a final command of, "Leave it!" she dropped the anchor noisily on the deck, then carefully worked her way back down. She panted and hooted as the whole group praised and tickled her. Mike jumped in the middle with an open play face.

Savage smiled. "When you have two of the smartest chimps in the world and the greatest trainer who ever lived in your midst, you might as well use them. Well done, you guys! Now if you'll watch our belongings and most importantly the dinghy as we're running out of them—let's get to work."

The mentioning of the dinghy put them all back in a somber mood. They knew the creatures belonging to the footprints had moved it in the night, and if they hadn't had a second one on the ship, they'd be facing a long swim back through waters that they didn't want to have to test for sharks and unknown currents.

"I wonder if whoever or whatever took our dinghy had planned to cut us off from our ship?" Consuelo wondered aloud.

"I think we took a hell of a risk last night by not returning to the safety of the ship," Ken said. "While I'm reluctant to split us up, I'm thinking we'd be best served if Lester, Girlie, Mike, Mark and Consuelo returned to the ship, kept in radio contact and made sure our ride home is safe." Ken looked out at their vessel swinging on her anchor in the relative calm of the leeward side of the nearest island that sheltered the cove. "I don't like leaving our ship attended by just GuGu and that Spaniard."

Mark shook his head, visibly upset. "But you may need me here in case of trouble!"

"You, young man, happen to be the best sailor in our lot. I don't want anything to happen to the ship or you. That ship not only is, as I said, our only way home but also our contact with the world outside and our food cupboard."

"But ..."

"No more of this. It's getting late."

The group set to work on making a rope ladder to scale the ship. Several times more, they relied on Girlie's climbing skills to bring ropes up to them. Mike picked up the idea quickly and joined in.

Ken was emphatic about having a safe and secure exit off the vessel before they searched it so it was afternoon before they were rigged to his liking. Once satisfied with their work, he sent Mark and company back to camp to make ready to return to the mother ship while the rest began the strenuous climb up the makeshift rope ladder to the tilted main deck above.

Savage was the first board the wreck, and with his first step, nearly fell through the rotted planks of the main deck. Even teak didn't weather well when left uncared for in the tropics. The ribs of the iron hull had fared a little better—at least they supported him when he stepped from one to the other. One by one they made their way up the ladder.

They slowly worked their way around the vessel, stepping gingerly as they searched for clues that would reveal her identity and what had happened to her. It was a slow and dangerous process. They found Bobby's small and light frame indispensable in working in the especially tight openings or crossing rotted decking. They tied ropes around their waists and to each other, much like mountaineers.

Or as Bobby complained after coming out of an especially tight spot, "… more like spelunkers."

CHAPTER 24

Mark and Consuelo worked hard, packing the small dinghy with what the team no longer needed and prepared to leave with the first load. Mark grinned nervously back at Lester. "We'll be right back for you if I don't sink this damn thing in the breakers."

The little engine roared to life as Consuelo held the dinghy pointed into the foam of the surf. Mark ran them expertly through the surf, only once nearly pitching it over in a breaking wave at the back of the surf line.

Lester thought how Mark and Consuelo had been a great choice to bring along with their youth and handy skills. He thought they made a handsome couple, as well. Obviously, this adventure was drawing them closer together. Memories of how he and Karen had been when they were young settled on him like a dark cloud. He quickly forced his thoughts back to the business at hand.

He watched Girlie and Mike as they lay resting in nests of leaves they'd each meticulously made. Lester had told Mark to take his time as he wanted to wait until everyone came back from the investigation of the wreck before he left the beach and the rest of their belongings unguarded. As he waited and watched in the heat, he grew tired and nodded off. He awoke to the sounds of Girlie and Mike pacing around the camp, softly hooting and whimpering.

He looked at Girlie. "What's wrong, girl?"

Girlie ran behind him as though trying to hide. She placed one hand on his shoulder, clumsily swung her other in the direction of the trees and pointed. Her lips trumpeted a soft hoot—the classic trumpet hoot used by chimpanzees to alert danger. Girlie was afraid.

Suddenly Mike flared up, making a loud trumpet hoot, and charged into the trees.

CHAPTER 25

"There's a way in through here." Bobby's head popped up from a jagged hole in the deck. "It looks like we can get further into the ship if we climb down this way". Bobby disappeared but his voice echoed from below. "Come on!"

The group pushed on deeper into the wreck, carefully working their way below decks, following Bobby's lead. The roar of the breaking surf as it boomed through hollow ship told them the tide was coming in again. It grew louder as they worked their way to what had once been the lower decks. The smell of rust and decay filled their nostrils. Sea birds had made their nests in the shelter of the wreck, leaving the stench of guano.

Bobby stopped to re-pump the Coleman lantern to brightness. Its hiss was reassuring as they left the sunlight above, feeling like miners delving deep into the bowels of an unknown shaft.

Ken judged from the coolness that they were well below the level of the sand. He broke the silence: "The elements are swallowing this ship whole. In a few more years, she'll be completely buried from view."

"As long as we're not buried with it—it feels more like a tomb than a wreck." Bobby held the lantern up above his head, looking back at the rest of them, and paused longer than usual. "The ship seems in better shape down here below the waterline or whatever it is."

Before too long they stumbled onto the remnants of a broken and ajar door that opened into what looked to be an officer's cabin. Bobby was the first to peer in, holding the lantern out ahead of him. Shadows danced off the crusty walls. Water dripped from above, hissing off the lantern.

"This looks like it might be the captain's cabin." Bobby held the lantern closer to what had once been the cabin door. He picked up a corroded brass plate and wiped the salt and green with his thumb as the others crowded around for a closer look. They could just make out what they thought to be a Russian name and a coat of arms.

Bobby pulled out a small notebook from his jeans and held it next to the plate. "Bring the light closer." He paused, reading and comparing his notes to the engraving on the plate. "This ship," he said, looking around at his friends, "is the *Orion,* and we are standing in the captain's cabin."

"Right," Savage said, "that's confirmed it. As much as I think we should get out of here before the tide floods the lower decks, we need to stay a little longer and take a look below".

Ken nodded toward the darkness down the long passageway. "After you".

A dread fell over them as they worked their way deeper and down a rusting ladder into the darkness below. They could just hear the muffled concussions as the rising tide pounded the ship's hull. The decks below had been less disturbed by the elements and the passing of time. They stepped over and around debris that had been scattered in the ship's last struggle. The lantern set their shadows dancing against the confines of this dark and lonely coffin.

Bobby stepped forward and tentatively led the group, pausing here and there to get his bearings and then gingerly moving on. It was slow going, picking their way through the piles of wreckage. He paused for an unusually long time, holding the lantern ahead of him and looking downward. "This looks like the way down to the engine room and cargo storage compartments. My guess is that we'll find the lowest level of the ship down there." Bobby turned toward the rest of the group, holding the light so they could all see each other clearly. "Something's not right. Have you noticed it?"

"Besides us being in a decaying wreck where one wrong step could send us plunging to our death or where the rising tide could trap and drown us— no, I don't find anything abnormal, Bobby." The rest of the group laughed nervously, affirming that Savage was voicing their thoughts exactly. Savage didn't laugh.

"Skeletons, Fred, the remains of the dead." Where are they? This ship must've been manned by say forty officers and merchant seamen, at least. Not to mention the passengers we think they had on board. I can't believe they all made it out." Bobby's shadow danced in the light against the ceiling.

Ken nudged Bobby. "Let's get below before we have the tide and waves to fight. It was hard enough to get on this ship without that, and we won't have Girlie and Mike to fetch us things when we have to climb off."

Hunt pulled a small flashlight from his pocket and shone it down the passageway before them. "I don't relish the thought of drowning down here in this cavern. Let's get on with it. I've been saving this for a rainy day."

"Anyone else have any treasures before we head down?" Bobby leaned on the first step of the ladder that led down into the darkness.

Hunt stepped forward and helped illuminate their way down. Below, they saw a larger gallery where several passageways headed in different directions. As they made their way down the ladder, they felt the whole ship shudder followed by a muffled boom.

"What the hell was that?" Bobby almost dropped the lantern.

"My guess is the tide is gaining on the ship. Let's see what there is to see and get the hell out of here. There's always tomorrow."

"I hope," Bobby said.

233

After several false starts they made their way into a large gallery. Huge wooden crates lay strewn and splintered asunder as though they'd been smashed in haste. At the far side of the cabin, they could just make out what was left of several large, steel-barred cages that had been torn and twisted open.

Ken kneeled next to one of the biggest cages. Its door was twisted off at the hinges. "Over here, gentlemen," he called to the rest.

The found him examining what looked to be a large lower jawbone. Bobby held the lantern where they could all get a closer look. They stood in silence, each caught in their thoughts as they stared at what Ken held in his hands.

As though lecturing in a university hall, he held the jaw in front of them, pointing at it as he spoke, "You'll notice that we have a hominid-like lower mandible with ape-like dentition. Particularly notice that the incisors are similar to what we'd find in a great ape such as a chimpanzee, while the jaw structure is not as robust as we'd expect—my friends, colleagues, I hold in my hand the find of the century."

"And I'd guess that radiocarbon dating would place it in the present," Savage said.

"I'll say it again. Don't you find it odd that there are no other remains in this whole ship?" Bobby emphasized "remains" by drawing it out. "I mean, we've been at this most of the day, and this is the only artifact that we've found, if that's the right word for that thing you're holding, but who or what twisted the hinges off that steel door?"

"I have to admit this place seems picked pretty clean," Ken said. "In fact, it seems that much of what I would've expected to be on this ship, especially way down here where it's more protected from the elements is not here. It almost seems that all the useful items have been removed—salvaged."

Everyone looked nervously around them. They stood in the area of the ship where cargo would've been stowed, but it appeared that the area had been converted to accommodate the transporting of live animals. Several large steel cages were bolted to the back walls. Cargo crates lay broken open, tables were turned over and smashed, and the debris of what had once been a floating laboratory covered the room.

They couldn't tell if all this wreckage been caused by the grounding of the ship or by some kind of salvage. Their feet crunched broken glass as they moved about. The whole gallery looked to be ransacked. A musky smell mixed with the dampness.

The hull shook with greater force and echoed with the reverberation of the pounding waves. In the darkness, illuminated only by the glow of Bobby's lantern and the piercing of Hunt's flashlight, it felt as though they were trapped in a huge drum that was being pounded on by some giant unknown hand, and the pounding grew louder.

The team worked bravely and diligently in the last hours in the depths of the ship, searching for more evidence of what had happened to the ship and its contents. The lack of light and slippery rubble hampered them, but they were intent on searching and not leaving.

Finally, when they couldn't stand the fatigue and strain of being there any longer, Ken pulled them from their search, his voice echoing with the rhythm of the pounding surf. "We've done enough down here. Let's get topside."

"Hold on!" They could tell Hunt was excited by the pitch of his voice, though they couldn't see his face in the shadows. "I've got something." The group closed in around him as he knelt in the shadows wiping the splintered deck with his handkerchief. They squeezed in for a closer look as he blew the sand away between wipes to reveal two rows of carvings. He motioned to Bobby to bring his lantern closer. "Someone or something has carved this," he whispered tracing his finger over the deep grooves and continued, "two lines above six."

Savage kneeled and said, "The same as in Danny's cage."

"The same...," Bobby's voice trailed off to the join the silence of the others. Only the soft stream of the lantern could be heard until the hull shook with an incoming wave.

Ken broke the spell and said, "As I said, it's time to get topside."

CHAPTER 26

They stood in shock, speechless. The beach was deserted and their camp demolished. The sand was plowed up in disarray with equipment strewn all over. The group gazed out to an empty bay. The *Si Como No* was gone.

Savage knelt by what was left of the smoldering campfire. "I can't make out much here. Whoever or whatever attacked the camp trampled any tracks that might give us a clue."

"Here's something!" Bobby stood holding a wristwatch at the edge of the jungle near where the trail began. "This is Lester's, and it looks like it was torn off in a struggle." The leather band was broken at the basal, the clasp still intact. "Karen gave it to him; see there's an inscription."

Savage took the watch from Bobby; holding it in the light, he read, "To Lester on our first wedding anniversary, to the best husband and chimp trainer in the world, your loving wife, Karen, Berlin, 1938."

The group stood in silence, gazing up the trail. Bobby hastily pocketed the watch. "I'll keep this until we see him again—and the others."

We're going in there." Ken pointed up the trail. "We have to find them." His jaw was set, accenting his chiseled features. "We're going to find them if it's the last thing we do." He began picking up what was left of their things. "Salvage what you can. We'll probably not be returning here."

They found to their relief, that while most of the equipment had been thrown around, it had not actually been damaged. They were surprised that only a few cans and packets had been broken open. But they were disturbed by how they'd been opened.

"How much force do you think it takes to do this?" Savage held the two halves of a can of peaches. Syrup and fruit dripped out from the bottom of the halves covering the jagged metal edges where it had either been bitten or torn in half. Everyone looked nervously around.

"From now on everyone stays close together. Is that understood?" Ken stared at Bobby.

"Then let's get going," Bobby said, anxious to head out.

Ken was struck again by how much courage and heart filled this little man. He was a lion trapped in a little person's body.

The group started down the path. Bobby and Savage led the way with the rest loosely taking up the rear. They glanced from side to side as they entered the twilight world that existed under the canopy of the jungle even at mid-day.

The trail followed a stream that wound its way through the jungle. They found themselves crossing it occasionally, which slowed their progress as they had to pick their way across slippery rocks. They remained especially alert at these shallow crossings where the stream widened and quieted, making it possible for them to hear muffled stirrings coming out of the darkness around them. They had the feeling they were being watched. Soon they needed flashlights to make their way and weren't sure if day was passing to night or if they were being closed off from the world of light the deeper they went into the jungle. They became hypersensitive to the moment, losing track of time passing, as though they'd entered some kind of limbo.

Their pace slowed as the trail narrowed and became tangled with vines. They could feel the path changing from sand to a damper, spongier floor mixed with dead vegetation. It became more difficult to push on as the trees and vines seemed to close in around them. The occasional sound of someone in the group stumbling and cursing broke the silence.

Several times upon stopping for a short rest, Ken thought he heard footsteps and stirrings behind them in the darkness. Sometimes the sound continued for a few steps and then stopped abruptly as though someone or something had realized they'd stopped.

"Did you hear that?" Hunt whispered.

"Shh! You'll frighten the others." Ken peered into the darkness. "There's nothing we can do right now but to continue on and be ready."

"Ready for what I wonder." Hunt pushed ahead of Ken who stood listening as the others picked their way down the trail.

The air was damp and humid, stifling, and the insects ruthless in their feeding. After what seemed to be an hour without a word, the group stopped in unison, exhausted.

"Christ! This is insane." Bobby's high-pitched voice sounded even higher than usual. "I can't see a damn thing. I don't want to step on a snake or worse."

"It's the 'worse' I'm worried about," Savage said in a strained voice.

"Let's light the lanterns," Bobby yelled to no one in particular.

He lit one, then immediately shut it off. Huge moths and other flying insects drawn to the light pelted them like stones, almost knocking Bobby over. Worse, they sensed something even larger lurking around them just outside the pale light.

Bobby repacked his lantern, mumbling, "This is no good. Let's try a flashlight and keep going. I have no desire to spend the night in here."

The commotion caused by the insects must have carried well into the jungle as it stirred what sounded like the hoots and displays of a very large troop of chimpanzees, though they couldn't see far enough into the darkness to be sure. Branches broke all around them, and they sensed a number of bodies moving through the treetops. The group froze when they heard a deeper set of cries drown out everything else. The cries grew louder, seeming to close in on them, and then they faded, leaving only the sounds of the jungle.

"Christ! I didn't like the sound of that. I think we'd better move a little more stealthily before we disturb something more than apes," Ken said as he worked his way up to Bobby and Savage.

"I think we may have already." Savage reached into his pack and pulled out a machete.

"Do you think those were chimps?" Bobby asked.

"I hope so," Ken replied. "At least the first cries sounded like chimps. Now let's keep moving and remember—stay together." He strode on, swinging his flashlight in the darkness.

The rest of the group stirred to life, as though waking from a dream, and quickly followed its dim light, which didn't seem to attract the larger insects. But they were reluctant to use their flashlights, just the same.

They kept at it for what seemed like hours. It felt as though they were sleepwalking in a very bad dream. Just when they thought they couldn't take another step, patches of sunlight streaming down through breaks in the canopy encouraged them onwards. It appeared that the trees were thinning. Up ahead, but out of sight, what sounded like a very large waterfall roared, and a cool mist drifted down the trail, giving them some relief in their efforts. As their eyes adjusted to the growing light, they were able to see that the path had widened and several trails routed off in different directions. After some discussion, the group stuck to what appeared to be the most worn route and cautiously continued toward the roar.

Bobby was the first to step out from under the canopy into the bright light of day. The group stood blinking as they took in their surroundings. A giant waterfall plunged deep into a valley in front of them. Its cataracts billowed up clouds of cooling mist which blew across the rocky clearing where they stood. The group drank in the fresh moving air. A steep footpath climbed up to a jagged ridge that towered high above them. They could just make out faint traces of it as it skirted along the edge of the steep gorge.

Ken pointed up toward the ridge. "Let's follow this path up to the top. It should give us a good vantage to get our bearings."

"I wonder who or what made this path," Hunt mused.

"Hunt's right. Keep your eyes and ears open." Ken looked back to the opening in the jungle from where they'd just come, half expecting to finally see who or what was following them.

Just as they turned to begin their climb, a huge chorus of piercing cries rose up out the jungle, sending a massive flock of birds into flight above the canopy. The whole jungle came alive with the calls and cries of its inhabitants. The group stood listening and looking back in the direction from which they'd come.

"I've spent the better part of my adult life in jungles like these," Savage said, almost shouting above the racket, "and I've never heard or seen anything remotely like this."

"Me neither." Without hesitating Ken turned and started up the path.

They found the track hard going after their exertion in the jungle. The afternoon sun beat down mercilessly. From time to time, Savage stopped and knelt, followed by the rest, and cupped sips of water from small pools that collected in the rocks from the overspray of the falls. "Don't forget to fill your drinking bottles and keep an eye out for any tracks or signs. It's going to be hard with all these rocks."

As Hunt put the cap back on his water bottle, a reflection caught his eye. Something shiny lay just next to the small pool of water. He picked it up and called to the others, "Just when I thought we were on a wild goose chase." He held up a gold ring with a small emerald.

"This is Consuelo's," Ken said. "She always wears it." The group gathered around him for a closer look. "Her mother gave it to her on her Quinceanera. I think, gentlemen, this was not

241

lost but left here for us to find—to let us know that they'd come this way."

"So, we have clues that may account for Lester and Mark," Savage said as he gazed up the trail.

"I'll take this as a sign that they're all together including Mike and Girlie and unharmed because I can't bear to think of it any other way," Bobby said as he busied himself repacking his gear. He pointed at the ridge above them. "We need to get up there where we can get a better idea where this path leads."

"Okay," Ken said, "we've been at it for a good hour and it doesn't look any closer, but we've gained some altitude. Take a look below." They guessed they'd climbed at least five-hundred feet above the clearing. The endless green of the treetops swelled out around them.

The waterfall they'd discovered formed part of a ribbon of water that wound its way through the jungle toward the sea. From where they stood they could see that the trail they'd followed through the jungle ran along this river. And better, the ridge they were climbing gave them a panorama of the lay of the land, a view that would only get better as they gained elevation.

The wind blew cooler as they struggled up the rocky backbone toward the summit. The rocks got looser and the hill steeper the higher they walked. With a final push to the top that sapped what was left of their waning energy, they fell together on their backs, panting and looking up at the harsh tropical sky. No one spoke for a while, including Bobby.

Ken leaned over the outcropping. "Anyone still have their binoculars?" He could make out a clearing and what looked to be a cluster of shacks far below. A tendril of smoke rose out of the clearing. Bobby handed him his binoculars, and Ken spoke as he scanned the valley and the clearing: "There's men outside several of the shacks. A small fire looks to be used for cooking. There's an iron pot hanging above it. Hold on ..."

"What? What do you see?" Bobby reached for the binoculars.

"Damn it, Bobby! You're bouncing me around." Ken elbowed Bobby.

Savage put his hand on Bobby's shoulder and pulled him back.

"Two men in khakis are taking plates to the large building." Ken peered through the glasses for several minutes, then handed them to Savage. "They look like some kind of soldiers."

"Any signs of our people or …?" Savage asked as he raised the glasses.

"No."

"I think we should wait up here awhile." Savage continued to scan the area. "I don't like the look of things down there." He froze for a moment and focused for a closer look at two flags draping from a makeshift pole in front of one of the buildings. One was Soviet and other was the same flag that had been in the photograph Bobby had sent them—the photograph that had brought them to this lonely part of Africa. It seemed so long ago that they'd studied the contents of that packet in the relative safety of the compound—ages ago.

"I agree. As anxious as I am, I think we should wait until dark to make our next move," Hunt said as he tried to arrange his pack on a rock to lean his head against.

"Okay, but let's try and get some rest before evening." Savage lay down next to Hunt.

They made themselves as comfortable as possible and shared food and drink. They set up a watch rotation and rested for the first time since they'd left the wreck on the beach. The strain and exertion of the day made it easy for sleep to silently ambush them as the tropical twilight faded to the darkness.

They stirred to the sharp cries of a troop of macaques. The moon lit the evening with a glow so bright that they cast shadows as they moved around. Except for a few lights that flickered from the buildings below and the smell of wood fires, they couldn't see or hear another sign of life in the compound. They grew anxious for their friends.

"This whole thing doesn't make sense," Ken said, looking through the binoculars. "I think they were taken captive or we would've found them dead or left for dead right on the beach." He put the binoculars down. He'd kept watch while the rest napped, and now his skin had a waxy hue and dark rings had settled under his eyes.

"You need to get some rest. Here, give me those." Hunt took the glasses. "If anything has happened to Lester—or any of them ..." He continued the watch while the others shared what food they had with Ken.

"I think we should work our way down there for a closer look," Hunt whispered after a while. "We can't stay here forever, and I don't fancy sitting on the outcropping waiting for company. We've been lucky so far."

The group argued as to what course to take, but no matter how they dissected it, they came down to the same decision. They'd have to go down to the clearing below to have a chance of finding their friends. So, finally, too tired to discuss it any further, they gathered what little supplies they had left and started down a trail that seemed to head in the right direction. They spoke only in whispers as they snaked their way as quietly as they could along the winding path, ducking under the thick under growth that covered the trail. They soon realized that they'd picked a little-used path off the ridge. Before long, it was hard to find their way, and they had to push themselves through waist-high grasses, making more noise than they wished.

Finally, they knelt in the bushes at the edge of the clearing near a bamboo wall. In the moonlight through several gaps, they could make out that most of the camp was in disrepair, and many of the buildings looked to be abandoned.

The jungle hemmed in around the cluster of rough, wooden buildings with tin roofs set in the middle of a red-clay clearing. Jungle vines covered several of the buildings, and in some places, trees grew out of holes in the roofs. A few of the buildings closest to the path they'd come down still seemed inhabited. Music drifted across the clearing, apparently from a radio as there was as much static as music.

"Brahms in the Jungle from what I can hear." Ken crouched at the edge of the clearing. The others huddled in behind him, trying to get a better view into the window of the shack nearest them. The place seemed to be coming to life. Small groups of soldiers loitered, smoking cigarettes on the porches of several of the shacks. Occasionally, a small group walked across the clearing from one building to another. The aroma of the kitchen distracted them and reminded them of how long it'd been since they'd had a real meal.

"Do you smell that cooking? God, I'm hungry," Savage whispered to Bobby. "I can't remember the last time I had a real sit-down dinner."

"Three days ago, on board the *Si Como No*," Bobby said. "I smell garlic and maybe onions—what do you think, Fred?" He smiled at Savage.

The shadowy forms of two soldiers passed close to the wall they were hiding behind, stifling their musings before Savage could reply.

"This isn't working," Bobby said when the men had passed. "We need to get closer." Before anyone could react, he popped up, scrambled up a tree, and dropped down an overhanging limb, and sprinted across the open ground to the corner of the closest building.

They watched him inch his way toward the open window where the music was playing. Occasionally, the light streaming out was blocked by what they supposed were people moving. The rattle of glasses and occasionally the sound of laughter came from inside. Someone began singing out of tune to the music, followed by more laughter and mock applause. Bobby finally reached the window and ducked just below the sill.

Savage could no longer stand it. "I can't wait here while the smallest one of us does the biggest job. Hell, I study apes, so I guess I can try to climb like one." They watched his awkward struggles up the tree until he disappeared into the branches. A few minutes later he dropped with a dull thud. He knelt looking from side to side before sprinting toward Bobby in a weaving fashion, trying to stay out of the patches of light that streamed from several of the buildings. Ken and Hunt looked at each other momentary and followed at a slower pace.

"Careful, keep low," Savage whispered.

"Christ! You scared the bajesus out of me!" Bobby pulled Savage down below the windowsill. "Sh-h-h-h-h-h! Let's try to get a look inside."

"Careful." Savage moved in unison with Bobby toward the opening of the window. The squeak from an opening door startled them, and footsteps came down the wooden steps on the other side of the building. They froze in the darkness. Two men turned the corner of the building and walked right toward where they hid, pausing in the darkness a few feet away to light cigarettes. It sounded as if they were arguing though neither Bobby nor Savage could understand what they were saying. The men were so engrossed in their argument that they didn't seem to notice them glued against the building in the darkness, barely breathing and only a few feet away.

The two men finally continued walking toward what looked to be a large warehouse in the center of the compound. They almost brushed Bobby as they passed by.

Bobby sighed and was just about to whisper when a shrill chorus of ungodly cries broke the stillness of the evening. The two men's shouts mixed with the cries as they entered the warehouse. "*Allez. Allez!*"

Ken had never heard anything like it. While ape-like, the strange and unsettling cries didn't match any species he could identify. They rose in intensity, piercing and prolonged, and were finally muffled when the two men closed the door behind them.

"Come on! We've got to get a closer look, Fred." Bobby left the darkness by the building and ran, as fast as his hunched little body would permit, across the clearing towards the building.

But before Savage could follow, a bell clanged. It sounded like an alarm being franticly rung by hand. Lanterns lit up in several of the shacks and men streamed out from all directions, their boots treading across the wooden porches and steps toward them. The shrill, ungodly screams drowned out their shouts. Bobby suddenly found himself surrounded by uniformed soldiers pointing rifles. Savage was pushed toward Bobby and could just make out Hunt and Ken's forms being escorted in the same direction.

A small, stocky man walked toward them, awkwardly trying to button his military tunic with one arm. A sharply creased empty sleeve was neatly pinned where his other arm should have been. He paused, taking in the scene before him, seemingly ignoring Ken and his group for the moment. He turned and said something to one of his men, inaudible because of the screams. The man saluted and quickly ran off toward the building. The stocky man looked at Ken, yelled something in French, then smiled and, meeting his eyes, said, "I just want them to stop that infernal racket."

CHAPTER 27

"Christ! Did you hear those screams?" Mark peered through the crack of a shuttered window in the shed they'd been unceremoniously thrown into after their capture. They didn't know how long they'd been locked up without food or water, and the shutter on the window made the heat unbearable. The only hint of fresh air whiffed through rusted iron bars above the door.

"Do you see any of our people or Girlie?" Lester winced in pain as he struggled to get up from a makeshift cot in the corner. Consuelo steadied him to his feet. He looked old and wasted. He'd suffered the most from their ordeal of being captured. But both Mark and Consuelo suspected his concern for Girlie was weighing on him the most.

"No—I can't make anything out. It's too dark out there." The cries subsided as Mark tried to pull himself up onto the windowsill to look through a wider crack to get a better view. He winced as excruciating pain rose up the back of his head to greet his eyes. It'd been stupid, he thought, to put up a fight with a whole platoon of soldiers. After their captors had run the creatures off, they'd been thoroughly searched and bound.

When Mark had attempted to intervene and stop a soldier from frisking Consuelo, he'd received a blow from his rifle butt. They'd been forced down the trail, marching for hours. Several times as they made their way into the jungle they'd been attacked by what he thought were the same creatures from the beach. He found it odd that none of the soldiers had actually shot to kill. They seemed more intent on scaring the animals off than actually harming them.

"That bastard really hurt you! What'd you think was going on?" Lester gingerly tried to stand on his own and walk. They'd all been roughed up during their capture on the beach.

"I don't know, but it sounded like all hell was breaking loose out there—did you hear those cries?" Mark dropped down from the windowsill, massaging his head.

"They reminded me of Oliver a little." Lester slowly made his way toward the window with Consuelo walking close by him. "They had the same high-pitched screech that Oliver used to make when he was excited ... more like birds than chimps."

"Or human screams. I don't ... you saw those things on the beach ..." Consuelo frowned as she tried to look out from behind the men. She rubbed the bruises on her small wrists. The soldier who'd searched her had bound her wrists so tightly that she'd screamed.

After the ruckus with Mark, another soldier, obviously his superior, had given some curt orders in French, and the man sullenly loosened the ropes. This had given her the opportunity to slip one of her hands free during their march through the forest. She wondered if she'd ever see her ring again; she hoped her friends would find it when they came to rescue them. *Would they come?* "We've got to get out of here and find the others. Who do you think these people are?" Consuelo put her hand on Mark's shoulder.

"Belgians, Russians and Congolese, mainly."

The sound of jingling at the door made them turn. A stout little man in a khaki uniform stood there with a large ring of keys. He tried each one, attempting to open the lock on the bars, but the fact that he was missing an arm hampered his progress. "Sorry, I make a better soldier than a jailer." He looked at Consuelo and smiled. "Would you mind helping me, mademoiselle?"

Consuelo hesitated, looking back at Mark and Lester for a moment.

The soldier seemed to grasp their hesitation. "Please, I mean you no harm. I'm just not very good at anything that requires dexterity as you can see. We know who you and your friends are. We've had a chance to board your ship, the *Si Como No*, I believe you call it? Your guides seemed in a hurry to leave, but we'll interview them."

Mark nodded and motioned Consuelo toward the door. The man smiled and nonchalantly handed her the keys. Still rubbing his head, Mark wondered if this was the old good cop/bad cop routine or some other kind of trick.

Consuelo opened the door after a few tries. The man rolled his one arm out in front of him and exclaimed, "*Voila!*" Casually taking the keys back, he continued, "Now, if you will all follow me, I'll make sure you have the opportunity to freshen up before dinner and meet some people you will mostly be glad to see."

The man started out, turning his back to them as he led the way down a long hallway that had barred doors to either side. His whole manner was casual with little concern to the possibility that they might all bolt on the spot. Somehow, they didn't feel threatened by him. It was so different from how they'd been treated on the beach and on their way through the jungle.

Except for the missing arm, they were all struck by how much he looked like one of the soldiers in the photographs that Bobby had found in Mexico. He looked to be in his mid-sixties, though it was hard to be sure. He walked with the spring of a man much younger and showed the weathered, olive skin of someone who'd spent years in the tropical sun. A military service revolver hung low from his left waist, carelessly bouncing with his step.

They followed hesitantly down a hallway without a word, casting questioning looks at each other, and stepped out into the tropical night onto a veranda that wrapped around the building. They followed the man across the clearing toward what looked to be an open dining patio coarsely covered with weathered corrugated metal overgrown with flowering vines. Kerosene lanterns softly lit the tables, illuminating the silhouettes of small groups of diners. The strange cries had subsided, and all was quiet except for the stirrings of the jungle that surrounded them.

Mark, Consuelo and Lester drank in the outside air. In a confusing turn of events, it seemed they'd been promoted from prisoners to guests. Mark was contemplating what action they should take next, when he caught sight of the rest of their company. They sat lounging with coffee as though they were on vacation. He yelled in delight, "Bobby!"

Bobby jumped up, his high-pitched voice setting off some caged birds on display in the dinning patio. "I didn't think we'd ever see you guys again!" He ran over to them, knocking over a chair. Two guards stood on alert, but their escort motioned them off. He remained in the background observing closely.

Ken followed and the rest ran forward. They huddled together in an embrace; no one moved or spoke for a long and delicious moment.

Savage broke the silence. "What the hell happened to you guys? We'd almost given you up for dead."

"Well, you guys don't look so good yourself." Mark paused, looking them over, struck by how tired and battered they all looked. "I can't really say exactly what happened; it was all so fast. We'd just returned to the beach, and all hell was breaking loose."

Soldiers handed them steaming cups of coffee which they took gratefully, then wandered over to the tables and sat down.

"Girlie, saw them first," Lester said, "so we weren't caught completely by surprise."

"Saw whom?" Ken asked.

"The creatures, of course. I hate to think what would've happened ..." Lester pointed at the guards, "if these guys hadn't

251

shown up." He frowned at their newfound host. "Though I didn't much care for how we were treated afterwards."

"Were they …?" Savage asked.

"Yes," Mark replied. "Though we only got a glimpse of them, fortunately."

"They were huge," Lester said, "at least six feet tall. They stepped right out of the jungle and had us backed up against the water. There were six or seven of them. Girlie went wild. I think she threw them off for a moment. They just stood there, and I mean stood, erect and straight, staring at us."

"While all of us just stood there frozen with fear, Mike charged right into the middle of them. That seemed to throw them into confusion and gave us a chance to make for the dinghy and get some distance from them," Consuelo said.

"If it hadn't been for the chimps delaying them, we wouldn't have stood a chance," Mark added.

"So, you guys don't have them?" Lester asked with concern. "I just assumed—"

"No," Ken interrupted. "We haven't seen any signs of them—though we did hear what we think were chimps in the jungle."

"The last we saw of them," Mark said, "they were in the trees with some of those monsters climbing up after them. From what I could see, they definitely had the advantage of being more agile at climbing."

"They forgot about us in the confusion, but not for long. That's when the cavalry arrived." Lester nodded at their escort and the guards.

The little one-armed man finally joined them at the table. "We'd been watching you since your ship dropped anchor. We were unsure of your intentions, so we—how should I say?—waited and watched. That's until your welcoming party showed up on the beach.

"We'd been following that troop of devils for some time; lucky for you that we had—or we wouldn't have been there. We don't often get so far from home." He became thoughtful and quiet for a moment. "But now I think it's time for some introductions—and from *you*, some explanations—we don't often get visitors way out here. Allow me to introduce myself, Major Jean Francoise at your service." Their host executed a slight but precise bow. The empty sleeve of his tunic dipped out in front of him slightly, and he absently straightened it. His thin brown hair was waxed and neatly combed from the side to cover the tanned flesh of his balding head. His forehead and eyes had wrinkles that hinted that he was used to smiling a lot.

Ken faced Francoise. "First, may I inquire ... are we your prisoners?"

Francois reached out and lightly touched Ken's upper arm. "I apologize for holding you in such a manner. After we paid a visit to your beautiful vessel ..."

Ken and Savage stiffened and glanced at each other at the mention of the *Si Como No*.

"Please don't be concerned about the welfare of your ship. It is safe and under our care. That was a big chance you took, leaving her in these waters with such unsavory characters as guides—but I can understand the circumstances." Francois bowed his head to Consuelo. "Ah, but I digress. We now realize that the famous primatologist Dr. Kenneth Turner and his equally noted colleague Dr. Fred Savage and company are our guests. You're, of course, free to come and go as you please—*after* we clear up why you've paid us the honor of a visit." Francoise looked out at the jungle. "I wouldn't recommend coming or going just yet. The jungle is full of surprises at night."

Ken noticed a slight change in the tone of Francois' voice when he alluded to the purpose of their visit. He'd been almost too casual, so Ken decided to keep their purpose to themselves for the present and try to divert the conversation. "For now, we'd be pleased if you would help us find Girlie and Mike, our chimps. We seemed to have left them on the beach in all the confusion."

Francois smiled knowingly. "But of course! Tomorrow we'll take a fieldtrip into the jungle—after a tour of our little facility."

He stood and motioned everyone to follow. "Now let's get you all settled in and some dinner in your stomachs."

CHAPTER 28

They rose early the next morning, driven to find Mike and Girlie, even though they'd not recovered from the events of the last few days. They squinted against the morning sun as they stepped out of their quarters. A small group of soldiers stood before them, making ready for a patrol.

The age of the soldiers' equipment surprised Mark, especially the weapons. Many of the soldiers carried Pre-WWII Tommy Guns, while the officers were equipped with .45 Caliber Colt service revolvers holstered in brown leather that snapped over. Once again it reminded him of the photographs Bobby had brought back from Mexico. After all their research, everything about their new surroundings seemed familiar.

The whole demeanor of their captors had evolved to that of hosts. The soldiers basically ignored them now. They discovered that they had the freedom of the compound, or at least parts of it; they were stopped at the large tin building from which they'd heard the cries from the night before. The guards had been polite but firm, silently stepping in front of them, thus blocking their entry. They gestured them back toward the soldiers in the main staging area.

Bobby said under his breath, "We need to get inside that building before we make our escape."

"And how do you propose we're going to escape?" Ken asked, surveying the twelve-foot-high fence weaved into what looked to be an impenetrable jungle surrounding the clearing.

"By the looks of things around here, they must make trips to resupply and what not. They must have a route and a means out." Bobby looked up a wide, sandy trail that led out from a gate that swung from a guard tower.

"Let's concentrate on finding Mike and Girlie for now," Lester said. "This is these guys territory, and I say we work with them until we get them back safely."

Bobby nodded in agreement.

Finally, they headed out. One moment the soldiers were joking and milling around as they packed gear and loaded their weapons and the next they flicked their cigarettes, packed up, and filed out a trail similar to the one on which the group had arrived. The soldiers paid little attention to them, seeming more intent on the work at hand. The jungle swallowed them almost immediately as they marched down a meandering trail that seemed to follow the river above the falls and mountains they'd so meticulously climbed.

"We must be headed to the headwaters of the same river we followed when we left the beach but on a lower route," Bobby observed.

"That's right. You have a good sense of direction, Bobby." Francois had dropped back from the lead and joined their group, which was lagging behind. They were not used to marching at the rate the soldiers had set.

"Why are we headed up river? Isn't that the opposite direction from where we last saw our chimps?" Ken asked.

"I have something to show you first." Francois said something in French to one of the guards who nodded and ran up the line.

Hunt panted. "God, he's like the Roadrunner."

"Or Wily the Coyote." Bobby frowned.

The terrain was varied and the trees not as thick in this part of the jungle. The going was easier than the day before, which was good since they were still tired from the exertion and strain of the events that had brought them to this part of the world.

Though unspoken between them, they understood that there'd be no attempt to escape until their group was whole again and they'd had a chance to investigate what they'd come for.

They climbed for what seemed hours until they reached a wide-open valley where they could see the gleam of several wide bends in the river as it meandered in its effort to carve a broader path. This open and fertile country contrasted with the closed and dark jungle they'd just negotiated.

They had lunch amongst the ruins of an abandoned village on the sandy banks of the river. Only a few of its grass huts still stood. They pushed on for a short while longer, passing several more settlements in similar states. It puzzled them as the valley was fertile and game plentiful.

This prompted Mark to ask Francois the obvious question: "Where are all the natives? This valley looks like it could sustain several villages and hundreds of people."

Francois tapped his finger to his nose. "You'll get your answer shortly."

They marched on in silence, their curiosity perked.

They moved into the open, spread out, and walked more stealthily, which slowed their progress and made them nervous. The group stopped often to listen and watch. Finally, they cleared a small rise that skirted a line of low-hanging cliffs in front of them. They kept their heads down just behind the rise and surveyed the area with binoculars. A variety of colored layers of sandstone striated the cliffs. Erosion from countless eons had created a honeycomb of caves and catacombs that opened into gaping mouths at ground level. It seemed out of place in this lush-green valley of smooth rolling hills.

Francois laid his binoculars in the grass and tapped Ken, silently getting his attention. Ken took the binoculars and scanned the hills. At first nothing caught his attention except what looked to be the ruins of yet another abandoned village, then he saw something moving at the mouth of one of the caves. He tried to focus but only caught a glimpse of someone or something in the shadows of the overhanging cliffs.

Just as he was about to give up and hand them back, a flock of ibis flushing up from the thickets closer to them drew his attention. He froze at the sight of what appeared to be a small hunting party returning in the direction of the caves.

The creatures were huge. He judged them to be at least six-feet tall, and they walked upright. They reminded him of Danny or the pictures he'd seen of Oliver, only they were much larger. Some carried what looked to be short fabricated clubs made of bone while others were loaded with game.

After some time, Ken handed the glasses to Savage. "Take a look back into the Pleistocene."

The wind shifted in their direction, and they caught the sounds of greeting hoots. The hunting party moved quickly toward the caves, and several other creatures bounded out of the shadows to meet them.

The light was brighter away from the caves, so Savage got a better look. The diversity in sizes and shapes struck him. While some were huge and very hominid-like in structure, others were more chimpanzee-like and walked less upright, but they all seemed to cooperate as a troop, much like any band of primates or aboriginal people. There seemed to be a division of labor, but as far as he could tell, no range in age as they all looked to be adults. At this distance, he couldn't tell if there were both males and females.

"I'd kill to get a closer look," Savage said excitedly.

"I'm afraid that's exactly what you'd have to do under these circumstances," Francois replied quietly.

Savage noticed that the soldiers were very alert and on edge with their weapons ready.

Francois continued, "This is one of two troops that have formed that came over with us and survived the shipwreck. Of course, the other you met on the beach yesterday."

"You've been studying them all these years? These are from the *Orion*?" Ken interrupted, barely containing himself.

"Yes and no," Francois replied gravely. "Only a few escaped

when the captain ran us aground."

"So where did the rest come from?" Mark asked in a tense voice. Consuelo looked on quietly.

Francois stared back at the sacked and abandoned village they'd just left.

Ken followed his eyes and it dawned on him. "Oh, my God, are you saying some of them were fertile and they …?"

Francois nodded. "The few that escaped swept over these villages like wildfire. We were in no position to protect anyone but ourselves at that time. They were killing and breeding machines for a time. Nature abhors a vacuum, but in time a sort of equilibrium or neutrality was reached between them. That is until you showed up. These creatures don't seem to be breeding anymore."

Just as Ken was about to say something, one of the officers of the patrol interrupted by pointing to the clearing. Several large creatures moved purposely in their direction across the field that separated them.

Francois sprang into action. "It's time to move out. Our presence has been detected, and as you can see they're very large, powerful, and smart and we really don't want to kill any more of them; as I said, they're not thriving very well."

The patrol beat a hasty but silent retreat back the way they came. The soldiers were very efficient and professional, covering their retreat with an armed rearguard and posting scouts on their perimeter in typical military fashion as they made for the cover of the jungle.

Ken couldn't get the image of the creatures out of his mind as they marched on, especially the one that had gazed his way. More than the creature's size stuck with him: the human-like proportions; the way it moved with a coordinated grace that was unlike the clumsy gait of any primate he'd ever seen walking upright; its lack of hair, less than a typical great ape, which exposed and accentuated the enormous muscles of its arms and chest. Its thighs reminded him of some of the body builders he'd seen in Venice Beach growing up. But the creature's eyes burnt into his memory the most: savage, almost golden, piercing and cunning. When it'd looked his way, his blood froze, making him fear that its menacing gaze would catch his.

The afternoon was fading into dark when they finally neared the edge of the tree line and struck the trail that headed back to the beach where they'd lost Mike and Girlie.

At last, Ken thought. He felt ashamed that he'd not thought about Girlie and Mike while they'd been off on their adventure.

But instead of continuing to the beach, the patrol turned and kicked their heels for home. He stopped, surprised, and Lester, Bobby, Hunt and Consuelo huddled next to him, all realizing they were about to head in the wrong direction. They were not going to spend another night without attempting to make their group whole.

Francois came up from behind. With a knowing look he said, "You'll find that my men have been busy in our absence. I think you may want to wait here for a few minutes." He walked on.

Ken and the group shared puzzled frowns, wondering if this was some kind of a trick. Just as they were about to turn up the trail that led the other way, to where they'd last seen Mike and Girlie, they heard familiar hoots. Mike and Girlie broke out of the trees and raced to meet them. Two soldiers followed but kept their distance to allow the reunion of old friends in privacy.

After a long embrace, Lester and Girlie walked quietly off toward the compound hand and hand. Both looked worn but determined. Lester's cheeks were salted with tears. He didn't look back or speak.

Mike, on the other hand, made the rounds hugging everyone. He hooted and somersaulted in their midst, receiving applause and laughter as a reward.

Ken stood silently watching Francois walk away, overwhelmed with emotions of relief and gratefulness. At a distance, Francois paused and looked over his shoulder. Ken tapped his heart, closed fisted, in thanks as he nodded to their little one-armed friend. Francois simply waved and turned before fading into the tall grasses of the clearing, following the trail that led to their new home—at least for a while.

Mike stood watching Ken, head cocked quizzical and signed, "Hide-and-seek. Play. Play. Chase."

The spell was broken. They all laughed as Ken replied in both speech and sign language, "God, it's all a game to you, right?"

Mike hooted and stomped, setting the whole forest off in an uproar.

It was late afternoon and they were all tired when they turned towards the compound. The smell of the cooking fires alerted them that they were near before they actually reached the guard gate. The chimps hooted with food-grunts.

They retired to a large dormitory that'd been cleaned out and furnished for them. A corner had been screened off with curtains to give Consuelo some privacy, a bouquet of wild flowers vested in a gourd set at the drawn opening.

Very chivalrous, Mark thought as he looked at the curtained-off area and the bouquet. He smiled. *No, very French.*

A large cage that looked similar to the ones they'd found on the wreck sat adjacent to the building. The fruit and water that had been left in the cage set the chimps off again.

Ken noticed that most of the furniture in their room had been salvaged from the ship or made from flotsam that looked to have been found on the beach. Pointing at a mahogany seaman's locker he observed, "I think we've discovered where all the booty on the *Orion* ended up."

They made their way to an open bathhouse set at the edge of the tree line and came back refreshed and hungry, and savoring the fragrance of dinner cooking.

Bobby lagged behind the rest, drying his thick brown hair with a small towel. "I just saw the cutest, little green snake on the ledge above the faucet." This set the camp in an uproar. Two men and the first woman they'd seen went into the bathhouse and dispatched it. It turned out that green vipers were to be taken very seriously.

261

One of the soldiers sat them down and gave them a lecture about not putting their hands, feet or butt anywhere they couldn't see. Further, he instructed, everything in the jungle either bites, stings, or strangles.

"So, it's just like show business." Bobby set everyone laughing. It appeared he was getting his humor back.

They dined in a large mess hall at a table near the kitchen with the officers. The spacious building had a thatched roof of palm supported by thick hand-hewed, hardwood beams and trusses. Smoke wafted up from the wood cooking fires, creating a haze in the dining area, which was peopled with at least forty soldiers and what they thought to be civilian scientists. Each group sat separately from one another, conversing enthusiastically while occasionally pausing to look their way, which made them feel conspicuous and self-conscious.

Since their arrival, they'd not had a chance to associate with anyone other than the soldiers and then mainly Francois. They could not be sure if this was by design or circumstance.

"Well, I see you are all getting comfortable with our routine." Francois settled in at their table. "May I recommend our local fig wine while we wait for dinner?" Before anyone could answer, he ordered one of the officers to fetch them a bottle. "We're having Poulet Basque with pommes frites tonight, and I can attest that this wine pairs handsomely."

Dinner was a delicious affair, and, they thought, amazingly appointed considering that they were in the middle of the jungle far from civilization. The jungle and their hosts' ingenuity had provided them a very good living. As the wine loosened everyone up, the story of this isolated compound unfolded.

Few of the original castaways who'd survived the storm and the shipwreck some forty years before remained. Their floating laboratory had been caught in one of the worst storms in history, and their captain chose to ground the ship in an attempt to save the crew and its cargo. It had been an amazing display of seamanship, but the downside of this effort was that the all the creatures that survived had escaped into the wild.

The survivors had endured great hardship in those early years, but with a herculean effort they'd built their compound from the salvaged materials of the wreck and the natural resources surrounding them. It'd been an amazing feat of engineering thanks to the knowhow of the soldiers and scientists. They worked well together in those early days and had carried that tradition on, instilling it into their replacements.

Once they were safe and secure, their little party of castaways had set about the effort of protecting and studying the creatures which were now loose in one of the most wild and isolated parts of the world. They couldn't have found a better place to carry on their work in secret. Providence had been good to them.

Ken was just about to ask a question when pandemonium broke out in the back of the hall. Lester had brought Mike and Girlie inside. He found it interesting to watch the reactions of the soldiers and civilians alike. First, they were alarmed but that changed to delight as they realized that the chimps meant them no harm.

Mike and Girlie quickly won over the crowd with their humor and charm. Soon both were running through the crowd playing games of tickle. They seemed to bring a level of collective relief to a community that seemed always on guard, a point not lost on Francois, who laughed with the rest. This seemed to be the ice-breaker they needed to mix with everyone. Introductions began, and questions and, more importantly, answers were shared.

As the evening wound down, Francois pulled the group together. "I'd like to show you one more thing if you're up to it this evening."

Ken nodded. His team looked at each other tentatively.

They stepped out under the dark tropical African sky, feeling relaxed for the first time in weeks. A sickle moon hung just above the trees. The stars shone bright with the different colors of the galaxies of the Milky Way. Bats darted overhead, their high-pitched screeches piercing the night.

Anxiousness revisited them as they crossed the compound and made their way toward the tin building from which they'd heard the screams the previous evening. No one spoke. When they reached the door where a guard stood sentry, he turned and followed them inside.

A line of brass oil lamps hung from the rafters, dimly lighting the way down a narrow hallway that led to a locked door. They heard the deafening screams long before they reached the animals.

"The ones making this infernal racket are the ones we've manage to recapture." They could barely hear Francois over the screams.

The brute power of the captives even set Lester back. Six massive creatures lunged at them, slamming against the steel doors of the cages. All were similar in appearance to the ones they'd spied that afternoon, but standing so close to such brute power and aggression struck them mute with awe. They were more human than apelike in appearance, but the screams sounded like no human cry, and their behavior was more savage then any great ape they'd seen. The beasts' aggression was pure malice.

Lester walked past them and stood close to the last cage at the end of the row; a cage that seemed to be empty. Francois stopped a guard who raced to pull Lester back from reach. Screams subsided as an older creature stirred in the back of the cage and moved to meet Lester.

Lester smiled and touched the back of his outstretched hand. "Hello, Oliver. So, our search for you has finally ended, old friend."

Oliver squinted with one eye open and panted quietly. He stretched the back of his hand out toward Lester, nodding his head in excitement. The other creatures silently watched this tender greeting of old friends. Francois and the guard looked at each other in amazement. Ken and company were the only ones not surprised.

CHAPTER 29

The morning warmed in the tropical sun. Ken and Francois breakfasted on the terrace, a popular place where people often interrupted them.

"We succeeded the first year in capturing the original hybrids that'd survived and escaped into the wild. Not many made it. Most drowned, as I almost did." Francois pointed to the building that housed Oliver. "We've housed them here ever since." He absent-mindedly stirred his coffee, deep in thought.

Ken thought how different everything appeared in the morning light compared to that first evening when they'd dined, frightened and exhausted. The castaways had made this a comfortable refuge in the middle of nowhere. Francois sipped his coffee. His cup and saucer rattled, bringing Ken back to the present. "So where did those others come from that we observed in the caves and the ones that attacked us on the beach."

"The hybrids were relentless. They were killing and breeding machines. Even our Soviets scientists are afraid of them. They raided all the villages in this whole area, running all the natives out. There's a superstition that surrounds this whole area now, which is helpful as it keeps people out, making our job easier. No one comes here—at least until recently." Francois had a pained expression. "You saw the results of their work in the valley yesterday. Actually, the creatures living in those caves and the ones you encountered on the beach are results as well, so to speak."

"What do you mean by 'results'?" Ken asked.

Francois lowered his voice. "They're the offspring that resulted from those village raids."

"My God!"

"I'm not sure God had anything to do with this. They're the results of Stalin's great Soviet experiment that went awry—that we unintentionally set in motion. We're responsible and we've been trying to contain it ever since."

"How?"

"By capturing the original hybrids who were fertile—the ones you saw last night—and doing everything in our power to contain the others, including finding and bringing back the two we lost to Belgian animal traders in the first few years." Francois nodded to where Oliver was housed.

"You mean Oliver!"

"Yes," Francois replied gravely.

"The other is Danny," Mark said as he and Consuelo clattered up the wooden steps behind them, startling Francois and Ken out of their dark conversation.

Francois motioned them to join them. A uniformed attendant brought them juice. "We were successful with retrieving Oliver in Mexico, but I'm afraid our reach wasn't as far as the W-A-T-C."

Ken and Mark looked at each other in surprise. Consuelo put her hand on Mark's shoulder, surprised at the mention of the Wild Animal Training Center.

Francois chuckled. "We've tracked both of them since they were trapped and traded from here, but we just didn't have the resources to get them back until luck brought Oliver within our reach down in Mexico."

"So, you're hoping that we're going to help you in your efforts?" Ken asked, gazing out toward the direction from which they'd come what seemed so very long ago.

266

As though on cue, Lester walked past them, accompanied by two scientists, towards where Oliver was housed. Lester was so busy answering questions that he didn't notice them sitting up on the terrace.

Francois' voice took on a serious tone. "It appears you already are. Besides Lester here, Bobby and Fred left early this morning with one of our patrols to track the location of the creatures we last met on the beach."

Mark interrupted, looking at Consuelo, "Well, we'd love the chance to see your biomedical facilities. Are you equipped to analyze blood and hair samples?"

Ken threw his hands up in dismay. "I guess I don't have much to say about this—looks like everyone has made their decision. I wonder what's left for me."

"Sign language, Dr. Turner."

* * *

The team's relationship with their hosts evolved amazingly quickly from that of guests to members of this tight-knit community. The adversity of living in such isolation, with such a dark secret, in such a wild place, had made everyone very suspicious of outsiders, which, until now, they rarely encountered.

They seemed to make an exception in Ken and his team's case. Within a few months they were welcomed into the community. The fact that Ken was a famous scientist and his research with chimpanzee communication had wide notoriety certainly gave him and his associates a lot of credibility.

Also, agents working for Francois' team had brought back intelligence about Ken's attempt to protect Danny and Oliver from Vandusen and the US Government. Even after they'd succeeded in getting Oliver back, Francois had been afraid to make contact regarding Danny.

While they'd appreciated their effort to protect Danny and Oliver, they feared it would bring attention back to Africa. They'd gone to great lengths to keep their work covert and had developed a sophisticated cover. The Congolese government thought they were simply a conservation organization involved in primate research and rehabilitation.

Ken and company were surprised at just how much these people knew about the wide world outside. For all their isolation, there'd been a considerable amount of comings and goings over the years. The hardships of living in a tropical rainforest had taken its toll on them. Very few of the original soldiers and scientists remained.

But more than just people had been replaced. Ken and team were amazed at the extensiveness of their research library and at how sophisticated and up-to-date the equipment was in their labs. Ken commented that they had a better collection of linguistic and primatology volumes than he had back home at his own facility.

But fortunes were changing; up to the present, the remoteness of their facility had protected them from the casual visitor—that, and bribes to the local authorities. But as the years passed and technology and travel improved, they were finding it harder to keep their secret.

More people were stumbling into their facility unannounced—various research expeditions, adventurers, and even the odd pirate tramping through what had once been a white area on the map. In fact, just recently one of their patrols had observed a survey crew working along the river. Their agents determined that the government was planning a dam project of all things. And it would flood the very valley where they'd contained one of the tribes of creatures. They'd gone to great lengths to contain the hybrids well away from that crew. All this work was risky at best and took its toll on everyone because they realized that their whole existence was threatened.

To further complicate matters, they'd brought some of the problems onto themselves. Over the years, as they made sporadic visits to the outside world to resupply and recruit, suspicions were awakened and rumors had followed.

Because of these rumors, the scientists at the facility felt they were running out of time to successfully breed a truly safe and useful hybrid creature. And when Francois learned of Vandusen and the government's involvement, he feared that even Ken, who though well intended, may have led them right to their part of the world—especially with the disappearance of GuGu and the captain before their capture of the *Si Como No*. They couldn't be sure how much those two had observed and if they were friend or foe. As a result, they placed their soldiers on high alert, doubling their recon patrols.

But they were scientists first and the research continued. Ken and company had been able to contribute a considerable amount. Ken and Mike dedicated themselves to working with Oliver and the other captive hybrids slowly teaching them sign language. Mark and Consuelo worked closely with the lab people, analyzing the breeding protocols, blood samples, and DNA. Savage worked observing the creatures in the wild. And Lester, Girlie, and Hunt helped fill in the gaps in the history of Danny and Oliver, as well as teaching basic handling and training techniques. Lester had taught the scientists how to create a relationship with the captive hybrids that actually had them quietly curious instead of fearful, which reduced the screams considerably.

* * *

The group huddled together to discuss their future.

"I really feel we should stay longer. This is a chance of a lifetime," Savage said emphatically. The fieldwork he'd managed to accomplish observing the two tribes of creatures in the wild would be groundbreaking. He felt as if he'd been put into some kind of time machine, making it possible to witness the ascent of humans, the dawn of early man.

But Ken and Mark, while making great strides with their linguistic research, felt time was running out before they'd have to return or cause even more suspicion. They were torn, hesitant to leave the scientific find of the century but realized that their very staying could endanger it.

"If we don't come back after my sabbatical, the university will pull all stops out looking for us. Right now, Mary has created a good cover back home." By radio, they'd been in almost daily contact with Mary through Raven. "Also, Raven will be wrapping up his movie in another month. It'd be best to return under his cover."

But they were reluctant. The progress they'd made with Mike was incredible, as well. They'd been very careful not to use sign language in front of the hybrids but rather have them interact only with Mike. They'd built a cage adjacent to the hybrids and exercised Mike in full view. It wasn't long before he began communicating with them. The hybrids picked up sign language quicker than the chimps had, which opened up the whole question of how sophisticated their language skills might become. The degree of intelligence they were observing from the captive hybrids was staggering, much higher than that of chimpanzees in general, including Mike.

* * *

Ken put down the radio headphones. His hand trembled. He was truly animated when he shared the news. "Mary will be coming with Danny as soon as Raven can make the arrangements.

"And Vandusen?" Mark asked.

"So far there's no news concerning that ghost."

It was as though Vandusen had dropped off the face of the earth since their last run in with him and his agents. But, somehow, they knew they hadn't seen the last of him.

"I don't like the idea of Mary traveling with that freak, Danny." Lester frowned with concern.

"Oh, I didn't mention. Dr. Raven will be with them—it's his show. The movie just rapped which is a perfect time to play another shell game with our animals."

Bobby asked, "How the hell are they going to get here?"

Ignoring Bobby, he said to Francois, "Raven wants to talk to you concerning this landing strip you have, something about a Cessna." He handed the microphone to him.

* * *

The twin-engine Cessna made one pass before it banked steeply and lined up with the dirt field for its final approach. They'd spent the last month lengthening and clearing the old field to accommodate the plane. Ken could barely contain himself. It'd been months since he'd seen Mary, and he'd missed her humor and quick intelligence. He missed the feel of her.

Raven had orchestrated the whole move brilliantly. In the bustle of shipping animals home and trainers back and forth, he was able to slip Mary and Danny into the mix and get them over to Africa. Obviously Raven had experience in such matters.

Ken wiped the sweat from his brow as he stood waiting in the lank and humid air. The plane bounced down heavily, stirring clouds of red dust from under each wheel before it taxied to where they stood. Ken and company shaded their eyes from the debris flying up from the revving engines.

Francois and a patrol of soldiers watched with curiosity as they anticipated instructions for the off-loading of Danny and the reception of their new guests. No one tried to speak, preferring to wait for the engines to wind down.

They could barely contain their excitement when the cabin door swung open and the steps dropped down. Mary appeared first. The wind blew her red hair across her face and kicked up her light sundress to reveal her shapely legs. Butterflies visited Ken. Swirls of dust blew up from the newly cleared runway, pelting them with small stones that kept them back as they waited for the propellers to finally come to a rest.

Francois placed his hand on Ken's shoulder. "This is the end of a very long journey for us. Danny is finally returning home."

It occurred to Ken that he was not the only one who was excited at the arrival of the plane.

Raven emerged next and helped Mary down the steps. But something seemed wrong. Mary and Raven paused, nervously looking back at the open door. Neither seemed themselves.

Vandusen stepped out, and the whole welcoming party froze at the sight. He nodded and shot a flare. Instantly an army

271

of men in camouflage fatigues surrounded them, guns leveled. Two Huey helicopters rose above the tree line with speakers blearing in English, French and Russian requesting them to surrender, drop their weapons and raise their hands.

Francois smiled apologetically at Ken. "I just can't follow that order."

He awkwardly unholstered his service revolver and fired a single shot that rang so loud that it woke the sleeping jungle, echoing off the distant hills. All hell broke loose like the cracks of doom on the last day of the world, and Ken knew no more.

* * *

The creature stood nervously watching the raging gun battle below. His cold amber eyes smoldered with rage at the sight of the humans. His nostrils burned from the caustic smell of the smoke that rose from the clearing below where the humans lived. He vaguely connected the pops he heard to the smell.

Suddenly a loud concussive sound startled him, sending confusing messages of fight and flight to his brain. His hair stood on end across his back and his shoulders and up the nape of his neck. He grimaced as primeval urges rose up in him to attack. But the large, noisy birds that hovered overhead frightened him, holding him back.

The complicated cross-wiring of his heredity sent contradicting signals that made it difficult for him to make sense of all the confusion. The harmony of his world was disturbed. He gripped the smooth bone handle of his club with his large muscular hand before he turned and signaled to the others. His clan followed silently, sifting into the trees like the fragments of a very bad dream that would linger in the shadows of the jungle.

CHAPTER 30

Ken came to with a splitting headache. He pushed himself off the wet stone floor of the cell and looked groggily around. Everything around him was blurred and spinning. He tried to think back to what had happened but couldn't remember anything after the blinding flash and deafening explosion.

I must be in one of the chimp cages. But why am I alone? A dread swept over him as he feared that he might be the only one who had survived. He immediately thought of Mary and chastised himself for asking her to come.

He stood stiffly. A wave of nausea consumed him. He leaned over and vomited. His throat burned from the acidic bile that kept welling up. He peered down the corridor at the other cages but had trouble focusing on anything.

Finally, he composed himself enough to shout. "Is anyone down here?"

Loud cries sent his head throbbing with more intensity. Moaning, he covered his ears before cradling his head in the crook of his arm. No human replied. Apparently, he was alone except for those damn animals.

I must be in a part of the building that houses Oliver and the creatures.

Again he shouted in frustration. "Where in the hell is everyone, dammit?"

"Actually, we're still counting bodies. You seem to be the only one of your colleagues accounted for so far. Our little corporate takeover was messier than expected." Vandusen stepped out of the shadows of a far corner where he'd been watching with amusement. "That little Belgian caused a lot more trouble than he's worth."

Ken's eyes flashed with anger at the sight of him. "If anything has happened to my wife or friends, I won't stop 'til I put you in the ground."

Ken's anger seemed to amuse Vandusen. "Really? I thought all you professors were non-violent. You know "make love not war". I'm sorry, but I don't think you're in much of a position to do anything. But we can talk later." Vandusen hugged the wall as he strolled out past the screaming creatures. Ken hunched down in the corner, wincing in pain.

He awoke later to the jingling of keys.

"We brought you some roommates." Vandusen nodded to two of his armed men who shoved Raven and Mark into the cage. The bars clanged loudly behind them. "Oh, as I'm sure they'll tell you, your wife and that other little bitch haven't been found yet. You better hope we find them before some of the other residents of this God-forsaken place do. As you've no doubt heard, these things have carnal and insatiable appetites. Vandusen walked off with two guards, laughing at the prospect of the creatures finding Mary and Consuelo.

Before Ken could respond, Raven quickly reassured him, "Mary's okay. We saw them both get away".

"Where are they?" Ken felt guilty that he'd not thought of Consuelo's welfare. He couldn't think of anything but protecting Mary. He felt completely powerless.

"I saw them make it to the tree line with Lester and Bobby. Don't worry they'll never let anything happen to the girls." Taking in their surroundings, Raven's eyes rested on a rusted bucket that served as their toilet. "Actually, I think they're better off than us. I'll take the jungle over our digs."

"What the hell happened?" Ken asked.

"All hell broke loose after Francois fired that shot," Mark replied as he pulled himself up on a wide stone ledge that framed a barred window to have a look outside. Dropping down he continued, "One of those damn helicopters fired a rocket too close, I think, and the rest is history."

"What do you mean too close?"

"I think they were trying to take us—or at least you, alive and in one piece," Raven replied. "I think that's why we all made it, more or less. Francois threw a wrench into their plan by firing on them. He got a few before they returned fire."

"What happened to the rest?"

I think Hunt got away, as well. I don't know about Mike and Girlie. I don't think Vandusen has them or I'm sure we would've heard about it."

"And Francois and his men?"

Ken gravely shook his head.

"All of them?"

"Either dead, wounded or, for a few, captured. The place is in a wreck except for this building. They avoided firing on it."

"Francois, dead?"

"I couldn't say." Raven paused before continuing. "He's a brave little man, crazy but brave—I'll give him that."

They stood in silence, each trying to visualize the events preceding the ambush. The sound of a familiar but unpleasant voice followed by the hoots of the hybrids jarred them from their thoughts.

"Well, well. So, we're together at last! A little less for wear but all safe and sound just the same."

"Childs!" Mark exclaimed.

CHAPTER 31

"Clean up this mess!" Vandusen yelled, furious. Their surprise ambush had gone very wrong. Half the compound was destroyed, and God knew how much harm had come to the animals, equipment and scientists. "Amateurs!"

Bauer and several of his men frowned, puzzled at his reaction. Their engagement had been by the book, like clockwork. Being a man of few words, preferring action, he simply replied, "Surprise and secure, and if fired upon, return fire—that's our standing orders."

Vandusen glared at them. "Goddamn it. Do a damage assessment. We need to get this facility up and running ASAP. See who's still here and able to perform their duties and what's still intact. This is a fucking disaster!"

Bauer gave the order, and his men sprang into action with military efficiency.

Vandusen could hardly believe his eyes: so much destruction in such a short time. The collateral damage had been huge. Most of the buildings were damaged or destroyed. As he surveyed the compound, an occasional shot rang out—Bauer and his men dispatching the critically wounded. The walking wounded were rounded up and herded into what was left of the mess hall. Those not dealing with the wounded busied themselves extinguishing spot fires or drenching the smoldering debris of Bauer's handiwork.

Vandusen righted a table and chair on what was left of the terrace. A large, gaping hole framed with wood splinters made it difficult to find a suitable place to set up. He swore under his breath as he tried to get settled.

Bauer finally returned to make his report, and it was even worse than he expected. They would have to repair the aging and damaged generator. All the facilities and labs ran off it. It would take weeks of reconstruction to put the place back in order. They still didn't have a full inventory. As far as he could tell they could only account for about half of Turners group and, more importantly, his chimp Mike was missing.

The only good news was that the laboratory had remained intact, so not all was lost.

Next, they'd have to sort through Francois' men and get them working again under the new "management," since Francois was among the missing. Vandusen's spirits rose a little at the prospect of what he was going to do to that little Belgian shit when he caught him. He was finally nearing his goal despite this little set back.

"So, what's next?" Bauer seemed relieved at his boss's apparent change of mood.

Vandusen made a note that he'd get more out of this idiot with a carrot than a stick. He smiled and said, "We're going to get these people working with us instead of against us and as quickly as possible. The less time they have to think—the better."

Bauer frowned, looking dubious.

Vandusen smiled menacingly. "These people just don't realize the significance of their work. How useful it could be to our government to have smart killing machines on the battlefield that would be more expendable than humans." He paused, gathering his thoughts. "Creatures that would not be encumbered by the flaws of human morals or ethics, and at the same time, when lost in battle, wouldn't be missed or, how should I say, counted in the dead. These people just need to be motivated—that's where you and that little shit Childs come in."

Bauer eyes narrowed. "You're talking about creating some kind of psychotic monsters."

Vandusen nodded. "No, not creating—our friends here have already accomplished that. As I just said, they've missed the practical application of their work and need a little guidance from us to get them on the right track."

Bauer didn't like what he heard. It wasn't how Vandusen planned to use the animals but rather the possibility that he and his men might be out of a job in the very near future—a job he really enjoyed.

Vandusen, watching the play of emotions across Bauer's face, immediately sensed his train of thought. He quickly reassured him. "Not to worry. We'll always need to train these creatures in the art of war, human style. The agency will need the finesse of a good man like you." Vandusen emphasized "man."

Bauer relaxed a little. "So, what're your orders, sir?"

Vandusen's dark eyes hardened. "Bury the dead and dying— but be sure to leave some holes in the ground for those who don't want to cooperate."

* * *

Childs took Vandusen's direction very seriously. He would do what it took to force these arrogant bastards to cooperate. His frustration grew each day as they refused to help. They were slowing the project and making him look bad. He feared Vandusen would question his usefulness. He knew where that could lead.

Even though Mike and Girlie had been sighted in the jungle nearby by their patrols, they had been unsuccessful in capturing them. And Ken flatly refused to help retrieve Mike. They wanted that little shit so they could continue the sign language work they'd heard about.

They'd quickly found out the progress Turner's group had made before Vandusen and his men had "liberated" the compound. Bauer had been very persuasive with the captives. He found out everything.

But Ken's group was too valuable for Bauer's methods, so Vandusen had assigned Childs with the delicate job of convincing them. However, Vandusen was beginning to lose confidence in him, which frightened him. To impress Vandusen, he desperately needed the cooperation of Ken's group. Their lack of cooperation frustrated and enraged him.

The final straw had been when he offered freedom in exchange for repairing and setting up the damaged labs. Ken and his friends just silently smirked at him.

So, with the help of Bauer, he'd enacted plan B: withhold food and water from both them and the animals they seemed to care so much about. It was brilliant. Break the bodies and the minds will follow.

As the days passed Childs took to his new work as a jailer. He taunted both the creatures and them humans with piles of fruit placed just out of reach in clear view. Some days he gave them a little water and others days a little fruit. They were weakening and losing hope.

* * *

Mark stood weakly, staring at the plate of fruit just out of reach. "Take your shirts off," he whispered.

Savage and Raven looked at each other quizzically but complied. Mark quickly began rolling and tying them together. He paused, looking at Raven. "Give me your boot."

Oliver and the creatures watched with interest as Mark clumsily swung the boot toward the plate of food. After several attempts he succeeded in pulling some of the fruit to the cage. They gobbled it down. The creatures began to hoot and beg.

Ken quickly signed, "Shut up!" and to their amazement the creatures complied.

"We can't take it all, and we have to hope a guard, and not Childs, picks up the plate later or they'll know." They nodded, looking longingly at the remaining fruit now in reach.

Mark surprised them by rolling a handful from their precious supply to Oliver. They sat silently eating their shared spoils.

It was days before the opportunity arose again, but when it did, it took a surprising turn. This time after the usual and predictable taunting, Childs gave all the pile of fruit to Oliver. Childs left content, pleased in thinking he was using the food to set them against each other.

They were shocked when Oliver shared it with them—not only the other creatures but also them. An unlikely bond had formed which they needed to keep very secret.

CHAPTER 32

"Hold up, Bobby! The girls are lagging way behind." Lester bent over, trying to catch his breath.

They were moving too slow, but Consuelo and Mary just couldn't keep up. They'd not stopped since they ducked under cover of the trees hours ago. A thick layer of smoke that lay like a fog, hampered their progress, blinding them. Bobby thought the whole compound must be ablaze.

He waited impatiently, straining to see Mary and Consuelo. Just as he started to double back to find them, they stumbled out the thick haze. "Here they are."

"Bobby! Please, we need to rest." Mary could barely speak. Consuelo threw herself on the ground, heaving.

Bobby realized they'd not been going farther without a break. "Okay, five minutes, no more. I'm sure they saw which way we've come. We've got to put some miles between us and fast."

Mary panted so loud it was hard to understand her. "Where the hell are we going?"

"We'll make for the beach—and the ship—as soon as we're rested."

"Terrific." Mary closed her eyes in pain and dropped, face down.

They'd been lucky to make their way out of the ambush, but Bobby had been quick on his feet. As soon as the first shots were fired, he sprang into action, grabbing Lester, Mary and

Consuelo and made a run for it. When they reached the cover of the trees, they decided to make it for the *Si Como No* as quickly as possible.

They figured that since Vandusen and his men had come by their own means, they may have not dealt with their ship as yet. In fact, they may have not even known where it was anchored. There could still be some of Francois' people on board who could help them or at the very least they could warn them— besides the ship had a radio. It was a long shot, but it was their only option.

Bobby rested with the others, his back against a tree, and woke with a start. The jungle was pitch black and stirring with noises. Branches cracked nearby and overhead. The smoke had cleared, and stars shone above through the treetops. Something or someone was definitely nearby and moving in the canopy above them. A limb fell with a crack, almost landing on top of them. He nudged Lester and signaled him to silence, pointing upward. Mary and Consuelo still slept where they'd fallen exhausted.

"There's something up there," Bobby whispered.

They could just make out two dim silhouettes moving directly above. They stiffened and fumbled around in the darkness, feeling for a rock or stick or anything with which to defend themselves. Bobby motioned to Mary and Consuelo. "Wake them up."

Before Lester could move, someone or something dropped from the trees and knocked them to the ground. Mary and Consuelo woke up screaming. Lester grabbed a handful of hair before he recognized a familiar hoot and smell. "God damn it, Girlie, get off! You scared the hell out of me." Girlie ignored his protests and climbed all over him, showering him with affection.

Mike stood back on the narrow path they'd been following. He pointed in the direction from which they'd escaped and made the signed for hide several times. At first, no one paid attention, being caught up in the emotion of reuniting, but his manner became so agitated that they felt a sudden sense of urgency.

"What, Mike?" Bobby signed. He'd learned a few signs over the last several months but had to slow Mike down.

"Bad. Run. Hide." He whimpered as he signed, pointing back the way they'd come.

Bobby walked up the path several yards and stopped. Looking back at the group, he realized how vulnerable they were, gathered there in the middle of the path. "We need to get the hell out of here. Anyone following us will come this way."

They no sooner stirred into action than they heard footsteps tramping their way up the path. Bobby signaled them to follow him off the path, up a bank under the cover of the trees. Mike and Girlie scaled the large trunk of a tree. They lay still in the shadows of the moonlight, barely breathing for fear of being seen or heard.

Bobby peered through the branches and could just make out the clearing they'd left. The sounds of the jungle seemed to grow as they listened. The minutes ticked by, and they heard no further footsteps.

Bobby relaxed a little, thinking their keyed-up emotions were feeding their imagination. Taking Bobby's lead, Lester and the girls began to stir, but they'd no sooner stood when six large, dark forms broke into the clearing. They froze in their positions.

The creatures spread out like shadows, searching every inch of the clearing. They meticulously worked their way to the edge of the bank and paused. What appeared to be the leader tilted his head and stared up the bank to where they hid. Other creatures followed his gaze.

Bobby's heart pounded so hard he feared the creatures would hear it. Just as he was about to signal the others to bolt, a rustling came from the treetops behind the creatures, followed by the cracks of breaking limbs. The creatures shifted their attention and took off in the opposite direction, following the noise.

"Thank God for Girlie and Mike," Bobby remarked as he gathered himself up.

"They're playing a dangerous game. I hope they don't cut it too close." Lester pushed himself up off the soggy ground.

"Let's get out of here. Finding our way to the ship's making way more sense now—even if we're not sure where it is or who's on it," Mary said.

When they found the ship the next day, Bobby searched through his pack and found the pair of binoculars he happened to have with him when they escaped. "It looks like someone's on board." The *Si Como No* rode the swell at her original anchorage. Apparently, Francois had ordered it back to the cove where it was more protected and hidden.

"Let's have those." Lester reached for the lenses.

"Hold on, I see someone on board now."

"Who?" Mary asked.

"Francois." Bobby handed the binoculars to Lester.

"Do you see anyone else?" Consuelo nudged them for the glasses.

"Not yet, but we need to do something. It looks like they're pulling out."

Lester ran out from under cover and tried to signal them. They could see the smoke from the engines even though they couldn't hear them as the wind was blowing in the wrong direction.

"Christ! What do we do, Bobby?" Mary ran out to join Lester who was waving wildly on the beach.

They saw the splash of the anchor as it rose just before the vessel started to make way. The whole group raced down the beach wildly waving and shouting. Bobby ran to his waist in the surf about to swim.

Just as the ship turned, showing its stern to set a course out of the cove, a loud report rang out over the water. A bright orange flare rose up in a strike and floated effortlessly above them. Startled they turned around to see GuGu and Omar running down towards them. At first Bobby thought they were running to help get the attention of those on the *Si Como No* until they heard the cries in the jungle following them down to the beach.

GuGu ran right past them into the water. "Everyone get into the water as deep as you can. They might not have figured how to swim." Omar stood at the edge and knelt, aiming his rifle. He paid little attention to the wave that slapped his back. The creatures broke onto the beach and charged. Omar opened fire and GuGu leveled his flare gun. One of the creatures stumbled and fell bleeding in the sand. Several stooped to pick him up as more shots rang out, drowning out the cries. But the creatures kept coming.

"Swim for it we're out of ammo!" GuGu yelled.

Several of the creatures tentatively waded into to the water and followed after them as they retreated deeper into the waves. Bobby swam, and the rest could barely touch the bottom with each surge. Some of the creatures still pursued them.

Several shots rang out in rapid succession. Bullets buzzed all around them. Spouts splashed up as the rounds hit the water; some finding their marks. The frothy foam of the surf turned red. The creatures retreated, screaming. Several floated face down in the water.

They heard the hum of the inflatable coming towards them. Bobby and Lester waited as GuGu and Omar helped Mary and Consuelo into the rubber boat.

They took turns standing guard as they had to make several trips to get everyone on the ship. Lester shaded his eyes, scanning the treetops for signs of their chimps. There'd been no signs of Mike or Girlie since the night before when they'd decoyed the creatures away from their group. Bobby frowned as GuGu worked the tiller of the little inflatable on the final bumpy run to the ship.

"I think those two chimps can take care of themselves just fine," Lester shouted over the roar of the outboard and patted Bobby's shoulder. "Don't worry, they'll show up. We'll find them—or more likely they'll find us, soon enough."

Bobby nodded in agreement. "But I wonder how well we'll do without them."

They rode the rest of the way in silence, hoping to catch sight of their chimps.

Soon after, they scrambled on board.

"You made it!" Bobby embraced Francois and the others gathered around, beaming with relief.

Francois smiled weakly. "Yes, thanks to these two." He nodded towards GuGu and Omar who stood back against the console of the wheelhouse of the ship. "If I hadn't stumbled onto them after I reached the jungle, I don't know what would've happened."

"It's mutual, believe me." Looking over at Omar, GuGu continued, "We spent a long time in the jungle not knowing what happened to you guys or our ship."

Bobby thought the Belgian looked worn out. He noticed several bruises and a large, infected gash on his forehead. Omar and GuGu didn't look much better, and the rest of them looked worse.

The noise of cabinet doors opening and slamming drew their attention; Mary rummaged around the galley looking for a first aid kit. Consuelo joined in the search.

Smeared with dirt, clothes hanging in rags, hair lank from the relentless humidity, they looked like a band of ragged castaways, and they dripped with perspiration, making everything they touched damp.

Francois grimaced as Mary gingerly cleaned his wounds. In the relative safety of the wheelhouse of the *Si Como No*, they finally had a chance to let the adrenaline wash away. They settled down and took stock of their present situation. Of their original group, Lester, Bobby, Mary, and Consuelo had escaped the ambush at the compound. They could only guess what had happened to Raven, Ken, Mark, and Hunt.

Their mistrust of GuGu and Omar had been unfounded. In the end, they'd risked much to help them. Raven had been right about trusting GuGu. After the initial attack, which seemed like so long ago, they'd abandoned ship, escaping just before Francois's soldiers boarded it. They had been living in the jungle ever since, waiting for a chance to recapture the ship when providence once again brought them on converging paths.

They debated for several hours on a plan for their next steps.

"So, it's settled," Bobby said finally. He felt tired and wanted to rest before they did anything else.

"We can move the ship to an anchorage closer to the compound," Omar said in his thick Arabic accent. It took a moment for his words to sink in.

"What are you saying?" Bobby asked.

"I know a cove that's less than ten kilometers from the compound, as the crow flies, as you Americans would say—it's less protected, but we wouldn't have to stay long if we stick with the plan, and it works."

No one spoke as each imagined what could go wrong. What if they were discovered by the helicopters? Outgunned and outnumbered, they wouldn't have a chance. What if the creatures caught them somewhere in the jungle, especially with Mary and Consuelo? What if Ken and the others hadn't survived? They couldn't bear the thought of them coming this far and losing everything. They kept their thoughts close and didn't share them.

Finally, no one had the energy to say another word. Some found their old cabins on the ship, while others simply slept where they sat. Morning came early with a deafening downpour accompanied by thunder and lightning. The crew raced around with buckets and pans, collecting the sweet, fresh water that poured off the roof of the wheelhouse. Fresh water in the tropics was valued above all else.

CHAPTER 33

"What's it been? Two weeks? And you're still giving us this same crap about being patriotic? These are bad people, Childs. Don't you get it?" Ken couldn't take his eyes off the heaped tray of fruits Childs balanced on his arm. Neither could the rest of the group or the creatures in the adjacent cages. Ken had to catch his breath before he could continue. "Do you really think that when Vandusen gets what he wants that he's going to let us go? If you had any brains at all you'd realize that includes *you*. You need to help us get out of here." Ken wobbled unsteadily, hardly able to stand.

The group was not faring well. They'd been confined for several weeks in one of the small animal cages next to the creatures. No news from the outside or knowing the welfare of their friends made their confinement even worse. Days at a time without food and water and the tropical heat took a toll on them physically. Raven and Savage helped Ken sit back down on the crumbling stones of the cell. Exhausted, he said no more.

Childs was getting worried. Vandusen grew more impatient by the day, and Childs realized that he was in way over his head, but he couldn't think of a way out. He was afraid that his charges were going to die, and he'd seen what happened to those who disappointed Vandusen. He tried not to show his fear and rage at their lack of cooperation.

He decided to take a different tack. "Mr. Vandusen has assured me that as soon as we get this facility up and running and the research back on track, he has no further use for us here and we will be free to return to the States. The government will be very grateful and will support us and our research very generously for our cooperation."

"You can't be that stupid," Ken replied, his voice weak. "We all know too much. Vandusen will never risk letting what happened here get out." He made a final jab. "And stop referring to us as *we*. You're nothing more than one of their lackeys." The group glared at Childs with contempt.

Childs flushed with anger. "Okay, day four without food. Oh, and that includes these pets you're so fond of." He walked over to Oliver's cage, taunting him with the plate of fruit, which set the creatures off food grunting and begging. Their delight quickly changed to rage when Childs noisily set the tray down just out of reach.

Laughing, he stood, picked up a slice of papaya, and ate it slowly, letting the juices run down his chin. "Yum, that's good." Loudly smacking his thin lips, he chewed, exaggerating his delight, then kneeled at the tray and sampled several other fruits. "Oh, look what we have here: coconuts, papayas, mangoes, figs—yummy!" "

The creatures slammed against the cages in a frenzy. Some tried to shake the bars loose—a deafening racket. Ken and his group looked nervously at each other, hoping the caging would hold.

Childs obliviously enjoyed his game—one he'd been at for several days now. In this, his final attempt to get Ken to cooperate, he didn't know who he hated more, Ken and his pompous friends or the creatures next to them. The game gave him a sense of control and, more importantly, revenge against the whole lot of them.

Oliver extended his arm, palm up, in a classic begging gesture, which caught Childs' attention. "Oh, poor baby, are you hungry? If your pals over here weren't so damn arrogant and cooperated, you wouldn't have to suffer. Hell, you could have this whole tray of fruit."

He stepped closer, very attentive of Oliver's reach, held another slice just out of reach and watched with amusement. Oliver straining with all his might could just touch it with his fingertips. He jerked his hand back and licked his fingers. This set Childs laughing uncontrollably and Oliver lunging in frustration. Childs was in ecstasy.

"You fucking coward! I'd love to see you do that if that cage wasn't between you," Mark yelled, both frightened and appalled at what he was seeing. The others stared with contempt and concern. The bars moved at the base where they were bolted to the stone floor. Some of the stones were loose.

"Oh, really? Watch this." He stepped in closer, holding a slice out again. Each time Oliver grabbed for it, Childs awkwardly pulled it back, laughing hysterically when Oliver grasped only air.

Mark elbowed Ken and whispered out of the side of his mouth as Raven watched in disbelief, "Oliver is man fishing. Childs is dumber than I thought."

CHAPTER 34

Vandusen needed help to roll one of the rotting beasts over on its back. He retched from the putrid smell of death. His whole crew had wrapped bandanas over their faces despite the sweltering heat. Fermenting decay seeped from the bloated bodies, and clouds of flies swarmed. Giant ants clustered over the dark stains that spotted the beach. The men fanned out, looking for clues to what had happened on this lonely beach.

He counted three more well beyond the breakers, floating in limbo with the tide. The sharks made them dance a macabre jig. Vandusen frowned, puzzled. Looking around, he felt uneasy. Large footprints, along with blood trails, lead into the jungle. The smaller human prints lead the opposite way into the water.

"They either fed the sharks like these brutes or someone had a fucking boat."

"They have a boat, sir." Bauer held up an oar with "*Si Como No*" stenciled on one side.

"And apparently they're armed." Vandusen held several shell casings in his palm. The brass gleamed in the sun, making them squint. He shook the casings absent mindedly as he took in his surroundings again, hoping to make some kind of sense out of this mystery. Clearly there'd been a brutal struggle with these monsters. But what had happened to the rest of them? He mentally tried to follow the footprints and piece together the sequence of events.

And where had the survivors gone off to? He wondered

what would bring any one to such a remote and forsaken part of the world. His gaze settled on the rusting hull of the *Orion* for a moment. "I wonder ..."

"Wonder what, sir?" Bauer was antsy to leave before darkness fell.

"Nothing—forget about it." He took a final look around and gave the order to head back.

* * *

From the treetops overlooking the cove, Mike and Girlie watched the humans finally leave.

Mike tapped Girlie and signed, "Hurry. Follow. Now."

Girlie nodded and pointed in the direction of the trail.

They brachiated high in the canopy where the sun still shone bright. Using their powerful arms, they flung themselves from limb to limb with purpose, flying like birds.

All creatures made way for them.

CHAPTER 35

Oliver's massive arm shot out so fast that he had a hold on Childs before anyone actually realized it. But his screams drove it home. Complete pandemonium followed. The creatures that could reach from the adjoining cages took hold of Childs as well, ripping with determined violence. Childs let out a shrill, primeval cry that froze them in horror as they watched Oliver pull his arm off in one jerk. Blood spurted in gushes, splattering everywhere.

Oliver left Childs writhing on the floor, his blood squirting in weakening beats. He ran up and down the length of his cage, scraping the bloody limb along the bars. It made a dull thumping sound as the bone bounced off each one. He licked the protruding bone and hooted in delight. Several of the creatures took advantage of Oliver's momentary inattention and grabbed the other end. They tried to tug it away and a fight broke out which turned into a macabre tug-a-war.

Finally, Ken stirred from his shock, and summoned everyone into action. They tried to pull Childs out of reach, but Oliver let go of the arm and grabbed Childs by the head. To their horror, they realized that he was faintly whimpering, still alive. Sitting on the floor with each foot spread out against the bars for leverage, Oliver slowly pulled Childs' head off his body.

Holding the bloody head in the air, he let out a triumphant cry. Childs eyes were still blinking, and his lips quivered almost as though trying to mouth something. Ken and company froze at the shear brutality of what they were witnessing.

Oliver slammed the head on the floor violently several times until the brains spewed out. He ignored the begging gestures of the other creatures as he dipped the slimy gel out with his long index finger and ate with appetite.

* * *

"The helicopters are guarded." Francois handed several hand grenades to one of his men. "You know what to do."

The soldier nodded and headed out to ready his men.

Francois and his group had marched through the jungle most of the night. It'd taken longer than they'd expected to reach the compound. The moonlight lit their way, so bright that it cast shadows and made it easy to see the lay of everything.

Bobby wondered how they were ever going to get down past the guards undetected and find the rest of their group. Guards were everywhere. Besides the ones they could see at the obvious places like the gates and several buildings, they caught the glow of cigarettes on several of the roofs.

But all seemed pretty lax considering what had happened over the last several months, and Vandusen's men seemed unaware or unconcerned of the danger they were in. They'd seen several bands of hybrid creatures roaming the jungle just on their trek from the ship to their present position on the hill above the compound. Francois and his men were very concerned that the numbers of these creatures were growing. He guessed that some had left the valley where they'd contained them for so long.

He realized that Vandusen and his crew had no idea of the magnitude of unintended consequences they'd set into motion with his objective of using the creatures for military purposes. Because of his ham-fisted blundering, they now had these creatures loose and uncontained. Without Francois' soldiers on guard, the creatures would be free to roam anywhere they pleased; and populated areas were just a four-day march downriver.

They watched as Francois' ragtag team left to destroy the helicopters and retake the facility. Fortunately, Vandusen had not killed all of the Belgian's men. Some had escaped in the confusion of the ambush, and others had been on patrol or guarding the *Si Como No* when it'd happened. They had about thirty men still fit for service, and they hoped to free more when they attacked.

Francois' plan was simple. Recapture the facility and neutralize the enemy. Bobby didn't want to know what "neutralize" meant with these military types.

Bobby and the rest of the group were far less ambitious. Find and rescue the rest of their team and make for the *Si Como No* and home.

* * *

"The keys aren't on him," Hunt shouted over the screams as he searched Childs' limp body.

"They're over there," Mark yelled, pointing to a clipboard and set of keys hanging on a hook by the door.

"Damn! We've got to get them before someone comes. Even these idiots are bound to know this racket isn't normal." Ken unhooked his belt buckle as he eyed the distance from their cage to the door.

Hunt busied himself with the grim task of unclothing Childs. They knotted their belts and shirts together to make a rope like they'd done before. Unfortunately, the keys were farther away than they'd reached before, and they hung on a hook several feet up the wall. But this idea was their only hope. God only knew what would happen when someone came looking for Childs and discovered what had happened. The group worked feverishly, ignoring Oliver's grim meal.

After many attempts, Ken finally threw down their makeshift rope, exhausted. "It's no use—the keys are too damn far." They'd been at it for too long. They were running out of time.

"Let me try." Hunt put out his hand.

"It's too late." They could hear someone fumbling at the door. They waited anxiously. In their agitated state, the creatures didn't notice.

Puzzled, they watched as the knob turned several times, but the door didn't open. Finally, after even the creatures realized someone was at the door, it swung open, revealing Mike hanging on it. He jumped down and raced to their cage, being careful to stay out of reach of the creatures, while Girlie kept watch in the hallway. Mike reached through the cage to them, hooting and greeting.

The creatures quieted down and watched Mike closely, except for Oliver who attended to his meal.

* * *

"We're ready, sir." The young lieutenant wore an intent expression as he waited for the go ahead from Francois to destroy the helicopters.

"Very well, but remember—surprise is everything. Don't pull the pins until we fire the flare." Just as the young man jumped into action, Francois grabbed his sleeve and added, "Oh, and protect that plane." He nodded and signaled to the rest of his men to follow through the hole they'd cut in the fence.

Mary and Consuelo remained behind on the hill where they'd be safer. From their vantage, they'd have a view of everything that was about to happen and could serve as spotters. Two soldiers had remained behind with a radio.

The dark figures of Francois and his men spread across the compound like ghosts.

* * *

"Come on, Mike. Bring 'em here, boy." Ken watched as Mike tried to grab the keys off the hook. He jumped several times, trying to reach them, but they were too high. Finally, he climbed up on the doorknob, swung the door to the wall, and grabbed them.

"Good boy. Good Mike—now bring 'em here." Ken held his hand out through the bars towards Mike and gestured him to come.

Mike bounded along on all fours with the ring in his mouth, but just before he reached Ken, he stopped suddenly. Oliver was gesturing for Mike to come to him. To their amazement, Mike turned and went to Oliver.

They screamed in unison. "No!" Ken frantically signed to Mike. "Come. Out. Out."

Mike sat near Oliver, ignoring them at first, and then began looking back and forth from the men to the hybrid as though trying to decide what to do. He sat in easy reach of Oliver, who'd laid down his grim meal and was shaking the door and pointing at the keys.

Just as Mike turned to come to Ken, Oliver signed, "Out. Out. Please. Out."

To their horror, Mike climbed up the bars of Oliver's cage and handed him the keys. Before anyone could react, Oliver opened the cage door. Ken and the others were stunned. Oliver walked passed Mike with deliberation and, ignoring the cries of the other creatures, came towards Ken, who retreated in fear. The group huddled on the opposite wall, unable to speak.

Oliver fiddled with their lock until he opened the door and signed, "Out."

Ken and others stared at him in terror and disbelief. They couldn't move. Oliver looked them up and down, his giant frame filling the opening. As though understanding their fear, he stepped back and pointed the way out. Ken jumped into action and they darted past Oliver and out to freedom, Mike and Girlie following. Oliver stood watching them leave, keys dangling in his enormous hand, ignoring the screams of the other creatures.

They raced down the hallway, stopping at the door that opened to the outside. Hunt cracked the door open as the rest looked back, expecting the creatures any second. Their eyes no sooner adjusted to the bright lights on the parade ground, when they flickered and went out. All became pitch black. Before they could say anything, a bright flare shot up above them, illuminating everything, followed by two deafening explosions. The flash blinded them.

Men poured from the mess hall and shots rang out from all directions, some buzzed overhead, making them duck.

Raven spurred everyone into action. "Let's make for the gate."

Savage grabbed Raven by the arm. "What about the creatures?"

"I think they can take care of themselves just fine. Now, let's move."

Mike and Girlie led the way across the compound. Using the confusion to their advantage and the fact that the guard at the gate lay dead, they had little trouble reaching the cover of the jungle, which was fortunate since they were all too weak to run or put up much of a fight.

Just as they were about to head up the trail they'd come in on so long ago, Mike stopped them and signed, "Hurry. Home. Now."

Ken stopped them. "He wants us to follow him."

"Let's go. He may know where the others are," Fred said.

Mark nodded. "It's not like we know where we're going."

They followed Mike up the hill that overlooked the compound. As they gained elevation they were able to see the flashes of gunfire and more explosions. Flames engulfed the helicopters, so bright that they illuminated the field all around.

The Cessna's still intact," Savage said in amazement.

Mark pointed at it. "This has got to be Francois' work. Mike and Girlie may be able to help us find the others!"

Mike jumped up and down and impatiently signed, "Hurry. Now," then he darted up the hill.

They stumbled into the clearing as dawn broke. Smoke rose from the compound in several places, but the shooting had subsided. Mike broke in, hooting, surprising the two soldiers and awakening Mary and Consuelo. It was a long time before anyone could part Ken and Mary or Mark and Consuelo. The world could've ended and they would've continued to embrace.

* * *

"The compound is secure, sir."

"Well done, Lieutenant." Francois bowed sharply as he couldn't salute. He felt pleased with the operation, except for losing all the creatures. Noticing a worried look on his subordinate's face, he asked, "What's bothering you, young man?"

"Their leader, Vandusen, and his other associates are not among the dead or captured."

"Search every nook and cranny and turn every rock they could've crawled under. I don't want them roaming around here causing more mischief."

The lieutenant bowed briskly and headed toward the building where they kept the creatures.

"Lieutenant! I'm afraid you're not going to like what you find in that building. Better take some men to help with the-ah-clean up."

The soldier looked at him quizzically but turned on his heels and began barking orders. Francois made a note to keep this young officer around as he'd been very brave and resourceful during the engagement. In the heat of battle, he'd ordered his men not to fire on the creatures when they swept through the compound, making for the jungle. He kept his nerve even when one attacked his men. He single-handedly charged, firing over its head until it ran off.

* * *

What had happened to Vandusen's flunky, Childs? It looked as though he'd gotten too close to the cages, probably distracted by the attack. But who'd let the creatures out? It was disturbing. Worse, the men were unsettled by some of the casualties they found in the field. Some had been so violently mauled that they'd shot them to end their suffering. Their limbless torsos lay withering in the heat, screaming as they bled to death.

Even the battle-hardened soldiers among them found it horrific. Several soldiers making their reports interrupted the lieutenant from his dark thoughts. He spent the rest of the day overseeing and mopping up, but not before he sent word up the hill that all was safe and secure—at least for now.

* * *

"Let's pull ourselves together, or apart, and head down to where there's probably still food and water and a chance to clean up." Bobby smiled as he watched Mary and Ken untangle from their embrace, an embrace that seemed to have lasted for hours. Marks and Consuelo did the same.

They were just about to head down the path that led to the compound when they froze in fear. Oliver and several other creatures stepped out of the trees. The soldiers grabbed their rifles, but Ken yelled, "Don't shoot!"

The soldiers looked at each other, confused.

"Steady everyone!" Lester stepped forward. "Hi, old friend." Oliver engulfed Lester in a hug. Everyone gasped. Lester, a tall man, barely came to Oliver's chest. The other creatures stood watching silently.

Mike and Girlie moved up next to Lester as they untangled.

Oliver looked at the group with sad, almost tired eyes. No one moved. He pointed to the shadows of the trees and signed, "Home."

Another creature stepped forward next to Oliver—Danny. His hair was soiled and he had several seeping wounds. He looked weak, but he still stood erect in the heat of the sun—almost proud.

They turned and disappeared like shadows into the jungle.

Mike ran forward, agitated and hooting. He tapped Ken on the leg and signed, "Go. Go. Go now, friend." Then he followed Oliver.

Everyone screamed at once, calling him. Ken ran into the forest screaming, "Mike, Mike. Come!" but he came back alone. Mike was gone.

* * *

"I think we've stayed long enough, my friends." Ken embraced Francois. The entire compound had turned out to say farewell. Raven, Bobby, Hunt, and Mark were leaving on the *Si Como No* with GuGu and Omar to head back to the States under the cover of Raven's movie. Mary, Consuelo, and Ken would leave on the Cessna. They found it hard to leave, especially with so much left to do. Vandusen and Bauer were still unaccounted for, and they would continue to try and account for all the creatures.

"I don't have the words. Come back soon." Francois' eyes watered as he struggled to hold back the tears. So much had happened which had bonded them together. They shared the secret of the creatures.

"Next summer at the latest—anyway we're not all going." Ken looked at Lester and Girlie and smiled.

Lester smiled, holding Girlie in his arms. "Francois is going to need a decent animal person around, and I'll keep an eye on that scoundrel, Mike."

Francois beamed. "That we will, and that we'll do!"

Ken nodded. "You better."

Mary, Consuelo, and Ken boarded the Cessna after making the rounds of good byes and promises.

Lester, Girlie, and Francois stood and watched the plane take off. It banked steeply, gaining altitude to clear the mountains.

Girlie looked at Lester and signed, "You. Me. Airplane. Fun."

Francois and Lester laughed.

Lester shook his head. "My god, it's contagious."

They walked off toward what was left of the mess hall with Girlie trailing behind. The cooking fires were lit.

CHAPTER 36

Oliver and Danny stepped out of the grasses into the open where they knew they were in clear view of the caves. A cry echoed from the cliffs. Almost instantly, several creatures poured out of the shadows of the mountain and grouped together to meet them.

Oliver and Danny stood still, waiting, as the creatures surrounded them. The largest of the band came forward to meet them. He stood a head taller than either of them and carried a large bone club decorated with markings and notches. He closed to within a few feet, grimacing and baring his teeth. His light skin and lack of hair contrasted with theirs.

The rest of the band pushed in closer. Oliver and Danny were outnumbered. They stood silent, measuring each other. The only sound came from the breeze hissing through the grass. The shadows grew with the setting sun.

Finally, Oliver stepped towards the creatures, but they drew back, raising their clubs. He ignored their aggression and confidently held out a large piece of bark with carvings of two notches above six others. The leader closed in and carefully traced the two notches with his index finger. He held up his club and pointed at the same markings carved in the worn bone.

Oliver pointed at the two notches again, paused, then pointed to Danny, and then tapped himself several times on the chest. The leader stared for a long time before stepping forward and embracing Oliver. The band, Oliver, and Danny became one in the quiet of the wilds.

CHAPTER 37

The hearing had dragged on all morning before a tired and haggard committee called recess for final deliberations. Tempers had flared. The members of the University Hearing Panel were clearly angry and frustrated. The hearing had been requested by the president of the university who wanted to get to the bottom of what he called, "Irregularities surrounding the operation of Dr. Turner's research facility."

Ken and his group had been as honest as possible, considering they were committed to the welfare of the chimps. Apparently, the committee suspected that Ken, Mark, and Savage had not been completely forthcoming when it came to the details concerning the absence of the chimpanzees and the disappearance of Mr. Childs or their simultaneous absence during the summer.

"I can assure you, gentlemen, that the chimps are being well cared for at the Wild Animal Training Center. Their temporary placement there is very important to the assessment of the progress of our work. There is nothing in our NSF grant or facilities agreement that direct us *not* to place our chimps elsewhere when we deem it appropriate." Ken saw by the reaction of the committee that he'd not been very convincing as to why they'd been relocated.

"But it does not give you explicit permission, either." The provost only just controlled himself. His voice was strained, and perspiration beaded on his forehead.

Ken would do anything to protect his colleagues and, more importantly, the chimps—even lie. They were caught up in a complicated philosophical dilemma. The administrators viewed the chimpanzees as an asset of the university, and the fact that they'd been moved without their approval put Ken and his colleagues in a very uncomfortable position. On the other hand, Ken and his group saw the chimps as beings, non-human beings for sure, but beings with basic rights that needed to be protected and were not assets to be exploited by them or the university.

The disappearance of Childs was far more bothersome. To explain what may have happened to him would require them to divulge their interest and search for the hybrids: a direction that they'd not been funded for and certainly brought up considerable ethical issues. Worse, it implicated them in a crime, possibly murder, and the association with several unsavory sorts that brought into question their appropriate fitness to continue working at the university.

Watching the play of expressions on the faces of the committee members prompted Ken to wonder again how much certain elements of the university actually knew about what had happened in Africa. He and his colleagues had suspected a link between Vandusen and company and the university, with Childs somehow in the middle. He really didn't like that little weasel. And then there was Melon who always seemed to be associated with their misfortune

The room fell silent except for the embarrassed coughs of a few of the committee members who'd been watching Ken intently. It took a moment for everyone to settle.

The provost spoke for his group. His voice echoed off the dark paneled walls of the chambers, giving the proceedings an ominous tone: "Before we share our decision, we would like to ask you one final question, Dr. Turner, for the record and I remind you that you are still under oath."

Ken smiled, but nerves fluttered in his belly. "Certainly."

The provost, a little man with a booming voice, stacked and organized a pile of files in front of him. Looking over his thick bifocals, he said, "It's a two-part question, actually. Do you believe it's possible to interbreed humans and chimpanzees, and have you ever been involved or are you aware of any such research being conducted presently or in the past to that end?"

Ken hesitated only briefly. He shook his head. "No. I don't think it's possible, and I have no knowledge of any such research."

The provost's eyes narrowed and he looked Ken up and down for what seemed an eternity before he turned to the committee and conferred briefly before he spoke: "That, sir, is your final statement?

Ken affirmed with a nod.

"Then it's the finding of this committee that while several irregularities have occurred by your team, Dr. Turner, we do not have enough evidence to take further action at this time other than to order you to return the animal subjects under your charge to the facility immediately. A letter to that effect will be hand delivered to you and a copy placed in your file. This looks very bad for you and your colleagues, sir." The provost paused to let this sink in. "I would further caution you that there is still a civil investigation underway into many of these irregularities, particularly regarding the disappearance of one of our graduate students, Mr. Gordon Childs. We expect you to fully cooperate with all authorities in this matter."

Before anyone could react, Ken stood, starling the others with his abruptness. "Let's get out of here."

The committee watched as they filed out and conferred with the provost in whispers.

The bright light outside blinded them for a moment. Bobby lightly bound down the steps that led to a large, open commons in front of them. The rest followed more sedately, their eyes adjusting to the mid-day sun. A clear spring day in Reno without a cloud in the azure sky, the freshness of the air and smell of the awakening earth contrasted starkly to the closed and stuffy chambers in which they'd been confined for the last several days.

They could just make out the snow-capped Sierras jutting up behind the university library on the opposite side of the commons. Many of the trees bloomed, showering petals on the new growth of the lawn. Students lounged around, studying between classes, and soaking up the warmth of the sun, like lizards.

This idyllic academic scene made their predicament and the stakes for which they'd been playing all the more ominous in contrast. It didn't seem to dampen Bobby's spirits. He, in fact, seemed immune to the seriousness of their situation. He'd been summoned as a witness to the hearings at the suggestion of Reno Sheriff's Department who had been in close cooperation with the administration upon learning of the disappearance of Childs. They'd sent a homicide inspector over to interview them upon their arrival back from Africa. The sheriff suspected foul play, but with the absence of a body or motive, they'd not filed any charges—not yet, at least.

"I think we did pretty well in there considering—don't you?" Bobby smiled back up at them from where he waited at the bottom steps.

Mary frowned at him. "I'm glad you think 'we' did pretty well. The fact is, Fred and Ken could've been, and could still be, suspended from their positions, and the funding could've been cut for the whole program." Mary had been allowed to attend but hadn't been questioned.

"Or-r-r-r, everyone could get a 'get out of jail card'. They really don't have any proof," Bobby replied.

"Why don't you speak a little louder, Bobby?" Savage frowned. "I don't think the students, down there on the lawn, heard you."

"We've been lucky," Ken said, joining Bobby at the foot of the steps. "They really don't need much. This isn't a court of law, you understand. It's a University Administrative Hearing Panel." Ken thought of the all the possible outcomes, and none

306

of them were very inviting. "They're not held to the same rules of evidential proof as a court of law, and don't forget there's Dr. Melon and the NSF site visit. He wasn't real happy with us and has reported so to the university."

Chaney looked back up the steps toward the administration building. "It's a damn kangaroo court if you ask me."

"It gets worse," Mary said in a strained voice. "I saw a school reporter milling around and talking to one of the university cops on our way out."

"Christ," Ken muttered under his breath. "That's all we need now: some damn student reporter writing a story that's picked up by the outside press."

"I doubt that'll happen. If there's one thing I've learned about the university, it's that it likes to take care of its own housekeeping. Anyway, the hearing is closed for now." Mary paused thoughtfully. "I wonder what act two will bring?"

"You really think there'll be an *act two*?" Bobby said.

The rest of the group looked at him in disbelief.

As they started across the commons, the young reporter Mary had mentioned caught up to them. "Dr. Turner, sir, I wonder if you'd answer a few questions?"

Ken turned toward the reporter and froze. Savage nudged Mark and nodded toward a newspaper a nearby student was reading. Her hand partly covered the article, but they saw enough to read: Massacre in the Congo suspected! The bloody, dismembered bodies of several UN relief workers were found in a deserted coastal village. The team had been investigating rumors of large apes attacking small villages along the Congo ..."

Ken jerked the paper from the startled student, turning his back to the reporter as he read. The group peered over his shoulder. The reporter hesitated behind them. Ken whispered to himself, "My God. They're on the loose, and they're *almost* human."

Mary squeezed his hand. "No—they're *more* than human ..."

A Note from the Author

It would be immensely helpful to me if you could write a review for *Almost Human* and publish it at your point of purchase. I need your reviews to help find the readers who will enjoy my work.

Also, please sign up to my newsletter to hear when *More Than Human,* the sequel to *Almost human,* is published and receive some true stories of my life with chimps **FREE**. Just type the following web address into your browser:

http://bajamotoquest.com

Then scroll to the bottom of my blog and click on where it says:

PLEASE SIGN UP FOR MY NEWSLETTER.

And please stay in touch:

Follow "@KenDecroo" on Twitter
Like "Ken Decroo" on Facebook

About the Author

Kenneth L. Decroo believes you must live a life worth writing about. Before he became an educator and consultant for universities and school districts, he worked for many years in the world of research and wild animal training in the motion picture industry. He holds advance degrees in anthropology, instructional technology, and education. He lives and writes in the San Bernardino Mountains of Southern California with his wife, Tammy. When not writing and lecturing, he loves to ride his BMW adventure motorcycle down the Baja Peninsula to beaches and bays without names. More about his adventures can be found on his blog, http://bajamotoquest.com.

www.ingramcontent.com/pod-product-compliance
Lightning Source LLC
Chambersburg PA
CBHW030624110726
47901CB00002B/305